The Beach at Painter's Cove

Also by Shelley Noble

Forever Beach

Whisper Beach

A Newport Christmas Wedding (novella)

Breakwater Bay

Stargazey Night (novella)

Stargazey Point

Holidays at Crescent Cove

Beach Colors

The
Beach at
Painter's Cove

A NOVEL

SHELLEY NOBLE

wm

WILLIAM MORROW

An Imprint of HarperCollins*Publishers*

HarperCollins
PUBLISHERS
Since 1817

THE BEACH AT PAINTER'S COVE. Copyright © 2017 by Shelley Freydont. All rights reserved. Printed in the United States of America. No part of this book may be used or reproduced in any manner whatsoever without written permission except in the case of brief quotations embodied in critical articles and reviews. For information, address HarperCollins Publishers, 195 Broadway, New York, NY 10007.

HarperCollins books may be purchased for educational, business, or sales promotional use. For information, please email the Special Markets Department at SPsales@harpercollins.com.

FIRST EDITION

Designed by Diahann Sturge

Library of Congress Cataloging-in-Publication Data has been applied for.

ISBN 978-0-06-243907-9

17 18 19 20 21   LSC   10 9 8 7 6 5 4 3 2 1

*To all my readers who love the beach
and the stories it reveals about us*

The
Beach at
Painter's Cove

Summer 1962

THE PAINTER'S COVE GAZETTE

Muses by the Sea, ancestral home of the Whitaker family and renowned artist colony, was the scene of a public garden party last week where local residents were invited to meet and greet those artists currently in residence. Hosts Wesley and Leonore Whitaker greeted new arrivals and mingled among the guests. Their children, Maximilian (Max), Jillian, and George were charming in their roles of junior hosts to the children of Painter's Cove, while their aunt Fae Whitaker entertained them with face painting and storytelling.

The Present

JILLIAN YORK ADJUSTED her sunglasses and dashed off her signature with a flourish before handing the tablet back to the cabana boy. She smiled slow and sultry in an attempt to recapture the feeling of stepping off the red carpet to a horde of autograph-seeking fans, scribbling her signature before she was whisked off to someplace famous by someone rich and hand-some.

Well, at least that last part was still a reality. Henri was handsome enough, frightfully rich, and moderately intelligent. But the tab at the beachfront bar was the only thing she'd been signing for quite a while and the exclusive image of Saint-Tropez was beginning to dull along with her reputation as one of Hollywood's most desirous and desired actresses.

She hated to admit it, but it was about time she called her agent and had her start looking for an appropriate role.

She lifted her hand languidly, flashed her recently mani-cured fingertips. The waiter appeared. He was more attentive than her public—or Henri for that matter.

"Un téléphone, s'il vous plaît. J'ai besoin d'appeler les États-Unis."

He made a sharp nod and walked away. Jillian watched his progress across the poolside, his neat little butt tightening with each step. Sunglasses were a wonderful invention. Jillian leaned back in the chaise and sipped her daiquiri.

Unfortunately, it was time she got her own butt back to work or she'd wake up one day with nothing but character parts on her dance card.

"STEPHANIE BANNISTER, YOU pick that up and do what you're told. I don't need this attitude from you."

Stephanie snatched her duffel bag from the carpet and scowled at her mother. "It's not fair. What about the dance? What about my new dress? It's my first dance *ever*. I have to go."

"I'm sorry, but I'm not sure when I'll be back. And you know we always visit Grammy Leo during the summer."

"But in August right before school, because Dad makes

us—Wait, you're leaving us there? But why? Where are you going?"

Steph turned on her whine voice. It usually worked for her drama queen little sister, Amanda. It never worked for Steph. "Why can't I stay here with Jackie? Her mom won't mind."

"Just hurry up."

"But when are you coming back?"

"I don't know. You kids always have fun with Grammy Leo."

"No, we don't. Grammy's okay, but she lives in that creepy old house. And crazy Aunt Fae lives in the cellar and never comes out."

"No she doesn't. She has her own house. She just doesn't like children. Go."

Her mother gave her the look.

She'd better move it or she'd be stuck at Grammy's without her cell phone. Steph dragged her duffel bag into the hall.

"Don't forget your swimsuit."

Yeah, right. Like she was going to waste her new bikini on Grammy's private beach.

FAE WHITAKER STRAIGHTENED up and arched her back. The concrete was getting hard on her knees, even with the gardening pad Adam suggested she use. She'd collected a crowd of people, mostly day-trippers who were just passing through town or had heard about her drawings and had swung out of their way to someplace else to take a look.

Her chalk paintings stretched out in three directions down the sidewalks that trisected the town square park. She chose a dark yellow stick, leaned over to add another layer of hair to the Little Mermaid. It made the tresses dance across the concrete, swirl as if it really were hair and not something that would start to disappear with the first footstep, the morning dew, an afternoon shower. Fade until it was no longer recognizable, and finally became a blank canvas for her next drawing.

Most folks thought she was eccentric. BJ Tuttle at the Beach Junque Store called her batshit crazy. Of course he was the one who started the whole ad campaign. Come see the crazy old lady and her disappearing pictures.

He wanted her to put a hat out like the musicians in the subway stations in Manhattan. She'd refused. Though there were days when she'd get home and find bills stuck into her knapsack or even in the pocket of her art smock. It was amazing what people were willing to pay for.

After she became a "legend" thanks to BJ's hype in several local newspapers, he'd wanted to charge admission. He'd even gone to the town fathers to suggest it as income for the town, with BJ of course taking a healthy commission. Fae refused.

That's all she needed . . . publicity.

Chapter 1

Isabelle Whitaker never carried her cell phone to a museum opening. Besides being gauche and self-important, there was no place to conceal it. And she couldn't hold it. Gallery receptions were two-handed affairs.

But tonight her crew was in the basement of the Cluny Museum packing out an exhibit they were transporting to the Washington Modern. Isabelle was curating the move and overseeing the installation, but she was also responsible for a current exhibit being feted this evening.

Not being able to be in several places at once, she'd admitted defeat and tucked her phone inside the wide elastic belt she'd stretched around the waist of her little black gallery dress.

"Isabelle, come meet Irwin Frazier." Delmont Feinstein, the director of the museum motioned her over. "Isabelle is one of our brightest and most requested young designers."

Isabelle shook Frazier's hand and felt the vibration at her waist. "And on call this evening. I'm afraid I'm being summoned."

"Nothing wrong downstairs?" Dell asked.

"I hope not. Excuse me." Issy stepped away and reached for her phone.

"Very committed," she heard Dell say. "Always on top of things. Things don't go wrong when Isabelle is on the job."

She sure hoped he was right. She headed for the freight elevator as another vibration drifted above the laughter and conversations of the art patrons.

"This is Isabelle."

"Aunt Issy?"

Isabelle covered her ear with her free hand. Three women passed by, coming from the ladies' room. *Lovely exhibit,* one of them mouthed in Isabelle's direction. Issy smiled, nodded. "Excuse me? Paulo? I can barely hear you. Do we have a problem down there?"

"Aunt Issy?"

"Who is this?"

"It's me, Mandy. Amanda Bannister."

"Amanda?" Why was an eight-year-old—nine-year-old?—calling her this late. It was almost ten.

A burst of laughter rose above the general conversation. Isabelle looked for a quieter corner. She strode toward the double glass entry doors. They swooshed open ahead of her. And closed just as swiftly behind her. She was caught in the totally soundproof entry foyer of the museum.

"Amanda?"

"Can you please come? Grammy is in the hospital and there's no one to take care of us." Amanda started to cry.

"Amanda! Stop crying and tell me what's going on."

"Miss Whitaker?" A deeper male voice came over the line. "This is Detective Sergeant Al Griggs."

Police, Issy echoed as thought processes slammed shut and she waited for the worst. "What's happened, what's going on?"

"Is Leonore Whitaker your grandmother?"

"Yes. What is wrong?"

"She's in county hospital in stable condition. However, I have three children here—Stephanie, Amanda, and Griffin Bannister—who say they are living with her. With Mrs. Whitaker in the hospital, there is no one to care for them. If no family member comes forward, I'll have to turn them over to social services."

"Social services? They have parents." Dread encircled her, tied her up. She and Vivienne had never gotten along, but— "What happened to their parents?"

"At this time we don't know. We're attempting to reach them but have had no success."

"There's my great-aunt, Fae Whitaker. She lives with— near—my grandmother."

There was silence on the other end, then, "They say they haven't seen her."

Isabelle glanced into the museum. Caught Dell's eye. Gave him a thumbs-up.

"The housekeeper? Mrs. Norcroft?"

"There didn't appear to be a housekeeper. How long has it been since you've talked to your grandmother?"

"Last month." Isabelle thought back. "Or the month before maybe. I've been busy."

"There was no one home besides the children and Mrs. Whitaker. Do you have a number where your great-aunt can be reached?"

"No, I'm afraid she doesn't have a phone." And even if she were home, they'd never find the path to her cottage.

Delmont was giving her the eye from the other side of the glass. He was getting impatient.

And how would she explain this? Her grandmother was in the hospital, her sister, Vivienne, had abandoned her three children—like mother, like daughter—and Issy had to take the first shuttle out tomorrow morning to install a Midcentury Modern retrospective at a Washington museum.

"Detective . . . Griggs, could I talk to Amanda, please?"

She heard the policeman call Amanda over.

"Can you come? Please." The please was more of a wail.

"Amanda, where's your mom and dad?"

"I don't know. Can you come? Steph says she'll run away if we go with those other people. They're going to put us in jail."

"No, they aren't." Though that hardly was comforting to a frightened nine-year-old. Ten-year-old? She couldn't even remember how old her nieces and nephew were. Not the closest family on the East Coast. Or anywhere, for that matter.

"They will!" This also ended on a wail.

Delmont had excused himself and was walking her way. What a mess.

"Where did they go? Why did they leave you with Grammy? Are they coming back tonight?"

"I don't know. She packed up our suitcases and said we had to stay with Grammy."

"When was this?"

"Three days ago and we've eaten all the soup. We could starve."

"Mandy, stop crying. I can't understand any of this. Where is your mom?"

Amanda gulped back a sob. "I don't know. She said she'd call, but she hasn't. And her phone is turned off and she went to look for Daddy."

A faint voice echoed in the background. "Shut up, stupid."

That had to be Stephanie.

"Does Stephanie know where they are?"

"No."

"Let me talk to her."

A faint argument in the background while the phone exchanged hands.

"Steph, this is your aunt Issy. Do you know where your mother is?"

"No. She just left us here, and I was supposed to be at the dance. And—ugh. Never mind." There was a clunk. Steph must have put the phone down.

Isabelle shot her fingers through her asymmetrical haircut. Of all the times for her sister—the perfect homemaker and country-club wife—to pull a bunk. It didn't make any sense. Except maybe it did. Could deserting your children be hereditary?

Isabelle gritted her teeth. Why couldn't she have a family that just stayed put?

But if Vivienne had really taken off, and Aunt Fae was not capable of caring for the children, someone would have to deal with the situation. Probably not George. Her uncle had pretty much told the family what they could do with themselves.

And as for Isabelle and Vivienne's mother, Jillian? Not even nominated for the award.

That left Isabelle, who, in incomparable Whitaker style, was about to be screwed over one more time.

Dell opened the door. "What's up?"

"Ms. Whitaker? Are you still there? I need someone to take custody of these children."

She glanced up at Dell. *Just hang up the phone, Issy. Think of your job. Let them take care of themselves.* Except there was Grammy.

The doors closed behind Dell and they stood face-to-face. Dell was frowning. Issy swallowed; if he thought he was annoyed now, wait until she told him the team would have to take the D.C. shuttle without her. She couldn't leave her grandmother alone in the hospital and her nieces and nephew held by public services. Even if they were Vivienne's kids.

"Yes, Detective Griggs. I'm on my way." She ended the call.

"Sorry, Dell. That was the police. I have a family emergency. My grandmother is in the hospital and my sister has disappeared and left her children." Might as well not mince words. Her family had been making scandals for several centuries.

"I need to take care of some things. There is no one else. I can drive up to Connecticut tonight." *Get someone from the town to stay with them until she could locate Vivienne and make her come get them.*

"Connecticut?"

"I can be in D.C. by tomorrow morning." *Afternoon . . . evening for sure.* "Deirdre can process the paperwork and Paolo will get the trucks unloaded. I'll be there in time for the installation." *Paolo could even start the installation, if necessary.* "And we can Skype until then if there's an emergency. But there won't be." *She could take care of both things. Family and work. It wasn't the first time.*

"Issy, I'm counting on you."

"I always come through."

"Don't let me down." He nodded sharply then strode back

into the museum looking as if nothing had happened. Well, for him, nothing had; he'd still be golfing in the Hamptons tomorrow.

Issy detoured to her office to pick up her laptop and the hard-copy installation specs, then took the elevator downstairs to give instructions to her unsuspecting staff.

She didn't take time to change and her heels clicked across the concrete floor of the loading dock, where her assistant Deirdre—as beautiful as she was vapid—was checking off crates on her tablet. She glanced up, gave Issy a quick glance that said a mouthful. *What are you doing down here wearing those four-inch heels instead of upstairs where I should be instead of in the basement in overalls.*

If only she could be that articulate verbally.

"Family emergency?" she said, when Issy explained what was happening. "But you're not married."

Paolo had strode over in time to catch the comment.

"She has other family. Most of us do. Mother"—he seam-lessly skipped over father to—"sister, grandmother . . ." He looked toward the ceiling where four floors up the cast of Rodin's *The Thinker* was on loan from the Cleveland Museum.

Issy bit her lip. They always "looked to *The Thinker*" when Deirdre was being passive-aggressive, or just plain obtuse, and exasperation got the better of them. Like now.

He eased Issy out of hearing distance. "*Cara,* what's up?"

"Besides the fact that my sister dumped her children on my grandmother three days ago and isn't answering her phone? My grandmother is in the hospital and my great-aunt is MIA."

"Shit."

"Pretty much. There's no one but me. The cop said they would have to turn the kids over to social services."

"No way. Go do what you have to do."

Issy nodded. "Thanks. I'll catch up with you tomorrow."

Paolo was her dream design assistant, a Goya body with the hair and face of a Botticelli angel and the soul of Michelangelo. He worked hard because he loved the art, he had a good eye, and a good heart; he was the one Issy turned to when she needed a second opinion. Sometimes even when she didn't really need it, just to hear what he had to say.

"Go. We'll see you when you get there." He gave her a quick kiss on the cheek and went back to work.

She took a second to watch him walk back to the truck. She often just stood back and watched him, admiring his work, the way he moved. There was nothing sexual about the attraction either way. Just appreciation. And that was fine with her.

But tonight she didn't even have time for appreciation. It was already close to eleven when she reached the parking lot, where she added her laptop to the suitcase she'd packed that morning and pulled her SUV onto the Harlem River Drive North.

She pressed on the accelerator. "Vivienne Bannister," she enunciated to her phone system. She waited while it connected, went to voice mail. "Where are you? Grammy's in the hospital, they're going to send your kids to social services. Call me."

Hung up. Considered for a second. It was worth a shot. "George Whitaker."

Her phone started ringing. At four rings she began to plan her message.

"Hello?"

"Hello, Uncle George. It's Issy."

"Issy," he echoed in a tone somewhere between surprise and suspicion. "Working late?"

"I'm on my way to Painter's Cove."

"On a Thursday night? Odd time for you to take a vacation, isn't it?" To his clients he was impeccably suave and persuasive. To his family he was just irritated and dismissive.

"Doing triage."

"What?"

"Grammy is in the hospital."

There was a slight pause. "Not dead?"

"No." Issy picked up on the slight tremor of concern and thought better of her uncle for it.

"I talked to an officer who said she'd fallen, maybe had a slight heart attack. I'll know more once I get there."

"I told Wes to make better arrangements for her. She shouldn't be staying in that house alone."

"She has Mrs. Norcroft," Issy said, but she was thinking, Why doesn't George call Wes "Father or Dad" like a normal person would? Or for that matter, why did Issy and her sister call their own mother Jillian. Like claiming relationship was something to be ashamed of.

"A housekeeper almost as old as Fae and Leo. This is what happens when—"

She cut him off; she'd heard it all before and it was just going to get worse.

"Vivienne has left her children with Grammy."

"What?"

"I don't know exactly what happened. Evidently Vivienne left them off with Grammy and no one has been able to get in touch with her."

Her uncle barked out a laugh. "Well, the fruit doesn't fall far from the tree does it?"

Issy winced. "I'm on my way there now, but I have to be in D.C. tomorrow. What should I do?"

"Turn around and go back. Wes left Dan Bannister in charge of the estate. Let him handle it."

"That's just it. No one seems to know where Dan or Vivienne is."

A derisive snort from the other end of the call.

"Uncle George, the police are talking about sending the children to social services."

"Well, there's your answer. Let them go." He hung up.

Issy hung up. How many decades would it take for her to get it? This family would never be a "family." Respected art patrons for generations, the Whitakers had nurtured strangers but couldn't seem to help themselves.

FAE WHITAKER AIMED at the dark second-story window, pulled her arm behind her head, and threw as hard as she could. She heard the plink when the pebble hit the glass—a paltry sound—and no light came on.

She hiked up her skirt and grabbed a handful of small rounded rocks. Threw the whole batch, which nearly overturned her and knocked the wreath of flowers from her head. The pebbles made the nice sound of hail hitting glass. A light came on. Not the one she'd been aiming at but another one downstairs.

She snatched the wreath off the ground and shoved it back on her head. She climbed the steps to the porch, where she waited until she heard scuffling behind the door. "Ben Collins," she hissed. "I need your help."

The door opened, momentarily blinding her with light. Then she made out the shapes of Ben and his sister, Chloe. Ben looking like young Lochinvar; Chloe's curly hair, a halo of gold. For a moment Fae could only stare.

"Fae?" he said. Ben's voice was croaky, like he'd just awakened from a hundred-year sleep.

Chloe moved him aside and took Fae's arm. "Come in. What's the matter? What are you doing out so late?"

Fae hadn't expected to see anyone but Ben. Chloe lived in town. Fae didn't know why she was here, but she was glad to see her. Ben and Chloe had been best friends with Issy from the day she started kindergarten and had been a constant part of the Whitaker family since. They'd know what to do.

Chloe led her to an old armchair. She sat down and was nearly swallowed up by the sagging cushions. Her headpiece slid down over one eye. She snatched it off and put it on the trunk that served as a coffee table.

Ben was walking slowly toward them, frowning and trying to smooth down his cowlick, a hopeless endeavor. He'd been fighting with that cowlick since he was a boy.

He sat down across from her. He'd managed to shuck on jeans and a T-shirt. Chloe was still dressed in her nightshirt that told the world that girls just wanted to have fun. Girls wanted a lot more than that, and Chloe knew it as well as Fae.

"I saw the ambulance." Fae watched Ben and Chloe's faces, waiting to see their reaction, if they knew something they weren't telling her.

"When?" Ben asked.

Fae looked toward the window and the dark night. "A little before moonrise. About nine o'clock.

"I was coming back from the Renaissance Faire. I meant to take the bus home, but I stayed late at the storytelling because a nice young family offered to drop me off on their way to New Haven. I should have come home earlier like I planned."

"I'll make tea," Chloe said, and slipped away.

Ben slid over to sit next to her. He took her hands. His hands were strong, warm, but rough, an outdoorsman's hands.

"Fae, tell me about the ambulance."

"I saw it on the road as we were coming home. We all opened a window and sent a prayer to whoever was inside. They dropped me off at the gates of the Muses and I stopped by to let Leo know I was back. All the lights were on, but she wasn't home."

"Maybe she went to visit friends."

"I called the ones I knew. None of them had seen her."

Chloe returned with the tea things and placed them next to Fae's wreath of flowers.

Fae took the wreath back and pulled it down over her hair. She crossed her arms to ward off bad possibilities.

Chloe unfolded an afghan and draped it across her shoulders. Fae smiled at her, but that wasn't the kind of cold she was feeling.

"She was in the ambulance. I should have flagged it down. Gotten her out. But I didn't know." Fae looked from Ben to Chloe. "There is nothing wrong with Leo. She's strong as a horse—or is that an ox? I never get the two straight." She took a teacup from Chloe. "I've only been gone a week. She shouldn't have been in that ambulance."

"Maybe she wasn't," Ben said.

Fae watched him stir sugar into his tea. "She was. They have her, she'll be so upset."

Ben put his cup down. "You mean she was really in the ambulance?"

"I said she was." Fae put down her cup and pushed the floral wreath back from her brow. *Why did the damn thing keep sliding off?*

"I'm sure she's okay," Chloe said, looking sympathetic.

They were both looking sympathetic, and thinking poor old

crazy Fae. Just humor her. Well, maybe she was crazy, but she didn't need to be humored. She needed to get Leo home, where she belonged.

"Did you call the hospital?"

"I did."

"You did?"

"Yes. On the house phone. She's there."

"What did they say?"

"They asked me if I was a family member. They could only speak to family members. I said yes. Then they asked me if I was the mother of the children." Her mind went cloudy for a minute. She looked from Ben to Chloe. "What children?"

Brother and sister exchanged looks.

"Children?" Ben asked.

"Did you ask for details?" Chloe asked.

"I hung up."

"Why?"

"What children? I don't know about any children."

Chloe sat down next to her. So young and sweet. "We don't know about any children either. There is some reasonable explanation, so don't you worry. Do you want Ben and me to drive you to the hospital?"

Fae shook her head. "I can't go there."

"Fae, have you maybe smoked a little too much weed tonight?"

"Ben!" Chloe gasped.

Fae dashed away a big fat tear. Shook her head. "I can't go because . . . Look at me. I've been camping out at the Renaissance Faire for a week."

"I see your point." Ben agreed.

Fae put down her cup. "I shouldn't have come." She started to stand.

"Of course you should have," Ben said, standing right where she wanted to go. "And I apologize."

Fae tried to side step him.

"Fae, it's all right."

"No, it isn't. My nephew George has been threatening to have me locked away since I danced at Wes's funeral last year. George has never appreciated me. Even as a child. He has no sense of humor whatsoever."

Ben laughed, but Fae knew it was just to make her feel better. "Then he'll put Leo in a home. It will kill her to be away from Wes." She hung her head. "It will kill me, too."

"He would never do such a thing," Chloe said.

He would and gladly. George Whitaker was a bitter man. But Fae wouldn't burst Chloe's bubble. There were few enough happy spirits in the world, and Fae wouldn't be responsible for making one less. "I can't go to the hospital, but I have to get Leo out."

Chloe put her arm around her. "Ben will be glad to drive over to the hospital and find out what's happening, won't you, Ben?"

"Absolutely. And how am I to get information when I'm not a family member?"

"You'll figure out a way. You've gone out with your share of nurses. Flirt. Bribe them. Or wheedle and beg. Whatever works. Fae and I will wait here drinking tea and eating some of those lemon curd bars I made yesterday. You're going to call us as soon as you find out anything, so don't forget your phone."

As the door closed behind him, Fae sent him a silent prayer to carry with him. And love to see him through. Even strong, young men sometimes needed a little help from their friends.

Chapter 2

Issy made the drive in record time and only slowed down long enough to get her bearings in the parking lot before she blew through the doors of Coast General Hospital. A wooden information desk curved along the wall of the lobby below recessed lighting that did nothing to enhance the features of the receptionist. Issy stopped to ask for Leonore Whitaker's room number.

"Third floor, cardiac. But visiting hours are over."

"They sent for me," Issy said.

"Oh." A sympathetic smile. "You go ahead, dear. Take the elevators on the right to the third floor. You can ask for her at the nurses' station."

"Thank you." Issy had stayed relatively calm on the drive from Manhattan, but now her nerves took over. She waited impatiently for the elevator, which seemed to be stuck in the basement, then made the interminable ride to the third floor.

The nurses' station was just off the elevators; a nurse walked her down the hall to room 317 and held the heavy door for Issy to precede her.

Issy stopped just inside. Her grandmother lay on her back, so still, covered by a sheet and a light hospital blanket. She was tall, thin, with wisps of white hair framing her face. She didn't look sick or frail, except for the IVs trailing from her arm and the monitors beeping green and red like the controls of a spaceship.

The nurse nudged her into the room.

Issy tiptoed toward the bed. "Grammy?" she said quietly.

"She's been sedated, so she probably won't waken while you're here. It's nothing to be worried about."

Issy nodded distractedly.

"The doctor is making his rounds. He should be by shortly. I'll make sure he speaks with you before he goes. Would you care to visit with her while you wait?"

"Yes, please."

The nurse left the room and Issy pulled a chair to the bed. She sat down, slipped her hand beneath her grandmother's and gently closed her fingers around it.

"Grammy? Grammy, can you hear me?"

LEONORE WHITAKER KNEW this place. A young girl at the general store had told them about the cove; it was on private property, but there was a footpath to the sea through some artist's place, called the Muses. They all decided to go. It had been a hot dusty ride from the music festival where they'd hung out for three whole days.

Leonore longed for a bath, but a refreshing swim would do until she got home. If she went home. Her new friends were driving to California, or Colorado, or Canada. Any of those sounded fine to her. But first a refreshing swim.

Just don't be too loud, the girl told them. They don't mind people coming there, but you have to be respectful. Of the land and the art.

They parked the van and found the opening to the path, walked single file through trees and bushes past patches of tall beach grasses. Until they came out onto a rocky ledge surrounded by beach roses that grew right down to the water.

It was a secluded place, a stretched-out orb of water with a narrow opening at one end where you could see ocean on the other side.

They were perfectly alone except for the gray patches of slate here and there where roofs appeared like pieces of a collage among the tree leaves.

Her friends didn't hesitate; they stripped and splashed into the water, but Leonore stood back, just breathing in the salty air.

"Come on, Leonore."

She stepped out onto a rock that jutted over the water. Pulled her shift up over her head and let it drop to the rough granite. Then she stepped to the edge.

And there he was, half hidden by the trees on the opposite shore. He had something in his hand. A paintbrush. They'd disturbed a painter at his work.

Leonore stretched her arms to the side, lifted her face, then her breasts, to the sky. Felt a tingle of exhilaration and dove into the water.

He was waiting for her on the other side. She broke through the surface, sucked in a deep lungful of air, and saw him, or the bottom half. Khaki trousers and Birkenstocks worn with socks.

She looked up and fell irretrievably in love. He held out his hands, helped her out of the water, and led her through the woods to a meadow of cornflowers where they made love in the high grasses. She never went to California or Colorado or Canada. She stayed with Wesley Whitaker. Beautiful, kind, loving Wesley.

ISSY FELT HER grandmother's fingers tighten slightly around hers. "Grammy?"

Leo's eyelashes fluttered. Her eyes opened. "Wes?"

Issy swallowed. "No, Grammy. It's Issy. You're going to be fine."

"Issy?"

"Yes, I'm here now."

Her grandmother smiled but it wasn't for Issy. Her fingers relaxed and Issy knew she was asleep.

Her grandmother didn't waken again, so when the doctor stepped into the room a few minutes later, Issy kissed her cheek and followed him into the hallway.

"Dr. Rajneesh Prasad," he said, shaking her hand. "My father, Dr. Neeraj Prasad, was Mrs. Whitaker's cardiologist before he retired. And I am honored that Leo chose to stay with me for her care. You are her granddaughter?"

"Yes. Isabelle Whitaker. I just drove from Manhattan. How is she? Is it serious?"

"She is resting comfortably and we are monitoring her closely. She was not very clear on what happened. Whether she had a dizzy spell and fell, or if she fell first. The upshot is she has a mildly sprained ankle, a few bruises, a bit of dehydration. She was complaining about a pain in her chest. That's why I've decided to keep her here a few days for observation and to do some tests. Check everything to the fullest."

"But she didn't have a heart attack?"

"A mild angina attack, to which she is prone. Something that can be treated with drugs and rest. But I do not feel comfortable with her staying alone in that large house. Are you planning to stay? She'll need someone with her."

"My great-aunt Fae Whitaker lives on the property."

"Yes. I see, then I'd suggest a home-care attendant."

An attendant? Neither Leo nor Fae would go for that.

"It's early yet, time to discuss the future. How long are you staying?"

"I don't know," Issy said. *Tomorrow morning?* But how could she leave? "Long enough to make sure she'll be taken care of."

"Good, good, then we'll talk at a later date. In the meantime, don't worry. She is in excellent hands."

He said good night and strode off down the hall.

Issy turned in the opposite direction in search of her nieces and nephew. She followed the sound of a television broadcast to a green-walled waiting room where a female police officer sat at a square Formica table. Amanda slumped at the table beside her, her cheek smashed into the remnant of a vending machine snack. Griffin was curled up asleep on the black Naugahyde couch.

A skinny teenager was slouched in a chair, head bowed over her phone, earbuds planted in her ears and thumbs flying over the surface. For a split second hope that Vivienne was at the other end of that text swelled in Issy's brain only to be snuffed out as Stephanie raised her eyes and glanced at Issy without slowing her relentless thumbs, and lowered her gaze back to the screen.

The officer stood and gave Issy's dress and heels the once-over. "Can I help you?"

"Isabelle Whitaker," Issy said stretching out her hand.

The officer looked at it and Issy let it drop. "Are you from social services?"

"No, I'm their aunt. I talked with Detective Griggs."

"I'll notify him you're here." She pulled a radio off her utility belt and spoke into a cloud of static. "The aunt is here."

A crackly voice answered. The officer hung up and motioned for Issy to sit down.

Which she did, gratefully. She should have changed into jeans and running shoes. Her feet hurt, she was exhausted, and this might take a long time.

The television played on, none of the children roused, though Issy was tempted more than once to pull the cellophane wrapper away from Mandy's face. Stephanie didn't look up again.

Issy heard the detective's footsteps just seconds before he entered the room, barely giving her time to stifle a yawn and smooth the front of her dress. A few minutes later he would have found her, like Amanda, facedown in the Yodels.

"Ms. Whitaker?"

His voice boomed over the lowered volume of the television. Griffin sighed and fell back asleep. Mandy's head lifted, she saw Issy. "I knew you'd come get us."

She launched herself out of the chair and threw both arms around Issy's waist. Issy, to her discredit, wondered if she would find chocolate smears on her dress when she boarded the shuttle in a few hours.

Griffin sat bolt upright. "Mommy?" He looked around, spotted Isabelle, and burst into tears.

Stephanie didn't bother to look up.

"Easy, guy. She'll be coming for you soon." At least Issy hoped so.

"I want her now."

So do I, Issy thought. So do we all.

"Have you heard from their parents?" Griggs interjected.

"Not yet, but I'm sure there's an explanation."

"They left us!" Amanda cried, and clung to Issy.

She peeled Amanda from her waist. "Did you talk with your mom or dad after they left? They're probably just out on a date."

Amanda shook her head. "She packed our suitcases and said we had to stay with Grammy. And left us. Steph got really mad."

"Shut up," came from Steph's lowered head.

Issy ignored her. "When did they leave?"

Amanda shrugged. Looked at Detective Griggs. Maybe Issy should just be posing her questions to him; surely he had questioned the children. He didn't seem too intimidating, about five-eight, chunky, black buzz cut, wearing shirtsleeves in deference to the weather.

"She said the mother dropped them off after her ballet lesson. She goes to that on Monday. They drove straight to Mrs. Whitaker's, where she left them. She didn't tell them when she'd return."

Issy looked toward Steph for confirmation, but she was deliberately ignoring them. Issy felt a punch to the gut.

Man, did she recognize that expression. She'd worn it plenty of times during her own childhood. So what if you've got a famous mother, if she didn't even bother to come to your school play, parents' night, graduation, your—fill in the blank—or if one day she dropped you off at Grammy's and never came back for you.

Issy would give everyone that same look as she died the death of a thousand humiliations. "Or a weekend away. Even parents get vacations."

"Do you think that's what they did?" Amanda said hopefully.

"I want to go home," Griffin cried.

Issy turned her attention to the detective. "You didn't find out anything?"

He shook his head. "I can put out a missing persons on them, but I need a member of the family to authorize it."

Issy nodded. She didn't see much else they could do. What if there really was something wrong, and this wasn't just Vivienne pulling a Jillian York.

"She's calling on Saturday."

Issy and the detective both swiveled in the direction of the voice. Steph was still bent over her phone. She hadn't moved but Issy knew the voice belonged to her.

"Why didn't you tell us this before?" the detective asked.

"You didn't ask." Stephanie never looked up from the phone.

"In that case, Ms. Whitaker, if you'll sign for them, they're all yours."

"Mine?"

Mandy and Griffin straightened up. Even Steph's thumbs paused before taking up again.

"If you're willing."

Wasn't that part of the reason she'd just driven from the city? And who else was there? She looked at the kids. Amanda and Griffin were looking tear-streaked and hopeful. Stephanie still hadn't even glanced up but Issy knew what she was thinking as surely as if she were in her place, and oh heavens, how many times had she been right there?

"Sure."

The room seemed to relax. The detective exhaled audibly.

"Just until your mom comes to get you. Can I take them home?"

"Locally?"

"Yes, we'll be staying at my grandmother's home at the shore. It's called Muses by the Sea. You might know it." She gave him the address.

"You'll be sure to inform me when you've made contact with one or both of the Bannisters. If you don't hear from them and need to take the next step—" He handed her a card.

"Thank you."

He cocked his head and looked speculatively at her. "Are you sure you're up for this?"

Issy looked at him in mock surprise and lowered her voice. "A bawling five-year-old, a histrionic nine-year-old, and a sullen teenager? Piece of cake."

He held the clipboard while she signed it then raised both eyebrows. "Will you be okay? Shall I try to find someone to walk you out?"

"Thanks but we're good. Come on, guys, we're going to Grammy's."

Griffin slid off the couch and glommed to her side. Amanda latched on to her belt, which stretched with each step she took as she ushered them toward the door.

At least Stephanie had stood and was shuffling behind them on her own steam.

This must be the way pack mules felt, Issy thought as they lumbered down the corridor toward the exit. *Pack mules.* She must be really tired. Of course she was. Long days, longer nights. Missed meals and little sleep. One installation opened tonight. Another leaving in a few hours, maybe already gone. And how was she going to make it back to Queens in time for the early D.C. shuttle?

What was she going to do with three children? She supposed she could just put them all on the shuttle with her and get Deirdre to find someone to babysit. Or get Deirdre to babysit. Just deserts.

Somehow none of that sounded like a good idea. What if Vivienne came back and they were gone? Holy cow, she'd have Issy arrested for child abduction.

But Issy couldn't stay here with them. Maybe Great-Aunt

Fae would be home when they got there, though Issy wasn't sure she was up to taking care of them. And where could Fae possibly be? Amanda said they hadn't seen her. Several scenarios passed through Issy's mind, none of them with a happy ending. She pushed the images away.

Maybe Mrs. Norcroft would be willing to oversee them if Issy offered her more money. But could Issy leave her grandmother in the hospital with no family members to watch out for her?

She'd just have to fly back and forth until the exhibit was installed, launched, and running. She looked at her phone to see if she'd somehow missed Vivienne's return call. Nothing.

She stifled a yawn. First things first. Get these kids to the Muses and find someone to watch them until she could find her sister or make permanent arrangements.

What on earth had her sister been thinking to leave them with their great-grandmother? Leo was in great shape for someone who was eighty-three—four? But she couldn't take care of three kids. Fae was younger by about six or seven years, but she would never be a reliable child-care provider. Fae was the least reliable person Issy had ever known, though she loved her dearly.

They were several feet from the exit when the door whooshed open; a man rushed in and barely managed to skid to a stop in front of them. His arms stretched out as if he might grab them—Issy's first thought—or was trying to herd them—before he said, "Sorry, sorry," danced around the little group, and headed to the information desk.

Issy knew just how he felt. The call in the middle of the night, the rush to the hospital, she just hoped his ride didn't end in heartache.

She gathered Amanda and Griffin closer and was about to lead them out when she heard the man say, "Leonore . . ."

Issy stopped, causing a boomerang effect with the youngest children.

"Whitaker."

"He's talking about Grammy," Amanda said in a whisper.

"Do you know him?" Issy whispered back. He was dressed in wrinkled jeans and a T-shirt, holey running shoes with no socks, and with his hair sticking up like he just woke up.

She squinted at him. He looked slightly familiar. She guided the others back toward the information desk. "Excuse me."

He'd just turned in the opposite direction toward the bank of elevators, but he completed the turn all the way back to Issy in an awkward pirouette.

"Are you talking to me?"

Issy nodded. "I heard you ask about Leonore Whitaker."

"Yes."

"I'm . . ." She stopped, really looked at him, kind of sandy hair, grayish-blue eyes, nice enough face. But it was the hair, the way it stuck up on one side like he'd just gotten out of bed . . . "Ben?"

He jumped as if one of the kids had goosed him; Issy quickly looked around for the culprit, but they were all standing behind her.

"Ben Collins?"

"Yes. Do I know you?"

Issy grinned, started to laugh. Totally inappropriate. It must be fatigue . . . she hadn't had much sleep in the last week, but this was no time to get punch-drunk. She tightened her mouth. Shook her head. Covered her face with her hand. Snorted a laugh.

Griffin started to cry.

"Aunt Issy," Amanda moaned. "You're scaring us."

"I am so sorry. The stress of the evening. I heard you ask about my grandmother and I thought . . ." What? That a total stranger could tell her what the hell was going on. But he wasn't a total stranger, and maybe he would have a clue.

"I'm Issy Whitaker. Chloe and I were in the same grade at school." They'd been unlikely comrades, porcelain complexioned and blond, Chloe was a mother's delight, cheerful, neat, with a streak of mischief she kept well hidden by a naturally happy disposition. And the dark-haired, dark-eyed, sullen Isabelle, who wouldn't recognize her mother in a crowd, who felt more comfortable among the cigars, brandies, and arguments of middle-aged artists than on the playground. And yet they'd become friends. Ben was Chloe's older brother, a science nerd and worshipped by his sister and her friend Issy.

"Issy? Good grief. I would never have recognized you. You've—" He seemed to stall for words.

"Grown?" Issy supplied. She felt another giggle about to erupt. What was wrong with her? She slammed down on it.

"That, too. How is she?"

"The doctor said it was a mild—oh God, I can't remember the name—" She took a deep breath. "Something to do with her heart, but minor and some bruises and dehydration and she'll be fine."

She was surprised by a yawn. "Sorry. I'm just sleep deprived and not thinking clearly."

"I can understand. Don't you work in Manhattan?"

"Yes I was at work when the hospital called. I came straight from the museum, which is why I'm . . ." She gestured to her dress, the worse for a two-hour drive and Mandy's sticky fingers.

"They look like they hurt like hell," he said, gesturing to her shoes.

"They do. I'm not sure why you're here. Did the hospital call you, too?"

"Actually Fae asked me to come."

"Fae? Where is she? The kids said—"

"These are your kids?"

She shook her head. "My sister's. Evidently they're staying with Leo and Fae for a while."

He blew out air. "That's what she meant. I was beginning to wonder."

"About what? Where is Fae? Amanda said she wasn't there." This time she managed to cover her yawn with her hand.

"You look beat. What are you going to do with these guys?"

"Take them back to the Muses for now."

"And not make us be orphans," cried Amanda.

"You're not an orphan," Issy said, too tired by now to even be annoyed.

"But we're starving," she complained.

"I want to go to McDonald's," mumbled Griffin, and started to cry again.

"Oh, man up, Griff," Steph said with disgust, and stuck her earbuds back in.

She couldn't have said it better herself, Issy thought. "Is Fae all right? Is she at home?"

"She and Chloe are both at my house. She's been out of town and she saw the ambulance drive away as she arrived. She sent me to see about Leo. It's a long convoluted story." He glanced around at the children. "Why don't I drive you all to the Muses and I'll call Chloe to bring Fae and some food, though I'm guessing those two will be asleep when they hit the seat.

"And that one." He flicked his head toward Stephanie. "We'll just plug her into the car lighter and reboot her."

Issy glanced at Steph just in time to see her eyes widen, then close as if she hadn't heard.

He scooped Griffin up. Gestured the others toward the doorway.

"Thanks but I have my car," Issy said. "I'll find a drive-thru on our way, and if you tell me where you live, I'll also pick up Fae."

"You're not driving anywhere tonight. You might yawn yourself into a ditch."

She knew he was right. Now that she was here, exhaustion was sweeping over her. "I have to be on the morning shuttle to D.C."

He stuttered to a stop. "And I suppose you're driving yourself to LaGuardia or Logan as soon as you drop these guys off."

"If there's someone to keep them. I have a huge installation beginning in the morning. I can be back by tomorrow night."

"Same old Issy," he said.

She wanted to ask him what he meant but she was just too tired.

"I'll drive your car, providing we'll all fit." He lifted his eyebrows in question.

"SUV."

"And Chloe can bring me back for my truck in the morning." He stuck out his hand and opened his fingers.

Issy didn't think about arguing; she dropped her keys in his palm.

Chapter 3

The familiar sound of gravel brought Issy bolt upright in her seat as her SUV passed beneath the wrought-iron arches of the Muses. She couldn't really see them, but she felt them in the darkness. For the briefest second she was a child and seeing the house for the first time. She didn't know then that it would soon be her home.

And here she was again. She sat still as the fog in her mind cleared. Grammy was in the hospital, Vivienne's kids were in the backseat, Ben Collins was driving them home.

She glanced to her left. Yep. Ben Collins was driving her car.

Issy pulled her skirt down in a futile attempt to appear put together and awake rather than lost in a total stupor. Only a few short hours ago she was at the museum, preparing for her next opening. Looking forward to a busy summer, and now . . .

"Sorry. I must have dozed off." She peered out the window. "You know I'd recognize that gravel anywhere. It has a crunch unique unto itself."

Ben flashed her a smile. "The sound of coming home."

"Well, I'm not sure about that." It had been her home, but

she hadn't thought of it as home for a long time. Tonight the old mansion and the grounds were lit up as if they were expecting her. They had been expected that night, too. She remembered it had looked like . . .

"Christmas," Issy said wistfully. "It's lit up like Christmas."

"I'm surprised you remember."

Issy cut him a look. She hadn't spent Christmas at the Muses since college. She hadn't visited at all since her grandfather died.

Ben pulled the SUV up to the front door and turned off the ignition. "All ashore who's going ashore," he announced.

He got out and opened the back door, lifted a groggy Griffin to his shoulder then waited for Mandy to climb out.

Stephanie just sat there.

"Out," he said at the same time Stephanie opened the opposite door. She slid out of the car without looking up.

Issy opened her own door and practically fell out of the front seat. Yelped when her bare feet met the gravel. She leaned back into the car and rummaged on the floor until she found her shoes.

When she straightened up, the children had all stopped at the bottom step, their faces lifted to the apparition that had appeared in a nimbus of porch light.

Issy hesitated only for a moment before she recognized her great-aunt Fae. She was dressed in flowing gown of floral gauze. A wreath of flowers sat askew and slightly wilting on a head of wild gray curls. Perennial flower child from an era that ended before any of the others were born.

Fae raised her arms in welcome, but before Issy could move, the front door opened and Chloe rushed out holding a wooden spoon. Chloe Collins, blond and plump, funny and kind, and Issy's best friend since kindergarten.

"Issy!" she squealed, and wrapped arms and spoon around Issy, nearly knocking her off her feet. "You look wonderful. Ben, get those children inside, and then bring Issy's luggage in. You do have luggage, don't you? How long are you staying?"

She chatted as she guided Issy up the stairs and deposited her in front of Fae, before scuttling the children through the door. Ben grabbed Issy's suitcase and computer case before Issy could tell him not to, and followed his sister into the house.

"Aunt Fae." Issy gave her great-aunt a hug. Fae felt fragile, almost as light as air. As if she was becoming one of her paintings, slowly disappearing from view.

Fae just smiled beatifically. Issy's smile wavered. Did she even recognize Issy?

"It's all right, Aunt Fae. I talked to the doctor and she's going to be fine." Issy patted the older woman's back.

Fae grasped both Issy's hands in hers. "I didn't know. I shouldn't have gone. But Leo said she'd be fine and—well, she's not exactly alone, lots of people look in on her. And I was only gone a week.

"She didn't tell me the children were coming. I didn't know what children they were talking about."

"Who was talking about?"

Ben stepped onto the porch. "The hospital when Fae called. Chloe says come and eat."

"I didn't know about the children. I wouldn't have gone."

"I don't think Leo knew they were coming," Issy said, finally able to loosen her aunt's hold and guide her to the front door. "According to Amanda, their mother packed their suitcases and drove them here. Nothing about making plans."

"Why would she do such a thing? Do you think something

happened to Dan? I—" Now she let go, but only to cover her mouth with her hand. "What did Leo say?"

"She was sleeping. It's late. She can tell us tomorrow." Except Issy wouldn't be here. But how could she *not* be here? Who was going to deal with this mess? It was abundantly clear that Aunt Fae was in no condition to care for anyone, maybe not even herself.

"They'll let us see her, won't they?"

"I'm sure they will." Issy walked arm in arm with Fae down the central hall to the kitchen, where the kids were already sitting at the table eating peanut butter sandwiches and slices of cantaloupe.

Chloe set a basket of homemade bread on the table. "I tried to interest them in gazpacho and quiche but they couldn't wait. The quiche will be ready in a minute. Have a seat. You, too, Fae."

There were three places neatly set at the opposite end of the table. There was so much Issy had to do, but she made for the wooden kitchen chair like it was a feather bed.

Issy's cell phone buzzed. All heads turned toward her as she fished it out of her bag. A text from Paolo. She shook her head. *Not Vivienne.*

Truck just left. Taking 6AM shuttle. U OK?

"Sorry, I have to make a call." Issy got up from the table and pressed her speed dial for Paolo.

He answered on the second ring.

"*Ciao, bella.* How goes it?"

She walked into the hall before answering. "My grandmother will recover. My sister left her three children here, and I have to make arrangements for someone to watch them until she gets back. I can do that tomorrow, but even so, I don't think I'll make the six o'clock."

"*Cara*, we're fine. The D.C. team can install this exhibit in their sleep. And the Cluny team will have to, since none of us has seen more than four hours in the last two weeks. So no hurries, no worries."

"I'll try for the eight o'clock; if I can get my aunt to care for the children, I can call for permanent care once I'm in D.C." She lowered her voice. "It's just a little dicey, the cop in charge suggested social services. I can't let them do that. I've been calling my sister all night but she doesn't answer."

"Do you think something has happened to her?"

"Not at this point, but it is unlike her just to dump her kids and take off. She's like supermother. A-team. Starring role."

Paolo chuckled.

"What?"

"Now I know why you so rarely speak of her."

"Why?"

"You don't like her very much."

"No love lost between us, that's for sure. A topic for another time."

"And several drinks," he added.

One drink tonight would put her under the table.

"I'll come straight to the museum from the airport. I'll give you a heads-up as soon as I know which shuttle."

"Issy, what I was going to say before we got sidetracked by your charismatic family is that Dell came down. I told him we could do the unload via Skype with you. Actually they don't even need us to unload but I kept that to myself. Don't want him thinking we're expendable. You take tomorrow, even Saturday, to arrange things there."

"I—" She started to protest, but she knew he was right. She'd be distracted the whole time. But she also knew that there was a handful of people begging for a job at the museum. Deirdre, for one, wanted Issy's. The pay was lousy but the perks . . . All that great art.

"Issy, Are you still awake?"

"Yes, just thinking."

"So stop it. Deirdre and I have got this. You take care of your family."

Issy's heart squeezed a little. "If you're sure."

"*Cara*, you're talking to me."

And to Paolo, family was everything.

"Thanks."

"And try to get some sleep."

"I will. Call me, anytime."

"Good night, Is."

"Night."

She ended the call as Chloe came down the hall, urging the three children toward the stairs and bed.

"I'll take care of these guys," Chloe said. "You go eat something."

"Thanks. And I just got a reprieve. I don't have to be in D.C. until day after tomorrow."

"Great; that will give us time to come up with a plan."

When Issy returned to the kitchen Ben was attempting to convince Fae to go home to bed. "Everything is fine. We'll go visit her in the morning. Issy needs her rest."

On cue Issy stepped into the room and yawned. She didn't mean to, but she was exhausted, and trying to get sense out of her great-aunt tonight was more than she could manage.

She went to Fae and gave her a hug. "It's all going to be fine. You'll see."

"Come along. I'll walk you home." Ben extended his elbow.

"That's not necessary. I know the way."

"But you don't want to hurt my feelings, do you?"

Fae sighed. "I know what you're doing. But very well."

When they were gone, Issy sat down to attempt a few bites of quiche. It was delicious, though a bit lukewarm by now.

Chloe came back in. "The two little ones are out cold. The teenager disappeared into her room and shut the door. I'll take that as she's fine."

She sat down next to Issy. "Wow. I can't believe you're here. I'm glad, though I just wish it hadn't been because Leo is in the hospital. The question is, are you going to stay?"

"I'm sorry, Chloe. I didn't mean to leave without a word the last time I was here. It's such a Whitaker thing to do. But things were such a mess. No one even told me Wes had died. I probably couldn't have made it back to the States in time for the funeral, but they didn't even try to find me. And for some reason, I just haven't made it back too often since then."

"Don't be so hard on them. Leo was distraught. Fae was . . . well, you know. George and Dan were at it. And Vivienne—"

"Vivienne saw her chance to queer me with the whole family."

Chloe shrugged. "At least this will give you a chance to square things with Leo."

"I can't stay. I have work that won't wait."

"We'll think of something."

"Thanks. So tell me what's going on with you."

"Well, I'm an administrative assistant at the local grammar school."

"What about culinary school?"

"I went for a year, but it was expensive and somehow it took all the love of cooking out of me. Just don't have what it takes, I guess."

"So you and Ben live together?" Issy asked, half curious and half just making conversation. It seemed so odd that they should reconnect so fortuitously at the moment Issy really needed some friends.

"No. Ben lives on the edge of town, close to his stinky old marshes. I just bought a bungalow downtown and I'm staying with him while I have the floors refinished. It's zoned for business and has an apartment above. I've been thinking about opening a tea shop."

She began clearing the table.

"You'd be great at it." Issy pushed her chair back to help.

They carried the dishes to the sink. Chloe turned on the spigot; the pipes creaked and banged; the water exploded out then ran in a slow trickle.

"That doesn't sound good," Issy said.

"It was supposed to be fixed," Chloe said over her shoulder. "A total overhaul of the plumbing."

Issy leaned on the counter next to Chloe. "Doesn't look like they got very far."

"No, it doesn't. Scott Rostand was contracted to do the job. I don't know what happened. He's working on the Cove Theater renovation. Guess it was a bigger, better-paying job. Though you wouldn't think it to hear them beg for money. Still, it's not like Scott not to finish a job."

"Doesn't even look like he started this one," Issy said.

The kitchen door opened and Ben walked back in. "Chloe, Issy's dead on her feet and you have her washing dishes?"

"I'm just kibitzing. And talking plumbing. Did you get Fae home okay?"

"As close as she'd let me. I waited, after she disappeared into the woods, for screeches, screams, or oofs. But nothing. I don't know why she's so secretive about where she lives. It's that yellow cottage on the cliff, right?"

Issy nodded. "It's just her way."

"I promised we'd take her to the hospital tomorrow."

"We?"

"We're not going to strand you here with those crazy kids." He took the drying cloth from her hand. "That's it for you. Off to bed. We'll finish here and lock up." He frowned. "You're okay staying here by yourself? Do you want us to stay?"

"No, you've both already done too much. We'll be fine."

"Then we'll pick you up in the morning, but not too early. Sleep in. We have the whole day to get things squared away."

"Thank you. Both of you. I don't know—"

"Enough. Get upstairs right now. Before I throw you over my shoulder and carry you up."

"I'm a little heavier than I was in grammar school."

"What? You don't think I can still throw you over my shoulder?"

Issy threw up her hands. "I'm going."

"Issy," Chloe said. "One thing. How did you recognize Ben at the hospital? He's not the scrawny geek he used to be."

Issy looked from Chloe to her brother and laughed. "I didn't recognize him. I recognized his cowlick."

Ben groaned and slapped his hand to his hair.

Issy grinned. "How many times did you show up at school looking just like tonight? I would have known that bedhead anywhere."

Chapter 4

It wasn't until the next morning, lying in her old four-poster bed, that Issy realized how dusty everything was. She'd been so exhausted last night, and so glad to see her old bedroom unoccupied by nieces or nephew, she'd dropped her clothes on the floor and climbed between the sheets without noticing the layer of dust that covered the nearby surfaces.

Except for the dust nothing had changed. She could be sleeping here five years ago, ten, or even twenty. She'd grown more selective in her surroundings since moving away. More selective and more minimalist.

She stretched and nearly knocked over a tall thin vase with a dead rose sticking out of the narrow top. She set it upright, trying to remember if the rose was left over from her last visit. Decided she didn't like the symbolism of that and reached for her phone and sat up.

Nine twenty-two. She'd not only missed the early shuttle but the next several. Then she remembered she wasn't taking the shuttle today.

The sun slanted through the window, but the air felt heavy

and thick, and she slid off the bed to wrestle the window open. A creak and a scrape and the sea air rushed in. Below her, the lawn, neglected now, rolled down to a beckoning beach. Beyond it, the sound danced blue as it met the sky.

Tempting, but she had a lot to do today.

Starting with an almost hot shower, delivered by clanking pipes. She towel-dried her hair and dressed in the black jeans she'd planned to wear for the installation—she hadn't packed beach clothes.

She tossed her work sneakers into the closet and exchanged them for a pair of black straw flats. Pulled out a deconstructed linen jacket from her suitcase, snapped it a couple of times, decided she'd go for shabby chic. Hopefully she would look acceptable for a meeting with her grandmother.

A basic application of makeup, a quick look in the mirror to make sure she looked neat and unfazed by all the surprises, and she carried her laptop downstairs to check in with Paolo.

The aroma of bacon and coffee wafted up the staircase and she was tempted to go straight to the kitchen. But the voices coming from there told her several people were up and she needed to get work out of the way.

At the bottom of the stairs, she turned right into the front parlor, but lingered just inside the archway. The parlor was one of those rooms that was always in shadow on one side because of the porch, and sunny on the other because of a large bay window, creating a play of light and dark—*chiaroscuro*—as they met in the middle.

Issy remembered stepping over grown men sitting or lying on the carpet, their arms outstretched as they passed their hands in and out of the bits of light.

It was a wonderful game that they gladly invited Issy to play.

Happy times, for her at least. But today the room was just dark, the air holding that lifeless sense when space is shut away. Even the familiar pieces lacked their vitality. The curved Queen Anne couch whose velvet cushions and horsehair stuffing scratched her legs in the summer. The portrait of great-great-grandfather Manus Whitaker looking down at her from above the mantel. The Tiffany lamp on the butterfly end table or the coffeepot that Russel Wright had created for one Fourth of July as a joke, but in his hands had turned into a work of art—except it wasn't there on the sofa table.

She looked around but apparently it was gone, broken or put somewhere else. It was sad in a way. Everything in the room had meant something at one time. But things changed, people left, objects were broken or forgotten. A shame to let it all go, but Leo certainly didn't need all these rooms. And Leo and Fae were both getting too old to manage on their own.

But the thought of her grandmother and aunt not at the Muses was too awful. They belonged here. Vivienne would just have to hire a service to help out Mrs. Norcroft, who was obviously getting too old to take care of the house alone.

Issy backed out of the room, leaving the memories where they belonged. She went across the foyer into the library. Here, too, it was dark, and she quickly opened the bank of heavy mulberry drapes, unleashing a curtain of dust motes as the sunlight began to pour in.

Issy sneezed and looked around. Two walls of built-in bookcases flanked the marble fireplace, both filled to overflowing.

Eclectic furniture, some antique, some created by artist friends of the family, vied for whatever floor space wasn't taken up by Wes's big kneehole desk. Paintings hung helter-skelter on the remaining walls, more glass lamps, Bakelite bowls, and modern sculpture rubbed elbows, sometimes literally, on the neglected surfaces.

She'd thought she would use the library as an office but it was just too cluttered. And the aroma of coffee wafting down the hallway was too enticing. Issy checked her e-mail on her phone, texted Paolo just to touch base, and went to join the others.

Chloe was at the stove turning over pancakes. Ben sat at one end of the table drinking coffee from a large crockery mug. A white laptop sat on the table before him. Amanda and Griffin sat along the same side, Griffin eating a strip of bacon, gradually working it into his mouth without using his hands, while Amanda gesticulated and informed her listeners of all the other gross things he knew how to do. Stephanie was MIA.

"Did you call Mama?" Mandy asked.

"Not since last night."

"And she's not going to try again until she has some breakfast," Chloe said.

Issy shoved her cell phone into her pocket, grabbed a cup off the table, and poured herself coffee. She took a sip and peered over Chloe's shoulder at the pancakes. "You didn't have to do this, but I appreciate it. Thanks."

Chloe put a plate at an empty place and shooed Issy toward the chair.

Issy was about to say she never ate breakfast, when she took a look at the pancakes. "Are those blueberries?"

"Yep, fresh from Jensen's farm market this morning."

"Who got them fresh from New Jersey yesterday," added her brother.

"I didn't hear you complaining when you ate the first stack," Chloe said.

"I was just being polite. It's still a bit early for the local ones," he explained.

He smiled at Chloe in the same old way as he had years ago, when Issy had longed to have a family like theirs, a mother who stayed home, a father who went to work, and who were as close and caring as Issy and Vivienne's mother, Jillian, had been unavailable.

Issy had a loving if unorthodox home; two grandparents and a great-aunt and a fascinating array of artists and musicians and sometimes actors—mostly stage actors.

Wes and Leo never cared for the cinema; Issy thought her mother must have destroyed any love they'd had for the medium when she dumped her two children on the doorstep and fled back to her glamorous, unencumbered life.

"What if she's never coming back?" Amanda wailed, breaking into Issy's reverie.

Griffin sniffed. "I want Mommy,"

Issy frowned at her niece. "Amanda, cut it out. She's coming back and you're upsetting your brother."

"I want Mommy." Griffin moaned.

Chloe turned to Ben. "Take him out of here before he gets any louder."

"Me?" he said, but he stood. "Hey, Griff, you want to go down to the creek? I think I saw a *Rana kauffeldi* last week."

Griffin's moaning trickled down to a whimper. "What's that?"

"A leopard frog."

Griffin's eyes widened. "No way."

Ben nodded. "Way."

Griffin slid off his chair and went to stand by the door. He must have dressed himself in the plaid shorts and SpongeBob

T-shirt several sizes too small for him and faded, obviously a longtime favorite.

"I want to see the leopard frog, too." Amanda snagged a piece of bacon off the platter and followed them.

"Is she still wearing her pajamas?"

"Their fashion-conscious mother would be having a fit," Chloe said as Ben and the two children went out the door.

"Then she should be here to dress them," Issy snapped.

"Guess you're not feeling forgiving this morning."

"Toward her? She just better have a good reason for this. She's dragged me from work—don't you have to work today?"

"Took a personal day."

"You didn't have to do that."

"I know."

"Thanks. She dragged us *both* from work. She deserted her children, who seem weird enough without all the extra stress. And landed Grammy in the hospital."

"You don't know that you can blame Vivienne for that."

"Oh yes I can. And God knows what else."

Chloe brought her coffee over to the table and sat down next to Issy. "Do you have any idea what Vivienne is up to?"

"Not a clue. Mandy said last night that she had gone to look for Dan. But she's such a little drama queen I didn't pay any attention."

"She didn't elaborate?"

"No, but I didn't encourage her with the police standing nearby."

"Are you worried about her?"

"Not yet. If Grammy hadn't ended up in the hospital, the kids could have come and gone and none of us would have been the wiser. Steph also said she was supposed to call on Saturday.

But if that's the case, why doesn't she just answer her phone? I tried to get her several times last night. It went straight to voice mail."

"Maybe she and Dan are having a romantic week away from home."

"Or she ran off to be a movie star and dumped her children on Leo."

Chloe sighed. "I suppose it would be better being raised by Leo than by Vivienne."

"True." Issy shuddered dramatically.

Chloe laughed and covered her mouth with her hand. "Not funny."

Issy shook her head, then spluttered out a laugh and they fell back into a friendship that had lasted through the years, even when Issy had been gone.

They were laughing when Ben dragged two dripping children back into the kitchen.

"Oh, dear," Chloe said wiping her eyes. "What happened?"

"These two rugrats decided they knew better than I did how to look for frogs. Squirt here slipped on a rock, Mandy grabbed for him and fell in."

"I tried to save him," Mandy said, her bottom lip jutting out.

"Both of them went in headfirst. It's a good thing we haven't had any rain lately." He winked at Chloe and Issy. "I would have had to chase them all the way down to the ocean before we could fish them out."

"We coulda drowned!" wailed Mandy.

"Shut up," came a voice from the doorway.

"Oh, goodie," Ben said. "Miss Sweetness and Light is awake."

Steph stood in the doorway, slouched on one hip and wearing what looked like the same clothes she'd been wearing the night before. Khaki trousers rolled up above Doc Martens and stained at both knees, white button shirtsleeves rolled to the elbow and looking limp and grayish. Then Issy recognized them. Steph was wearing Leo's old gardening clothes.

She didn't look at anyone and only moved aside when Ben nudged the other two past her with the admonition to go get cleaned up and "Don't leave your wet clothes on the floor, on the bed, or in your suitcases."

Steph wrinkled her nose as they ran past.

Chloe jumped up. "Morning, Steph. Sit down, I'll make you some blueberry pancakes."

"They're safe," Ben said. "Vegetarian blueberries. They don't eat teenagers." He grinned at her.

"I'm only twelve."

"Then you might be in trouble."

Steph rolled her eyes and sat down opposite Issy.

"Your outfit looks familiar," Issy said.

Steph looked up sharply, something flashed in her eyes. Anger, defiance? "Grammy Whitaker gave them to me. She said I could keep them."

Issy nodded. If Vivienne saw her lanky daughter dressed up as Leonore, it would push her over the brink. "They look cool."

"They're okay," Steph said, looking down.

"Are you short on clothes or is this a fashion choice?"

"I have plenty of clothes. I just don't want to wear them."

"Cool."

Chloe put a plate of warm pancakes down in front of Steph. Steph frowned.

"They're just regular pancakes," Chloe explained.

"Tofu's out of season," Ben said.

Chloe punched him.

Steph scowled at him and reached for the syrup.

"I made a grocery list," Chloe said. "Hope you don't mind, but the cupboard is pretty bare."

"You mean for once Mandy wasn't exaggerating about starving?" Issy asked. "And where is Mrs. Norcroft? Shouldn't she be here by now?"

Chloe shrugged. "I guess. I'm ashamed to say I haven't kept my eye on them lately. Between working and the bungalow, I've been remiss." She slapped her head. "I could have been bringing them dinner instead of fattening up Ben here. I know he throws half of what I make away."

"Only because you make so much of it. I have a freezerful and so do you."

"That just makes me feel worse," Chloe said, and sank onto a kitchen chair.

"Well, don't," Issy told her. "Leo's family should be making sure these things are taken care of. But you know the Whitakers, nobody talks to anybody."

But she was going to start. At least with Leo and Fae. She owed her grandmother and grandfather and great-aunt everything. They gave her a home when Jillian dumped Vivienne and her on them. They never resented the girls. Gave them love, and stability, and paid for their educations.

"I should have—"

"Both of you cut it out," Ben said. "The market still delivers. They weren't going to starve to death, no matter what the drama princess says. And I can pick up groceries today if you need me to."

"Absolutely not," Issy told them. "Thank you for making the list, but I can go to the store. I'm sure you have plenty of things you need to do."

"No, I don't."

She narrowed her eyes at him. Tried to remember what it was he did for a living. They hadn't crossed paths in years.

"No, he doesn't. He's already been tromping out in the marshes this morning."

"Dear sis, I don't tromp in the marshes. I delicately skirt them except when taking readings, and then I'm very careful not to disturb things any more than necessary."

Chloe gave Issy a sideways glance. Issy could tell she was fighting a smile. "Oh, sorry. I meant tiptoeing. Tiptoeing through the marshes . . ." she warbled.

"Very funny. Hey, Is, can I bum a ride to the hospital to get my truck?"

"You really need to ask? Just let me get my bag."

Ben was waiting by the SUV when she got outside, but she took a moment to look around. She'd been too exhausted to notice anything but the lights last night. And the dark concealed things that were so obvious in the daylight.

The massive oak trees that sheltered the house from the heat of the summer sun weren't the only things looking their age. The old American Gothic mansion where Issy had grown up and where some of the great artists of the century had stayed and played was in need of a coat of paint.

"Growing roots?"

Issy shook herself. "Just taking it all in. And wondering if . . . oh, here she comes."

Fae Whitaker hurried out of the woods and across the lawn. She was lugging a tapestry bag and had swathed a magenta crocheted shawl around her already colorful ensemble.

"Oh, good, I'm not too late." She walked right past Ben and opened the back door while Ben was opening the front door for her. "I never sit in front," she said, and climbed in. "It feels like warp speed."

Issy and Ben exchanged looks over the hood of the SUV and got in.

No one spoke at first. There wasn't much to say. Issy didn't know what they would find today and she was sure Fae was worried, too. She was worried for them both. Fae couldn't care for Leo. And Leo would refuse to go into a rehab center.

Neither of them would be able to stay at the Muses without help.

"Aunt Fae, is Mrs. Norcroft still coming in every day?" Issy looked in the rearview mirror.

Fae was holding tightly to her bag.

"Aunt Fae?"

"I heard you. No, she isn't."

"When does she come in?"

"She doesn't."

"She retired?"

"No."

Issy exchanged looks with Ben. Why couldn't her aunt just fill in the details without Issy having to drag them out of her?

"She didn't die?"

"No, of course she didn't die."

"Then what happened to her?" Issy asked, exasperation nearly getting the better of her.

"Vivienne fired her."

"Because she was getting too old?"

"For stealing."

Chapter 5

"Stealing? Are you sure?"

Fae looked out the window. "That's what she said."

"After what? Forty years? I don't believe it. What did she steal?"

Fae didn't like confrontation, but it was hard to have a conversation in the rearview mirror when the other person was looking out the window. And the person she should be asking was Vivienne. Something she would add to the list of growing questions she had for her sister—when she found her.

Issy tried one more time. "Are you sure?"

"I'm not supposed to talk about it."

"Says who?" Issy breathed in, let it out slowly. She had a long fuse usually. It didn't pay to get angry in her business, too many priceless pieces of art, too many rich and philanthropic art patrons, many of whom needed to be constantly stroked, not yelled at. But Issy felt like yelling now. If George hadn't fought with his father, George would be in charge and Vivienne wouldn't be able to wreck their lives because of her unending resentment.

But it was useless to get angry. It would just ricochet across the family and end up hurting those she loved most.

Issy pulled into the hospital parking lot. "Shall we drop you off at your truck, Ben?"

"I thought I would come up for a minute if they're letting non–family members in. Just to say hello and then I'll leave you girls alone."

"Yes, Ben, do," Fae said before Issy could answer, so Issy merely repeated her aunt's words. "Yes, do."

Leonore was sitting up in bed, her eyes closed, when the three of them tiptoed into her room. Even in a blue hospital gown with her hair unclasped and wisping at her face, her grandmother looked . . . regal, if a little tired. She was smiling almost as if she'd known they were coming.

Issy stepped ahead of the others and took her grandmother's hand. "Grammy?"

"Wes?"

"N-no, it's—"

"It's your granddaughter Issy," Fae said, so uncharacteristically loudly that both Issy and Ben started.

Leo's eyes fluttered opened. She frowned. "Issy? Oh, dear. What are you doing here? You didn't have to come." Her gaze flitted from Issy to Fae. "Fae, you shouldn't have worried Issy."

"But she didn't, Grammy," Issy assured her. "Amanda called me."

"Amanda?"

"So you can blame the little drama queen," Ben told her.

Leo sighed. "Amanda. Zestful."

Zestful—one of Leo's highest compliments.

"What you really mean is 'little hellion,'" Ben said. "Morning Leo. You look awfully chipper."

Leo pushed herself up on the pillow. "I look a fright. More tubes and wires than Frankenstein's bride. Please say you came to take me home."

"Not up to me," Ben said.

"I talked with the doctor last night," Issy said. "They want to keep you in the hospital for a few days for observation."

"But the children are visiting."

Issy let that pass. She and Vivienne had come for a visit, too; they came and never left. Issy just hoped Vivienne wasn't following in their mother's footsteps. Issy had been frightened and lonely at first, but she'd come to love Leo and Wes and the Muses. Vivienne had never let go of her anger at being left behind. She'd blamed Issy, Leo, Wes. Just about everyone but Jillian. She wouldn't do that to her own children

And she couldn't expect Leo and Fae to raise another generation of children; they'd already raised two.

"Don't you worry about the children. You just get better."

Leo sighed again, her breathing slowed.

"I think we should let you sleep," Issy said.

"I shouldn't be here," Leo said dreamily. "I should be there. I don't belong here." Her free hand pinched at the sheet.

"Leo," Fae said in that same loud voice. "You're in the hospital. People are here to help you. Lots of them nearby to help you."

Leo's eyes opened. "Oh." She looked around, closed her eyes.

"You're tired," Issy said, glancing at Fae. "We'll come back later."

Leo's eyes opened again. "Reach in that drawer and hand me my checkbook."

"I have cash if you need any while you're here," Issy said.

"I don't need a thing here. And you're not going to use your hard-earned salary to feed and entertain those children. We still have an account at Ogden's Market, but you'll need other things, too."

Issy got out the checkbook and a pen.

Leo wrote out a check and handed it to her, leaned back on the pillow, and let the pen slide from her hand.

"I'll try to get back this afternoon," Issy told her, but Leo had already drifted off.

Ben followed her to the door, but Fae held back.

"Can I have just a minute?"

As soon as Issy and Ben left the room and the door was securely closed behind them, Fae turned to her sister-in-law.

"Leo wake up."

Leo sighed.

"I know you're medicated but you need to listen."

Leo lifted her hand, waved it listlessly in the air. Fae captured it and held on to it.

"Don't worry. I'll be fine."

Fae looked toward the door. "I'm not worried about you. I'm worried about us both."

"You have your secret love to protect you. And I have Wes."

Fae's blood ran cold. It was times like this when Leo said things that made Fae really worried about both their sanities.

She was supposed to be the crazy one and she was—a little. She was different, allowed her mind to explore paths and byways, but she always called it back. It was Leo who sometimes slipped away and seemed to have no real reason to come back to them. Unlike Fae, who had the best reason ever. And if Leo did that, slipped into the past and stayed there where she had been truly happy, Fae didn't know what she could do to save either of them.

And with Issy here, they might be in real peril. Issy was observant, intelligent. It wouldn't take her long to realize that Leo was living somewhere else. What she thought of Fae was anyone's guess.

She reached inside her bag, pulled a necklace of crystals out, and pressed it into Leo's hand. Closed her fingers over it.

Leo didn't resist, just sighed in her sleep or wherever she was.

Fae whispered an ancient chant over the bed. Warding off the two things she feared most. That someone else would decide their future. And the ultimate fear—something everyone had to face one day—the fear of what happens to the mind when it grows old.

Just say it, Fae. Dementia, Alzheimer's. No matter how well you care for it, the mind can just slip away. And if you've challenged it in all sorts of ways, it might slip away that much faster. Because reality wasn't a game you played until you got tired or bored and you closed the board, shut off the screen, and went to bed.

It was a far cry from withdrawing from what was real and not knowing the difference.

And these days she wasn't sure Leo always did. And that would be their undoing.

FAE LOOKED SO disheartened when she came out to the hallway that Issy decided not to question her more about what had been happening at the Muses.

"She looked better today," Issy said. "She's just still groggy from the drugs."

Fae shot her a fleeting look, then nodded.

"Ben, would you mind taking Aunt Fae home? I want to get to the store and bank, then I have some work I need to do."

"Gladly, but I can do the shopping if you trust me. Chloe does."

"Thanks, but I can handle it. And Aunt Fae, can we talk later? I feel like we haven't had a minute to . . . visit," she finished, thinking that *pick your brain* might cause her aunt alarm.

"Of course, dear."

"Don't hurry," Ben told Issy. "We'll just be back at the homestead relaxing with Chloe and the Brats: Whiner, Moaner, and Slump."

"Sounds like an eighties rock band," Issy said.

"If only," he answered. "You don't mind my truck, do you, Fae?"

Fae shook her head.

Ben took her arm and they walked away.

Issy deliberated about going to the bank or the market first. The market was on her way and there would be someone at the Muses to accept the groceries if she was delayed at the bank.

The Whitakers had been shopping with one Ogden or another since Joshua Ogden had moved to the area a century ago, bought a small plot of land, a horse and a cart, and began selling vegetables to the few inhabitants that had congregated around the cove. His son built the first Ogden Market and his son had added on until it resembled the current market.

The aisles weren't all straight, the products not always organized in the most intuitive way. It didn't have the selection or the lower prices of the large chain stores out on the highway, but it was only a few minutes from the Muses instead of twenty to forty depending on traffic, which in summer could turn a trip for milk into a whole afternoon's event.

And it was local. Issy didn't even have to think about where to shop. She pulled into the narrow parking lot that ran alongside the one-story brick building.

She grabbed a cart from the line along the sidewalk and read the week's specials taped to the storefront windows as she rolled it to the entrance.

The ancient automatic door creaked open and Issy entered Ogden's Market: Feeding the Community since 1928.

It had two counters, one to either side of the entrance and exit doors, which invariably created a bottleneck on busy shopping days. Today it was empty and Issy didn't make it past the cash register before Mrs. Ogden called out, "Good heavenly days, is that Issy Whitaker?"

Issy stopped. Smiled. "It is indeed." It was impossible not to emulate Mrs. Ogden's cheery disposition.

Mrs. Ogden's face slackened. "Is anything wrong up at the Muses?"

"Leo had a little episode. She's fine but she's in the hospital and they called me."

"You?"

Did that sound like an accusation? Maybe the whole town thought she had been neglecting her family. And the truth was that she had been.

"I mean, is it that serious?"

"It doesn't seem to be."

"Well, I hope you stay awhile. They need you."

Issy smiled, nodded. The last thing she'd expected were recriminations, but that's what Mrs. Ogden's tone insinuated. Or maybe it was her own guilt.

Keeping Chloe's list in one hand and steering her cart with the other, Issy chose oatmeal and cold cereal, granola bars, flour, sugar, paper towels, toilet paper, and dish detergent. On to hamburger, chicken, and a rump roast, to the dairy case for milk, flavored yogurt, string cheese, eggs. Then to the fresh vegetables. When she finally made the rounds and was back at the cash register, her cart was filled and Mrs. Ogden had been replaced by her husband.

"Issy, how are you?"

"Fine, thank you. And you?"

He nodded. He seemed more serious than she remembered him. Though she could readily understand that; she was the only customer in the store. The highway had been taking a lot of shoppers out of the town.

She began to take things out of the cart and put them on the counter.

"Um, Issy. I don't know how to say this."

Issy looked up. "What is it, Mr. Ogden? Is something wrong?"

"Well. It's just . . . I can't keep putting groceries on your grandmother's account."

"I totally understand." Things must be bad. She couldn't remember a day when the Whitakers had had to pay cash at the market.

"You take credit cards?"

"Oh yes."

"What about delivery? I have a few errands I have to run."

"Certainly, Issy." He began to ring up her purchases, then stopped. "I hate to ask, but . . ."

What now? she wondered.

"Do you think they're planning to send a payment anytime soon?"

Issy blinked. "I'm not sure I understand."

"Your grandmother's account hasn't been paid in over three months. I understand if she's having financial problems, but I can't continue to carry her. Things are just too tight here. I'm barely staying open as it is. I'm very sorry."

"Wait. Are you saying no one has paid for groceries in months?"

Mr. Ogden nodded. He looked like he might cry.

"There must be a mistake. My grandfather—" She stopped. She assumed that Leo had been left well off. Surely Uncle George must know what her circumstances were. His sense of duty—and pride—wouldn't allow his mother and aunt to live in poverty. And if there was a problem he didn't know about, he wouldn't want it spread all over the neighborhood that his mother was living in straitened circumstances.

"How much do they owe?"

He looked around to make sure no one was listening. There was no one in the store; still he leaned forward. "Almost two thousand dollars."

Issy had to force herself not to grab the counter for support. Vivienne and Dan were supposed to be managing the estate. Obviously someone was not taking care of business.

"I'll pay for the groceries today and I'll find out why you aren't getting paid and remedy the situation, if you can just wait until next week. I have to go to Washington tomorrow but"—Issy jumped off the deep end of the pier—"I'll be back on Wednesday. If I can't get this worked out this afternoon, I promise I'll get it worked out by then."

Mr. Ogden nodded jerkily. "I hated to have to bring it up—"

"Don't worry about anything. Obviously the mess-up is on our end. I'll look into it."

"Thank you." He finished ringing her up. Ran her credit card, and they arranged to have the groceries delivered as usual. Issy said good-bye and walked into the midday sun, stunned. If Leo had meant her to pay the Ogden's bill with her check for two hundred dollars, she was nowhere close.

Maybe she just didn't have a clear sense of what things cost. As far as Issy knew, her grandfather had always paid the bills. Leo had never had to worry about a thing. Surely he had made all bills a part of the trust.

She drove to the bank wondering if she should have just paid the arrears and called it a day. But she couldn't really afford to drop two thousand dollars without knowing if she would be reimbursed or not. And with Vivienne still gone and silent as to her whereabouts, Issy decided it was better to keep her own funds.

By the time she reached downtown, she had worked herself into righteous anger. They had waited to call her about Wes's death until it was too late to get to the funeral. Maybe they thought that Paris to New York was too long or expensive to spend on a funeral, even for one's grandfather.

By the time she got back, the funeral was over, and George, who was fuming that Wes had chosen Dan to administer the estate over him, wasn't speaking to any of them. Issy could understand why. George was the artistic black sheep of that generation, the only Whitaker who showed no interest in art or artists. Dan, on the other hand, was from another old Painter's Cove family. He had a flare for entertaining if not a true artistic sense. But Issy supposed it was easier for Wes to relate to Dan than to his own stiff-lipped son.

Issy snagged a parking place a half block away from the bank, outside the Cove Theater, established in 1870 and still presenting live plays from local theater groups and smaller bus and truck tours of Broadway shows. There was a large red banner stretched across the front: BUILDING FUND.

She walked down the block to the First Coastal Bank. It was fairly crowded and she had to stand in line for a teller. She endorsed the check and pushed it and her ID across the counter.

The teller smiled and keyed in the bank account. Looked at the screen and turned back to Issy.

"I'm sorry, there aren't enough funds to cover this check."

"Sorry, my grandmother is in the hospital and probably just got confused. Aren't all the accounts linked? I know there are several. Can you take it from another one?"

"I'm sorry," the teller said, looking around and finally catching the eye of someone whom she motioned over.

A middle-aged woman stopped at the counter. "Can I help you?"

Issy looked from the teller to the newcomer's name tag: BANK MANAGER. MRS. TALBOT.

"Could you check on this account for me?" the teller asked, blushing faintly.

"Of course, if you would come this way." She led Issy to the other side of the room, where a glass partition separated four desks. Mrs. Talbot stopped at the first desk, motioned Issy to sit, and then sat down at her computer screen.

"This is the Whitaker account."

Issy nodded. "Several of them."

"And you are?"

"Isabelle Whitaker." She explained who she was and why she was here. "Is there something wrong?"

Mrs. Talbot frowned at the screen. "Just a minute, please." She picked up the phone. "Mr. Kilpatrick, do you have a minute? Ms. Whitaker is here inquiring about her family's account." She hung up. "Just one moment."

No money in the account, no one had paid the grocery bills. Dan and Vivienne missing. Issy was getting a nasty feeling about where this was leading.

She recognized the bank president immediately. "Mr. Kilpatrick," she said, relieved.

It took a minute for him to place her. "Isabelle Whitaker. I can't believe it. Is this little Issy?" He turned to Mrs. Talbot. "I helped Issy open her first Christmas club account, must be twenty years ago."

"More," Issy said.

"So now, what would you like to do today?"

Issy's hands had begun to shake. "My grandmother is in the hospital."

"Oh, I'm sorry to hear that."

"She'll be okay, but she gave me a check to cash, and evidently there are no funds in the account."

"Oh, we'll remedy that in a jiff." He motioned Mrs. Talbot to the side and sat down in her chair. He frowned at the computer screen. Keyed in a string of numbers. Letters? Code? Waited, frowned. Typed more.

"Could this be an obsolete account?" Issy asked. "Maybe Leo got confused when she wrote the check?"

Mr. Kilpatrick continued to scroll down the page.

"I think, Issy, we should go down to my office."

He took her elbow and politely ushered her past the desks and through a heavy wooden door. They stopped inside a square room, paneled in dark wood and large enough for filing cabinets and a big desk.

"This is what happens when big banks take over smaller ones; new people come in to run something that has been run fine since its birth."

"What?" Issy asked.

"In an earlier time I would have been made aware of this immediately. But the computer didn't pick up anything unusual. I would have. Any banker worth his salt would, but this was done in a way to slip in under the radar."

"What was?"

"The withdrawals." He turned the screen to face her. "Money has been systematically withdrawn since the beginning of last year. Someone has cleaned out all the accounts."

"There must be *something* left." Issy's heart flipped up to her throat and lodged there. She cleared her throat, forcing it back down. "What about other accounts?"

"They were all consolidated several years ago when Wes changed his will. To make things easier for your grandmother and Fae."

"You're telling me there's no money left?"

"Not a red cent."

Chapter 6

Stephanie sat cross-legged on her beach towel and turned up the volume on her iPhone. She could still hear the waves. Boring. Well, it wouldn't be if she were with her friends. But no. She'd gotten dumped here with Mandy and Griff.

Her mother didn't even give her time to call around and invite herself to someone else's beach house. She'd only stayed long enough to unload the kids and left, just saying she'd be back as soon as she could. Did this mean she was sticking them here for the whole summer?

Or leaving them for good? Everyone knew the story of how Jillian had left Steph's mom and Aunt Issy with Grammy and Grandpa Wes, but her mom would never do that to them. Never.

Her mother could sometimes be a whack job, especially when it came to "the finer things in life." It wasn't like she didn't have a new foreign car, clothes and jewelry, and trips to the city. They lived in a huge house in Guilford. It wasn't like they were starving or anything.

She heard a car engine, stretched to see over the rocks that lined the back of Grammy's beach. Ben's truck was parked outside. She probably should go back.

She hadn't told Chloe where she was going. Not that it took a great stretch to figure it out. You didn't wear your bikini into town.

Chloe just said, "Don't forget your sunscreen." Chloe was okay. She was going to be a chef. That was so cool. You could go anywhere in the world and be a chef.

Steph groaned and scooted against the rocks. Crazy Aunt Fae was coming down the beach path. Her hair, long skirt, and oversized shirt were all blowing in the wind, almost pulling off a Free People look, but not quite.

She was bound to see Steph and then what? She'd probably stop to chat, ask if they'd heard from her mother, though Steph was going to call her Vivienne from now on like they did their grandmother, Jillian—who they never saw anyway.

That thought made her a little sick to her stomach and now she couldn't see Great-Aunt Fae from where she was sitting. How was she going to know when she was gone? What if she looked up and the crazy old bat was looking down at her?

She crouched along the rocks then peered over the top. Caught a brief glimpse of floating skirt as her aunt moved across the lawn to the trees. Steph pulled herself up and then stood on tiptoe to see better. Fae was skipping—skipping—through the woods.

Too weird. But where was she going? Aunt Fae lived in a cottage somewhere on the property, but Steph had never seen it. Fae didn't invite people to visit.

Well, Steph would invite herself. She scrambled up the rocks and started down the path, leaving her towel and shoes on the beach. She'd just have to remember to collect them before high tide.

Steph made sure to stay far enough back so that Fae wouldn't hear or see her, slipping in and out of the shadows like a shadow herself. That's the reason she was fully surrounded by trees before she became aware of how damp and dark it had become.

She could still hear the ocean, but she couldn't see anything but the woods. Even Fae was becoming dimmer as she flitted past trees and bushes. Steph wanted to take a quick look around, but she was afraid to take her eyes off Fae, who seemed to be moving faster now. So fast it was like she floated along the ground.

Steph blinked hard several times. Fae was getting farther ahead. What if she suddenly disappeared? Would Steph be able to find her way back?

She thought she saw a door peeking out through some vines to her left. Her heart thudded like crazy until she realized it was one of the old cabins where people used to store their paints. When she turned back, Fae was gone. Gone.

And of course the path forked in two directions. Which one did Fae take?

Stephanie squinted down the left path and saw the roof of another cabin, but it was old and falling apart. Nobody would live there. She must have taken the right fork.

Steph hesitated. This sucked. Why did she have to come here? She wanted to be in her own room, getting dressed for the dance. This was so not fair. She whimpered, then chastised herself for being a baby. *Follow the right.* At least it might lead back to the beach and she bet Fae would want a view of the ocean.

Listening to that voice of reason and trying hard not to wonder if it was just taking her farther away from civilization, she forced herself to walk on. She really wished she had stopped and put on her Crocs. The pine straw was soft enough but there were plenty of other things that stabbed her feet.

And then she stepped into sunlight. It was so sudden she had to close her eyes and take a couple of steps back into the protection of the trees. When her eyes recovered, she looked out from the canopy of leaves. There was a big meadow off to the left and a bunch of rosebushes that lined the other side of the path and spilled over the shore to the water.

Fae was walking up the steps of a cottage that was painted yellow and white and had a front deck, partially shaded by a big white umbrella. It was perched right on the edge of a rock, facing the water like the prow of a ship. The back was surrounded by trees, so that from the woods you might never know that it was there.

Steph formed a silent *wow*. It was like every fairy-tale cottage she'd ever seen in a book.

Before Fae got to the door, it opened and a man stepped out.

Steph bit back a screech and pressed behind the nearest tree. What if he was a burglar? Before she could decide what she should do, the man pulled Fae into his arms and kissed her. Right on the mouth. A deep one, like the kind they showed close up at the movies.

WTF? Aunt Fae had a boyfriend? Maybe she lived with him. Eww. Totally gross. She didn't want to imagine Aunt Fae getting it on with this old geezer. Except, for an old dude, he looked really good. White hair, long and all swept back from his suntanned face, then he looked up . . . right at her. Stephanie stepped behind the tree. When she looked out again, he'd turned away and stepped into the shadows of the eaves, so that Steph couldn't see him well anymore.

Then he and Fae went into the house.

Man, Steph was so tempted to go peek in the window to see what they were doing, but that would be just too weird. Aunt Fae had a lover? No. Impossible. Guys couldn't get it up when they got old. Look at all those commercials during football games.

When Aunt Fae came back outside, she was alone and carried a tray holding two glasses, a pitcher of what looked like lemonade, and a plate of some kind of cake.

Steph's stomach growled. She pushed her fist into it to shut it up.

Fae poured lemonade into the glasses and sat down, but the old dude didn't come back.

Steph's mouth was so dry she could cry.

"Well, are you going to crouch there in the bushes all day or are you going to come out and have some lemonade and orange loaf cake?"

Steph froze, afraid to move.

Her eyes felt so big she was afraid they might pop out of her head. *She knows I'm here.* But how? It was just plain spooky.

Aunt Fae turned toward where Steph was. Steph shrank back. Like she wouldn't be surprised if her crazy great-aunt morphed into some fairy-tale witch and zapped her into a bug.

But she just waved for Steph to come down, and Steph went.

"Have a seat and some lemonade," Fae said when Steph reached the little porch.

There were still only two glasses.

"But what about the old g—the man who was here?"

Fae raised her eyebrows. "What old geezer?"

"The man. He was on your porch, then you both went inside. And then you came out alone."

"Ah," she said.

Stephanie waited, she didn't like having to be patient, and she figured Aunt Fae was thinking of an excuse for him being there.

"Is he your boyfriend?"

Fae laughed. It sounded like those little bells people—losers—wore on their hats at Christmas. "What would I do with a boyfriend?"

Good question, Steph thought. "So who was he? The handyman?"

Fae leaned closer to her. "Well, if you must know." Her voice had taken on a sound that pulled Steph closer, she couldn't stop herself. "You are one of the few lucky people to witness a changeling in the flesh."

"A changeling?"

"An elf, to be precise."

"No way. Elves are tiny and have pointy ears and wear little pointy hats. And besides," she added abruptly, "they don't exist."

Fae cut off a slice of the yummy-looking loaf cake. She slid it on a plate and put it in front of Steph. "Well, I daresay, *Elf on a Shelf* doesn't exist except in the mind of a marketing department, but faeries, elves, and all sorts of fey people do, and they don't look like you think they do."

Steph raised her "skeptical" eyebrow to let her great-aunt know that she wasn't buying it.

"Have you read *Lord of the Rings*?"

Steph shook her head. "No but I saw all the movies."

Fae sighed. "Well, in *Lord*—"

"I remember. There were elves but that was just Orlando Bloom wearing prosthetic ears."

Fae sighed more deeply. One of those sighs people make when they're disappointed in you. Steph had experienced plenty of those. Yet the idea of an elf was taking hold in spite of her best rational efforts. The old guy did kinda look like Orlando as an old guy.

Fae pushed herself out of the chair. "Have another piece of cake. I have something for you."

Steph wondered if she was going to drag the "elf" out to the porch and try to pass him off as anything but an old dude. But she only came back with a big book.

Fae put it on the table and turned it around so Steph could read the title. "It isn't Tolkien but I think you might like it. Some of the stories are a little risqué, the satyrs are . . . you know . . . and male faeries adore beautiful women and can be very virile. But the elves . . . the elves are incomparable. So don't show your mother."

Steph grinned. "Thanks."

ISSY WANDERED OUT of the bank in a stupor. There was nothing left. The money that was supposed to last a lifetime and beyond was gone. She couldn't comprehend it; she didn't know what to do about it. She climbed into her car, unaware of the stifling heat, the blistering seats. There was no money.

It had to be a mistake.

She considered going back, asking them to check again, but that would be useless. The money was gone. Unless Dan Bannister had moved it to a different bank.

In small withdrawals instead of one big check? Not likely.

Not likely but possible, Issy insisted, clinging to her last hope. Yeah so if that was the case, where were the checks and where were Vivienne and Dan?

So help her if she ever saw her sister again, she would beat the crap out of her. Dan, too. Except Issy didn't even know how to throw a punch.

There was only one thing to do. And she didn't expect much help; she certainly hadn't gotten it the last time she'd called. She called anyway. And he actually answered.

"Uncle George. It's Issy." She suddenly didn't know where to begin.

"Is Leo—?" he prompted.

"She's okay. She had a fall, a dizzy spell or something. They're keeping her in the hospital for a few days for observation."

"I see. They'll probably want to check her into . . ." His voice buzzed out until he said, ". . . rehabilitation center. Our family always uses—"

"Wait, we've already been through that; she refused to go. I'll be lucky if I can get her to sleep in Mrs. Norcroft's room downstairs until she's more stable."

He snorted. "And where is Mrs. Norcroft going to sleep?"

"At her sister's on the other side of town, where she is now because Vivienne fired her for stealing."

"What? That's preposterous. She's probably just trying to save money. Tell her I said to hire her back. Oh, that's right, she's disappeared. Along with the deadbeat husband. I don't suppose they've returned?"

"Not yet."

"I doubt if you had the good sense to turn her offspring over to the state, did you?"

"No, they're at the house with Chloe Collins. Remember her?"

"Vaguely. Where are you?"

"At the moment sitting in my car outside the First Coastal Bank."

"Don't tell me you need money already and you can't get into the bank account. Get Leo to write a check."

"I did. She wrote a check and I tried to cash it. There's no money."

"Ridiculous; she probably wrote it on the wrong account."

"Mr. Kilpatrick took me to his office. Listen, Uncle George. There is no money. In any of the accounts. I couldn't even cash a two-hundred-dollar check."

"It must be some kind of glitch. Or he was looking at the wrong accounts."

"The glitch is there is no money left. And I don't think we can blame this on Mrs. Norcroft."

"No, dammit. I think we can blame this on Dan Bannister. But is Roy Kilpatrick sure about this?"

"Yes. What are we going to do?"

"You're going to do nothing and say nothing. I'm going to make a few discreet inquiries, beginning with Kilpatrick. Maybe things aren't as dire as they seem at first glance. Dan might have decided to move the funds to another bank for a higher interest rate."

"You think that might be it?" Issy asked hopefully.

"Perhaps, but I think it more likely that Dan and Vivienne absconded with the money. I'll check it out. Anything else I should know?"

Issy didn't want to confide in George. It would just make him angrier and more bitter. But it couldn't be helped. She was out of her element.

"They owe the market two thousand dollars. I don't think Leo and Fae have any idea that there is no money."

"And they are not going to find out."

"How can they not? I don't know what bills have been paid and which haven't. Mr. Ogden said he hadn't been paid in three months; maybe no one else has either."

"Issy, I'm depending on you to keep your head. There's no reason for this to become public knowledge. A scandal like this would be bad for the family and my reputation as a financial investor. And I don't intend to air the family's laundry in public just to exonerate myself from accusations of sheer incompetency at best."

"But you didn't do anything wrong."

"No. Dan Bannister did that, but when it hits the fan, it hits everyone."

"That's terrible. But if he did take the money do you think we'll be able to get it back?"

"Not if he's already spent it or hidden it. So it's best to prepare yourself to prepare Fae and Leo when the time comes."

"Prepare them for what?"

"For going to live in a state-supported facility instead of a posh assisted living cooperative that we'd planned."

"Uncle George. You wouldn't do that to them."

"I'm not paying for my father's follies."

"Why can't you just let it go?"

"That's what I intend to do, and I suggest you do the same. Not that I expect you to listen to my advice. They'll suck you dry if you let them and be totally oblivious about it the entire time. I can't tell you the times I gave them advice only to be ignored. I could have kept this from happening, but Wes was determin—" He broke off.

"So you won't help?"

"I'll make a few inquiries, have my secretary research state facilities. But I will not bail them out financially. You do real-ize we're talking millions. I don't know how much exactly. Wes didn't confide in me. No telling how bad it is. But the con-tents of the house should bring a good price at auction. And the house is standing on prime real estate."

"You can't."

"We have to think of what's best for Leo and Fae."

"And if it's sold, they won't have to go to a state facility?"

"I don't know, Issy. I'm not sure that it can be sold, and even if it could be, it wouldn't sell in time to help Leo and Fae. I'll call you when I learn something."

"But, Uncle George—"

He hung up.

"Thanks." For nothing. Still it was useless to argue. His animosity toward the family seemed out of proportion to a few loans and not being named caretaker of the Muses. If she'd hoped for a bailout, it wouldn't be coming from Uncle George or anybody else that she could think of.

It looked like the only thing standing between Fae and Leo and the old-folks home was Issy.

And she had to go to Washington.

"Hey, how's Leo?" Chloe asked as she took a double-sized casserole dish out of the oven. "I meant to ask Ben when he dropped Fae off, but he went straight to work. And Fae didn't come in, just hightailed it across the lawn to the woods."

Issy went to the sink and poured water into a glass. "She seemed better today. She wants to come home."

"They're not going to send her to rehab?"

Issy held up a finger while she guzzled down half of her water. The taste was so familiar that she forgot for a minute that their life was on a crazy spiral out of control. Instead she hovered in an endless summer of beach days and impromptu evening concerts, artistic temperaments, and Fourth of July fireworks.

"Sorry. She's refusing to go. Says she can take care of herself." Issy looked at the ceiling. "Do she and Fae look after themselves? Fae said Vivienne fired Mrs. Norcroft for . . ." She hesitated. She didn't want to start any rumors about the housekeeper, especially with the missing money hanging over their heads. Or not hanging over their heads, as it turned out. They were out of money. How was she supposed to deal with that?

"Issy, if you're worried about me saying anything, I already know. Ben stayed long enough to tell me. For stealing. It's a crock, but Mrs. Norcroft must be devastated. To be accused of stealing after she's worked for this family for decades; it's just mean-spirited. I've never seen Ben so angry. I confess I feel like punching Vivienne's lights out myself."

"Right now you'd have to stand in line," Issy said. "But first things first. Where is Ben?"

Chloe's face lit up.

"I just want to ask his advice about maybe moving Grammy downstairs at least until she's stronger."

"He's gone to check on some tests he's doing in the salt marsh." Chloe sighed. "I swear he'd tramp around in the mud all day if left to his own devices. What he needs is another interest."

"Like changing the back parlor into a bedroom suite?" Issy smiled. She knew that wasn't what Chloe was talking about. Chloe had been marrying off her older brother since he was sixteen and they were ten.

"Like trading in his bachelor life for marital bliss. But in spite of all the hard work I do, he's still single. I'll never have nephews and nieces."

Issy coughed out a laugh. "I have three that are yours for the taking."

Chloe made a face. "They're a little spoiled, aren't they?"

"An understatement. Vivienne was always one of those nothing-but-the-best kind of people. Sort of like our mother, only totally opposite. No bright lights, big city for her. She wanted the big house in the burbs, with the designer kitchen. She was born hardwired to HGTV. Her first words were probably 'granite countertops.'"

"Highly overrated," Chloe said.

"You're probably a quartz kind of girl, right?"

Chloe grinned. "Yep, though now all I have is imitation something."

"Hasn't held you back. Dinner was delicious last night."

"Thanks. I made lasagna for tonight. I thought the kids might like it."

"I'm sure everyone will." Issy pulled out a chair and sat down. "What am I going to do?"

"Well," Chloe said, sitting down beside her, "you're going to let Ben and me help you."

"Chloe, you're my best friend, the sister of my heart, but I need to make immediate arrangements for Leo and then find some kind of care for the children until their mother returns . . . *if* she returns."

She chewed her bottom lip. "Do you think Mrs. Norcroft would consider coming back—if I begged?"

"Maybe, but Mrs. Norcroft is getting older, too."

"I know." What she needed was someone strong and agile.

Someone who could care for an eighty-four—five?—year-old lady who thought she was thirty-five, keep one eye out for Fae, and still be able to manage kids. And who would work cheap.

What she needed was herself.

She was strong. She cared about the family. She was affordable. And there was no one else. She could finish up the D.C. installation via Skype. She had two weeks' vacation time due. Two weeks. Hardly any time at all.

The thought turned sour in her stomach. Hardly any time at all to fix her family situation, more than enough time to lose her job to an ambitious assistant. Everything inside her was screaming "get on that shuttle. If you don't, you'll never leave."

It was just like twelve years before, standing on the drive, trunks packed, waiting for Ben to pick her up in his truck and drive her to the university. Only then she hadn't wanted to leave. She'd actually begged them to let her stay.

The Muses was her home. The only place she'd ever known. Her family. A family who didn't run away.

But the truck came inexorably through the gates. When she turned back to Leo and Wes, they were arm in arm, smiling at her. No sadness at seeing her leave. And she wanted to run back to them and beg them once again to let her stay.

But they had discussed her future. They were excited for her getting out into the world. They assured her that the Muses would always be her home. But already she could feel the invisible chasm opening up between them as Wes and Leo turned to each other and Issy knew things would never be the same.

Ben stopped the truck, jumped out, and put her suitcases in the bed.

"Get a move on. Adventure awaits."

Easy for him to say. He was out of school and living in a shack on the marshes.

He put the truck in gear and drove out to the street, Issy looking back as her grandparents turned *sfumato*—blurred through her tears.

"You're going to be fine, kid. It's going to be an adventure." They turned left and suddenly the Muses was out of sight. Issy had never looked back.

Until now.

She glanced up to find Chloe watching her, and she knew what she had to do.

She couldn't leave them like this. It was time to call Dell and explain that she needed to take her two weeks' vacation now.

You're going to be fine, kid. An adventure. She'd worry about the rest later.

Chapter 7

Steph went to her room after dinner. She'd been hoping Aunt Fae would come back, but she didn't. Issy was there, though, and Issy wasn't happy about it.

You could tell just by looking at her. She smiled and everything, but she wasn't there. Not really there. Most of the time these days her mom and dad weren't there, even when they were. And now they weren't even there physically.

This was really beginning to suck. The only thing that didn't suck was Great-Aunt Fae, even though Steph hated to admit it. Her dad said she was a crazy old coot, and maybe she was kind of crazy, but in an okay kinda way.

Steph tried looking through the trees to see if any lights came from the direction of Fae's cottage, but there was nothing. She was pretty sure she could find her way back there, but maybe not in the dark.

She didn't exactly believe her aunt about the man she'd seen being an elf. Maybe it was because she'd gotten the image of *Elf on a Shelf* in her head and couldn't get it out. She'd read books about humanlike creatures and shapeshifters—she'd loved *Twilight*. She'd even read a few other vampire books, and come to think of it, there were faeries like Fae described in one of those. Her mother found them and took them away, saying they were inappropriate.

Her mother should get a clue. Some statistic said kids today knew more by the time they were Steph's age than their great-grandparents learned in their whole lives. Sometimes Steph wished she didn't know so much. But tonight she wished she knew if there really were other kinds of beings.

Changeling. Maybe that's what *she* was. It would make a lot of sense. She wasn't like Amanda or Griffin or their mother.

She locked the door, pulled the book Fae had given her from under the pillow, and opened it to the first page. It was kind of dull at first. An introduction about the science of otherworldly beings and various cultures they were found in.

She skipped over some of those parts, she could always go back. She read on and was just thinking about going to bed when the book mentioned the Elf King, which made her think of Legolas in the movie. And he did sort of look like the man today, except younger with long light hair and clear skin, tall and . . . And that's when she got to the good part.

ISSY STOOD JUST outside the kitchen looking both ways down the dark corridor. The kids had gone to bed. Chloe and Ben had gone home. Now it was just her and the house.

The house she loved. A huge house that suddenly felt claustrophobic.

She'd called Dell; he'd reluctantly okayed her vacation. She'd called Paolo, who of course completely understood. She'd scheduled a Skype meeting for the team the next morning.

She missed her work already. She always felt whole when

she was working, as she saw her exhibit designs become a reality. Maybe what she did wasn't fine art, but a bad installation could kill an exhibit.

Issy was proud of her work. She was afraid if she stayed away, she would lose it. Hers was a competitive field. For all their sublime artistic reputations, museums were places of cutthroat competition. The pay was poor, the hours were long, but it attracted passionate and talented people, some of them willing to throw you under the bus to get your job. Deirdre came to mind.

But it couldn't be helped.

Issy looked toward the front of the house, where the rooms lay in shadow. The Muses was such a huge part of all their lives. For more than two centuries, it had been a haven for artists, a meeting place of great minds, great ideas, rowdy fun, and heated arguments—and after World War I, free love and booze.

But the rooms that once had a function now pretty much served as homage to a past that would soon be gone. The furniture was fading, the wooden floors were dull, and Issy bet the whole place needed dusting and cleaning.

Maybe George was right. He'd been trying to move Leo and Fae into an adult community since Wes's death. They both adamantly refused to go. And Issy selfishly agreed with them.

But tonight she wasn't sure. And maybe they wouldn't even have a choice.

She turned away and traced her way through a warren of silver cabinets and larders until she came to the small apartment where Mrs. Norcroft had resided for as long as Issy could remember. She immediately knew Leo would refuse to stay in the servants' quarters. It would have to be the music room.

The music room, like all the other rooms she'd inspected, was crammed with the past. If the contents hadn't been so interesting, so old, so artistic, the family might be called hoarders. As it was, a lot should be cleared out. You couldn't even see what was there in the haphazard way things were placed around the room.

She picked up a green Arts and Crafts–style vase. Turned it over looking for an artist's mark, but the light was too poor to see. They needed to make an inventory.

She picked up another piece, an ashtray. And smiled. She remembered making it in the third grade. Her teacher had been upset that she would make an ashtray. Smoking had fallen out of favor by then—except at the Muses.

Definitely needed to catalog the good pieces, put aside the sentimental ones, and discard the rest. A giant yard sale, hopefully after she'd returned to her life in Manhattan.

At the door she turned and looked back into the room. Actually they weren't destitute yet. At least monetarily. They could always sell a painting or two. Some would bring small fortunes. If she could convince Leo to part with any of them. Then they could afford some repairs and to hire someone to care for the two old ladies.

Until that money ran out and they had to sell another painting, then another. She covered her face with her hands as the image of disappearing artwork took over. She didn't want them to become one of those families that had to sell things to stay alive. First a piece or two, leaving only an unfaded rectangle of wallpaper where they had hung. Until more and more empty places appeared and the walls became a patchwork quilt of loss.

She didn't want that for her family. Well, not for Leo and Fae. The rest of the family be damned. They'd all turned their backs. Walked away. Even the distant relatives didn't bother to stay in touch. Herself included.

Issy walked out of the main house to the conservatory, a massive glass structure that stretched across the back of the mansion and overlooked the sound. In its day it had provided light and southern exposure for visiting artists. Warmth for comfort while reading a book or having tea. Today the panes were dingy and covered with debris and leaves, their transparency dimmed by a layer of salt and sand and pollution.

Beyond it the lawn and gazebo had once been the scene of afternoon teas and town fetes and badminton. Sometimes impromptu dances would form, many of the ballroom variety with an orchestra and punch. Other times they devolved into the Isadora Duncan kind that invariably ended with nudity and a romp down to the beach to frolic in the waves.

Everything was just depressing and unkempt now. She unlocked a set of French doors and pushed them open. They creaked on their hinges and Issy stepped outside.

The night was dark and the waves were gentle, and for once she didn't feel the magic of the past or the present, just the cool night air. But as she walked down the lawn toward the beach, some of the tension gripping her began to ease. For a second she was a little girl, her head in Grammy's lap, drowsy before the large beach bonfire while Wes read from *The Diary of Frida Kahlo,* which had just been published.

Occasionally Grammy would cover Issy's ears with her hands, but Issy didn't understand the words. She just liked the way they floated around and around in her head until her eyelids grew heavy and the next thing she would know it was morning and she was in her own bedroom upstairs overlooking the sea.

And she'd wonder who had carried her upstairs like a sleeping princess, and she'd dress and run down to the kitchen for Mrs. Norcroft to make her breakfast, because she knew better than to wake any of the others because they would have "heads." Which Issy learned had more to do with brandy and champagne than anatomy.

She turned back to look at the house. Well over a hundred years old, large and rambling and filled with the history of an entire art movement, as well as the lives of friends, colleagues, and strangers who just stopped in.

It had withstood fire and storms, no easy feat being situated so close to the sound and the cove. But Mother Nature had spared it so far. Issy just hoped it wouldn't be her generation of Whitakers who oversaw its downfall.

She had no illusions about being able to do her job for the museum while taking care of the situation with the Muses and her family. The buck had stopped with her. She could let George take over. Put Leo and Fae into some assisted living place where they really would go crazy. Sell off the Muses to someone who would raze it and put up a luxury condominium. Cut down the woods and roll out golf course sod. Add an infinity pool that flowed into the cove, where the town would no longer be welcome, and skinny-dipping would only be allowed to members of the association, if it was allowed at all.

The cove would be congested with Jet Skis and boogie boards crammed together at the deep end near the boulders where the epic beginning of Leo and Wes's great love story had unfolded. Drive their ATVs through the meadow where, according to Leo—with much blushing by her children and grandchildren—Max had been conceived.

And the knoll where Max and Wes were buried?

Issy couldn't let it happen.

Not to the family, or the art or the memories. There was over a hundred years of artwork adorning the walls, the shelves, the tables, the closets of the old house. Masterpieces and mistakes, the poorly executed and the heights of the craft, all nestled together higgledy-piggledy. The architecture itself was a historical example of American neo-Gothic.

If they lost the house, some pieces would be sold at an estate sale; others carted away. The better pieces would end up in museums or private collections, where the only context would be the typed information plaques by each work.

Moonlight on Painter's Cove by Adam Ellis. 1968, donated by Mr. and Mrs. whoever bought it at auction.

The viewer would never know that on the nights of the full moon, whoever was staying at the house went down to the cove beach and danced until the moon rose high in the sky. Nor that if you could see beyond the frame, just off to the right, they would be there, iridescent in the night, spinning and laughing and celebrating life. Nor that *Moonlight* was the last painting Ellis had finished before he drove his automobile off the bridge and into the sea.

Every work there had its own story, no matter how small, and each deserved more than a small cardboard tag.

How could George even think of selling?

Issy shivered and started back toward the house, rubbing her arms and walking a little faster on the dew-slippery grass.

A light on the second floor went dark. Steph's room, she thought. Worried about her mother and father. Or maybe just tired of texting her friends.

Issy knew what she had to do.

Muses by the Sea was her family's heritage. Not just financially, but artistically and civically, and most of all, historically. It was an icon. The place where many young artists got their start, where tired ones found rest and rejuvenation. Where those in despair were healed and sent out to carry on. Where her grandfather and her uncle Max were buried on the knoll and the Coastal Art style was born.

The Whitakers had a responsibility to preserve that past, perhaps to promote its future. Besides, Leo would never leave the Muses and Fae would never leave her.

And Issy? That was the big question she'd have to answer in the next two weeks.

WHEN ISSY ROLLED out of bed the next morning, it was too early to Skype Paolo and Deirdre at the installation. Too early for the kids to be up. Too early even for Chloe to be in the kitchen making breakfast as she insisted on doing until Monday when she had to go back to work.

Issy made coffee and carried it into the library, where she set up her laptop and spent the next couple of hours alternating between double-checking the layout of the Washington installation and wondering how she could save her family.

Her first cup grew cold and she went back to replenish it. Still too early to call Paolo and no new ideas about what to do about the Muses. She drank her coffee standing at the kitchen window, her mind as blank as an empty canvas.

In the morning light, it was pretty clear that Vivienne and Dan, whether through intent or inefficiency, had lost the money from the estate . . . was it even possible that they'd stolen the money and fled the country?

It seemed so ridiculous. As much as she and her sister didn't get along, and as much as Vivienne had resented being abandoned by their mother, Issy couldn't imagine her cheating her family and abandoning her own children. Though it seemed that's just what Vivienne—as well as their mother—had done.

No way was Issy going to take in her sister's kids. She didn't have the time or the inclination to be a mother. Certainly not to those spoiled brats.

Something banged above her head. Issy picked up her coffee and fled to the library.

At nine o'clock she logged into Skype. "Morning, gang."

Deirdre smiled back at her; Paolo, standing beside her, didn't.

"So what's up? How's it going?"

"The understructure is mostly in place," Paolo said. "Here." He lifted the laptop and panned slowly around the exhibition space.

The walls were clear and already fitted for the new hangings. Crates of paintings stood around the perimeter of the room, waiting to be hung. Another group were being held at the end of the room along with several display cases that would be put in place once the first series was hung.

"Looks good," Issy said when she was once again facing her two assistants.

Deirdre glanced quickly at Paolo. "We do have one problem."

"Hit me with it."

"We're ready to hang numbers one fifty-one, -two, and -three, but there's a spatial question."

Issy consulted her specs. "Where's the problem?"

Deirdre shouldered Paolo out of the way. "It's with number one fifty-three. The old frame went in for repairs and the temporary one is larger, which skews the layout."

"Didn't all this get checked off before we left?" Issy said.

"It did," Paolo said, his head moving back into the screen. "Several frames were sent to the fabricators. I just called them and asked them to remeasure the original one. They measured. The original is smaller than the new one, but the new one is the same size as the specs we sent."

"So we sent out the wrong measurements?"

"Sure looks that way."

"Don't look at me," Deirdre said. "I just typed what was on the sheet."

"Double-checked your figures?"

"I always do. They were obviously measured wrong."

Which Issy had entrusted to Paolo.

"Well, let's see what we can do." Issy pulled her tablet out of her briefcase. Opened to the D.C. Modern file and brought up the schemata of the installation. Zoomed in on paintings 151 to 153.

They were talking about a couple of inches each way. Even in the smaller space of the D.C. Modern, it wouldn't be a problem.

"Thanks for pointing it out, but I think we'll be okay."

"Fine. Just thought you should know."

"Yes, thank you. I should. Now, why don't you two bring me up to speed on the rest of the installation."

IT WAS GOING to be a busy day, Fae thought as she walked up the narrow path toward the Muses. And she also knew it was going to be stressful. She and Leo were in a pickle, no doubt about it. George threatening to put them in a home. Dan letting the place fall to pieces. Issy pulled away from her job in the city.

That wasn't what they wanted for her. They wanted her to be able to leave and come back at will, not disappear and never return—and not to be trapped here. Now, if they weren't careful, she wouldn't be given the choice.

And that wasn't fair to her.

Fae had known this would happen. Not all of it. Not how or why or when. She didn't have a crystal ball or ESP or an ability to commune with spirits, though plenty of people thought she had all three.

Ever since she was a child she'd been able to feel things. She couldn't predict train wrecks or tornadoes, or who would get into Harvard or be married first. But she knew other kinds of things.

Most people just didn't pay attention. And even when they did they very rarely understood. Fae could feel energy aligning itself, right and left, yin and yang, light and dark. She didn't know how she knew these things. But she did.

She'd just been a kid when she told their mother that poor Mr. Sheraton needed help to feel better. But she didn't know that he would soon take his own life.

"Don't fret, Fae," her mother said. "He's fine."

"Hell, he's the life of the party," her father said.

He was still the life of the party a few weeks later when he took his father's shotgun to his head.

Some people had blamed Fae, like it was her fault for mentioning that he was unhappy. It was weird the way people reacted when they didn't understand something. How they would search for someone to blame. Always looking outside themselves.

Hell, Fae didn't understand most things, but she never lashed out because of it. It got around school that she put curses on people. She couldn't; there was no magic in her, not that kind anyway. She just felt things.

And she felt the moment when her friends stopped being her friends. She'd been lonely at first. Then she discovered the hippies. Flower Power. Make love not war. It didn't matter to them that she was a little odd; they were odd, too. Or a little old: there were plenty of other older dropouts. Dropped out of the wrong job, the wrong life, the wrong mind-set. It was a vibrant, active, thoughtful time of brilliant creativity. Artists of all kinds ready to push the parameters of life and art. Vonnegut, Kesey, Salinger. Ginsberg, Peter Max.

Psychedelia was in. It had been Fae's happiest time.

Happiest until she met Adam. And then it was euphoric or heartbreaking depending on the day, the hour, the year. No one knew about them. Not even after Adam's death.

The crunch of gravel snatched her from her thoughts. Ben's truck came to a stop at the side of the house.

Fae slipped behind the scrub oak and waited until he went inside. She wasn't sure why she hid; she was going there, too. She just needed a few more minutes to herself. Time to figure out what to do. Then she would go inside and ask them to call a cab to take her to the hospital.

She came out from behind the tree and hurried across the circular drive to the front porch. She'd pick up the mail on her way to the kitchen. That would give her a little more time to corral her wandering thoughts. The mailbox sat next to the front door. It had been there since the house had been built. A rectangular brass box heavy with patina.

She lifted the top, pulled out the mail, pushed it closed. She didn't much care about the mail. It was mostly circulars and politicians' promises and ads for hearing aids and burial insurance. She could hear just fine and so could Leo. And as for graves, Leo would be buried up on the knoll with Wes and Max. Fae would be buried in town in the family plot, maybe. Or maybe she wouldn't be buried at all. She might float away on a funeral pyre.

She went inside and dumped the mail on the side table. Noticed there was another letter from the power company. She stuffed it in the pocket of her madras tunic and went into the library.

She already knew what she'd find. She crossed to the desk, pulled at the top drawer. It was locked. She fished in the cut-glass catchall bowl for a hairpin. Unlocked the drawer with it and tossed it back into the bowl.

She pulled the drawer open. Just as she thought. She closed the drawer—no reason to lock it now—and made her way to the kitchen.

"Just in time," Ben said. "Do you want a lift to the hospital?"

"Please. If you're going," she said, and sat down.

Chloe set a mug of coffee down on the table in front of Ben. "Fae, would you like some tea?"

Fae shook her head.

Ben looked over his mug at her. "Is everything okay?"

"No."

"You're not worried about Leo, are you?"

Fae shook her head. She should just show him the letter and ask for his advice. Leo kept saying Dan would take care of it, but it wasn't looking like Dan was coming back. And she didn't want to worry Issy with it. She had her life and her work and Leo was adamant about not burdening her with their "problems." Actually they were really only Leo's problems, but Fae had promised Wesley to look after her.

She reached into her pocket and pulled out the crumpled bill. Pushed it across the table. "I think we need your advice."

Ben took the letter, opened it, and read. "Fae. You haven't paid your electric bill in three months."

She knew that, Leo knew that. Dan was supposed to take care of it. But Dan hadn't.

Ben shook his head, looked at his sister. Fae knew they were thinking, Those poor old women, too old to take care of themselves. Well, she could tell him, she and Leo could take better care of themselves than Dan could do. Or would do. She'd tried to tell Wesley. George had tried to tell him. But you couldn't tell Wesley anything.

Dan pandered to him, talked about the importance of family and art and keeping tradition. And Wesley Whitaker, who had held his own with some of the great talents and minds of the century, bought it hook, line, and sinker.

Even after the bills started to mount up Fae couldn't get Leo to take action. Because there was no convincing her that her beloved Wesley had made a mistake in whom to trust.

And now it was left to Fae to break their trust and tell someone. She didn't want to burden the Collinses, they were always so kind and helpful, but she didn't know who else to turn to. Certainly not George. And not Issy; Leo had made that perfectly clear.

"You might as well see the rest." Fae walked out of the kitchen and back to the library. Ben and Chloe followed her. She went straight to the desk and pulled open the top drawer.

"Good heavens," Chloe blurted out. "There're so many."

"And what the hell are they?" Issy asked from the doorway.

Chapter 8

I ssy!" Fae threw up her hands, sending papers flying into the air. "Why aren't you gone? I mean, aren't you supposed to be in D.C.?"

"Yes. But I changed my mind," Issy said, coming into the room. "What is all of this?"

"Nothing. Just a few . . ." Fae trailed off as she bent down to pick up the papers that had fallen to the floor.

Issy snatched up a pile before she could get to them. She looked at one, slid it to the back, and looked at another. "What the heck? Have any of these been paid?"

Fae shrank back.

"Issy, lighten up," Ben said. "She came to get help and was just showing us these when you came in. Why don't we all go sit down, preferably over coffee, and try to all get on the same page."

He put his hand on Issy's shoulder. She knocked it away. She wasn't ready for any more surprises and the last thing she needed was sympathy.

They went back to the kitchen, Chloe guiding Fae with a protective hand.

"Sorry," Issy said to Ben, who had fallen in beside her. "Knee-jerk reaction."

"It's okay. If you're going to lose it, I'd rather you lost it with me, or even Chloe, than with Leo and Fae."

"I didn't mean to, but what else can possibly go wrong?"

"It's a few unpaid bills. You can work out a deal with the utility company."

Issy bit her lip. This was probably how Fae felt before showing the Collinses the utility bills. Wanting to protect the family. Wishing the problem would just go away. But Issy would have to tell them the rest. It was stupid not to. Maybe between them they could come up with a plan. And she couldn't protect Fae or Leo from the actuality of their situation much longer. Maybe they even knew about it.

"It's a lot worse. It's—" She stopped. Mandy and Griff were coming down the stairs.

"We're having a breakfast picnic," Chloe chirped. "Hurry up and let's get ready." She effortlessly handed off Fae to Ben. "Come on, you two."

The children scrambled after her.

"Where's Steph?" Issy called after them.

"Reading some book. She wouldn't come down."

"First, coffee," Ben said. "And tea for Fae," he added, depositing Fae in a chair at the table. She'd started to cry and Issy hurried over to her. Put her arms around her. "I'm sorry, Aunt Fae. I was just so surprised. I've had a rough few days and I took it out on you. Forgive me."

Mandy and Griff were watching, wide-eyed. Chloe grabbed a tablecloth and napkins from the pantry and sent them outside to cover the picnic table.

Fae patted Issy's hand. "I didn't want you to find out. Leo was very insistent that we not burden you with our problems."

Who else could they have burdened? George? Jillian? Dan and Vivienne were supposed to be taking care of them and had failed miserably. Maybe even cheated them. Who was she kidding? Definitely cheating them. There was no money, no way to stay afloat, and Issy didn't have a plan.

Once coffee was made and Mandy and Griff were settled outside, silence fell on the four people sitting around the kitchen table.

Issy put down her cup. "How long have you not paid the utility bills?"

Fae had been holding her mug of tea, letting the steam curtain her face. But her hands jerked, tea splashed, and she quickly put down the cup. "We never pay any bills. We never see them. Wes left it all in Dan's hands. The bills go directly to him. He handles everything.

"Until last fall." Fae took a sip of tea. Frowned into her mug, and Issy wondered if she was reading tea leaves and had forgotten they were talking.

"Aunt Fae?"

"A letter came to the house. It said we were past due and to call the utility company. Leo said there had to be a mistake and she would call Dan. We didn't hear any more about it and thought everything was fine. Then they sent a man around. I paid them something. Just until they figured out the glitch.

"But it happened again; I paid them again, but I told Leo that I wasn't going to keep spending what little we had on things Dan should be taking care of.

"She didn't want to bother him, so I called. He was shocked, said it was the first time he heard of it. Made it sound like Leo hadn't called him. And that he would straighten it out. But he didn't. How could he not have noticed the absence of utility bills?

"And now Vivienne and Dan have both disappeared. Left their children. Who would do such a thing?" Fae's mouth clamped shut and her eyes widened. "Oh, I'm sorry, Issy. I should hold my tongue when I'm upset."

"No need to apologize, Aunt Fae. And we don't know that Vivienne has left for good. Mandy said she'd gone to 'look for Daddy.' Maybe all isn't lost." *Pipe dream, Issy. Don't plant the seeds of false hope.* Things were looking pretty bleak.

"Steph said she was supposed to call today. If she doesn't, I think I should fill out a missing-person report, don't you?"

"I suppose we must."

"Is there anything more?" Issy asked. "Are there other bills you know about?"

Fae shrugged. "I mostly live in my cottage, take care of myself."

"You do have electricity and heat?"

"Of course I do, but Dan doesn't pay for it."

"Then who?"

"I do. I have a little stipend. It pays for me and helps out Leo. No one could live on the stingy allowance Dan gives us. But please don't tell Leo any of this."

"Why? She needs to know."

"What good will it do? Wesley trusted Dan and now Leo trusts Dan. That's a given."

Issy nodded that she understood. In Leo's eyes, Wesley could do no wrong, ergo . . . "But you don't trust Dan."

"I never did. I told Wes not to put him in control, George

told him. But Wes knew what he wanted." A tear fell into her tea. "What he wanted was Max. Max was artistic, sensitive, cared about people. And he died in that senseless war.

"When Vivienne married Dan, Wes reimagined him into Max. There was no reasoning with him."

She rummaged in her large pockets, brought out a handkerchief, and wiped her nose. "Max would have taken care of us willingly. Even George would have seen that we didn't go without."

Fae put the handkerchief away. "We'll just have to pay the bills ourselves. Leo can only draw money from one account without Dan's signature, but there may be enough money in it. Did you notice when you cashed her check?"

Here it was. Issy would have to tell them. Her stomach seized up; for a staggering moment she thought she was going to be sick right at the table. But she pushed it away.

"Or I could put some toward the payment and hopefully Dan will fix it when, or if, he gets back."

Issy was pretty sure Dan wasn't coming back. She was more than ever convinced he and Vivienne had taken the money and run. Now the others would have to know, too. Even if George's people found the money, he'd said the chances of getting it back were slim. They needed to take care of things now.

"It's not just the utility bill, Aunt Fae." Issy hurried on before she lost her courage. "The market bill hasn't been paid in months."

Fae covered her face with her hands.

"That's okay," Chloe said. "People sometimes get behind. It happens to everyone. Mr. Ogden will understand."

Ben shot Issy a concerned look.

"There's worse."

Fae moaned.

"I went to the bank. The accounts are empty. They've been completely cleaned out."

She heard Chloe's intake of breath, Ben's expletive, and Fae's cry of pain. Issy felt numb, depleted, as empty as the inside of a blown egg—and about as fragile.

The Whitakers were broke and they were about to lose everything.

No one said anything for the longest time; they just sat looking at each other.

Issy glanced at Fae, trying to gauge how much of this she was taking in and if she was coming to her own conclusion. "None of this is your fault or Leo's."

"Dan is responsible for everything," Ben said, an edge to his voice Issy had never heard before.

"And they blamed Mrs. Norcroft," Chloe added indignantly.

"We need a plan," Issy said. "George said he would look into things, but—"

"George knows?" Fae let out a keening sound that made them all jump.

Chloe and Issy both rushed to her side. Fae grabbed Issy's wrist. "You mustn't let him."

"Let him what?"

Fae shooed the question away with a flutter of both hands. "I have to think."

"Aunt Fae. I think we all need to think together on this one."

"You don't understand."

"Then enlighten us."

"Leo mustn't know."

"Why? She's going to have to be part of the decision making," Issy said. "Because decisions have to be made."

"It will kill her. Such perfidy from her own children. Go back to the city, Issy."

Issy's breath caught on a stab of pain.

"Fae." Ben's voice was like a douse of cold water. "Issy is trying to help you."

"I know," Fae moaned. "But she can't and it will drag her down with us."

"What are you talking about?"

"He'll put us in a home." Fae began to cry in painful gulps. "I promised. I promised."

"You mean *he* promised. George promised not to insist on assisted living?" Chloe said.

"What? Oh, he's always threatening to send me, but it isn't up to him."

"Do you mean Dan?" Issy asked.

Fae nodded.

Issy's fist clenched under the table. "He's threatened to send you and Leo away from the Muses."

"If I mentioned the bills to George."

"Well, Dan's not here, and we won't let that happen," Issy said as brightly as she could. She was pretty sure it sounded close to hysterical.

She saw Ben frown at her. He knew as well as she did that nothing could stop them from losing their home if they didn't come up with enough money to keep it.

And Issy couldn't accomplish that alone. She was used to making her own decisions. If she needed a second opinion, she went to Paolo. She wished he was here. He had more experience with family than she did, raised by two old ladies and a sister who resented her. It wasn't exactly experience to inform a good decision.

But Ben and Chloe came from a big, close-knit family. And they cared about Fae and Leo. She could depend on them to help.

"She'll have to be told," Ben said. "But we'll wait until she's settled back at the Muses. Maybe there's some factor we don't know yet."

The screen door banged and Mandy and Griff ran in.

"We're dying of boredom," Mandy cried. She stopped cold, and held out a hand to keep Griff behind her. "What?" Her face crumpled.

"Nothing," Chloe said, jumping up. "It's just grown-ups having coffee."

"No, it isn't. Aunt Fae is crying and Issy's mad. When is my mom coming home?"

Griff started to cry.

Issy just sat there and watched. She felt sympathy for Mandy and Griff but she didn't know how to deal with them and didn't want to. Chloe was all over it.

"Everything is fine, we were just trying to decide what to do."

Which was true, thought Issy, but not in the way the kids took it, because they immediately starting making suggestions—the movies, the beach, walk to town and buy ice cream, go to Fun Town; they'd gone to Fun Town last year.

"You can come to town with me," Fae said, standing up. "I'd meant to go to the hospital before story hour but it's getting too late. Would you like to go to story hour and then you can get ice cream?"

"Yeah! Yeah!" They both jumped up and down.

"I'll go get my things and when I come back we'll begin the parade."

"We'll need parade clothes," Mandy said. "Come on, Griff. Let's get crazy."

Chloe laughed. "Issy, you and Ben discuss a few things. I'll go rouse Steph and get these two into parade mode."

The kitchen emptied out to silence. An awkward silence.

Issy got up and poured them both more coffee, then went to the sink to look out the window. Somehow it was easier to say things with her back turned to him.

"I'm sorry you and Chloe got dragged into this mess. I had no idea."

"We didn't either. I don't even know what to say, except I'm sorry, Issy. I'm kind of clueless in general, according to Chloe. I get involved in water temperatures and marsh environment to the exclusion of other stuff. But Chloe is good about checking up on people. And I know she's always making Leo and Fae food and dropping it off. And I'm sure she didn't have a clue either, or she would've put her nose right in it, and badgered me until I did, too."

"You've already done more than I could hope for and Chloe is great with the kids. I think all of us Whitakers missed that gene."

"You didn't. You just haven't tried it yet."

"Let's just say these three aren't inspiring my biological clock to start ticking. I should have kept better tabs on Leo and Fae. If I'd stayed in touch with Leo, I might have been aware of any incipient problems. I'm really good at doing that with my work. I pretty much stink at it with my family."

"I think it's them more than you."

"Thanks." She turned around. Found him standing right there. He put down her coffee cup and gave her a hug.

"Why did I let myself drift away from my family?"

"Because they hurt you. They didn't mean to. Did you know that Leo and Fae—and Wes—cried after you left for college?"

Issy pulled away. "They did? But they made me go."

"They pushed you to go so that you wouldn't ultimately feel trapped and resent them for it."

"I would never . . . they didn't say that."

"They didn't have to. Leo and Wes always felt they'd driven their own children away because they'd held on to them too tightly. They wanted you to be free to make your own choices."

"But I—I didn't choose too well." Issy covered her mouth with her palm.

"Hey, I didn't mean to make you cry. Chloe will have my head."

"You didn't. We're just a lachrymose family."

He chuckled. "I just thought you should know."

She looked up at him. "I'm glad you told me. I don't know why we're all so secretive and I don't know why they thought I would feel trapped here. I loved it here."

"Maybe you loved it too much."

"You know, for a scientist—"

"I know. I should stick to Phragmites and sediment accumulation. I just wanted you to know that . . . well, you can count on Chloe and me for anything we can do. We're not financially useful, but whatever we have—"

Issy eased away and they both turned to face the window.

"George says they'll have to go to assisted living. The state-run kind. He said he wouldn't help them financially."

"What? You think George would let the family go bankrupt? Have the house go on the auction block?"

"He said as much."

"It does make sense, in a way," Ben said. "I think Fae was

only half right about George and Max. George might not have the artistic talent his brother Max had, or the passion. He has a passion, just not for art, and I know he turned it against the Muses and the family when Wes went over his head to Dan. Maybe even before. But can he force Leo to sell?"

"I have no idea. Does she own it? Is it protected? I don't even know what Wes's will said. They didn't invite me to the funeral."

"That's why you weren't here?"

"I was in Paris. By the time they bothered to tell me he was dead, it was too late for me to book a flight."

"Ah, Is. Leo was inconsolable. She wasn't thinking straight. Fae had to do everything. Not who I'd put in charge of any organization. At the last minute Vivienne stepped in and . . ." He trailed off. "I'd better get going. My Phragmites are waiting. Hang in. I'll be back in time for dinner."

"She what?" Issy called after him.

"She took over the details." The door slammed after him.

Vivienne. Of course. Issy had been making allowances for her sister ever since they were little. It was Issy's fault they were at Grammy's. Vivienne was old enough to remember their life in Hollywood and thought of it as home. She missed her mother more than Issy did. But now, at last, Issy was done making excuses for her. Right now she'd gladly scratch her eyes out.

But Vivienne wasn't here and Issy was. And it was obvious she was the one who was going to have to fix the mess.

She didn't have any savings worth speaking of. New York was expensive and museum work didn't pay all that well. Whether they finally reclaimed the money or not, she needed money now. She didn't even know where to begin. George? Vivienne? Dan? Giant fails.

There was one person who did have money and, as far as Issy was concerned, owed them big-time.

And Issy had her cell number. She hadn't used it in years, but today she didn't think twice. She walked out to the conservatory, where she knew she wouldn't be disturbed, and made the call.

It rang several times.

Issy was about to hang up when "Take that, you filthy bastard" erupted loudly from her phone. A loud crash. A thud.

"Hello?"

"Hello, Mother."

"What? Who is this? You must have the wrong number."

"Jillian!" Issy demanded before Jillian could hang up.

Silence at the other end and finally, "Vivienne?"

Issy stopped—a disappointed sigh. "No, this is Isabelle. Your other daughter." She crossed to the couch. Looked around to make sure she'd shut the door, then switched to speakerphone and put the phone on the glass-top table by the window. No reason to get any closer to her mother than absolutely necessary, and if she wasn't holding the phone, she wouldn't be tempted to hurl it across the floor. The conservatory floor was stone and an outburst of temper would mean a trip to the Apple store.

"Oh, Oops. It's you. How are you, darling?"

Issy grimaced. "I'm fine."

"And Vivienne?"

"I have no idea, seeing how she's missing. She dumped her children with Leo and Fae and disappeared. Sound familiar? Leo is in the hospital."

"Oh, dear, what's wrong with dear old Leo?"

"Your *mother* . . ." Issy paused long enough for the *mother* to sink in. Jillian never called anybody by anything except their given name, not even her daughters, and she didn't even call Issy by her real name. They in turn were never allowed to call her Mother, Mom, Mommy, or any of those ordinary endearments. Just Jillian.

"She fell. She'll be all right but not all right enough to take care of three motherless children."

Issy paused again to make sure no one was listening. Her talks with her mother inevitably ended with Issy's humiliation, and since she'd already had to bare her family's troubles to Ben and Chloe and cried in front of Ben, she wanted to make sure she would endure this without witnesses.

"We're in a bind. I'm supposed to be in Washington, D.C., but I drove up here first to check on things." She waited, hoping to let her words sink in so that Jillian would actually offer to help without Issy having to ask. But *Is there anything I can do?* were words not in Jillian's vocabulary.

"Well, that's such a relief. I'm sure you're handling it just fine. I'd feel so guilty being here in Saint-Tropez instead of . . . home."

Give me a break, Issy thought. Home to Jillian was wherever her next part and next man were.

"Jeez, Mom," Issy said, knowing it would infuriate Jillian and mentally kicking herself. Stupid to make someone angry when she was going to ask for a favor. "Aren't you the least bit concerned that your daughter, your *other* daughter, is MIA?"

"Vivienne? Don't tell me she's done a bunk. But really, who could blame her? Between that deadbeat husband and those—how many children are there now?" Jillian sniffed for the benefit of her audience—Issy. "She's never even brought them to visit. Some people can't forgive and forget."

Issy looked at the ceiling. Some people would love to forget and Issy was one of them. No such luck. "Nobody blamed you. And no one is blaming Vivienne. We're concerned. Vivienne has always been devoted to her children, she wouldn't just disappear."

"Like me, you mean? That was an unkind thing to say, Oops. I did what I thought was best for the two of you."

Issy gritted her teeth. She hadn't said it and she was still being blamed for saying it. You couldn't win with her mother. She always managed to turn everything around and make it about her. Issy took a breath. Let it out. "Fine. But now it's time for you to step up to the plate."

"Me? What can I do? I'm half a world away. Call George."

"I have. He says if Vivienne doesn't come back, the kids will have to go into foster care. He wants to put Leo and Fae in an assisted living facility and sell the Muses in order to support them there."

Issy heard a thud, turned to look, but no one was there. The house was falling down around them. Then she saw a book on the floor by the couch. And on the couch was Steph, sitting bolt upright.

Issy grabbed the phone, killed the speakers.

". . . Muses?"

"What?" demanded Issy, jamming the phone to her ear.

"Sell the Muses? He can't do that. It belongs to the family." Jillian's voice dropped dramatically on *the family*. Issy really hated it when she did that.

What had she said that Steph might have overheard? She needed to end this conversation now, but she needed money more.

She carried the phone to the French doors, opened them with one hand, and walked outside. At least there was no wind today, so she could still hear.

"He'll never talk Leo into selling. Though . . ." Jillian trailed off and Issy could smell the beginnings of conniving all the way from Saint-Tropez. "Besides, he doesn't have power of attorney, does he?"

"I assume Dan has it. Right?"

"How should I know? No one tells me anything. Though really it should be George or me."

"There's nothing I can do about that," Issy said, continuing to walk away from the house. It would be just like Steph to follow her.

"What do you expect me to do?"

"Nothing. Like you said, you're half a world away." Which was a good thing, because Issy had no doubt that Jillian York would sell the Muses in a New York minute even if it meant leaving her mother and aunt homeless.

"I'm in a bind. I'm working in Manhattan at the Cluny Museum."

"I know, dear, around all those rich art patrons. Have you met anyone yet?"

"No. And I don't make enough money to support all six of us."

"You could remedy all of that with a little effort."

"I'm not like you," Issy spat. Immediately tempered her voice. "I need you to—"

"Oh, Oops. You know I'm busy."

Issy flinched. "I don't need you to do anything but write a check. I can't support the family on my museum salary."

"What about the maintenance fund that what's his name is overseeing. What is Vivienne's husband's name?"

"Dan. He's missing, too. All I know is the bank accounts have been cleaned out. I just need funds to keep things going long enough for me to sort this out." She'd been thinking low, a few thousand, but what the hell, it was time for Jillian to start paying them back. "Say fifty thousand."

She heard Jillian choke. Probably on expensive champagne.

"I'll pay you back." *Chickenshit. You have no backbone when it comes to your mother.* "Eventually. But there are repairs needed on the house, kids, doctors, food, and I have to hire a full-time housekeeper, one who can drive. It's the only way to make this work. I don't have nearly enough in my savings."

"But, Oops, I don't keep that kind of money available, everything is tied up. You know I never spend my own money for the day-to-day business of things."

Not as long as there were men on earth. "So you won't miss it."

"Really, darling."

"Look, you can't let me—us—down. I have to get back to work, I have a tour starting, and incoming exhibitions to oversee. Are you going to leave your mother, your aunt, and your grandchildren out on a limb—a homeless limb?"

Issy waited; couldn't even hear breathing, but she didn't think Jillian had hung up.

Issy hated the way she always turned into a simpering needy child around the one person who would never love her. But this was more serious than her feelings or Jillian's. She for once wouldn't be the one to hang up.

"Well, actually . . ." Jillian said. "It will take a little time for me to figure out what's what."

Issy plowed on. "It would be best if you just wired the money from Saint-Tropez," she said gently, afraid of rupturing the tenuous situation. "To my bank account since I'm not sure Leo's is secure. But quickly."

"This is so much to take in. I'll get back to you, darling. Ciao." The phone went dead.

It was so abrupt that it took Issy a second to realize Jillian had hung up without even getting Issy's account number. Issy powered off. "Ciao. Thanks for nothing. And don't call me Oops."

JILLIAN YORK TOSSED her cell phone on the bed in her luxury suite at the Hotel de Paris. Her arm was still aching from where Henri had grabbed her before throwing her to the bed and storming out of the room.

No one treated her that way. Of course she'd been rather stuck with him until a few minutes ago. And then voilà, a call from little Oops. Begging for money. How quaint.

And how fortuitous for Jillian. She just might see a way out of this mess after all.

She dragged her suitcases out of the closet, opened them on the bed, and began throwing her clothes into them.

Her family needed her.

And though she didn't have two pennies to rub together, she had something much better.

Herself.

Chapter 9

Steph watched Issy walk back to the conservatory. Now what did she do? She couldn't exactly pretend like she hadn't heard. She was stuck.

She'd spent the morning reading in bed, and when she finally had come down to breakfast, they were having a heated discussion in the kitchen. Fae was crying and Steph wanted to run in and tell them to leave her alone, but no one ever listened to a kid, so she just took her book out to the conservatory to wait until they finished.

That's why she overheard Issy's conversation with Jillian. She didn't mean to listen, but at first she thought maybe it was her mother on the other end. And by the time she realized it was really her grandmother Jillian, it was impossible to sneak out without Issy seeing her—besides, the conversation was too interesting.

Now she wished she hadn't stayed, because Issy said the same things Stephanie was trying not to think. She'd almost convinced herself that she hadn't heard what she thought she heard. Her mother screaming at her father late one night.

"You bastard. You'll go to jail." Steph had thought maybe she was just mad at him over something and was exaggerating. Her parents fought a lot, her mother was never happy. Steph had read on Facebook that some people enjoy their own misery. Steph was afraid her mother was one of those people. She really hoped she wouldn't turn out to be one of those people, too.

Then Issy had said the thing about foster care, and Steph knocked the book off the cushion. She only heard Issy's side after that, but she got the drift. Leo's money had disappeared and they thought her mom and dad had taken it.

Maybe they were already in jail. And how was Steph ever going to face her friends again? Well, she wouldn't have to, would she? They'd all be put in foster care and never see each other or their family again.

Maybe she wouldn't have to go. She was pretty old. She could stay and help Grammy and Fae. She could read to them when they got too old to read. If they didn't get put in the old-folks home.

It was just awful. And here was Issy stomping toward her. Steph could tell she was pretty upset. Angry even. She'd yelled, "Don't call me Oops" before she hung up.

Steph took a breath, planted her bare feet on the cold marble floor, and waited for the storm.

Issy stopped in front of her.

Steph willed herself not to move away.

Then Issy smiled, not a happy smile, but one of those smiles that were actually kind of sad.

And Steph just blurted out what rose to the top of her thoughts. Not *I wasn't listening.* Not *Are my mom and dad crooks?* Not *Are we all going to foster care?*

But . . .

"Why does she call you Oops?"

Then Issy's face got all soft, which was even worse because Steph knew it was how people looked when they were trying to hide something, like a broken heart.

"I was a mistake."

Steph shook her head. "No, you weren't. A surprise maybe."

"And just what does a twelve-year-old know about it?"

Steph lifted her chin. "I know what it means. That Jillian didn't want you and Mom."

"She wanted your mother. I screwed everything up."

"That's what my mom says. I don't believe it."

"Thanks. Let's go get some breakfast." Issy linked her arm in Steph's.

"Is my mom coming back?" Steph asked.

"I hope so," Issy said. "I sure hope so."

They walked back through the conservatory and had reached the hall when Mandy and Griff barreled down the stairs dressed in the most ridiculous outfits Steph had ever seen. Except that she kind of remembered wearing them herself. A long time ago. When she was a kid. Which she wasn't anymore.

Not that being an adult looked all that great at the moment.

It made her stomach feel a little queasy. She wanted to ask Aunt Issy more about what was happening, but Mandy and Griff were whooping around like nutcases.

"Steph, look at us," Griff yelled. He had a beret on his head that was slipping over his eyes. Someone, Chloe probably, had drawn a big black mustache on his upper lip. He had a feather boa around his neck and an old book satchel across his shoulder with a plastic sword sticking out the top.

Mandy twirled in front of them, which lifted the satin scarf she'd stuck in her shorts to make a skirt. She had on a hat with a huge fluffy feather sticking out of it and a long strand of pearls around her neck.

Chloe was laughing as she came down the steps behind them. "They found the dress-up trunk."

"Grammy lets us play with it," Mandy told Issy. "All the time."

"Those pearls aren't real, are they?" Issy asked.

Chloe shrugged. "They were in the trunk."

"I'm going to get something to eat," Steph announced, and marched off to the kitchen.

FAE KEPT A steady hold on the old red wagon as it rattled and jumped behind her. She usually took the shortcut through the woods to the town square, but today she wanted to make sure the children came to story hour. Those three needed a little imagination, a little outdoors, a little color in their life.

Steph especially. That girl needed someone to teach her to soar. How could Dan the "artiste" and Vivienne "the nothing but the best" fail to notice that their oldest daughter had an imagination waiting to explode. That they were keeping her confined, like a banked fire on a cold night when what you really needed were flames.

It wouldn't be easy. The girl was twelve, a little old to throw over her old habits or the peer pressure that was defining her. But she never would be totally happy if she didn't open up, look around, see things that others didn't bother to see. She was already wearing Leo's old clothes, looking like she knew something was missing but didn't know what. At least she had the instinct to try.

Fae figured that responsibility had been dumped right in her lap. Usually she just showed up at the reading spot un-announced and unnoticed. Dressed in overalls or one of her everyday long skirts. Today she went all out, with lots of fabric, and color and jewelry. She had dressed with Steph in mind.

A gauzy skirt that fell to her ankles, a paisley design in purple and aqua and gold whose hem lifted and danced with the breeze. A white peasant blouse hand-embroidered in Gua-temala and a sleeveless smock to keep the chalk dust from get-ting on her clothes. She'd tied a scarf around her head to keep her hair from falling in her face while she drew. Most story-telling days she wore it pulled back into a ponytail, sometimes in a bun, but today she let it "frolic," as Adam often said. *Wild* was a more apt description.

She'd worn a plethora of crystal jewelry, opals for inspira-tion, abalone for emotional balance (not to mention that it was good for arthritis, which Steph didn't need but Fae did after an hour of kneeling on the pavement). She carried cubes of calcite in her pockets, one of which she would give to Stephanie for inspiration. And necklaces of quartz and citrine for positive energy. Hopefully she had all her bases covered.

The wagon rattled along behind her and she rattled along in front. As she neared the Muses, the two young children ran out and down the steps. They'd found the dress-up trunk.

The sight of those clothes always brought a pang to her heart. She and Wes and their brothers and sisters now long dead had created stories and plays and went on wonderful adventures from that trunk. Then it had been relegated to the attic until Wes and Leo's children were born, and then it saw another generation. Max and George playing at pirates.

The older Max, tall, lean like his father, and graceful in his eye patch and ruffles. George, younger, slower, determined to hold his own, but never quite succeeding. And all the while Jillian flourishing satin scarves like the dramatic diva she would someday become. And later, Vivienne and Issy came . . . Vivienne never wanted to play anything. At eight, she was already filled with resentment.

And poor innocent Issy. Barely four, not understanding what was happening, desperate for love, some show of kindness. She spent hours alone, dressed up in the clothes from the box, dressing her dolls and stuffed animals, or Leo or Fae when they had the time.

She'd been such an undemanding child, while Vivienne demanded your constant attention, sulked and cried piteously if you didn't coddle her. And they had. Even though they knew it wouldn't help her navigate life.

Wes and Leo were committed solely to each other; their own children suffered and their grandchildren suffered. They'd loved them all, but not like they loved each other. Fae did what she could but she just wasn't very good at it. That's one of the reasons it was important to unlock little Steph's potential. She reminded Fae of Issy a lot, undemanding, but deep, and as closed off from the world as any well-treated twelve-year-old could be.

"Aunt Fae, Aunt Fae," Griff and Mandy yelled in chorus, running toward her. "We're coming to story time."

"Chloe said you'd let us walk with you. Can we?" Mandy asked, practically batting her eyelashes. Definitely took after her mother and grandmother. Fae would have to make her a necklace to keep her guided on the light path.

"Ple-e-e-e-ese," Griff added.

"Of course you may." Fae looked around, just a tad disappointed. "Where's your sister? And Issy?"

"Inside," Mandy said as she sashayed around the wagon. "Can we blow the bubbles, too?"

"Me, too?" Griff echoed.

"Once we get to town, we'll all blow bubbles. Are we all ready?" Fae looked back to find Issy and Steph standing in the doorway. Neither moved, indecisive, wanting and not wanting, two of a kind, the real Whitaker gene.

"Well, I am," Chloe said, stepping between them. "Come on, you two. You can't wig out on us."

Fae reached into her huge tapestry bag, found several more long scarves, handed one to Chloe, then stood at the bottom of the steps holding out the other two like the offerings they were. She could already feel the excuses forming in both of their minds.

"You can't leave Chloe to take care of both of these children by herself," Fae said so softly that her words must have carried on the breeze, because Issy started.

"I'll just get my wallet." She disappeared inside.

Fae lifted one scarf up to Steph. "Didn't you read my book last night?"

Steph shrugged, but she was caught. She came slowly down the steps, but instead of letting her take the scarf, Fae tied it around her head, the long tails trailing down her back.

"The Gypsy Bride."

Steph rolled her eyes but she continued out to the wagon.

Issy HAD SO much to do, so much that she was going to march down the sidewalk with Aunt Fae, Raconteur and Fading

Picture Lady, blowing bubbles and reinforcing the common thought that not only were the Whitakers philanthropists and art patrons, but were just a little loony to boot.

When Issy was little she didn't mind it. She loved coming to town with Aunt Fae. Mainly because it made her a Whitaker. She didn't remember ever calling herself a York. Maybe because no one, including Jillian knew if she was really a York or the product of one of Jillian's wild Hollywood nights. There had been plenty of speculation, the media had a field day, Issy had been clueless then. She was barely four when her mother dropped both her and Vivienne off at the Muses for good.

From that day forward, Issy was a Whitaker. Vivienne was a York and she never let anyone, especially Issy, forget it.

Well, today was not the day to break a family tradition or rain on anyone else's parade. She took money and a credit card out of her wallet and hurried back outside.

It was only a few blocks to town. They passed houses and businesses and by the time they reached the parklike town square, they'd been joined by others, children and adults and pets. Fae stopped to hand out bubble wands along the way. And by the time she dropped her tapestry bag on an empty space of sidewalk, they were surrounded by tiny floating rainbows.

Everyone spread back to give Fae space while she took chalk and rags from her bag and laid them to one side. Pulled out a green gardener's kneepad from the wagon and placed it in front of a blank piece of sidewalk. Knelt on it and reached for a piece of chalk.

The crowd settled around her, some looking over her shoulder, others sitting on the grass. The bubbles continued to fill the air.

"Once there was a farmer who took his young son to market

day." As she talked, she began to draw. "It was late when they left the market and the man pulled his sleepy son up behind him on the old farm horse."

A curve appeared on the sidewalk. A sweep of brown chalk. The horse? An oval of pink. Dots of blue and more dots of orange and brown.

"'Hold tight, my son, and do not fall, for I won't stop once we enter the forest.'"

Story and picture progressed together. Not one word was lost as she leaned over her drawing, and she never stopped the flow of chalk as she spoke.

Issy recognized the story, or at least the subject matter. A Goethe poem about the Elf King, who stole sleeping children and killed them for his revenge. Not exactly a story for impressionable young children. But often Fae appropriated characters from other stories for her own tale.

Issy glanced around; no one appeared to be afraid. No young mother was dragging her screaming children away. Griff and Mandy were practically breathing on Fae's neck.

At first Issy let herself be beguiled by the story. Why not? Shouldn't she soak up every bit of memory before it was gone forever?

Fae's words buzzed in the air around her as fanciful dark trees began to surround the man and his son.

"'Do you not see him, Father? He's come to steal me away.'"

Gradually she noticed that Steph wasn't watching the drawing, but the crowd.

"'I see no one.' 'Hurry, my father. He draws near.'" Fae drew their cloaks flying out behind them, the horse straining forward.

What—or who—was she looking for? Issy started watching the crowd, too. Steph had said her mother was going to call on Saturday. It was Saturday. As far as Issy knew, she hadn't called. Is that why Steph was scanning the crowd?

"'Look, my son. Ahead I see a light.'" Fae crawled along the edge of pavement and a sunburst of color was sketched above the horse's head.

"'It's he,' cried the boy."

The crowd leaned closer as another figure appeared before them, tall, lean, with flowing hair.

"'I come not to harm you, boy, but to show you the way home.'" Fae drew an arm and a pointing hand. And at the very top, a triangle turned quickly into a little cottage with light filling the windows and door.

"And the father and son rode toward it, safe and happy to be home."

The story ended. Fae rested back on her heels. The drawing was finished. An entire story in one scene. It had all happened seamlessly. Story and drawing, separate but together.

And a story that had a tragic ending, in Fae's hands, had been made happy again.

No one moved, held there by the spell she had cast.

Steph sighed.

Issy stepped close. She didn't know kids, but she did know about missing your mother. "She'll be back soon."

Steph's head snapped toward her. "Who?"

"Your mom, isn't that who you're looking for?"

Steph shook her head.

Issy frowned. "Then who?"

"The Elf King."

Boy, HAD SHE read that wrong, Issy thought as they walked back to the Muses with their ice cream. The vote had been unanimous. Dessert before lunch. And since there was no one around to say differently, that's exactly what they did.

But Issy's mind was on Steph rather than ice cream. The girl was just too hard to read. Had Fae even mentioned the Elf King in the story? She tried to remember what she'd been reading at Steph's age and drew a blank. It certainly hadn't been *"Der Erlkönig."*

Fae seemed distant, Issy thought. But she remembered that sometimes it took a while for her to come back to the world after story hour, she became so involved in the story. She'd cast a spell over her audience. Even the sullen Steph. Looking for the Elf King among the people watching. Afraid that she, too, was about to be snatched from her family?

Or maybe she was just being sarcastic. It was hard to tell with almost-teenagers. Issy didn't come into contact with them very often.

It was only natural, Issy supposed, that Steph should get captivated by Fae's magic. Issy had grown up with Fae's stories and they never ceased to fill her with wonder. Fae had a real gift for storytelling, for drawing, though not much talent for—or maybe it was just a question of a lack of interest in—coping in the day-to-day world.

Magic wouldn't help them much now, Issy thought, though she'd be totally happy if Fae could conjure up someone to show the Whitakers the way home.

Chapter 10

After a late lunch that no one really wanted thanks to the ice cream, Issy and Fae drove to the hospital. They didn't talk on the ride over. When they got out of the car, Fae said, "I hope she's feeling better." And fell silent again.

Leo was feeling more than better. Actually she was a little irritated. They found her sitting in a chair, fully dressed and ready to go home. Her hair was swept up in her usual twist and Issy wondered how she'd managed it or if she'd conned one of the nurse's aides into doing it for her.

"The doctor discharged me hours ago."

"Why didn't you call?" Issy asked.

"I did. No one answered. I left a message."

"You know today was story hour," Fae told her. "We were all at the park."

Issy didn't mention that Leo should have called her cell. She probably didn't know Issy's number. And Fae didn't have a cell or a landline. Something they might have to negotiate in the coming days.

Leo struggled out of the chair.

"Just a minute, Grammy. Are you sure Dr. Prasad said it was okay for you to go home? Did he leave instructions?"

Leo turned to Fae. "I need to go home. Wes will wonder where I am."

"Yes," Fae said. "I did make sure the flowers were watered and the weeds pulled. I told you I would. No cause to fret."

She'd stepped in between Issy and Leo to say this and it sounded more like an admonition than a reassurance. And it really didn't make any sense. Had Leo just said that Wes missed her?

"I'll just go talk to the nurse," Issy said, and left the room.

"Yes," the nurse said. "I think she wore the doctor down, poor man. But he said she's fit as long as she takes it easy. He left instructions for you and said to call him anytime." She handed Issy several sheets of paper. "He phoned in two prescriptions. The directions are on the top page. The pharmacy said they would deliver them."

"Thanks." Issy read them and made a quick call to Chloe to apprise her of the situation and to ask her to get the kids to help her prepare Mrs. Norcroft's rooms for Leo.

"I'm on it. Are you going to be able to get Leo into the SUV?"

"I didn't think about that. I think so. It's not one of the really high ones."

"I'll call Ben to come and help her out."

"Don't interrupt his work. You've both done way more than I could possibly ask."

"Nonsense. Now let me go round up my cleaning crew." Chloe hung up.

Leo balked at having to be taken out of the hospital in a wheelchair. That it was a hospital rule did nothing to change her mind. But she lifted her chin and held the blue-flowered cane the hospital had issued her like a scepter as they proceeded down the hall.

Issy and Fae walked behind her.

"Like members of the court," Fae said under her breath.

With help from a male nurse and a little maneuvering, they installed Leo in the front seat. Ben was waiting to help her out of the car when Issy came to a stop at the front door of the Muses.

She went up the porch steps leaning on Ben's arm, but when she reached the foyer and Chloe and the children met her with "We fixed up a nice suite downstairs for you," she recovered completely.

"Thank you, dears. You're all so thoughtful." She smiled at them, cupped Griff and Mandy's cheeks. Stopped in front of Steph, who was wearing another Leo outfit, with Fae's scarf tied around the waist.

"Where did you get that old thing?"

"I like it." Steph crossed her arms as if she expected Leo to rip it off her. But Leo took her by the shoulders and whirled around. "I remember buying that. It was here in the village, when Agnes Starling decided to open a boutique. Poor Agnes. In those days hardly anyone came through town. There were so few full-year residents that I always made a point to pick up something whenever I was in town. She moved away once her children were grown. I don't know what happened to her."

"Aren't you getting tired, Leo?" Fae asked.

"What? Not at all. Issy, take this child to the mall and buy her some clothes if she needs them."

"I don't need them. I like these clothes."

"You're a darling," Leo said. "And, Chloe, Issy says you've

been holding our little household together in my absence, and on your weekend off." She took Chloe's hand and squeezed it affectionately.

"We all appreciate it and I'm sure Mrs. Norcroft will when she returns. But you needn't have bothered for me. I told Issy and Fae that I had slept in the same bedroom since the day I married Wes—except of course when we were traveling or when the bedrooms needed repainting. And I'll sleep in my own room tonight." She somehow skirted the little group and was reaching for the banister when Issy dove to stop her.

"Grammy, the doctor said, no stairs."

"He said," Leo said, shaking Issy's hand away, "that he didn't want me running up and down the stairs all day like a teenager."

She started her sweep up the stairs, Issy and Ben both following behind her. She made it almost to the top before she had to rely on the cane. And had to stop on the landing to catch her breath. Then ignoring both Issy and Ben, who had come to a stop on each side of her, she walked down the hall to her room.

"I think I'll take a little rest before dinner," she said, and closed the door in their faces.

"And you wonder where your mother and the madcap Amanda get their dramatic flare." Ben gestured to the stairs. "Shall we?"

"Incredible, just incredible," Issy said as they walked back down the stairs to where the welcome-home party was still standing in the foyer.

Chloe laughed. "Kids, you have just experienced what it's like to be bowled over by a pro."

"Mandy's probably taking notes," Ben said under his breath.

Issy smiled. She probably was. Griff had already wandered off. He'd found a bag of wooden blocks, broken metal soldiers, and some early die-cast cars. He'd been occupied with them ever since. Hadn't once complained about there being nothing to do.

And, Issy noticed, he hadn't once reached for his game tablet.

Chloe clapped her hands together. "I'll get dinner. Anyone want to help?"

Mandy shook her head. "I'm tired. We cleaned for hours." She managed to slump and sigh on the last word. She wandered off.

"Are you upset about the clothes thing?" Issy asked Steph, who was scowling again. She shook her head.

"So no trip to the mall?"

This headshake was fast, sharp, and meaningful.

Issy didn't know what it meant exactly. Or why. But if it was important for Steph to wear those old clothes, it was fine by her.

"Will you stay for dinner, Aunt Fae?"

"What? Oh, I should be getting home."

"There's plenty," Chloe said as they started back toward the kitchen.

"And there's happy hour," said Ben, who had wandered off and met them as he stepped out of one of the many pantries. "A 1997 Margaux. I think Wes would agree that having Leo home is worth a little celebration."

"I'm sure he would," Fae said. "I will stay for a quick glass."

They all went to the kitchen, including Stephanie, who Fae swept up as she passed. "You can show us all the hard work you put in for Leo this afternoon. She appreciates it. She's just a creature of habit."

They all detoured to Mrs. Norcroft's rooms. They were spotless, even the windows had shed their normal coating of salt rime.

"Nice job," Issy said, probably too brightly. The emptiness of the rooms hit her unexpectedly. The furniture was all there, the same dresser and side table. The same overstuffed chair. They were rooms Issy knew well. She'd fled to them when Vivienne had goaded her one too many times, when one of the adults made a careless remark, or when her feeling of otherness was more than she could handle.

Fae was sensitive, but she was often away. And Mrs. Norcroft was neutral ground. She didn't despise Issy the way Vivienne said the others did. Or if she did, she never let it show.

"I should visit her while I'm here," Issy said. "Let her know that we don't believe any of it."

"Believe what?" Steph asked.

Issy bit her lip. She'd just done what so many adults around her had done. Just accepted Steph's presence and didn't caution her tongue.

"Just a misunderstanding."

"You mean about the stealing."

"How did you know about that?"

"I overheard Mom and Dad fighting about it. It's amazing what you learn when adults forget you're around. I think I'll go read my book now. And in case you're wondering, I won't be listening at keyholes."

"Good, 'cause we're going to be talking about you," Ben said.

"Ben!" Chloe exclaimed. "You're incorrigible. Don't listen to him, Steph. He's just an overgrown kid."

Steph turned a very smug, exaggerated smile toward him, then left the kitchen.

"Those kids could all use a good—"

"I can hear you," came through the closed door.

"To the moon, Alice."

"What?"

"Nothing, go read your book."

He rummaged in the drawer, found a corkscrew, and went to work on the bottle. "She's beginning to grow on me."

"She needs our help," Fae said.

Chloe placed four wineglasses on the counter and Ben poured. "How so?"

"She's not living her own story."

"I know better than to question that one," Ben said, and raised his glass. "To Issy being home, to Leo being out of the hospital, and to fixing the mess so they can stay that way."

They all lifted their glasses, though Issy had gotten stuck on the fact that he thought she was here to stay. Did they all think that? That she'd taken the first excuse they'd given her to come home again?

Ben seemed to realize the implications of what he'd said, and choked on his wine.

Chloe, conveniently on her way to the pantry, whacked him on the back. "What he means, Issy, is that we're both so glad to see you and hope to see a lot of you while you're here."

She made a comic face at her brother, who blushed bright red. Issy decided it was because he was choking.

"Are you okay?"

He nodded. "That's what I meant," he spluttered. "Better with plants than with words."

"If that's not the truth," Chloe said. "Remember when Lissa Jenkins got her . . ."

More wine was poured, the kitchen filled with heavenly aromas.

"Boeuf bourguignon," Chloe said, "but we're calling it beef stew with noodles. I'm determined to develop Mandy and Griff's palates to appreciate something more complex than peanut butter and jelly, and if I have to use subterfuge to do it . . ."

Issy got out silverware. "Do you think Leo will want to eat in the dining room?"

There was a unanimous quiet while everyone pondered the possibility.

"No," said Ben. "No one dressed for dinner."

"Works for me." Issy set the table. Ben poured the rest of the wine and suggested opening another bottle.

"What is that noise?" Issy asked.

"What?" Everyone stopped to listen. Nothing but the creak of the heated oven, the whir of the refrigerator, and a distant hum.

"The kids must have the television on," Chloe said.

Laughter broke out as she said it.

"That must be it. I didn't know you'd brought a television downstairs. Aunt Fae?" Issy looked at her great-aunt but she seemed miles away. And knowing Aunt Fae, she might be, Issy thought.

"I'm sorry, Issy. I was thinking about something."

"Just that the downstairs television is a new thing."

"Leo put it in the back parlor. I think she gets lonely with . . . without Wes. Does it bother you?"

"Heavens no. As long as it isn't something on its way to

breaking down that we have to have fixed, I'm happy as a clam. She misses Wes, I know."

"Her other half is gone."

"Okay, everybody," Chloe said. "Let's not get morose. Ben, will you round up the children then go up to see if Leo wants to come down or if she'd prefer a tray in her room."

Fae snorted. "She'll be down. Mandy . . . now she's the one who would be having vapors and demanding trays in her room."

Ben left, only to be replaced by Griff, Mandy, and Steph.

"Ben's gone to get Grammy," Mandy informed the others.

"He said to give you this." Steph put another bottle of wine on the table.

They all sat down. Ben burst into the kitchen a few minutes later. "She's not in her room."

"Maybe she's in the bathroom."

"I looked."

"The other bedrooms."

"I did a quick run-through."

"I thought maybe I'd missed her when I was in the parlor with these meatheads."

"I'm not a meathead," groused Mandy. "Whatever that is."

"Something grown-ups watch on late-night television when they can't sleep because they don't have a girlfriend," Chloe said. "Shall we all go look? I'll put the food in a warming oven."

They fanned out, checked the downstairs rooms.

"Where could she be?" Issy said, panic beginning to blossom. "It's not like she could have gotten past us all and gone outside?"

"Why would she go outside?" Chloe asked.

"Oh," Fae said, and walked past them to the front door. They all followed.

"Do you know where she is?" Issy asked.

"I have an idea." Fae set off in the direction of her cottage and the cove, but when they all started to follow she stopped. "Stay here please. I'll bring her back."

Ben stepped up beside her. "If you think I'm going to let two—"

"Old bags," Fae finished.

He glowered. "Two of my favorite people wander around when it's twilight and easy to pitch over a cliff, you're—"

"Crazy," Ben and Fae said together.

"Please."

The one word and the way Fae said it was enough to stop them from taking another step. But they stayed and watched as Fae marched across the grass past the outbuildings, along the edge of the woods, and toward the shore.

"Of course," Ben said. "The knoll."

"It's where they buried your great-grandfather," Chloe explained to the children.

Steph moved closer to Issy.

Now Issy could see the figure seated on the knoll.

"She goes there a lot to visit," Chloe said. "Ben even built her that bench so she would be comfortable."

"Maybe I shouldn't have encouraged her," Ben said. "It could be dangerous for someone frail to lose her balance."

"Boy, you better never let her hear you talking like that," Issy said.

"I think it was a nice thing to do," Steph said.

Issy and Ben both turned to look at her.

"Well, I do."

"I do, too," Issy said.

Ben looked from one to the other. "You do?"

"I'm hungry," Mandy whined.

"Me, too," Griff said.

"Then let's go back to the kitchen and get dinner on the table."

WES LOOKED SO *handsome, dressed in a summer linen suit, the coat un-buttoned and the sleeves rolled up to his elbows. He stood straight in the skiff as the waves rocked the boat. The sky swirled blue and white behind him. The sky was always remarkable here. Artists came to the cove just to paint the sky. A larger wave lifted the boat and Wes caught the side.*

Be careful or you'll get a wetting.

He laughed. Come on down.

Leo held on to her round belly. We'd sink like a stone. The three of us together.

A whale would swim by and spout us back onto the shore. A grand adventure.

Where Graham and Ernest would find them, having come expecting a delicious dinner and instead finding an embarrassingly wet and straggling host and hostess.

She gestured for him to come to shore. And he sat down and began rowing to the sand. She leaned over the edge of the bluff, her hair whipping about her head in the breeze, and she watched as he jumped onto the sand and pulled the boat above the tide line.

And the baby jumped in her belly. Hooray! he seemed to say, because his papa was so clever, so strong, so everything in the world to her.

FAE WAS OUT of breath and as angry as a sweating wet hen when she reached the knoll. Even though she wanted to chastise her sister-in-law for being pigheaded, selfish, and worrying them all, she couldn't. First of all she was out of breath. And second of all . . . there was such a stillness surrounding the knoll that she didn't dare rush into that solitude and destroy it.

She stopped, then walked slowly until she was behind Leo. Leo of course didn't know she was there, didn't hear her approach, didn't feel her presence, she never did when Wes was nearby. They were for each other and the rest of the world be damned.

Wes had been gone nearly three years. Everyone had expected Leo to follow close on his heels. That's what old people did. First one, then the other. But not Leo.

Maybe she thought she had unfinished business here. She did, but none that she would ever admit to.

No, Fae thought, it was because to Leo, Wes wasn't really gone. She always said she could feel his presence. Fae couldn't feel him. She'd be angry if she did. Wes had no business hanging around, making life difficult. And he hadn't. She knew that, because like the good man her brother had been, he'd done the right thing; he'd died and crossed over.

In a way she wished Leo would accept that. She'd lead a much healthier life if she did. That or she'd have no reason to keep on living. Of course she did have reasons; four of them were waiting back at the house.

Fae had made up her mind. Let Leo live with her Wes. It was a purely selfish motivation. If Leo died, there would be a haggle over who got the Muses until they found out who really owned it, then they would go in for the kill. Metaphorically of course.

Fae wouldn't be able to help, because she would be trundled off to the old-folks home before she could name the first president of the United States. Most days she could recite the first five or six without thinking. There were other days she had to let it bubble to the surface.

Leo had more of those days. It had started right before Wes's illness. Fae had discounted it as caused by stress. And it probably was true. But it didn't recede.

At first rare episodes, they could live with that. But now it was becoming more and more common. The doctor wasn't concerned because Leo always concentrated when she was at an appointment. It wasn't dementia that worried Fae the most. It was the alternate reality that Leo lived in most of the time. Because between the past, the present, and the normal hardening of the arteries, Leo was becoming more than Fae could protect.

She sat down next to Leo on the bench.

"Did they send you to look for me?"

"They all came. It was all I could do to keep them away. Chloe's made dinner and everyone is hungry."

"I couldn't wait. I missed him. And he didn't know where I was."

"Of course he did. He always knows where you are. So you don't really need to worry about him. And we really need for you not to talk about him like this while Issy is here."

"I know." Leo took her hand.

Fae wished she did know how to cast spells. She would cast a spell of protection around both of them that no one could break. No, she wouldn't. She would cast just one around Leo and lose her forever. Because Fae belonged out here in the present. Finally. And it wasn't something she would give up without a fight.

"Are you ready to come back?"

Leo sighed. "If I must."

"You must." *For all our sakes,* Fae added to herself. *You must.*

Chapter 11

Issy waited on the front porch until she saw Fae and Leo approach then slipped into the house to tell the others.

"Now don't make a fuss," Leo said as soon as Fae led her into the kitchen and Ben hurried over to seat her at the head of the table.

"I hope you don't mind that we're eating in the kitchen and I'm serving from the stove," Chloe said.

"Not at all," Leo said. "We're lucky to have you."

"We are," Issy agreed as she began filling plates for the kids. "But she goes back to her own work tomorrow, so enjoy while you have her. After tomorrow you've only got me."

"I'm sure that will be fine, dear," Leo said, already distracted by the plate of beef Chloe put before her.

Between the two of them, everyone was served quickly, salad would be served at the end, European style, the way it always had been in the Whitaker household.

"This is yummy," Mandy said, her mouth full.

Griff nodded as he stuffed a piece of roll in his mouth.

Issy had visions of having to perform the Heimlich maneuver before dinner was over. And a cold wind of panic swept through her. Tomorrow there would be three kids and Leo—and her.

She'd deal with it when she had to, but tonight, Leo or no, there were some things that needed to be discussed and it might as well be now when they were all more or less captive at the table. And Issy didn't know any better way to do it than to just ask, so she did.

"Kids," she said. "Did your mom call today?"

They all stopped in various poses of eating, a perfect Norman Rockwell moment except that it wasn't.

Three heads shook the answer.

"She's probably busy," Leo said. "Is anyone going to pour me a little of that wine?"

Ben looked at Issy. She'd glanced at the doctor's instructions. It hadn't said no alcohol. She nodded.

Ben poured out a glass and set it at Leo's hand.

"I wanna see my mommy," Griff whined.

"Not as much as Issy does," Ben quipped. And strangely the boy stopped crying.

"And so you will as soon as she returns," Leo told him. "And until then we're going to have so much fun. Remember the plans we were making."

"Picnic on the beach," Mandy said.

"Fun Town," Griff said.

"If we can get Ben—oh, we have Issy's car," Leo said.

Issy had no intention of taking them to Fun Town. There was work to do and her two-week vacation was already slipping through her fingers. She hadn't even called Paolo to check on the exhibit.

"If we have time after we do some housecleaning." Issy gave

all three kids pointed looks. They groaned, even Leo groaned. "And you," she said, pointing to her grandmother, "don't even think about sneaking off with my car."

Leo smiled. "I haven't driven in years."

"And you're not going to start now."

"Which brings us to . . ." Ben interrupted. "How did you get past us tonight to get outside? I swear no one saw or heard you come downstairs."

"I didn't come down the stairs."

Fae dropped her fork on the floor and bent down under the table to retrieve it.

"I took the elevator."

"An elevator? When did you put in an elevator?"

"Oh, several years ago, when . . . Wes first . . . so I use it when I feel like it."

"How did I not know there was an elevator? Where?"

"Around behind the back staircase," Leo said.

"No more leaving the house without telling me."

Leo looked down her nose at Issy.

"Please, Grammy."

"Very well." Leo went back to eating. It seemed that for someone just out of the hospital, she had a very healthy appetite. That was a good thing.

"And don't you three get any ideas about using it," Issy said, pointing a finger at Griff, Mandy, and Steph each in turn. "I guess we'd better have it inspected. Ben, do you know—"

"A guy? Yep."

As soon as the kids were finished, they were excused to go look for fireflies outside.

The adults sat around the kitchen table drinking coffee, except for Fae, who sipped chamomile tea. Which Issy should be drinking. Between caffeine and adrenaline she was on overload.

"We need to discuss what to do about Vivienne. She was supposed to call today but she didn't call her kids and she didn't call me. I told Detective Griggs that if we hadn't heard from her by Saturday, I'd call in and report her missing."

"Well, she isn't missing," Leo said.

"Then where is she?"

"I don't know exactly. When she dropped off the children, she just said she had to go out of town and could they stay here. I said of course."

"Did she say when she expected to be back?"

Leo put down her cup. "She didn't know, but said not to worry about her. I think she and Dan may be having some marital problems. I know she'd wanted another child and he was dead set against it. I told her to take all the time she needed; we would be fine. And we would have been if I hadn't taken that fall. I'm so sorry, Issy, to drag you away from your party. You looked so lovely."

"Party? Oh, the opening. I was happy to be able to come."

"You're probably in a hurry to get back to work."

"No, I have vacation time. I thought . . . If you wanted . . . I would stay and help get things in order."

She hadn't expected to get derailed so easily. Leo was smiling at her, but Fae's eyes were trained on Leo, almost as if she didn't dare look at Issy. Is this why things felt so screwy? They didn't want her here. They were still nursing whatever bad feelings they had toward her because of the funeral?

How did they expect her to get to a funeral she knew nothing about? Or was it from before that? But she had visited whenever she could get away. Which, granted, hadn't been that often, and practically never since her grandfather died. Was it her fault? Had she estranged herself from the only people who loved her from some misplaced sense of being slighted?

"Of course they want you," Chloe said. She frowned at Issy, then at the two women. "They just don't want to be a burden."

Fae perked up at that. Obviously that feeling hadn't occurred to her. Ever since Issy arrived, it seemed Fae yo-yo'd between relieved to have her home and anxious to get rid of her.

"Grammy, do you want me or not? I totally understand either way."

Leo's lip quivered. "Of course I want you. Don't we—Fae?"

"Of course, we just don't want you to have to take off time from work."

"There, see?" Chloe said. "And Ben and I want you to stay, too. And whenever Leo and Fae can do without you, I plan on spending that time with you having fun. Some of the old crowd still lives in town and we meet nights at the pub and there's a new coffee bar in town, cute barista . . ."

Chloe babbled on while the air cleared, and when she finally trailed off, Issy said, "Well, regardless, I promised Detective Griggs I would call him and let him know if we hadn't heard from her by Saturday. And it's Saturday."

"I really don't think that's necessary," Leo said.

"Well, don't you think it's odd that she hasn't gotten in touch with her children at all?"

"I suppose, but Wes and I used to go down to the Keys. That was before cell phones, of course. We only called the children to let them know we had arrived. Then they saw us when we returned home laden down with gifts, piñatas, and huge straw hats and coconut dolls . . ."

More likely, Issy thought, Vivienne and Dan were on a romantic island spending Leo's money.

Leo seemed to have no inkling of what they had done. And the longer they waited, the harder it woud be to get the money back. George had said to stay out of it. But Vivienne was her sister. "One more day."

Leo stood. "I think I'll go say good night to the children and make an early night of it."

They all stood.

"Do you want me to escort you up the stairs?" Ben asked. "I'd rather you not use the elevator until I can get someone in here to inspect it."

Leo patted his cheek. "Thank you, Ben, but I can manage just fine. Really. You stay and enjoy your coffee."

"I'll be going home," Fae said.

They all said good night, then Issy, Ben, and Chloe sat down.

"I'd suggest we all run down to Fisherman's Den for a nightcap, but Issy looks dead on her feet."

"I'm not on my feet."

"I know, but I couldn't very well say 'dead on your butt.' My sister would yell at me."

"You are incorrigible."

Ben shrugged. "I'll try to get someone over here on Monday to check out the elevator, though I'd be inclined to pull the plug if she's going to be running off to Wes's grave all the time."

Chloe stood. "I'll get those guys upstairs and ready for bed."

Issy started to stand. "I should be doing that."

"From the looks of things you will be. I don't mind; besides, I like it."

"Cooking, cleaning, kids . . ." Issy trailed off.

"What?"

"Nothing. I'm impressed," Issy said, thinking that Chloe sounded like the perfect mate for Paolo. She mentally shook herself. Her family was falling apart and she was match-making?

Chloe left the room and Ben and Issy sat looking at the coffee in their cups.

"Thanks for bailing us out once again," Issy said.

"That's what friends do."

"Leo doesn't seem to know about the money or any of it."

"No," Ben agreed.

"It doesn't seem right to keep it from her."

"Fae just wants to protect her."

"Is that why she's trying to get rid of me? She thinks I'll hurt Leo?"

"Why do you even say that?"

"I can tell with every look they exchange, every sentence they don't finish. The stubbornness. The dismissals. 'Issy, what are you doing here? Don't you have to get back to work, dear?' I'm not stupid. I can read between the lines. Like they can't wait until I'm gone."

"I think you might be misinterpreting the signals."

"I only came because the police threatened to put the children in foster care and George is threatening to put Leo and Fae in assisted living. I know they would hate that."

"And you care about them."

"Of course I care about them."

Issy's throat started to burn; she stared across the room, away from Ben, to quell any tear that even thought about fall-ing. Why was she being so dramatic? Life was life. You took what you got. She had been lucky. She should be content with that. She just didn't know where she had gone wrong. And she was afraid she'd waited too long to make it right again.

Issy looked into her cup. It was about as murky as her feelings about her family.

A banging at the back door had them both on their feet. "What was that?"

"I don't know. Stay here." Ben warded her off with one hand as he started toward the mud room. Before he got to the door, Fae fought her way through the opening, dragging a huge faded duffel bag, and a small suitcase on rollers nearly hidden beneath several bags, one that looked like a computer case, and other assorted "stuff."

She made it to the middle of the kitchen, dropped the smaller bags onto the table, and let go of the suitcase and duffel bag, both of which fell heavily to the floor.

"What are you doing?" Issy asked.

Fae took two deep breaths. "Moving in. You can't handle Leo, those kids, the house, and cooking by yourself. If you're thinking Leo will be a help, forget it. I don't think she knows the difference between a saucepan and a measuring cup.

"Chloe has to go to work on Monday. So I'm moving in."

"But you hate leaving your cottage," Issy said.

"I do. But everyone has to do their part if we're going to keep life as we know it. And that includes me. I'll stay in Mrs. Norcroft's rooms, close to the kitchen, in case I get hungry."

She picked up the handle of the suitcase in one hand and the duffel in the other while Ben and Issy just stared. Then Ben jumped to life. "Wait. Let me get those for you."

Ben took the cases and Fae walked out of the room. Ben followed, looking bemused. Issy just stood there. Aunt Fae was moving into the Muses? Issy didn't have to look out at the night sky. She knew that pigs would be flying there.

Ben returned almost immediately. "What do you think about that?" he whispered.

"I'm shocked; what do you think it means?"

He took Issy's hand. "Not that she doesn't trust you. She wants to help."

Chloe chose that moment to return to the kitchen. Zeroed in on the clasped hands, which Ben dropped like the hot potato it wasn't.

Issy prayed he wouldn't try to explain.

"Fae's moved into Mrs. Norcroft's rooms," he said.

"Wow." Chloe looked from one to the other. "The world is full of surprises tonight. Mandy didn't even pitch a diva fit but fell right to sleep."

"And Steph?"

"Closed her door. I said good night through the wood. Not even sure if she heard me."

"It's hard for her."

"I know. With Fae in the house, do you want to sneak away to the Fisherman's Den?"

"I'd love to, but I still have work to do tonight. I haven't checked in with the installation since this morning. But can I take a rain check?"

"Absolutely." Chloe gave her a quick hug. "See you tomorrow."

"You don't have to. You've already done way too much."

"I have to. I promised Mandy and Griff I'd bring donuts. I think they're already tired of healthy eating. Makes you wonder what they eat at home. Night." She grabbed her bag off a peg in the mudroom and hurried out the door, leaving Ben and Issy looking at each other.

"Ya gotta love her," Ben said.

"I do. Thanks."

"My pleasure." He followed his sister out the door.

Issy waited until she heard them drive away before she took out her cell. She poured the last of the wine into her glass and went into the library.

Paolo answered on the fifth ring.

"I didn't wake you up, did I?"

"No, *cara*. How goes it?"

"It's going. Tell me how today went."

"You sound beat."

"Work will perk me right up."

"It's going fine."

"Paolo." Nothing was ever just fine with Paolo. His vocabulary was filled with descriptions. He, unlike most people, didn't have to answer with words like *fine*, unless he was at a loss for words.

"Paolo. Is everything all right down there?"

"What wouldn't be going right? How are things going there? How's your grandmother?"

"She insisted on coming home today and now my aunt Fae has moved in to help with things."

Paolo chuckled. One of the many things Issy liked about him. He had perfected the chuckle. "She and my nona sound like they came from the same pack."

Issy smiled but she blurted out, "They don't want me here."

"Ah, *cara*, how could they not want you there?"

"I don't know. I just know that things have never been the same since I left for college."

"Then perhaps it is time you made them not the same but better. Now I have a piece of news."

"Good I hope."

"If we can act quickly, but not if it takes you away from those who need you."

"What?"

"Dell called me today. Alphonse Guerrera contacted him about an exhibit they have in the works."

"Alphonse? What kind of exhibit?"

"Toulouse-Lautrec."

"Wow. Who do we have to sleep with?"

"That's the beauty of it. They requested you as the designer. Are you interested?"

"Interested? Did you have to ask? Of course. What an opportunity."

"That's what I told Dell."

"Why didn't he call me himself?"

"Because he either is miffed that you left him and wants to make you suffer a little first, or he knew you would jump at the chance and he doesn't want to feel guilty if you come running back to the city.

"Not to worry. I told him that you could work remotely."

"What timeline are we talking about?"

"They're expressing the specs to the museum on Monday. I can drive them up as soon as they get there, and we can look them over and then make a decision. If you have the time."

"I'll make the time. Fantastic."

"Thought that would brighten your day. So now get some sleep. You'll be doing double duty soon. And don't worry about the D.C. exhibit. It's almost hung in spite of Deirdre. I swear, why that girl decided on museum work is a mystery."

"To meet rich men."

Paolo let out an Italian expletive. "Did she say that?"

"No, but I called my mother, the movie star, today to ask for a loan. I'll tell you all about it when you get here. She was very disappointed that I had been working at the museum for so long and hadn't managed to snag a multimillionaire. Yes, that's the stock I come from."

"You are never dull, *cara*. See you in a couple of days."

Issy hung up, smiled. She felt better just talking to Paolo, and having an unparalleled opportunity handed to her was great, too.

Now to pull it off. But it was all clear as glass to her. Whether Vivienne came home or not, whether they recovered the money or not, Issy had two weeks to make things right. It was time to roll up her sleeves, literally, and do some serious cleaning. And as she cleaned she'd do an inventory with an eye to what could go, what could stay, and what they might sell if necessity demanded it. Fortunately, with Issy's connections, they would get good placement in any auction.

And—sometime during those two weeks while she solved her family's problems, Issy would find time to design the new exhibit. She could do it. She could get Fae to entertain the kids, maybe even enlist them in a little housecleaning. Leo could sit and tell Issy what she remembered of each piece and decide what to keep and what to send out to the veterans, the junkyard, or to the auction houses. Maybe Steph could be coerced into taking notes.

She was suddenly so energized that she thought she might start cleaning and cataloging tonight. But she reined herself in. She needed rest. She'd been running sleep-deprived for weeks now. She'd better be smart or she might end up too sick to design the new exhibit.

IT WAS JUST before dawn when Jillian York slipped the concierge fifty dollars and walked out the front door of the Hôtel de Paris. Two bellmen carried her luggage outside, where they deposited the pieces in the back of the taxi. They asked no questions, they didn't send well wishes to the family who was the source of the "emergency." They were used to people trying to sneak out of the hotel at night. Fortunately for her, Henri was stuffed with food, booze, and sex and was asleep upstairs in their suite with most of his credit cards and cash nestled all snug in his wallet. The rest were in Jillian's pocket.

ACROSS THE OCEAN, the moon was shining through the sliver of window between the frame and the curtain in Mrs. Norcroft's bedroom and it was driving Fae crazy. Moon-crazy. She wanted to go home. Wished she'd never let herself be talked into doing the right thing by helping Issy out. Of course she wanted to help Issy. She loved Issy and didn't want her to be burdened by their problems. And she needed to protect Leo. But couldn't she do both while sleeping in her own bed?

Obviously not, because she was here instead of there. This was the price of caring. At least most of Mrs. Norcroft's residual anger and heartbreak was gone, just vestiges trapped in the corners of the room. Tomorrow she would have to do a good cleansing. A good thing she'd brought her store of bundled sage.

STEPH SLEPT THE deep sleep of a girl on the brink of becoming a teenager. Neither innocent nor worldly, neither good or bad. A flower waiting to blossom into what no one, not even Steph, could guess.

ACROSS THE HALL Leo floated on her memories. Wes leading her across the meadow to his mansion that overlooked the sea. Wes carrying her over the threshold, both of them laughing so hard with happiness she thought they might tumble to the floor. Wes lying on the rubber raft in the middle of the pool, a martini in his hand, a book of Roethke's poetry open on his chest. Leo sitting on the side, her feet dangling in the water, her skirt spread out wide beside her, soaking up the water like a sponge.

Chapter 12

I ssy woke the moment the sun rose over the trees. For the first time since returning to Painter's Cove, she felt she had a plan. She wasn't sure where it would lead or why exactly she was doing it, but she would leave that to the future.

She dressed, made her bed, and went downstairs to put on coffee. Then she went to the library to organize her supplies.

By the time the coffeemaker beeped, she had pencils, pens, and markers lined up across the library table. Yellow notepads, a tablet of drawing paper and her laptop opened to a museum inventory template, and her iPad opened to her design program were set up strategically nearby.

She was pouring her first cup when Chloe came to the back door and tapped on the window.

Issy went to let her in.

"Chloe, you're going beyond the call of friendship."

Chloe smiled and walked past her to deposit two large bakery boxes on the table. "Because I'm the sister you always wished you had." She shrugged. "And you're mine."

The statement brought an embarrassing lump to Issy's throat. "You are."

"And I saw you holding my brother's hand last night. We could make it a reality."

"That wasn't what it looked like."

Chloe sighed. "It never is." She poured herself a cup of coffee. "You have to promise me not to exhaust yourself today. Ben said he'd meet us at the Den after dinner. He's out in the marshes all day."

Issy blew out air.

"Don't even start thinking of excuses. Just a friendly drink."

"What's the real reason for all this talk about Ben?"

"I'm considering going back to culinary school. And don't say it. After I just bought a store that I can't afford. I don't know what I want; he does know what he wants, but he'll be all alone if I go."

"Oh, jeez, Chloe. He's a grown man. Most people are alone."

"You're not."

"I was until this week. And now I have a grandmother who I'm not sure always recognizes me. An aunt who wishes I would leave. A mother who ignores me. A sister who hates me. And three children who I have absolutely no idea what to do with. Better to be alone."

"Maybe."

"I have to get to work."

"What are you doing?"

"Cleaning and cataloging the objects in each room."

"Not because you're thinking of selling the Muses?"

"It's not up to me. In fact, if we don't figure out some way of raising money, it might not be up to any of us."

"You'll figure out what to do."

Issy grabbed her coffee and beat a retreat before Chloe could embark on one of her pep talks.

"That got you moving," Chloe called after her.

Issy stuck her head back into the kitchen. "Flee before the Chloe pep talk."

"Isn't that a good thing?"

"Yes, but you keep goading and goading until you make us do what we didn't think we could do and didn't want to do until you badgered us into doing it." Issy grinned and ducked out the door.

"It's what friends do, so prepare to be goaded!" Chloe's words followed Issy down the hall to the library.

Issy put her coffee on top of the yellow tablet and opened up an empty page of her design program. It was going to be a daunting task. There was just so much stuff. She divided the library in quarters. Started in the northeast quadrant. Drew two rectangles to designate the floor-to-ceiling bookshelves. There were probably some first editions there. Not her domain. She'd hire someone to appraise them if it came to that.

She added a rectangle for the mantel, and another one to represent the framed flapper dress above it. The dress was said to have belonged to Lois Long, who, in a boozy stupor, left it behind to follow a story for the *New Yorker*.

Issy's finger hovered above the rectangle as an idea took form. She turned slowly a full 360 degrees. There were so many works of art and craft in the room, so many in *all* the rooms, and each one had a story. Some more interesting than others, granted, but many fascinating.

She thought of Lois's dress hanging in a museum, a placard saying, *This dress of sequins, bugle beads, etc., belonged to Lois Long, re-*

porter for the New Yorker *magazine in the 1920s. Known as "Lipstick," Ms. Long was the quintessential New Woman of the twentieth century.*

Yawn.

But the image of Lois Long stumbling down the stairs at the Muses after a day of art and debauchery, demanding that someone call her a cab so she could get back to the city before the midnight deadline . . . Grabbing one of the gentlemen's overcoats to hastily throw over her underthings, and snagging a bottle of gin on her way out . . . now, that was a presentation.

Issy could almost see her. She made another full circle as her mind exploded with exhibits, events, readings, guided tours— art in situ. Alive, the way it should be.

She stopped herself. Shoved the exploding idea aside, pushed it back where it couldn't sidetrack her. She was cataloging things for an inventory and perhaps for possible sale if things came to that.

She had a lot of work to do without wandering off on fantastic detours. She had to get back to the city and a new design that would be a golden rung up the ladder of her career.

For the briefest moment, the flapper reporter running half clothed down the staircase and Issy standing in her jeans in the library became one. Then, like all crazy ideas, it passed.

Issy's finger moved to the center of the screen. Placed a circle to represent a table. To its right, a smaller circle for the freestanding globe; another circle for the marble plinth with the bust of . . . someone, the two chairs with a small rectangle for the reading table between them.

She took a moment to check her graphics with the actual space. She'd have to use numbers to represent the artwork. Maybe she could convince Steph to collate everything on the inventory template.

In a few minutes she had a series of squares, rectangles, and ovals representing the paintings, drawings, and photographs in all four quadrants, using placeholders for the statues, ceramic pieces, photos, and memorabilia crammed together in every available space.

Art, crafts, junk. Great artist, friend of the family, children, passing strangers, all juxtaposed in a fascinating story of the Muses.

FAE TURNED OVER in bed, stretched. Her arm met air—and disappointment. Of course. She was in Mrs. Norcroft's single bed. She had the aches to prove it. She must have been crazy to leave the comfort of her life and come here to help the family.

Crazy old woman, what possible good could you do? You're more likely to cause the downfall of the house of Whitaker. And create such a scandal. Possibly go to jail. Was what she'd been party to punishable by law? She felt no guilt. Not one little ounce. Not even when she tried. Which wasn't often and certainly wasn't today.

She kicked off the covers and stood on the rag rug, old and faded like all the other junk in the house.

She heard banging and voices in the kitchen. She'd slept late because this side of the house faced west. Her bedroom at the cottage met the sun each day, each glorious new day. Today didn't seem so glorious. Did they even need her here?

Probably not. But she needed to be here. Needed to make sure Issy didn't realize just how far Leo had gone into the past.

Fae didn't blame her. Leo's past was a fairy tale, at least to Leo. Wes had brought her home one day. A scraggly, dripping-wet girl still in her teens. He walked right beneath the tree branch where Fae sat reading. And he called out without even looking up, "Come inside and meet the girl I'm going to spend my life with."

Fae slid down to the ground and followed them.

Wes and Leo's love for each other consumed them, and singed everyone near them. Fae envied them at times. Other times, denied her own love and miserable, she burned with her own fire—jealousy, bitterness, envy. But no more. No more. And yet she wouldn't desert Leo until Leo was with Wes again.

She didn't bother with a shower but put on a pair of overalls, light blue with stars on the pockets. Underneath the overalls she wore a man's T-shirt. Large, too large, but comfy and secure.

It was going to be a workday. She knew that as well as if Issy had told her in advance. At least she could help with that. She padded across the hall to the kitchen.

The two younger children sat at the table, eating a breakfast of eggs and donuts. Fae shuddered.

"I also have bran muffins," Chloe told her, and put the teapot and an empty cup on the table opposite Mandy.

"Can we watch cartoons now?" Mandy asked.

Her voice grated on Fae's nerves. Well, that was to be expected when you spent most mornings in quiet, if not solitude, in complete . . . completeness. Was that a word? It was definitely a state of being.

"Can we?"

But not this morning. "It's Sunday," Fae said.

"They have cartoons on Sunday."

"Don't you go to church?" Fae asked, just because. She didn't really care. And she had no intention of taking them. Wouldn't that be interesting? Lightning might strike. They'd enjoy that.

"All the time. It's so-o-o-o boring." Mandy slumped down in the chair.

"What about all the beautiful music and the stained glass? Surely that part isn't boring."

"Boring. Griff gets to play on Mama's phone with the sound off, because he's little."

Griff glanced up, his cheeks bulging with donut, one edge of his mouth smeared with red jelly.

Fae tossed him a napkin across the table.

"I have one," he mumbled through his mouthful of food.

"Then use it." Fae didn't understand children. Maybe because she didn't have any. She'd never wanted any. Her story hours were enough for her.

Griff swiped his napkin at his mouth, leaving a smear of jelly across his cheek. Had there ever been a time when she'd sat at the table stuffing food into her mouth with reckless disregard of her napkin? It was so long ago she truthfully couldn't remember. But she doubted it.

"Yes, I think you better go watch for a few minutes," Chloe said. "Wash your hands and face first and put the volume on low."

"Oh, we won't wake up Steph. She can sleep through an earthquake," Mandy said, obviously quoting someone.

"Shut up," Steph said, walking through the door. She was wearing Leo's trousers and gardening shirt with Fae's scarf still wrapped around the waist.

Fae's heart squeezed just a little. Couldn't anyone see? Didn't they hear how she was crying out for guidance? Not the guidance that would keep her from wandering off the path they'd chosen for her, but to show her the way to that special place inside her that Fae could feel beating like it was her own heart.

And for a selfish moment, Fae was glad Vivienne and Dan had stolen the estate's money and dumped their kids here. Steph needed the Muses this summer. Hopefully she'd be here long enough for it to matter.

"Sit down, Steph," Chloe said. "Would you like a donut or bran muffin with your eggs?"

Stephanie hesitated.

"She'll have both," Fae said, and took a sip of her tea.

ISSY FINISHED THE schemata for the library and took a sip of her coffee. Ice cold.

She headed back to the kitchen through the back hall. Halfway down the narrow corridor she noticed the red blinking light emanating from somewhere along the dark wainscoting. She followed it to a telephone cubicle left over from decades before —where Leo still kept her phone and message machine.

No wonder Issy hadn't known about it. There were several messages and Issy wondered—no, hoped—that one of them was from her sister.

She pressed the listen button. "Hello, is anyone there? It's Leo. I'm ready to come home." Issy deleted it.

The next one. A public-service number to call about something. Issy impatiently moved to the next caller.

And there it was. "Hello, Leo? It's me, Vivienne. Don't tell anyone I'm calling okay? There are just some things I don't want them to hear. I know . . . crazy, but just . . . I'm all right, so don't worry, not that you would after . . . But anyway. Can you . . . the kids awhile longer? Just tell them I love them. I don't . . . them . . . worry about me . . . home soon. First I . . . Dan. My phone's dying, so you might not hear from me until I can . . . to charge it. Just . . . thanks."

The call ended. Izzy rewound the machine, listened again. Tried to fill in the missing words from the dying charge. Just like Vivienne to rush out and forget to charge her phone. *I know . . . crazy?* What did Vivienne know was crazy? The way she was acting? That she and her husband stole a huge amount of money from her family? What about Dan? Issy could easily fill in the missing words in that sentence. *Dan made me do it, but as long as we're filthy rich, I'm going to enjoy it for a while.* Tell the kids she loved them. *If* she loved them . . .

Oh, why did she even try to second-guess her sister? At least Vivienne was okay. Issy could put off calling the police for a while longer.

But not for too much longer. She took her cup back to the kitchen, where she found Chloe, Fae, and her grandmother in lively conversation while Steph listened and picked at a bran muffin.

"Well, you'll be glad to know your mother called," Issy said, dumping her cold coffee into the sink.

The talk cut off to complete silence and Issy was left listening to the steady drip-drip of the leaking faucet.

"So she's okay. She said she loves and misses you guys." *So what if that was a little embellishment?* "And will be back soon." *Or something to that effect.*

Leo stretched out her hand; Issy took it and leaned over to kiss her cheek—and immediately wished she hadn't.

Leo sucked in a sob. "Oh, Issy, I'm sorry to have caused you such trouble. And over nothing."

"Trouble?" Issy looked from great-aunt to grandmother. "You're no trouble."

"I don't want to hold you back."

Issy pulled a free chair next to Leo. "You've never held me

back. You made me leave, remember? To go to college. Ben drove me to New York. I didn't want to go."

And she had neglected them since then. Is that what they thought? That she didn't care about them?

"It's just that I've been busy with my career. I travel a lot or else I would visit more often."

Leo patted her hand. "I know. I understand. Hollywood is so much more exciting than Painter's Cove."

"Manhattan, Grammy. I live in Manhattan."

"Hmm?" Leo gave Issy's hand a little shake. "Of course you do. Chloe says you're going to put us all to work this morning with this plan of yours."

Issy hadn't really thought about how she was going to pitch her idea to the family. She still didn't know how much Leo actually knew about their finances.

And she didn't want to be the one to tell her. And she didn't want to mention inventory and cataloging because it seemed a bit mercenary.

"I thought we'd start in the library. Dusting and vacuuming and cata—writing down which piece goes where."

"I don't think anything has been rearranged since I moved here," Leo said.

"Well, it's a good thing to do, in case there's a water leak or you need to up your insurance." She stopped. Looked at Fae, then to Leo. "You do have adequate insurance, right?"

"Dan takes care of all that," Leo said.

That answered one question. Leo didn't have a clue about what was going on. Issy added *check insurance* to her to-do list.

"Well, it's always good to update your inventory. Do you have one?"

Leo and Fae exchanged looks.

"Well," Issy said. "We'll do an update just in case."

"And the house needs a good cleaning," Fae added.

"Yes," Leo agreed. "With Mrs. Norcroft . . . not here."

"Good idea," Chloe said. "I'll get Mandy and Griff. And tell them their mother called and then I'll put them to work. It wouldn't hurt those two to do something useful for a while. Come on, Steph, you can help me drag them away from the television."

Issy took the moments of their absence to organize her "workforce." She heard the television go off and a minute later Chloe and Steph returned with the reluctant pair in tow.

"Mandy and Griff, you two and Chloe"—Issy shot an apologetic look toward her friend—"are in charge of the entranceway. Dust everywhere you can reach. Up the staircase; every spindle, even where it joins the wood tread. Then you can take turns vacuuming the floor."

"Aw," Mandy started.

"It's a very important job. Everybody comes through that front door. And it's very important that they are, uh, wowed by how sparkly it is. This is Muses by the Sea."

"Do famous people really come here?" Mandy asked.

"All the time."

"Really, Grammy?"

"Really. Once your grandfather and I gave a party for a Lithuanian princess and she brought two hundred people with her. We cleaned out Ogden's Market. They had to borrow trucks to deliver everything." Leo trilled a laugh.

Both kids looked blank.

"See," Issy broke in. "You never know who's going to come through that door, so it's important that everything looks its best."

"I wish my mommy would," Griff said, and the lip began to quiver.

Chloe jumped in. "Okay, troops, follow me." She marched Mandy and Griff into the cook's hall; Issy heard rummaging as she handed out cleaning supplies.

The rest of them went to the library.

Issy motioned Steph over to the desk. "So how are you with a laptop?"

She looked blank, then grinned. "As good as you?"

"We'll see. You and I will start in the library. I don't suppose you brought your laptop with you?"

Steph shook her head.

"Tablet, iPad?"

"I associate those with homework and I was sulking."

"Nose and face," Issy reminded her.

"I know, but I didn't really think she'd make me come. I missed the dance. My first one." Her voice wavered.

Issy felt it all the way down to her toes. Twelve is not a good time to miss a dance. Especially a first dance. "Sucks," she said. "You and I will start in the library."

"I can dust," Fae offered.

"I thought you and Grammy would—"

"Sit on our butts like a couple of old women?" Leo said. "We'll both dust."

"Actually," Issy said, "I need you to sit with Steph and tell her what things are, and if you remember the artist, or the circumstances of how it got here."

"We can take a picture of it with my iPhone," Steph said.

"Good thinking. Then we'll give it a number, enter that and the provenance—where it came from—and Grammy's information in the appropriate boxes. Got it?"

"Yep. It's a simple spreadsheet."

Steph was as good as she boasted.

Fae sat Leo in an armchair next to the desk. "And cover your ears when the stories get naughty." She grinned at Steph, who gave her a saucy look.

And Issy just stopped to wonder how Fae had managed in such a short time to bring the light to the kid's eyes.

They started on the wall next to the bookshelves. Issy read off a number. Described the painting. "Looks late nineteenth century. An allegory."

"Oh, the Blashfield," Leo said. "It was one of your great-grandfather's favorites." She chuckled. "It used to be in the front parlor but I don't think Wes's mother liked it very much. Or maybe it was just Blashfield that she didn't care for. She put the Maxfield Parrish there and relegated this to the library, where she said she hoped it got covered up in cigar smoke."

Steph looked at Issy for instructions. This could take a while. "Blashfield," Issy said. "Do the best you can with the spelling."

Steph typed it out. Got up to take a close-up with her phone. They needed another pair of hands.

They worked steadily for an hour, taking sips from water bottles, Fae humming as she dusted. When Leo tired, Fae would pull Issy and Steph into a circle and they'd dance in the center of the room while Leo dozed in her chair.

At first Steph was stiff and uncomfortable, but Issy fell back into her old childhood habits as easily as she could name most of the paintings on the wall.

Then they would go back to work. They could hear Mandy and Griff and Chloe chatting as they cleaned. Playing name games to keep them going when they lost interest. At one point Chloe had them singing "Ninety-Nine Bottles of Beer on the Wall." Vivienne would be horrified.

Issy was just about to call a lunch break when she heard a car on the graveled drive.

"Mommy!" squealed Griff and Mandy. Brooms clattered and footsteps bounded across the floor. Even Stephanie started in her seat, before recovering herself and sitting down again. But Issy was just as anxious as everyone else to see her sister. And once their fond hellos were over, she'd make her tell what exactly had happened to their grandmother's inheritance. Then she'd scratch her eyes out.

They all piled out to the porch as a black limo came to a stop at the front steps.

A limo? Paid for by the Whitaker estate no doubt. Issy had to count her breaths not to run out and snatch open the limo door.

"Mommy!"

Chloe clutched at Griff as he ran headlong down the steps, grabbing Mandy as she started down after him. They all managed to reach the bottom without mishap; Steph stood like stone next to Fae.

The driver ran around the limo and opened the passenger door.

The moment the first leg appeared, Issy knew something was wrong. Suntanned legs, stiletto heels. The second foot. The hand held out to take the driver's hand . . .

Mandy and Griff skidded to a stop.

Issy swore; she heard Fae breathe, "Ah, hell."

The woman tootled her fingers. "Do you have a tip for this delightful man? I seem to be out of cash." She smiled, flung her arms open.

Issy sucked in air and finally found her voice. "Kids, say hello to your grandmother Jillian York."

Chapter 13

All three kids gasped and clapped their hands simultaneously over their mouths, their eyes wide above their fingers like three "speak no evil" monkeys.

Jillian perused her grandchildren like they were aboriginal specimens: they seemed frozen on the spot, but Issy wasn't sure whether it was because they didn't recognize her, didn't know she existed, or because Issy had mentioned the dreaded—never to be spoken—word *grandmother*.

"You may call me Jillian." She turned to Issy and kissed the air in the direction of Issy's right cheek. Issy moved out of range before she could accomplish the second half.

"You didn't have to come. A check would have been sufficient," Issy said, desperately trying to get the upper hand and hopefully some cash before all hell broke loose, as it always did when Jillian was around.

"Really, Oops," Jillian said. "And leave poor Leo alone in the world?"

"She's anything but alone."

"Where is she anyway?"

Issy looked quickly toward the door and was relieved to see that Leo wasn't there. Fae had disappeared, hopefully back inside to prepare Leo for the shock.

"Inside?" Jillian asked over her shoulder as she breezed past them and up the porch steps. "Be a dear and get my luggage. And can someone *please* tip the driver?"

She stepped inside and the screen door slammed shut behind her.

"Get it your—" Issy's knees went weak. Was she crazy? She needed the woman's money. She was half aware of Chloe's arm slipping around her waist.

"You asked her to come?"

"I asked her for a loan. I wonder what she's up to?"

"Maybe she wants to help?"

Issy didn't bother to answer. Chloe had known Issy since kindergarten. She knew exactly how many times Jillian had ever bothered to visit.

"Should we take her suitcases?" Steph asked, finally breaking the spell.

"Is that really our grandma?" Griff asked.

"Don't call her that!" Mandy shrieked. "Her name is . . ."— her voice lowered dramatically—"Jillian."

"Oh, for heaven's sakes." Issy felt in her pockets.

"I've got a twenty," Chloe said, and handed it to the driver, who snatched it from her hand and drove off in a spurt of gravel.

"Thanks, I'll pay you back inside." Issy glanced at the pile of matching luggage and sighed. "Come on, troops, let's get the blankety-blank luggage."

Between the five of them, they managed to get the heavy pieces up the steps and into the foyer. "She can do the rest," Issy said. "Or she can come down and dress in the foyer, for all I care." More outrageous things had occurred in this foyer, some that Issy remembered and some she'd only heard about.

She didn't see how Jillian York, for all her airs, could hold a candle to the escapades of the guests at the Muses.

Jillian and Leo were seated together on the parlor sofa. *Stalker and prey,* thought Issy.

"Oops, I can't believe you put poor Leo to work, and her right out of the hospital. Well, it's a good thing I came."

"Oh," said Issy. "And just what do you plan to do while you're here? Cook her food? Wash her clothes? Take out the trash?"

Jillian's expression changed comically. "Really, there's no reason to be sarcastic."

"Oh, I'm perfectly serious. Anybody who stays here has to carry their weight."

"Tsk tsk, Oops." Jillian stood, walked to the window, and turned. "Actually I was hoping you would loan me your apartment in the city while I'm meeting with my agent."

"My apartment? You should have called first; I would have told you that I sublet it. Sorry." The lie came so easily to Issy's lips that it surprised her and disgusted her. She hated that she'd fallen into this game so easily. "So no. You can't. Maybe they have a vacancy at the Plaza."

Jillian threw herself into a nearby chaise. "If you must know, I don't have a penny to my name. I had to use Henri's credit card for my flight, but by the time I landed in New York, he'd canceled it. I had to spend the last of my cash to come here."

Issy's knees buckled. What little hope she'd had of getting money from her mother evaporated like smoke in the wind.

Leo smiled vaguely at her daughter. "Well, I'm sure we'll be glad to have you . . ."

"Jillian," Fae prompted. "And after such a long time. I hardly recognized you."

"Dear Aunt Fae." Jillian went through the air-kiss routine again. "I'd recognize you anywhere. Now, shall I take you upstairs, Leo? You must be tired."

Issy was sure she was up to something. And from Fae's expression, she thought so, too.

"Thank you, dear, but we were right in the middle of doing an inventory."

"Inventory? Why?"

"In case of theft," Issy said pointedly.

Fae stifled a gasp, which might have grown to a guffaw if left to its own devices.

Jillian lifted an eyebrow, an expression famous in the film world, on and off the screen. *Hauteur.* But Fae and Issy were inured to it and the children were too young to understand the point of it.

"Well, I'm tired. I didn't sleep at all on the plane." She gave Leo a kiss that almost landed on her cheek and went out into the foyer. Posed, framed by the double door. "Oh, you sweet things, you retrieved my luggage." She smiled, waited.

"I'm afraid you're on your own, Jillian," Fae said.

"The Impressionist Room," Issy added. "I believe that one is free."

There was a barely perceptible flash in Jillian's "cerulean" eyes. An instant of pique.

"I'm too old to carry bags," Fae continued. "The children are too young. And Chloe and Issy are busy."

"What about the ele—"

Stephanie's hand clamped over Mandy's mouth. "No manners," she explained, but didn't let go until Jillian disappeared from the doorway and they heard her bumping one of her suit-cases up the stairs.

"Why didn't you let me tell her about the elevator?" Mandy whined.

"Because she's not nice," Stephanie answered.

"She's a movie star."

"Stephanie is correct," said Leo, startling them all. "She isn't very nice."

"DO YOU THINK Leo knew it was her daughter?" Chloe asked as she and Issy were making sandwiches for lunch. "She didn't seem the least bit moved by seeing her."

Issy shrugged. She'd been wondering that herself. Actually she'd been wondering about a lot of things in the last few days. Leo confusing Issy with Wes in the hospital she had put down to the drugs. There were times since she'd come home when her grandmother seemed vague, but other times when she seemed as sharp as a tack. Especially about the past. She remembered everything that Steph had asked her about the various pieces they'd cataloged. A huge help.

And it was pretty clear by the way Fae had jumped in that she, too, wasn't sure whether Leo understood what was happening. Issy would have to have a talk with Aunt Fae before long. She might act like someone stuck in the sixties. Who was more comfortable in "the Otherworld," but Issy had long thought she wasn't as flighty as she acted.

"Issy, do you think Leo's . . . you know, all there?" Chloe asked.

"Not at all. Every time you give her a chance she's off with Wes, living in the glorious past. God, I hope I never have a love like that."

"What do you mean? Their love story is legend."

"And binding. I don't think she'll be happy—"

"Don't say it."

"Wasn't going to." Issy looked out the kitchen window. "They're not at the picnic table. Better pack up the lunch."

"Grab a tablecloth," Chloe added. "It'll be just like old times. Picnic at the cove."

Not quite, thought Issy. Now there would be no Wes, at least not in person, though he and Max would stand guard from their graves on the knoll.

"I've got your back, Is."

"Thanks."

"THAT WAS JILLIAN?" Leo asked.

"Yes, your daughter," Fae said. "Are you focused on this?"

Leo chewed on her knuckle. "How could I not have known? Of course it was Jillian. Those eyes alone." She looked up at Fae and Fae saw the fear in them.

"You're not losing your mind. You just keep wandering away. Plus her arrival was unexpected. It took me a second to figure it out."

Two actually, Fae thought. As soon as Jillian's second foot hit the ground, the feeling of dread that came over her was enough to know who was attached to those high heels.

"Now you know. Don't forget. And try to stay in the present for as long as she's here."

"She's staying?"

"She's broke."

"No. How can that be?"

And so are we. How can that be? Fae looked to heaven and then looked across the cove, where she could just see the top of her own roof. How she longed for just a moment to be on the front porch looking out to the sound and beyond to the open sea. "I don't know. We have Netflix. We keep up with the movies. She hasn't appeared in anything for a couple of years. Actually she hasn't worked steady since she divorced Trevor York."

"And brought the children here," Leo said dreamily. "I suppose we'll have to give her some money."

"Leo. Those children are grown now. We have no money. One of those children has cleaned out the estate and disappeared. The other just left her job to come save our butts."

"What do you mean? I don't understand you."

Fae huffed out a sigh. Threw caution to the wind and hoped she wasn't about to give her sister-in-law a heart attack. "Brace yourself. I didn't want you to know, kept hoping we could clear it up before it came to this. But things are out of hand."

Leo's gaze drifted away.

"Look at me." Fae took Leo's shoulders in both her hands and held her steady.

"Dan and Vivienne have stolen all the money Wes left in the estate accounts. And your personal account."

"No."

Fae held on to her. "We have no money. It's dire. Issy is trying to do what she can."

"No. Vivienne said she had something to do and she would be back. She wouldn't lie to us."

Fae sighed and let go of Leo's fragile frame. "Fine. Believe what you want for as long as you can."

Leo grasped at Fae's sleeve. "But we should send Issy back. She'll just get stuck here."

"Don't I know it," Fae said to herself. "She won't be bullied this time. She's determined to help. But she only has two weeks of vacation, and will have to go back to Manhattan, so just hold out until then. Okay? Just try to stay with us, please."

"But—"

"Or George will make good on his decision to put us in an old-folks home."

"Wes wouldn't let him," Leo said indignantly.

"Wes is dead. You're sitting at his headstone."

"I know that. But he set up the estate so that you and I would be provided for. That the Muses would be provided for. Would stay in the family."

"Well, unless you have a spare million or two hidden in your garter, Vivienne and Dan are living off the estate money in some South American country, and we are toast."

"Silly. No one wears garters anymore."

Gods and goddesses, give me patience. Fae caught sight of Issy and Chloe coming across the meadow. "Good. Here's lunch. Now remember. You were so surprised to see Jillian it's taken a while to sink in."

"It has."

"And don't mention the money situation."

"No."

"And whatever you do, don't talk to Wes while they're all here." Fae leaned back and looked at the sky. How on earth had they gone from peacefully living off the radar to becoming the Hotel Disaster-waiting-to-happen? And was there any way they were going to fake their way through it?

Issy and Chloe carried sandwiches, salad, chips, and a container of iced tea and cups across the lawn to the knoll where Fae and Leo were seated on a bench near Wes and Max's headstones.

"Ben made the bench for them?"

"They kept bringing down lawn chairs and he thought it was just asking for an accident. So he made them a bench."

Thoughtful as always. Issy could imagine the "family" barely waiting long enough for the will to be read before leaving without a thought for the wife and sister Wes left behind. But Ben and Chloe had stayed around to keep a watchful eye on them.

And what about you? asked a niggling voice she'd rather ignore.

"What?"

"What what?" Issy asked.

"You kind of growled. Don't you like the bench?"

"Huh? Oh yeah, it's great. Thank Ben for me."

"Thank him yourself." Chloe shimmied, as much as anyone carrying a bag filled with sandwiches could shimmy. "At the Den tonight."

Issy started to say she couldn't go out when her mother had just arrived. But why not? It wasn't like they intended to make up for twenty years of silence with a gabfest tonight.

Issy found a flattish place on the ground and spread out the tablecloth. Then stood and took a deep breath. She hadn't been this far out on the property since she'd returned. And as the salt air filled her lungs, a sense, not of peace but of belonging, filled her being.

The sky was blue as only a Connecticut beach sky could be. "Cerulean like your grandfather and mother's eyes," Leo used to tell Issy, and Issy was so jealous because Vivienne had those eyes, too. It wasn't until she went to college that she learned that cerulean covered a score of shades of blue. But to Issy the Connecticut sky would always be cerulean blue. And her eyes would always be brown.

To her left, the grassy knoll rolled down to the sandy beach of the cove, a teardrop-shaped inlet carved by the waves. Farther along, the sand turned into rocks, with lots of sheltered niches where the trees overhung the water, where painters painted, writers wrote. The water near the knoll was shallow and sloped down before disappearing into the depths of the far side, where a boulder that jutted out from the land and the woods and meadow began. Where years ago a young woman had thrown off her clothes and dove in. And surfaced where Wes Whitaker was waiting for her, where they'd both fallen in love.

Issy had done her share of skinny-dipping in the cove, but so far she'd never fallen in love.

She turned in the opposite direction toward the path that led down to the stretch of sandy beach that ran along the open waters of the sound. She could see the children's heads, bent over, looking for shells. Except for Stephanie, who stood near the point, ankle-deep in water, scanning the trees of the opposite shore.

Issy cupped her hands to her mouth just at the breeze kicked up, ruffling her hair and the sleeves of her shirt. She wanted to yell, *I'm home!* but settled for "Lunch is ready!"

They all scrambled up, though Steph moved more slowly, reluctantly, Issy thought. With only a half-eaten bran muffin for breakfast, she had to be starving. Issy certainly was.

She waited for Steph to catch up, wishing she knew something to say that would make her feel . . . what? Happier? Safer. Loved by her mother?

"Do people live in the woods over there?"

Issy jumped. She hadn't expected Steph to actually speak to her. "Well, it's all Whitaker property. Great-Aunt Fae has a cottage there, but she doesn't like unannounced visitors. There used to be quite a few small cottages hidden away in the woods. Though we weren't allowed to go there."

Steph turned her head to really look at Issy.

"They weren't dangerous or anything; some served as storage places, others held the artists' supplies, the cove was a favorite painting place. There were others for contemplation, or just to get away from the craziness of the houseguests. Occasionally someone would rent them for a few weeks or a whole summer. I don't think they all had running water. And, of course, sometimes they were used for, um . . ."

"Sex," Steph volunteered, then smiled that "gotcha" smile.

All right, twelve-year-olds were pretty sophisticated these days.

"This was an art colony, I was thinking more along the lines of late-night trysts, more romantic. Though I don't see why anyone bothered. Muses by the Sea was a free-love zone," Issy finished smugly.

"Did you or my mom ever use them?"

"For sex?" Issy's reaction ended on a squeak.

Steph gave her a "too dumb to live" look.

"No . . . No." Issy sighed. Embarrassed by a tween, it was pitiful. "Your mom always hung out with her rich friends at their places. And I . . . I never had a boyfriend until I went to college."

"What about Ben?"

"Ben wasn't my boyfriend. He's Chloe's brother."

"Chloe wants you to hook up with him."

"I'm not 'hooking up' with anyone. I may consider falling in love, if given the opportunity and the right person."

"So why not Ben, like Chloe wants. I think he's hot. Except for the stinky smell on his clothes when he comes in from the marsh."

Issy laughed. "Chloe wants to be my sister. We used to call each other the sister we never had. Because she only has brothers and because my sister didn't like me."

"Hates you," Steph said. "Don't take it personally. She hates the whole family. That's just because she's jealous."

They had almost reached the others and Issy stopped her. "That may be. Just promise me you're not planning on hooking up with anybody in any of the cabins. They're probably run-down and filled with spiders. If they're even still standing."

"Aunt Issy, I'm twelve."

"Just saying."

Chloe had the lunch things spread out on the tablecloth, and as soon as they sat down, she handed out sandwiches and tea like a pro. Fae joined Leo on the bench, but Issy stood.

Now that she'd started work on the art collection she didn't want to stop. Plus she needed to do some serious grocery shopping for this crowd, but she didn't want to have to go to the big chain stores out on the highway and slight Mr. Ogden's market. She'd just have to pay off some of their account and start having their groceries delivered.

And how long is your money going to last, paying for everything? Groceries, utilities. There were probably taxes. If you're going to steal someone's estate, you probably wouldn't be nice enough to pay their taxes first.

Anger surged up inside her. How could Vivienne do this? Grammy and Wes had given them a home, loved them, paid for everything. They'd sent them to college. Even Issy, who would just as happily have stayed home with them.

That was when the first crack in the fairy tale of her world view occurred. The first time she realized that maybe her grandparents had just been biding their time until they could be free of their responsibility and go back to their old life. Just the two of them. A ten-year chunk out of their life. More than ten—fourteen until they pushed Issy out the door.

Artists still came, the house was always filled with interesting people, especially in the summer. Issy had never felt like she'd cast a pall on the festivities. She never complained about the late-night noise that sometimes kept her awake, or the cigar and cigarette and pipe smoke. Or eating in the kitchen when a big party was going on. She liked the kitchen and Mrs. Norcroft.

Whom she would have to visit soon with her abject apologies. Maybe ask her to come back to work. *And pay her with what?* She had about enough money saved to feed the family over the summer, and if she didn't go back to her job she would have nothing left once that was gone.

All conversation had stopped and everyone was contentedly eating their lunch. Everyone but Issy. And when the others had eaten their fill and made signs of going back to the beach or taking a nap, Issy announced, "Okay, back to work."

"I'm ex-*hausted*," Mandy moaned, and fell onto her back in the grass.

"You watched television all morning and cleaned a few stair spindles," Issy said.

"You can't work when you have company. It would be impolite."

"We don't have company."

"Grandma is here," Griff said.

"We're not supposed to call her that," Mandy said. "Mommy said so."

"It's not fa-air," Griff whined.

"It's life with Jillian York," Issy said. "I'm going back to the house."

"I'll stay here with the kids for a while," Chloe called after her.

"And, Issy," Leo called. "Tell Mrs. Norcroft to set the dining table for dinner tonight. In Jillian's honor."

Issy waved and kept walking.

"I'll come with you," Steph said, and fell in step.

"You don't have to," Issy said. "Stay and hang out on the beach."

"I don't mind what we're doing, and if you don't need me, I can finish my book."

"What are you reading?"

"Something Aunt Fae gave me."

Issy nodded. *"The Otherworld,"* she guessed.

Steph looked sharply at her. 'You've read it?"

"A long time ago."

They walked along in silence until they were almost back at the house.

"I guess everyone in the family has read it," Steph said.

Issy stopped, sensing the girl's sudden disappointment, and in a moment of clarity that hit her hard, she understood her reaction. "Didn't she tell you not to tell anyone about reading it?"

"She said not to tell Mom. Because it's, you know—"

"It's not that. It's because only one person in each generation gets to read the book," she extemporized. "It's because you and I are special."

Chapter 14

Issy sent Steph off to read her book while she got organized. What she really needed was a little time to herself. She'd come close to bursting the kid's bubble and it had unnerved her. She of all people knew how important it was to have something all your own, something that picks you out from all the glamorous people surrounding you, from all the perfectly perfect people at school.

Aunt Fae had loaned Steph the book of stories for the same reason she'd let Issy read it all those years ago. Just a forgotten collection of Victorian tales of the Otherworld with some Victorian eroticism thrown in for good measure.

Not children's fare but wildly romantic and shocking for a teenager; a rite of passage into a special world. And Issy had almost wrecked it for Stephanie. Fortunately she'd caught herself in time.

Aunt Fae was good that way. For knowing just what you needed and when. Some people, including people in her own family, thought she was just an old hippie who'd never grown up, but they were wrong. Fae belonged to the spirit world, not peopled with real fairies and Elf Kings, but the possibilities of them. The possibilities in life.

She wondered if Fae had taken Steph to her cottage yet. It was a delightful place, a safe place, where Issy had stayed many times when she felt the differences between herself and the kids whose parents lived at home, or when the talk among the artists grew too passionate or theoretical. Or filled with despair. Once, when Henderson Clark had slit his wrists in a fit of depression, he'd rushed down the stairs crying, "It's red. It's red!" So startled by the color of his own blood that he fainted at Issy's feet. Issy ran to Fae's and stayed there for two days.

She wandered through the rooms rearranging cloisonné boxes, touching Fabergé eggs and pieces of sea glass, mainly remembering. She was acutely aware that her mother was upstairs, sleeping off jet lag and most likely several in-flight gin and tonics. She would come down for dinner refreshed and looking for a way to make their lives more complicated than they already were. And Issy would long to run to Fae's and take Steph with her.

Chloe came back ahead of the others. And they set the dining table as per Leo's request.

"You only got out seven plates," Issy said.

"I'm not eating with you guys, thank you very much. Besides, who will serve?"

"Nobody's serving. She's not the bloody queen. We'll put the food on the table and let everyone pass it around like a normal family."

"Fine, but I'm still not eating with you."

Issy gave Chloe an impulsive hug. "I owe you big-time."

"Then promise you'll come to the Den tonight."

"Deal."

They were just finishing up when she heard someone rummaging around in the parlor.

Issy headed for the door, not sure what she was going to say, but making sure her mother, like her sister, wasn't attempting to help herself to the artwork.

She found Jillian headfirst in the drinks cabinet.

She stood as Issy walked in. She was swathed, no other word for it, in silk pants and a tunic in a pearl-blue color that changed shades as she moved. Issy could kick herself for the admiration she felt.

She left you behind, remember.

"I swear this is the same bottle of vermouth that was here last time I was in town. Do you think McBready's is open on Sundays? I think we should order new everything. Do you have your cell on you?"

"No, I don't, which is academic, since we're all broke and we won't be ordering from anywhere."

"You, too?"

"No, not me, but I will be trying to keep all of us together until further notice."

Jillian put the vermouth bottle on the cabinet top. "Are you sure you're not exaggerating?"

Issy lifted an eyebrow. It was the mirror image of Jillian's. The only reason she knew this was because everyone who knew Jillian remarked on it.

Jillian broke first, gave a dramatic sigh, and reached for a glass. "We do have ice?"

"In the kitchen," Issy said, and left before Jillian could hand her the glass.

Issy went straight out the back to the lawn, where she couldn't be seen or found by Jillian or anyone else. She slipped into a sheltered nook out of the wind and called Paulo.

"*Cara*, how are things in Connecticut?"

"My mother showed up."

"In the flesh?"

"Yes. Evidently she's broke. Not only can't she lend us money, she had the nerve to ask to borrow my apartment."

He laughed. She felt better.

"Was the museum pleased with the installation?"

"Of course. And Mark Darwin said if you ever wanted to leave New York . . ."

"He says that every time I see him. I think it's a kind of flirtation."

"Perhaps. Anyway, everything went fine. Dell is going down tomorrow for the opening, and guess what, taking Deirdre with him since you're *en vacances*."

"Some vacation."

"So Mama is there. Do you want me to postpone my trip? I could overnight the specs to you. But really we should look over them together. Major coup for us."

"No. Come. Stay."

"Because of the plans or because you need reinforcements?"

"Both."

"I'll be up first thing tomorrow. Wait, I have a debriefing, but if I hurry that along, I can beat the afternoon rush-hour traffic at New Haven."

"Perfect. Bring your swimsuit."

They rang off, and when Issy walked back to the house, she felt almost cheerful.

Issy changed for dinner, but only into clean slacks and a T-shirt not saturated in dust and dirt.

Jillian sat in the parlor like she was the hostess, and Issy had to grit her teeth not to mention it. But as people often told her, Jillian wasn't mean-spirited, just self-absorbed. Issy never really understood the difference. She still didn't.

Leo had pinned up the wisps of hair that had blown free in the beach breeze. And changed into a pantsuit that managed to trump Jillian's. Griff and Mandy were relatively clean. Fae looked absolutely the same, except perhaps her hair was even more windblown than it had been at the picnic.

Steph got the prize for dinner couture. She came in after Fae, and was wearing what had to be one of Fae's summer shifts. Yellow, blue, and mauve, with a gathered shoulder cape that opened like butterfly wings when she moved.

She was looking at the floor when she entered, but cast a quick look at Issy from beneath her lashes as she passed.

Issy gave her a "nailed it" look back.

"I wanna wear a costume, too," Mandy whined, destroying the moment.

"It's not a costume, stupid."

"It's beautiful," Leo said. "Come, Stephanie, and let me see."

Stephanie stepped toward her.

"I remember that dress," Leo said. "Fae wore it to the open house we had . . . when was that?" She looked at Fae.

"Oh, 2004 or five."

"I remember it was a beautiful June day—"

"That it was, just beautiful. Shall we go into dinner?" Fae started toward Leo but Jillian stood. "Shall I help you up, Mother?"

Leo smiled up at her. "Thank you, dear, but I'm capable of getting out of my chair."

And she managed it just fine. Jillian did take her elbow going into the dining room.

"She's up to something," Fae said as she passed. "Be sure to count the silver."

Issy snorted. "We're using the stainless steel."

IT WAS LATE when Issy and Choe arrived at the Fisherman's Den, a mostly local bar and grill nestled between the road and the water at the far edge of Painter's Cove. Constructed of wood and stone, it had survived several fires and hurricanes, had been rebuilt more than once, and other than that had done absolutely nothing to keep up with the gentrification of the shoreline.

It was packed, even on a Sunday night. The music blared out into the evening along with a billow of smoke from the outdoor kitchen.

Chloe pulled Issy through the crowd, nodding at several people as she passed. Issy didn't recognize anyone, not that Chloe was giving her time to. They headed straight to the deck out back and several steps down from the main building, where it was considerably quieter, less smoky, and cooler by a good ten degrees.

Ben was leaning on the rail, a bottle of beer sitting on the eight-by-four that served as extra table space. He saw them and raised a hand to call them over.

When they reached him, he leaned over and looked into Issy's eyes, leaning so close that their noses nearly touched.

He swiveled his head toward Chloe without standing up. "I think she's going to make it." He straightened up. "Chloe gave me a heads-up about Jillian showing up."

Issy threw her head back and looked at the night sky.

"If you're going to howl at the moon, could you pretend like you don't know us?"

Issy dropped her head. "I wasn't going to howl. I was just communing."

"How was it?"

"It wasn't. I call for a loan and get her on my doorstep instead. Something I did in a former life no doubt."

"Well, the good news," Ben said, summoning a waitress, "is that she never stays longer than necessary."

The waitress appeared with two more beers.

"How did you know I still drank this label?" Issy asked as she took the bottle from Ben.

"I just assumed," he said. "My bad."

"Not bad. Lucky."

"But don't make a habit of it," Chloe added.

"It's a guy thing."

They drank beer, saw a few people Issy knew, danced a little, and fell into the way it always used to be, maybe the way it should be.

"You're dead on your feet," Ben said.

"I am not," Issy said, stifling a yawn.

"Well, you were dead on my feet. I'll drive you home."

Issy started to say that the Muses wasn't home. But it was and it would always be, no matter where she was.

She and Chloe hugged good night. "Thanks."

"Don't think you've seen the last of me," Chloe said. "Ben and I mean to stick around and make ourselves useful. Oh, I forgot to tell you. I'm taking Mandy and Griff with me tomorrow morning, if that's okay. There's a day camp at my school and I just happen to know the registrar. I told Fae."

"It sounds like heaven. And they had room for them?"

Ben laughed. "Chloe's the only one who knows how to run the new computer system the school installed."

"Well, double thanks."

"All right, come on, you." Ben took Issy by the arm. "Chloe, are you coming?"

"In a minute. I see some people I know. I'll meet you back at the house."

Issy and Ben walked arm in arm to the parking lot and Ben stopped her in front of a battered pickup. He opened the door and unceremoniously hoisted her into the front seat.

"This isn't the same truck you drove me to college in, is it?" Issy asked as they rattled out of the parking lot and onto the paved road.

"No. That one lost the battle of bumper meets bog. This is its replacement."

"Ben?"

"Yeah?"

"I haven't been too good about staying in touch."

"No, you haven't. But I expect you had your reasons."

"Had," Issy agreed. "No more. I can't tell you how—"

"Don't say thank you again. It's just like it always was. Back and forth, help out when you can, get help when you need it in turn. We're all the same. You're the one who's forgotten, so it seems odd."

"You're right. I had forgotten."

He turned into the drive of the Muses. The lights were off except the porch and vestibule.

"Good. It looks like they're all having an early night. You get them up early to help you catalog." He pulled to a stop in front of the steps and gave her a wicked grin.

"And I'll enjoy doing it," Issy said. She leaned over and

kissed his cheek. "Thanks," she said, and jumped out of the truck and ran inside without looking back to see Ben's reaction.

EVERYONE HAD GONE to bed. Steph was in her room but she couldn't sleep. She sat at the window reading. She was tired, but every time she lay down her mind started running like crazy. Like, what was with Issy and Jillian? And why did they let Jillian come home like she hadn't ignored them all her life. And what was going to happen to them, Griff and Mandy and her? What if her mom and dad never came back?

Grammy and Jillian had a big discussion about it. Jillian said they should definitely put out a missing-person report. She could go on television and make a plea for her child to be returned.

Then Aunt Fae reminded her that as far as they knew, she'd left of her own free will, and hadn't been kidnapped.

Steph wouldn't mind staying with Grammy and Aunt Fae except Aunt Fae normally lived in her own cottage, and the Muses was a really big house for just two people. And probably could get really spooky when there weren't a lot of people staying.

Her room was on the northeast corner of the house, so she could see when headlights appeared in the drive and came toward the house. For a minute she wobbled between hope and something else. She wanted her family back, but back without the yelling and the anger and her mother always carping on how Steph should behave and dress and act. But she also wanted to stay here where life was full of . . . specialness.

But it didn't matter. It was just Ben bringing Issy home from the bar. Issy went inside, Ben drove away.

If Steph was older she could have gone with them instead of

having to sit in the living room and listen to Jillian and Grammy talk. Aunt Fae took the kids to the other side of the room to play some game that she and Great-Grandfather Wes used to play when they were little kids, but it looked really dumb, so Steph had just looked around the room at all the stuff they'd have to catalog the next day.

Every room was like an episode of *Hoarders,* only good stuff. They needed a whole army to write down everything that was in here. Especially if Grammy was going to tell a story about every one of them. Though she had to admit it was pretty interesting stuff. Much better than the trips to galleries with her mother where all the paintings were named *Abstract #1, Abstract #2, Abstract #3.* And you had to look thoughtful and pretend like you knew what they were about.

Steph sat; she might as well get used to it because she just wasn't going to be able to sleep. Ever again. She'd be one of those people who can't sleep then goes crazy and dies.

She yawned, rested her elbow on the windowsill, and saw the first little circle of light. She sat up, moved closer to the glass, not taking her eyes off the little circle. It was going up and down like it was floating on the water; but it wasn't on the water, it was on the lawn and it was headed toward the woods.

Fairies? Stupid, there was no such thing as fairies. Maybe not fairies, but *faeries* maybe. They might exist. They might come and exchange children in the night.

They could take Mandy if they wanted her. But Steph was pretty sure they only took babies. She'd buy that, because Steph never felt like she belonged in her family. But if faeries existed, it was a long time ago. Aeons. These days there were just psychopaths and divorced people who kidnapped children.

The light entered the woods. She kept losing sight of it, then it would suddenly reappear, and she knew it was going through the trees. And it was getting smaller. She wanted to run downstairs and outside to chase it. But it would be gone before she could reach it.

Even now it grew dimmer; then it winked out altogether and didn't come back on. She waited for a really long time, and the next thing she knew it was morning.

Chapter 15

The next morning Issy drove across town to see Mrs. Norcroft. She hated that she had to meet the old housekeeper again under these circumstances. It was a daunting task. But someone had to thank her for her decades of service, apologize for the lies Vivienne and Dan told, and then beg her to come back to work.

It was nearly ten when she pulled up in front of the wood-frame house that belonged to Mrs. Norcroft's sister and saw the first indication that she might be too late. A "Sold" sign was stuck in the middle of a well-manicured yard.

Issy hurried out of the car and up to the front door. Knocked; waited until someone called out, "Coming." The door opened and a woman peered out of the opening.

"Excuse me. Does Mrs. Norcroft live here?"

"Depends on who wants to know."

Issy tried peering over the woman's shoulder, but she stepped to the side, blocking her view.

"Issy. Isabelle Whitaker, and—"

The woman stepped back and slammed the door in Issy's face.

Issy leaned into the door. "Please. If Mrs. Norcroft is there, I came to apologize. There's been a terrible mistake. And I wanted her to know. Please let me in."

This was worse than she could have imagined. Of course the family deserved any treatment they got, but she couldn't stand the idea of Mrs. Norcroft thinking they didn't trust her.

The door cracked open.

Issy didn't move to go in.

They stared at each other for what seemed like an aeon.

"I'm Mrs. Stone, Lila's sister." She opened the door and stepped back for Issy to enter.

The house was small and comfortable looking, furnished with plush couches and chairs.

"She's in the kitchen." Mrs. Stone lifted her chin and turned away. Issy followed her to a swinging door, which she held open for Issy. And Issy was hit with a familiar aroma of bananas and coffee. She breathed it in and indulged in a sigh of memory.

Mrs. Norcroft was taking pans of banana bread out of the oven. She put two pans down on a rack and saw Issy.

"Issy?" the housekeeper said tentatively. She was wearing a white apron, covering a blue-flowered shirtwaist dress, and her face was dusted with flour.

Such a familiar sight, it was all Issy could do not to throw her arms around her and beg her forgiveness. But she was an adult now, and besides, she hadn't done anything but ignore her family.

"Oh my Lord, I didn't even recognize you." Mrs. Norcroft's face fell. "What they said about me wasn't true. You know I would never take anything from your family."

"She wouldn't steal from anybody," Mrs. Stone added. "It was an out-and-out lie. Didn't even call the police 'cause they knew it wasn't true. And if that sister of yours sent you down here to—"

"Elsie, thank you my dear. But let Issy talk."

"Humph." Mrs. Stone crossed her arms.

So Issy was going to have an audience.

"First." Issy took a breath. "Vivienne didn't send me. I haven't seen her. She's disappeared and left her children with Leo."

"Run off with that no-good husband of hers," said Mrs. Stone.

Mrs. Norcroft pressed her fingers to her lips.

"Things are in a mess, Mrs. Norcroft. I had no idea. I didn't mean to neglect them; I kind of fell out with the others a while back. Well, we all fell out with each other. I just got busy at work and haven't visited or called as much as I should have. But that's all in the past now."

"You were always a volatile bunch. You sit down. Elsie, will you get cups down? I'm sure Issy would like some coffee."

Mrs. Norcroft gestured to one chair and sat down in another.

Mrs. Stone poured out three cups of coffee, placed them on the table, and sat down in front of one of them.

"I don't know what to say, except that I'm sorry."

"Sorry doesn't cut the mustard."

"Elsie, please."

"Well, it doesn't. The whole town knew what your sister accused Lila of. Most of them knew it couldn't be true. But any town's got its gossips and it was humiliating for her just to go to the market. The things people say."

"Well, none of it is Issy's fault."

"You say," Mrs. Stone said.

"It is my fault," said Issy at the same time. "If I'd stayed in touch, I would have figured out what was going on. I know you would never hurt us. And I'll be glad to tell the whole town if you want."

"Not necessary, dear. Fae's already taken care of that. She may be an old fool, so are we all. But she knows what's right and she sticks by it no matter what other folks might think of her."

Issy nodded.

Elsie Stone slapped the table. "And I say good riddance to Dan Bannister and that sister of yours, too. I'm cutting us some banana bread."

"That's for the church bake sale."

"Hang the church bake sale," said Elsie, and pulled a giant knife off the wall rack.

"What's been going on, Mrs. Norcroft? Do you know?"

"The long and the short of it, Dan Bannister starting ripping off Leo before Wes was cold in his grave. I didn't realize it at first but I wasn't surprised when I did notice. The Bannisters have always been a family that took what they wanted. Everybody told Leo not to let Vivienne get involved with him, but Vivienne was bound and determined to have the life of luxury she wanted. Well, she got it.

"No old family home for her. Had to have one of those big McMansions over near Guilford. Then the cars. Over here all the time with those bratty children sucking up to Wes. Anybody could tell where that was going."

Issy nodded.

"And if you had been around, missy. You would have seen it, too."

"They sent me away."

"They sent you to college. It's what parents do."

"I know that now. At the time I thought they didn't want me. And they . . ." Issy still choked on the words. "They didn't even call me to say Wes had died or tell me about the funeral. Nothing."

"Vivienne's doing," Mrs. Norcroft said, accepting a plate of bread from Mrs. Stone. "I heard her tell George she would take care of it. You were out of the country on a job. Such a brouhaha, between Fae and Dan when she found out why you weren't there. Lord, if that crazy woman could cast spells, Dan Bannister would still be hopping around your front garden.

"But there was nothing you could've done. It was already too late by then. You were always Wes's favorite, but you had a career and the Bannisters were always around, and he didn't want to burden you with his estate."

"Me? What about George?"

Mrs. Norcroft waved George away with a flick of her hand. "Wes got suckered in by that Bannister boy, and Leo never could see any farther than Wes.

"Wes could've left things in George's hands, but those two were like oil and water. Then Wes dies and Dan takes over. He did have the roof fixed, but it leaked with the first hard storm. Cut corners, you know."

"And the plumbing?"

"Hired Scott Rostand. He did four of the upstairs bathrooms, Dan didn't pay him, kept putting him off. Scott had no choice but to move on to another job. He's working at the theater now."

"We still owe him money?"

"I doubt if Dan ever paid him. It was about that time I

started noticing things were missing. I didn't want to think that Scott would have helped himself in lieu of payment. And I knew he didn't when things kept going missing after he had stopped working at the house.

"Then I wondered if Fae might have taken them. I don't know how Wes left her, but I was afraid that maybe she needed the money. I asked her right out."

Mrs. Norcroft laughed. "And she told me right back what I could do with my suspicions. She thought it was Vivienne and Dan."

"And she was right," Issy said. "Leo and Fae didn't realize what was happening. Leo still doesn't know what Vivienne did to you. She thinks you're on vacation."

"Bless her. Best not to upset her. What's done is done."

"I see that the house is for sale. It's not because of what my family did, is it?"

"No, no, child." Mrs. Norcroft reached over and took Issy's hand. "We're going down to Tennessee. Got a brother and another sister down there. Weather is nicer. Taxes are cheaper. Elsie and I always planned to move down there when we retired. And now we both have."

Issy squeezed the housekeeper's hand. "What a family."

"Can't pick your families. Just make the best of them."

"I guess." Issy looked up, smiled. "And you'll be okay?"

"Oh, sure. Wes left me a nice inheritance. I didn't plan on using it until I retired, but Vivienne retired me. Elsie and I might even take ourselves off on a cruise. I'd like to see some of those places all those folks at the Muses talked about. I'll miss Leo, though. She ought to get herself a nice little condo somewhere, but I know she'll never leave."

"Well, I wish you the best," Issy said, getting up and feeling a little teary.

"Take some of this bread to Leo and Fae. Make sure they get it and not those bratty children. Tell her I'll always remember the good times I had at the Muses, and the kindness of your family. But maybe this was a blessing in disguise, give me a chance to enjoy my retirement while I still can."

FAE DUMPED A box of cookies on a glass plate and dropped the whole thing on the sterling-silver tray, which sent several of the cookies sliding off. She stopped, stretched her arms open, and took a deep, cleansing breath.

"Never prepare food in anger," she said to herself as much as to Steph, who was watching her like she was afraid Fae might just flap her arms and fly out the kitchen window, which, as far as options went, wasn't the worst, even if impossible.

Fae returned the errant cookies to the plate and arranged the others in a circle. "Anger will attach itself to anything it can, and if it gets inside you, it can bore a little hole and attach itself to you, so you can't get rid of it."

"Are you angry, Aunt Fae?"

Fae turned to look at the girl, who'd knocked at her door in Mrs. Norcroft's rooms this morning looking for more clothes to wear. Fae had anticipated this request and brought a duffel bag filled with wonderful patterns and colors just in case. She was also prepared for the girl to turn up her nose at them.

She did at first.

She tried really hard not to want them, but she couldn't hold out against the magic of those fabrics. And now she and Fae stood side by side, both wearing a pair of patchwork overalls rolled up to the knee and faded tie-dyed T-shirts Fae had bartered for at the Renaissance Faire.

They were very colorful.

"Aunt Fae?"

"What? Oh, am I angry? Just annoyed, and that's not much better. And not at you. But there is a lot to annoy me these days. I should embrace the challenge, but you know, dear, sometimes I feel just too damn old."

"You're not old. At least not as old as Grammy."

"True. But Leo has lost her great love and that's made her older than she needs to be."

Fae got the sherry bottle out of the pantry and poured it into a Waterford decanter.

"Great-Grandfather Wes was her great love?"

Fae nodded and added several jelly glasses to the tray. They were what people called collectibles these days, but to the Whitakers they were just things that had never been thrown away. Fae didn't know if the ladies of the Theater Fund committee would appreciate drinking their sherry from Tweety Bird or Road Runner or if they would even take their star-studded eyes off Jillian long enough to notice.

A glance at the tray and she knew neither of them would manage to get it safely to the parlor, where the committee, Jillian, and Leo were waiting. She took the decanter of sherry. "Think you can get the tray to the parlor without losing anything?"

Steph shrugged.

"I say we go for it."

Steph smiled and Fae's heart sang. Because hearts could do that. And it was the first real happiness smile she'd seen from Steph. And Fae knew that for all her sins, she had been doubly blessed. "After you."

They went single file down the hallway. Steph taking baby steps with her eyes glued to the cookie plate, Fae holding the heavy decanter like it was an offering to a king—or queen—until they reached the parlor. They put the tray and the decanter on the coffee table in front of Jillian, who was lounging on the sofa like Goya's *La Maja*.

Jillian trailed a languid hand and Fae moved away before she could ask her to pour. Steph wasn't so quick and Jillian said, "Stephanie dear, will you hand the cookies around?" And lo and behold, the girl dipped an awkward curtsy and picked up the plate.

Leo coughed behind her hand and Fae bit her lip, willing herself not to laugh. It was just like some prank the two of them would have played in the past, and she prayed that this wouldn't catapult her sister-in-law into better times and make her totally incomprehensible to these adoring ladies.

The cookie plate made the rounds. Stephanie returned the plate to the coffee table and stood attentively. Jillian smiled at her.

Fae recognized that smile. "Yell, if you need anything else," she squawked, and steered the almost-teenager out of the room. "No more *Downton Abbey* for you, miss."

Steph spluttered. Fae laughed and they ran down the hall, giggling like they weren't all going to hell in a handbasket.

A BLUE SUBURBAN minivan was coming out of the Muses by the Sea drive as Issy was turning in. She didn't even feel a surge of excitement. She'd pretty much given up on ever seeing Dan or Vivienne again. And she doubted if Jillian was making a quick exit in a minivan, though that would be entertaining. She parked and took her two loaves of banana bread inside. She found Jillian and Leo sitting in the front parlor surrounded by glasses and a plate of cookies.

Jillian was looking smug; Leo looked like she was miles away.

"Entertaining?" Issy asked with a smile she didn't feel.

"Some charming ladies from the Cove Theater asked me to be their hostess at the fund-raising gala in September."

"September? You're planning to stay until September?" Issy asked, trying to keep the panic out of her voice.

"Unless you've changed your mind about lending me your apartment or my agent calls."

Issy shook her head. Not her apartment; she'd put her hopes on the agent.

"Of course you'll stay here," Leo said. "The Muses has always been open to artists of all kinds."

Jillian and Issy both yanked their attention from each other to Leo.

Leo blinked. Touched her handkerchief to her mouth. "Why would you leave when you just arrived . . . Jillian? I was hoping we'd have a nice visit."

Issy exhaled. Jillian didn't.

"Thank you. Mother, I'd love to."

"Oh, good," Issy said, wondering if she could parlay this new information into getting Jillian to take custody of the kids. It would never happen, plus she didn't trust Jillian enough to leave her here alone.

But she could put her to work in the meantime. "You know how they say many hands make light work? We have a lot of work to do." She snagged a cookie off the plate and left the room.

She didn't want a cookie. She wanted a nice lunch in the museum café or a hurried deli sandwich at her desk or . . .

She found Fae and Stephanie in the kitchen, sitting at the

table drinking lemonade and dressed like twin clowns from Cirque du Soleil.

"Do not, I repeat, do not clean up after that woman," she told them.

They both sputtered into laughter. Issy's mouth twisted into a smile. It was impossible not to give in to their mirth. "What did you two do?"

"Nothing," Steph said. She turned twinkling eyes on Fae. It was the most animation Issy had ever seen from the girl.

Fae put down her cup and looked seriously at Issy. "Stephanie made a spectacle of herself."

"We both did," Steph said, and the two of them burst into laughter. It took a couple of attempts, the words and laughter tumbling out together . . . "and then she . . . *Downton Abbey* . . . in jelly glasses . . . you should have seen . . ."

"Sorry I missed it." Issy's eyes flew to the ceiling, and she wondered if there might be a replica of *The Thinker* somewhere upstairs, which reminded her that Paolo was on his way.

She made a quick call to Ogden's. Explained to Mr. Ogden that she would have a check for half of what they owed plus the amount for the ordered food for the deliveryman.

He was totally amenable. "I knew it was just some oversight," he said brightly. "Now, what would you like me to send out?"

LUNCH CONSISTED OF soup and egg salad sandwiches at the kitchen table. It seemed odd with the five of them, four generations of the Whitaker family, together in the kitchen. Issy tried to imagine how Norman Rockwell would have painted the scene. And decided it was more appropriate for Edward Hopper. People together, but alone.

No one spoke. So after a few minutes, Issy said into the silence, "I think we'll clean the parlor this afternoon, if that's okay with everybody. I have a colleague arriving with some specs for another job tonight. It would be nice to run the vac and dust before he arrives. Okay with everyone?"

Leo, Fae, and Steph nodded.

Jillian had been studying her sandwich with distaste, and stood. "I'll just be in the way. I think I'll go into town and look for a charming little bistro. Is there a car I could borrow?"

No one answered. Not even Leo.

"Oh, well, the walk will do me good."

Issy wondered how she'd suddenly gotten money for lunch. She looked from Fae to Leo.

"Did one of you loan her money?"

"She said she didn't have a penny to her name," Leo said. "And you know how Wes always tries to help artists in need."

Across the table Fae's sandwich stopped halfway to her mouth. At the same time a shiver ran up Issy's back. Steph shot a worried look at Leo.

"Leo," Fae said in the gruffest voice Issy had ever heard her use. "That artist, as you call her, is your daughter, Jillian."

"I know, Fae," Leo said, and seemed to shrink in her chair. "I just forgot for a moment because I was thinking about something else."

"Well, don't," Fae said imperatively, but quietly. "And eat your sandwich. It's your favorite."

Steph moved closer to Leo, and after lunch she offered to go upstairs to see Grammy to her nap.

Issy and Fae stayed at the kitchen table and Issy knew she had to ask. "What's going on with Grammy?"

"Nothing. Nothing." Fae pushed back her chair. "Let's get

these dishes cleared if you want the parlor floors cleaned before your colleague arrives."

STEPHANIE WALKED SLOWLY next to Grammy. She didn't want to hover. Be like one of those helicopter moms. But Grammy needed someone to help her.

They went into Grammy's bedroom and Grammy thanked her, but she didn't leave. She loved this room with its big bed and shiny satin comforter, the big wooden wardrobe and the funny plastic chairs that some famous friend had made for them. It was like being in a fun house, Grammy's bedroom.

She helped Grammy to get on her bed and then took her shoes off for her.

Grammy was so sweet and smiled and thanked her, but Steph began to feel a little sick.

"Grammy?"

"Yes, dear?"

"Do you know who I am?" Steph held her breath, silently chanting *please, please, please.*

"Of course I do."

"Who?"

Grammy looked at her with those bright loving eyes. "You're my dear sweet girl."

"What's my name, Grammy?"

"Your name?"

Steph couldn't control her mouth. It twisted all ugly. "Please."

"You're Stephanie, silly. Did you forget?"

Steph shook her head, tears of relief rolling down her cheeks.

"Oh, dear, come sit beside me and tell Grammy what's wrong."

Steph climbed up on the bed. "I want to stay with you and Aunt Fae forever." She leaned her head on Grammy's shoulder and Grammy rocked them both side to side.

"Well, my dear, nobody can stay here forever."

"Please say I can stay."

"It's not possible, Issy. It's time for you to go. There's a whole world waiting for you. A world you'll miss if you stay here with all these crazy artists. You have to go. You'll love college. Besides, everyone wanted to go, it's not right to keep you.

"I'm tired now, Issy. Have Mrs. Norcroft help with your luggage and I'll have a little nap."

Steph slid off the bed, her nose was running. "Please Grammy."

Grammy lay back against her pillows. "We lost Max and then we lost Jillian and George. Wes says we have to let you go or we'll lose you, too. And we love you so much."

Grammy closed her eyes and Steph stumbled to the door. Stood in the hall. And then flew down the stairs to Aunt Fae and Issy.

"SHE DIDN'T KNOW me," Steph choked out as she burst into the kitchen. Fae turned around in time to catch her in her arms.

"Oh God," Fae said, and sat in the nearest chair, taking Steph with her. Steph clung to her, crying, while Issy looked on helplessly.

Then it was true, the little lapses that she'd noticed and dismissed as consequences of Leo's fall. Issy groped for the nearest chair, pulled it next to Fae and Steph, and sat. She'd known it, from the first day, she'd known something wasn't quite right.

Fae pulled Issy close and the three of them sat together while

Stephanie sobbed. Being together; sharing that moment when denial is shattered by devastating realization.

When Steph finally calmed, Fae said, "Tell us what happened."

Steph sniffed, Fae handed her a napkin. "We sat down and I asked her who I was, because sometimes it seems like maybe she doesn't know. And she said I was Steph, so I thought it was okay. And I said . . . Well, I said I wanted to stay here forever and she said I couldn't." Her voice cracked and she cried some more while the two women waited.

"Then she started calling me Issy. And said I had to go because if she didn't send you, you would go anyway and be lost to her, and they had to let you go because they loved you so much."

"She said that?" Issy asked, close to tears herself.

"Something like that."

Then they were all crying and hugging each other until Fae pushed the other two away. She took a deep breath and looked over Steph's head to Issy. "This is why we didn't confront Vivienne and Dan about what was happening. Why I couldn't go to George. If they guessed at Leo's state of mind . . . They're all just looking for an excuse to put the Muses up for sale."

"No," Issy and Steph cried out.

"And send you and Grammy to the old-folks home?"

Fae smiled. "Yes. I won't go. I'll run away before I let them do that to me. But Leo? She won't leave this house or Wes and Max and she won't be able to fight. She's not losing her faculties. At least not that it matters. She gets confused. I think it's because she spends so much time in her mind with Wes in the past. She's lost without him. She's just waiting to go to him, but it's not her time.

"And if that helps her get through the day, it's fine with me. But other people. Well, they already think I'm crazy." She smiled at Issy and Steph. "And I am, a little, but Leo isn't, not really. She needs someone to stay with her, make sure she eats and doesn't fall, things like that. But they can't send her away. It will break her heart; no one should be unhappy before they die."

Fae dabbed at her eyes with the backs of her hand.

"You and I can stay with her," Steph said.

Fae smiled . . . sadly, Issy thought. "One crazy old lady and a twelve-year-old? They won't allow it."

Issy leaned back in her chair. One more complication she hadn't imagined when she'd jumped into the car a few nights before and driven to the rescue.

The situation was a mess. And who could they find to live with her grandmother? And what could she do for the children?

"Did Wes leave everything to Grammy?"

Fae shrugged. "He left some things to other people—me, George, Jillian, Mrs. Norcroft, and—oh, I don't know."

"But she owns the house and the contents?"

"I'm not sure. John Renfroe would know. He did Wes's will. Why? How can that help us?"

Issy shook her head. "I'm not sure if it can. Right now we're going to clean this place from top to bottom. And then we're going to catalog the art, and if Grammy owns the contents of the house, we'll have to figure out which paintings to sell to keep the Muses afloat."

Chapter 16

S ell?" Fae asked incredulously. "Leo will never let you sell any piece. It's the legacy of Muses by the Sea. And before you point out that there will be no Muses to have a legacy, don't bother. It would take more than a couple of paintings to keep this old house from falling down. Then what, sell more? Let the art collection dwindle down like so much beach erosion.

"We might as well have been drawing with chalk for the last two centuries."

Steph cast an anxious look at Fae. "Aunt Issy, you have to do something."

"The land?" Issy ventured. "Can Leo sell a parcel of it?"

"I'm pretty sure it's in trust."

Issy hung her head. It seemed whichever way she turned, her hands were tied.

Don't alert the police about the missing money, from George. You can't sell anything, from Fae. Jillian, penniless, who'd moved in, lock, stock, and designer luggage. Issy couldn't afford to keep Grammy in the house on her museum salary. She couldn't even stay here to take care of Leo without quitting her job and then they would lose her income and the hideous spiral downward would just escalate.

"So here we are," Fae said. "Wes should have taken care of willing it over to some museum but he couldn't leave Leo without a home. And now it's turned into an albatross around our necks."

"And everything would have been fine if my parents hadn't stolen all your money."

Damn, Issy had forgotten about Steph's feelings in her own consternation. "We don't know that they stole the money. There may be some explanation."

Steph pulled away and hugged herself. "No, they're thieves." The resignation in her voice broke Issy's heart. But keeping secrets in this family is what had brought them to this; she just wished they had been a little more understanding in the telling of the truth.

"Well, that's their karma, not yours," Fae told her matter-of-factly.

"And you're part of this family," Issy added. "You and Mandy and Griff, so no worries, okay?"

Steph looked from Fae to Issy and strangely enough didn't break down again. She'd grown up a lot in the last few days; Issy just hoped it didn't break her.

FAE PULLED THE vacuum cleaner out of the back pantry. Steph and Issy rummaged around to find dustcloths, paper towels, and Windex.

"Parlor first?" Issy said.

They divided up jobs, with Fae dusting, Steph cleaning the windows, and Issy vacuuming. Issy could imagine what the ladies from the Theater Fund must have thought during their visit.

They had stopped to take a water break when they heard Jillian come in the front door. She took one look into the parlor, saw they were working, and headed for the stairs.

Issy went after her. "Oh, good. Just change into your work clothes and come help."

Jillian stilled at the first step, turned around in slow motion—posed as if Issy's aerosol can was a camera. Scarlett O'Hara in a peach silk pantsuit. Issy wouldn't have been surprised if her next words came out in a southern accent.

Jillian laughed a deep throaty disbelieving sound. "I would be so out of my element. I'll just stay out of your way."

"If you stay, you work. Like the rest of us. You have a family obligation." Who was she kidding? Her mother didn't care about any of her family, including Issy. "Or you don't have to stay."

"And where would I go? You won't loan me your apartment, even though you're not using it. One would think you'd be happy to have someone to keep an eye on the place while you're gone."

"I wouldn't, it isn't up to your standards, and you can't afford it."

"You'd charge your own mother rent?"

"Yep. Double."

For a second Jillian stood perfectly still. So still and expressionless that Issy had an almost irresistible urge to call "line" and just managed to stifle herself when Jillian's chin lifted. "Not funny, Isabelle. What on earth made you so bitter?"

You did. "I'm not bitter."

Jillian raised one eyebrow.

It pushed Issy right over the brink. "I'm not bitter, I'm pissed. I haven't asked you for anything in twenty-four years.

And when I finally do give in to ask for a loan—a loan—so that your mother and my grandmother can stay in her own home after my sister—that's your other daughter—robbed her blind. What do I get? You. Broke. What if I hadn't called? Who would you have sponged off then?"

"That is such a middle-class attitude. If I were you I'd be too ashamed to call myself Isabelle York."

"Well, it's a good thing I don't. I'm Isabelle Whitaker. Have always been. Because I'm not a York, am I, Mother?"

Jillian gasped, and for an eternity, they teetered on the brink; maybe finally her mother would tell her the truth, the real truth. But it passed.

The tiniest shift in the color of Jillian's eyes. And Issy's blood ran cold. *The color of lying,* Issy thought. The tabloid headlines rose in her mind. "Who's the Real Father of Jillian York's Surprise Child?"

Issy shuddered and the image fragmented and fell like so much glass. "So. Until your public calls again, make yourself useful." Issy tossed her a dustcloth.

Jillian caught it without taking her eyes off Issy. It was pure trained-actor reflex. And very effective.

And it cut Issy to the quick.

Jillian tilted her head, cuing Issy that she expected her to make the next move.

But Issy had nothing to add to this dialogue but hurt and humiliation, and she'd be damned if she'd let her own weakness sabotage the future of this family. She wouldn't let Jillian break her down.

She'd gotten better at dealing with Jillian over the years. It didn't make her a better person. She hated the way she had to treat her mother, but it was the only way to keep herself from feeling like the piece of toilet paper stuck to the bottom of Jillian's designer shoe. The only way to deal with the pain of knowing that your mother would never love you.

"This is not a spa. We're not your paid attendants, we're your family. Like it or not."

The chin lifted higher, the beginning of a huff. "That my own child . . ." Jillian finished the lift with a full-body 180-degree turn. *With the flash of her magic dishrag the evil queen swept up the stairs.*

Issy turned to find Steph and Fae standing just inside the doorway, watching.

Neither of them said a word, just followed Issy back into the parlor, where Fae plugged in the vacuum and handed it to Issy.

"I don't trust you to handle the breakables right now." Her smile broke the tension and they all exhaled.

"She acts just like a movie star," Steph said. "But"—she lowered her voice—"she's my grandma."

"Never mind," Fae said. "It's the moon on the wax. Everyone is full and getting fuller."

"And when the shit hits . . ." Issy said.

Steph snickered.

Fae gave them each a patient look. "I've sage in my pocket, and when we finish cleaning, I'm going to burn it in every corner of this house."

Issy took the vacuum cleaner. She was afraid it would take more than Fae's sage to cure what ailed this house and this family.

As she pushed the vac around furniture and moved tables to reach hiding dust bunnies, Issy tried to forget about Jillian or to care whether she had taken her words to heart and would reappear like a modern-day Cinderella, dustcloth in hand and dressed for the part. More than likely she was enjoying a post-luncheon gin and tonic in her room.

Maybe she was packing. Or pouring out her woes to Leo.

The problem of what to do with Leo and Fae and the houseful of memories suddenly seemed overbearing.

She was crazy to think she could actually salvage any of it, much less all of it. Even if she gave up her job and moved back to Connecticut, found work locally doing whatever. She couldn't support all three of them. She probably couldn't even pay the taxes on the house each year.

And if Vivienne didn't return, there were the three kids to consider. They'd have to go to Dan's family, if they'd take them. And if not . . . Maybe George was right and Grammy and Fae should go into assisted living. She didn't believe Fae when she said she'd run away. She wouldn't leave Leo alone in a strange place away from her home and Wes and Max's graves.

Fae couldn't do that. And neither could Issy. Damn Vivienne and Dan for their greed.

She thrust the vac under the tapestry chaise and it died. She pushed at the on-off switch several times. Damn, this meant a trip to the store for a new one, the last expense she needed right now.

The plug appeared in front of her face.

"What?" she asked, turning to face her aunt, who was holding the cord.

"Do you know how much negative energy you're spreading into the world?"

Issy bit down on her reply.

"Respect your surroundings; this carpet, these floors have held famous people, sensitive people, loving people. You played on this carpet, I played on it with you. You rode your tricycle—"

Issy snatched the cord from Fae's hand. Smiled through her teeth. "All right. I grabbed this cord from you lovingly, and now I'm going to plug it back in lovingly and finish the damn floor."

Issy marched over to the wall, hesitated as she bent over, and gently pushed the plug into the wall. And with it she let her anxieties, and indecision, and anger ease out of her. And when she stood she felt better and more determined to make things work.

"How come you're always right?" she asked Fae.

Fae just smiled. "There is no right," she said, holding an antique Turkish cigarette lighter in one hand and her dustcloth in the other. "Or left."

Issy laughed.

Fae gave the lighter a good scrub.

From the parlor they moved to the music room. At least that room was a little less stuffed with furniture and artifacts. The baby grand piano probably hadn't been played in years. Issy didn't even open the keyboard; it was amazing that the sea air hadn't eaten art and instruments alike.

There was a distinct pathway across the carpet, whether mowed down by the passage of feet and time or just cleared of dust by recent traffic. Issy followed it to the back of the room, where an alcove overlooked the terrace and the sound. The game table there would be a perfect place to roll out the specs for her and Paolo's new project.

Which reminded her. "I think I'll go clean out one of the bedrooms for Paolo on the outside chance I can convince him to stay a few days." She unplugged the vac and retracted the cord.

"I think we're almost done here," Fae said. "Steph, go help Issy. I'll finish up down here."

"She wants to cleanse the rooms without us," Issy explained.

"By burning sage?"

"Yep. But I'm sure she wants to cleanse us first." Issy pulled Steph to stand beside her, then took the stance of a prim school-girl while Fae dug a thick brush of white sage from her overall pocket. Lit it with one of the many antique lighters around the room. And ran it over the space surrounding each of them, chanting something under her breath. Then she handed it to Issy, who did the same for Fae except Fae did the chanting.

Then Issy and Steph went upstairs to prepare a room for Paolo.

She gave him a room at the end of the southern corridor. It had a wonderful view of the sound, and he wouldn't be disturbed by children running up and down the neighboring hallway.

When they went downstairs again, it was nearly four thirty and the rooms smelled like a huge pot-fest from the "good old days." Fae, Leo, and Jillian were seated in the parlor around the tea tray. Jillian was the only one who had started on the cocktails.

"Car coming," Fae said, and a few moments later a gray sports car drove up to the front of the house.

"How did you do that?" Steph asked.

"Do what?"

"It's Paolo," Issy told them, and ran outside to welcome him.

She'd hoped to have a couple of minutes to warn him of what to expect, but she should have known better. They all fol-lowed her out and stood on the porch like they were welcoming a returning prodigal.

He climbed out of the little car and stretched to his full height. Pushed his dark hair back from his face and smiled at Issy. He was dressed in black jeans and a gray stretch tee, and Issy could practically hear her family sigh in appreciation behind her.

"Cara," he said, coming around the front of the car, his arms outstretched. He gave her a double air kiss but lingered on the second one. "Welcoming committee or lynch mob?"

She laughed. "Oh, I'm so glad to see you."

He stepped away and reached into the car, brought out a fat metal tube. "Wait until you see."

Issy took it, dying to peek inside. "Did you bring luggage? I hope you can stay for a week."

"Be careful for what you wish for. Things are afoot. But yes, I brought luggage." He reached back into the car and brought out a metal suitcase. "Actually, I didn't unpack from D.C. I may need to do laundry."

She took his arm. "Did I say how glad I am to see you?"

No one moved aside as they walked up the front steps, but Leo stepped forward, both hands held out. "You must be . . . Paolo . . . Welcome."

Paolo smoothly dropped the suitcase, took her hands, and kissed her on both cheeks.

Leo smiled, years shedding from her, and in that instant Issy wondered if loneliness was pushing her mind into the past.

He barely had time to snatch up his suitcase before Leo took his arm and led him into the house. "I'll do the introductions once we have you settled with a nice drink. Too many names to remember after such a long drive."

Fae rolled her eyes and followed them in. Steph was staring

at Paolo as if he'd ridden in on a white horse instead of a ten-year-old Alfa Romeo that belonged to his father.

"My, my," Jillian said beneath her breath as Issy passed her. "I take it back, Oops. You have been busy at the museum."

"He's my colleague."

Jillian lifted her trademark eyebrow. "In that case . . ."

"Don't even think it."

Jillian flicked her hair and breezed inside.

Issy poked Steph. "Wake up."

"Wow," Steph said dreamily, and went inside.

Only Issy and Fae remained on the porch. "Maybe I should have met him off-site," Issy said.

"The face of a Botticelli angel," Fae said. "We'd better go in and save him from his admirers."

When they reached the parlor, Paolo was ensconced in Wes's wingback chair, Jillian was handing him a drink, and Stephanie was standing nearby still looking a little star-struck.

"See," Fae said. *The Adoration of the Whitakers.*"

Steph saw them and walked straight over. "Is he real?"

Issy frowned. "You mean, for real? Like is he really like that or putting on a show?"

"No, I mean is he human or fey?"

Issy looked at her aunt with a little consternation. How on earth had she taken a fairly sophisticated twelve-year-old and made her believe in the Otherworld in a few short days?

"I believe he's human," Fae said, and looked to Issy for confirmation.

"Of course he's human. Don't be ridiculous." Issy carried the metal tube over to the couch and sat down. Glanced at Paolo, who was totally absorbed in some story Leo was telling him.

It was nearly twenty minutes before Paolo said that he was on company time and he really should get to work.

The ladies protested, all except Issy, who was beside herself wanting to get a look at the plans he'd brought.

She jumped up. "I've set us up in the music room," she said, and practically dragged him out of the room.

STEPHANIE SLIPPED OUT of the parlor. Grammy seemed perfectly normal. She'd told Paolo all sorts of things about the artwork and the artists. She knew who Paolo was and talked about his work with Issy.

That made her feel a little better—a little, not much. She was still worried about what was going to happen to Grammy—and to herself. She'd been busy since her mother had dropped them off. Lots of fascinating things had happened and made her not think so much about whether her mom and dad were going to come back. They wouldn't leave Amanda, Griffin, and her, would they? Jillian left Issy and Steph's mom, but that wasn't the kind of thing you inherited, was it?

She went outside. She'd meant to come out earlier to see if she could find traces of whatever had been moving through the trees the night before. In the daylight it didn't seem that faeries could be possible, and she'd almost convinced herself it had been late fireflies, then Paolo showed up looking just like a dark-haired Legolas from the movie.

And suddenly the possibilities made a lot more sense. Issy said he was human, but maybe Issy didn't know. Did the Elf King know Paolo was here? Would they know each other? Were they enemies or friends? Should she try to warn him?

Or should she tell Aunt Fae.

But Fae wasn't in the parlor anymore. She wasn't in the

kitchen and she wasn't in her room. She might have gone home without Steph seeing her. She was good at that.

Steph went outside and walked to the knoll where great grandfather Wes was buried. She looked across to the other side of the cove. Saw the roof of Aunt Fae's cottage poking out of the trees, followed the line of beach rosebushes that stretched along the shore. A head appeared momentarily behind the bushes and she knew someone was in the meadow, but it wasn't Aunt Fae.

She scrambled down the grassy slope of the knoll until she was on the beach. And suddenly felt seriously alone. To her right, the sound looked like a painting, still and blue. Almost the same color as the sky. To her left were inlets, bushes, and tiny hidden beaches. Across from her at the back curve of the cove, a pile of boulders formed the platform where Grammy dove in and met Great-Grandfather Wes.

Everyone knew the story, even the part about swimming nude and making love. That was a little icky, thinking about parents and grandparents doing stuff, but the Elf King—did the Elf King have a wife? Was it Aunt Fae?

Steph started over the beach and her sandals immediately filled with sand. She kicked them off and grabbed the straps in one hand. The sun was behind her and she knew she should be helping with dinner, but she needed to see who was in the meadow.

She splashed through the water until she took a step and dropped down to her waist. Great. Grammy dove. Of course it was deep here.

She threw her sandals as hard as she could and managed to get them to a lower rock, then she plunged in clothes and all and swam to the rocks.

She heaved herself onto the lowest boulder—her wet overalls weighed a ton—grabbed her sandals, and climbed up the boulders as fast as her slippery feet would allow.

At the top she stopped to look around. Across the way, she could still see the trees and beach roses, but no cottage. There would be a path from the rocks. She bet she could follow it to the meadow. She quickly put on her sandals and stepped into the trees.

Today it looked familiar. She should have taken the path to Aunt Fae's, but she'd been in such a hurry to see that she hadn't been thinking about getting wet. Now her sandals were squeaking and bits of bark and dirt were sticking to her ankles and clothes.

It was cool, almost chilly, beneath the trees, but up ahead she could see sunlight. The meadow. She slowed, stepped off the path, and edged toward the light.

And there it was, completely hidden, green with little tiny flowers sticking their faces up like fairy creatures. *Stop it!* Not those kind of fairies. Those only existed in children's stories and Disney movies. She was after the real deal.

She crept closer. Scooted down to the edge of the grass and there he was, the Elf King. He was dressed in flowing clothes, not the kind her grandmother Jillian wore. Hers made her look kind of exotic and kind of trashy; the Elf King looked strong and amazing. His long silver hair glistened in the sun and rode the wind as he turned. Not young and not old, but like one of those creatures who could live hundreds of years and barely age at all. That was her Elf King.

He was moving in slow motion. Almost like dancing, but it wasn't. Probably some kind of elfin karate. His arms came up and then opened wide and his hands made a series of shapes.

He lifted his knee and put his foot down softly, then he lifted it and kicked, still in slow motion, then stepped again. And Steph bet even if she had been sitting right there, she wouldn't have heard him move.

The Elf King was preparing for battle. That must be it. Or why do all that karate stuff.

He stopped, turned his head in her direction. She didn't move, didn't breathe. She was afraid to creep away, afraid to stay. She was paralyzed, not with fear, but . . . He must have her under a spell.

He stepped toward her. "Hello there."

That did it; she broke and ran.

Chapter 17

I ssy led Paolo through the second parlor, past the door to what had become Leo's television room.

The music room looked one hundred times better than it had a few hours ago. A little vacuuming, furniture polish, and tender care had done wonders. The sunshine lit the back windows, and only a few streaks where Stephanie had issues with the Windex remained.

"Incredible," Paolo said, looking around. "Very eclectic artwork."

"And so much of it," Issy said, putting on her best gallery-visitor imitation.

Paolo laughed. "Are they all originals?"

"As far as I know."

"Even this?" He picked up a misshapen papier-mâché object that was supposed to be an apple.

She took it from him, the dried faded tempera paint left residue on her fingers. "Even this," she said, turning the apple in her hand. "I made this for Wes in art class in second—or was it third grade? Vivienne said it was stupid to give to Grandpa because apples were for teachers. But now that I think about it, it was totally appropriate. Living at the Muses was the best education I could have hoped for."

She put the apple down. "So show me these specs."

Paolo spread the sheets out on the table and anchored the corners with whatever was handy. A geode. A Chinese paper knife. A palm-sized book of poetry. The apple.

"So this is what they have. Four rooms of Toulouse-Lautrec."

"Okay. That seems straightforward enough."

"Not excited yet?"

"Sure, it's a great collection."

"But it will be really great when they get this . . ." He pulled a smaller sheet from the bottom. A brochure from the Costume Institute at the Met.

Issy smiled as she caught on. "They want us to present the paintings in 3-D using authentic period costume."

"How much fun is that?"

"How many rooms do we get?"

"Depends on how many full glass cases we can commandeer."

"Every spare one we have and can borrow or steal," Issy said, already imagining the configurations of the room. "Or even better . . ."

"Here we go," Paolo said, and settled back to listen.

"First, no exhibits alternating paintings and costume cases around the perimeter of the room. No 'A Stroll Through Montmartre' with an info plaque and a glass case with random clothing pieces. A: women's stockings circa . . . B: children's shoes . . . C: parasol." Issy walked away, came back. "We'll have to use mannequins. Possibly people in period costumes visiting a museum. Or . . . no, we'll have mannequins depicting the people in the paintings."

Paolo threw his head back and laughed. His laugh always made her feel . . . happy. "I told Dell you didn't need to be on-site to nail this one."

Issy rested her hip on the desk. "But I will have to get back."

Paolo immediately became serious. "Is there a problem with that?"

Issy shrugged. "There's no money. I can't support the family for more than a month or so. I can't stay, and yet how can I leave them?"

He shrugged. Shoved his hands in his pockets. "You are sitting on a gold mine, so to speak."

"I know, but Fae says Leo would never sell anything. They're so much a part of her existence. She seems to be living just to keep the Muses alive. Both her children want to sell it and move her and Fae into a home. It's a huge mess. And for once, I don't know what to do."

There; she'd said it. Give her an exhibit and she could make it work. No matter what kind of shape it was in. But an exhibit wasn't a family. And her family needed more than she knew how to give.

"You'll think of something. You always do. Now, come on. I think it must be happy hour. And I just happen to have brought two bottles of excellent Pinot Noir which never made it out of the car."

They rolled up the specs for the new installation and returned them to the tube. "I'll show you to your room, and then I'll tell Leo that we're going out to dinner. I don't think she'll mind, she seemed tired and I'm sure she would enjoy a quiet evening at home with the television. Unless you'd rather eat with this crew."

"I think you could use a night off. By all means."

"It won't be haute cuisine."

"Not a problem."

They were coming back downstairs from dropping off Paolo's suitcase when the front door opened and Mandy and Griff burst into the foyer followed by Chloe carrying backpacks and crafts and pictures drawn at the day camp.

"Hooligans!" Chloe said, laughing. She looked up and her smile transformed.

Paolo had stopped, one foot arrested in the air on its way to the next stair tread. "Ah, *bellissima madre.* Please tell me she's divorced."

Issy laughed and they continued down the stairs to where Chloe stood, smiling and soft and welcoming.

Paolo hurried forward. "Let me take those for you." He swiftly relieved her of backpacks and artwork and handed them off to Mandy and Griff, who were staring at him.

"You must be Paolo." Chloe stretched out her hand. Paolo took it, turned it over, and kissed the back.

This was accompanied by giggles from Mandy and Griff.

"Go put your stuff away, you two."

"Where's Grammy?"

"I think I heard her in the television room," Issy said.

Mandy and Griff ran down the hall.

"I want to show her."

"No, me first."

"No, I want to."

Chloe and Paolo didn't seem to notice.

"We're in trouble now," Issy said. "But we have a plan . . . for dinner at least."

"I got a pan of lasagna out of the freezer," Chloe said, pulling her hand from Paolo's. "There's enough greens for salad, but we'll need to make a serious grocery run soon."

"Already done. Ogden's will be delivering any minute now. But tonight we're going out, me, you, and Paolo—and Ben if he's free."

"What about the family?"

"They haven't starved yet, and I really think Paolo has done his duty for today. Not to mention I'm afraid Jillian is going to start hitting on him soon."

"Perish the thought. I'll call Ben."

"Great. Let me just tell Grammy and we're good to go."

Issy found Leo and Mandy and Griff watching television. Griff was wedged in the easy chair with Leo, his head resting in the crook of her arm. As Issy watched, Grammy gave him a little squeeze; he nestled closer and Issy could almost physically feel the comfort.

Climbing into that same chair with Grammy, on those days when the world was just too much, when she didn't understand, when she just needed someplace soft to nest. For a second she felt envious of Griff.

Mandy stood leaning over the padded chair arm holding up her picture and pointing to each person on the paper and telling their name and what they were like and whether she liked them or not. And Leo listened like it was the most interesting thing in her world.

Issy stepped just inside the door. "Grammy, do you mind if I take Paolo into town tonight for dinner? Chloe made lasagna that I'll put in the oven and I'll set the table and—"

Leo waved her away. "Of course, dear. You don't have to wait on us. We do know how to take care of ourselves, don't we, Griff?"

Griff just squeezed her tighter.

"I think we could all use a quiet evening at home. Maybe these two and I will even eat in front of the television. What do you say to that?"

"On the little tables with flowers on them? Yes. Yes," Mandy said, and jumped up and down several times.

"Sounds like fun," Issy said, wondering at the pleasure an old TV table brought to a child whose mother only cared about "the best."

Issy joined Paolo and Chloe in the kitchen. Paolo had tied an apron around his waist and was slathering garlic butter across thick slices of Italian bread. Chloe slid the lasagna pan into the oven. "Ben said to give him a half hour and let him know where."

Paolo finished the last slice with a flourish, wrapped the whole loaf in tinfoil, and put it on top of the stove. "I'll just go get the wine." He went out the side door like he knew the place, and Issy turned to Chloe.

"Well?"

"Well, what?" Chloe said, and started pouring out a bag of salad greens.

"I felt the earth move and I was standing several feet away."

"I don't know what you're talking about." Chloe dumped the bag in the trash and leaned over the table. "Okay, I do know what you're talking about. Wow. I had no idea. You said he was like El Greco. He painted the skinny guy with the scraggly beard, right?"

"I just meant he's tall and thin."

"How long is he staying?"

"We didn't discuss it. I'll see what I can do."

"I meant for you. Are you and he . . . ?"

Issy shook her head. "Friends and colleagues."

"Really?" She looked pensive. "Well, that's good, I guess."

"You guess? I saw that look."

"No, I just mean, there's still hope for Ben."

"I think you can get that out of your mind."

"But you like him."

"I do. I hope he likes me, but he's your brother."

"So brothers get to have lives, too."

"I like him; I do. But it would be weird. I've known him since I've known you. He's seen some of our less than savory moments."

"You're talking about a man who spends his day knee-deep in stinky marsh muck."

"True."

There was a commotion in the mud room and both of them went out to see if Paolo needed help. He pushed the door open, ushering a wet and dripping Stephanie ahead of him.

"I think we've had a wardrobe malfunction," Paolo said, and put two bottles of wine on the counter.

Issy came out. "Steph, what's wrong? Are you hurt?"

"No, nothing's wrong," she gasped. She looked from one to the other then at the floor. "I got wet."

"I'll say you did." Chloe tossed her a dish towel. "Dry those feet before you track mud across the floor. I spend enough time doing that with Ben."

Steph took the towel. Sat down and took off her sandals, which Chloe took out to the mudroom, carrying them at the ends of two fingers.

Steph shivered. "Where is Aunt Fae?"

"I'm right here," Fae said from the doorway to the house-keeper's quarters. "I suppose you'll be needing some dry clothes from my paltry selections."

Steph nodded.

"Then come along. Tomorrow I'll make an emergency stop at the cottage for supplies. This could be a long summer. Of course we haven't even started on the attic. No telling what gems we'll find up there."

Fae led Steph away.

"Did she say where she got wet?" Issy asked.

Paolo shook his head and took the corkscrew Chloe handed him.

"She was coming to the kitchen when I went out. I nearly ran into her. I excused myself, held the door open, but she shook her head then followed me to the car.

"I must say, Issy. You do have a colorful family. She asked me where I came from. When I said Manhattan, she said, 'No, really come from,' and I said a was born in Milan but came to New York when I was ten. She gave me such a look. Then she asked me if I was staying long. And I said at least until tomorrow.

"Then she nodded and clammed up. I got out the wine, she followed me inside and didn't say a word until you asked her if she was okay. Was she someplace that would get her in trouble?"

"No. Along the beach, sometimes the waves get rough in a storm, but not much undertow. There's a place near the boulders over in the cove that's pretty deep. The scene of Leo's 'infamous dive to love.' But I don't know why she'd be over there."

Issy shrugged. The cork was pulled out, glasses were poured, and the topic changed to where they were going to eat.

FAE RUMMAGED IN the closet for something for Stephanie to wear. Something not too old lady. Something flattering. Huh. She hadn't thought about flattering—*not true, Fae, you're a big liar, you think about the way you look every day*. She decided on a pair of gauze harem pants that would work if she tied them up and then folded the waist over.

"Are you going to get out of those wet clothes?"

Steph nodded, blushed.

And Fae understood. She didn't want to undress in front of her. "Just us chickens here," she said.

"What?"

"Nothing. Why don't you put on these and this shirt and call me to help you with keeping them up."

"Okay."

Fae put the things on the bed and went to stand outside the door. While she was standing there she tried to remember if there had been an age when she'd been embarrassed to get naked in front of other people. She chuckled to herself. If ever there was a time to dress and undress in the dark, it was now, when her skin was sagging and wrinkled, and her breasts and butt were headed south.

Too bad the classic painters didn't portray old people as they did young models. Beautiful naked old people, not just the hags of fairy tales and morality plays.

"You done in there?"

"Yes," came the muffled reply.

Fae went back inside. Steph stood in the middle of the little room holding up the pants with both hands. If she stayed at the

Muses much longer, Fae would have to search for the old sewing machine and do some serious alterations.

She wrapped a canvas belt around the girl's waist and folded the excess fabric over the top. "Where were you that you got so wet?"

"I fell in the water. I didn't know there was a big drop-off there."

"You were by the boulders?"

Steph nodded.

"Why did you go over there?" Fae didn't need to ask. She knew the answer. She could feel it as sure as she could feel the breeze through the half-open window.

"I saw him."

Fae picked up the soggy overalls and T-shirt. Flapped them out and hung them temporarily on the windowsill. Waited for Steph to say more.

Steph followed her to the window and whispered, "The Elf King. He was practicing his war moves in the meadow. Is he going to fight Paolo?"

This had gotten totally out of control. Fae needed to nip this right now. And yet she couldn't tell the truth. She sat down on the bed. Patted the place next to her.

Stephanie sat.

"You know how I said some people don't see things that other people do?"

Steph nodded.

"Well . . ." Fae hesitated, choosing her words carefully. Things were beginning to unravel. She'd known they would eventually and she was shocked that she was so unprepared.

"Aunt Fae?"

"Just because they don't see them doesn't mean they aren't there."

"Like the Elf King and the faeries I saw."

"You saw faeries?"

"Last night, I couldn't sleep. It was only one faerie but I saw his light in the woods."

"Oh Lord," Fae mumbled.

"What? Wasn't I supposed to see them? I didn't mean to. I was just looking out the window."

"No, child. There's nothing wrong with seeing faeries, but . . . but just don't follow them."

"Why not?"

Yes, Fae. Why not? "Let me explain. Some people . . . well, you know how the earth is a planet in the solar system?"

Steph nodded, but she was frowning.

"And the solar system is in a galaxy at the very edge of a vast cloud of galaxies? There are people who say that even something that large is small enough in the scheme of things to sit on a pinhead."

"That's weird. It couldn't do that."

"We don't know that, do we? But that's not really the point," she said, and hurried on. "Most people won't believe something they can't see or prove. Some people can see more than others."

"Like us?"

"Like us. We get into trouble trying to convince other people of what we see and believe, and they will never be convinced because they can never see what we do."

"So that's why you said not to tell Mom, not because of the sex stuff."

"Well, yes—but also because of the sex stuff. When you try

to trap that world, try to confuse the boundaries of the different worlds, then it disappears. You destroy it. It's sort of like Grammy living in the past so much. She's happy there. It doesn't do any harm until people mess with it. Then all hell will break lose."

"It isn't fair. She should be able to do what she wants."

"Exactly, if it doesn't hurt her or anyone else. And it doesn't. But some people can't see that, and because they can't, they want to force her into the world they understand."

"I get it. I think. Do you want the book back? I've almost finished it."

"No, no. Just keep it safe. It's old like everything else we have, but it's special. And so are you."

Steph nodded.

"Now let's go help with the dinner so Issy can go and have some fun with her friends."

Steph stood up and started for the door. Fae held it closed. "And don't worry about Paolo. Something tells me he's going to be just fine."

Chapter 18

They took Chloe's car to the restaurant since she had to get up for work the next morning and Ben was meeting them there, and could drive them home later.

"He said he'd meet us at Wharfside," Chloe said. "It's a little trendy, but not snooty yet, the food is good, and they don't rush you through dinner. Though I expect we'll end up at the Den afterward. It's only a couple of blocks—and worlds—away." She glanced in the backseat at Paolo. "It's the local hangout for about a hundred years now. No trip would be complete without a stop there."

"I'm intrigued," Paolo said.

"Ben may be a little late. He's coming straight from work; he tends to get involved and forget the time."

Paolo laughed. "Sounds like Issy and me. It's good to have work that you love."

Chloe sighed. "Yes."

"What do you do, Chloe?"

"I'm an administrator in the local elementary school."

"Sounds . . ."

"Boring," she said. "It is. I went to culinary school for a year, but it was just too expensive and I didn't really enjoy the environment."

"Besides," Issy said, "she already cooks better than most chefs I know. She's kept us fed since I got here. For which I owe her forever." She reached over and tweaked one of Chloe's stray curls. "Among about a million other things."

Chloe batted her hand away. "I like to cook."

"I love cooking," Paolo said. "Especially when someone else is doing the cooking and I'm doing the eating."

They laughed at that and in a few minutes they were pulling into the parking lot of Wharfside.

"I called ahead to make a reservation. Strangely enough, Ben doesn't like to eat outside. I mean he's always eating out-side, so when he goes to a restaurant, he's into the creature comforts, as he calls them. But there's a nice indoor porch with a really good view."

"Well, I agree with Ben," Paolo said once they were seated. "I enjoy the occasional picnic with champagne, but give me a waiter and a wine list any day."

Chloe laughed. She was obviously smitten. Paolo had that effect on most women; men, too. As far as Issy knew, he didn't have a girlfriend; he'd mentioned dates occasionally, but never anyone consistently. He said he would know when he met her, and he hadn't met her yet.

But Chloe was her friend and not to be trifled with. Issy laughed out loud at what she was thinking.

"What?" Chloe and Paolo said together.

"Nothing. I was just thinking."

"Well, no more thinking tonight," Paolo said. "Now, shall we wait for Ben or shall we order a bottle of something now?"

They ordered a bottle and it arrived at the same time as Ben.

"Sorry I'm late."

Issy stared. Ben Collins, he of the stinky clothes and uncontrollable cowlick, was wearing dress pants and a button shirt, though it was open at the collar and the sleeves were rolled up to his elbows. The cowlick was firmly gelled in place.

"You must be Paolo," he said as Paolo stood and reached across the table to shake his hand. He sat down, then frowned at Issy. "What?"

"I don't know. I expected muddy boots and a fish smell. But this . . ."

"I'd rather be in muddy boots, but I had to give a report at the lab today. I can go back and look for some old clothes if that would make you feel more comfortable."

"No. Sorry." She turned to Paolo. "When we were growing up, he was already mucking about saving the salt marshes. Which is a good thing, but he always had jars of disgusting stuff in his bedroom, in the mud room—"

"In the fridge," added Chloe.

"In the fridge," Issy said.

"I made a sign that said 'Do Not Touch.'" Ben held out his glass for Paolo to pour.

"But it was in the fridge," Chloe explained. "We thought it was iced tea."

Paolo made a face. "You didn't."

"Issy did."

"You didn't," said Paolo.

"I did," Issy said with a shudder. "It was disgusting. Really disgusting."

"Served you right," Ben said with a smile. "It was part of my plankton experiment for biology class. She wrecked my control group, but no one ever touched my specimens again."

Issy laughed. "Come on, we had some good times."

"Great times," Chloe added.

"We did." Ben's look went from Chloe to Issy and rested there. "Some of the best times. Weird." He shook his head. "These two drove me crazy."

Paolo laughed. "I know what you mean. She drives me crazy, too."

A moment passed while they both looked at Issy. Then Paolo said, "And now you're a marine biologist?"

And the conversation was back on track.

"Yes—"

"And working on his Ph.D. in marine ecology," Chloe added.

"Working is right, sold my soul to the university lab to pay for it. But I'm almost done."

"And what will you do when you're a doctor?"

"Muck about in the salt marshes, but the fish will respect me more."

"I had no idea," Issy said.

Ben gave her a look that lasted so long that she had to fight not to squirm beneath it. "I know, I didn't ask. I think it's great, Ben."

"Thank you."

He took a sip of wine and opened his menu.

"But you still have your cowlick."

His free hand went to his head, as she knew it would.

She flashed teeth at him. "Not tonight. You look very distinguished. So how's the flounder here?"

The flounder was delicious, grilled with lemon, and served with a vegetable salsa and fingerling potatoes. Everyone enjoyed their meal and they ordered a second bottle of wine.

Ben asked Paolo about the D.C. installation. Paolo gave him the bare essentials, but Issy thought he seemed subdued, which was weird because he always waxed eloquently over art. But it passed and soon he was expressing admiration for the Muses. "It's like an architectural compendium of great art."

"One that needs to be organized and weeded out," Issy agreed. "I started a little bit yesterday but it's going to be a long haul."

"I can help if you like," Paolo said.

Issy looked up. Interesting; was he planning to stay for a while? It would be great but was this about meeting Chloe? Already? It seemed unlike Paolo.

"How long are you planning to stay?" Chloe asked.

"It sort of depends."

Issy narrowed her eyes at him. "You're welcome, of course. Did Dell put you on vacation because I took time off?"

"Not exactly."

Her stomach started to churn. "Then what?"

"I quit."

Silence.

"Why? What happened? What about the new installation?"

Paolo studied his wineglass. "Shit happened after you left. Well, actually we didn't tell you about it."

"What?"

"One of the paintings didn't make it to D.C. For a few panicked minutes we were afraid it had been stolen."

"But it wasn't," Issy said.

"No, but Dell had to make a special trip down with the crate. He was pissed."

"What? He didn't call me."

"No. But he did say that if you had been there it wouldn't have happened. I agreed and told him it was entirely our fault."

"But you guys were checking things off when I left. How did that happen?"

"Evidently, I said I put it on the truck, but I didn't."

Issy gave him what they called the Look. "Wait a minute, you don't do the actual loading."

"No, but we double-checked each tag as the paintings were loaded onto the truck. Deirdre called it out, I checked it, and gave her a thumbs-up, she checked it off again." He turned to Ben and Chloe. "We deal with really expensive pieces. You can't be too careful."

"She must have skipped over something but checked it off anyway?" Issy asked.

Paolo shrugged. "Let's just say *I* didn't look at my cell phone once during the procedure."

"No." Unlike Deirdre, who was notorious for sneaking peeks to see who had texted, called, or messaged her. "You explained it to Dell?"

"I tried. It doesn't matter."

"It does, too. I'll call him first thing in the morning."

He covered her hand in his. "No. I've made my decision."

He sighed. "Sorry, guys, terrible dinner conversation, but it will be over in a second." He took a breath. "She told him the only reason I had the job was because I was sleeping with you. She said I really didn't do any work, was just kept around for show. I haven't slept with Issy, if anyone wants to know." He looked at Chloe first, then at Ben.

"I'll kill her," Issy said.

"No. I can't work with her, especially with you gone."

"But I'm only on vacation." Issy frowned. "Aren't I?"

"Of course, Dell's not a total fool. But I'm sure she's already hustled herself up the ladder to my position. And you'll be stuck with her."

"That's why she's in D.C. for the opening instead of you."

Paolo nodded.

"She'll be going after me next."

"She probably has already started. I was going to tell you, but when I saw what a mess things are here . . . *Cara*, don't worry about me."

"I can't believe it."

"So if you need someone to help catalog, I'm your man. Now, let's not let it spoil a lovely evening. Who needs more wine?"

They all left the restaurant feeling happy, even Issy, who, though she knew she had huge issues to deal with, and even more now that Paolo had quit his job at the Cluny, was suddenly determined to enjoy her friends.

It had been a long time since she hadn't been working like a maniac. Finishing one installation, already started on another, and looking out for the next. That didn't leave too much time for fun. It didn't leave too much time for reflection, either.

Is that why she worked so hard? She loved the work she did. But couldn't she love it just as much if she wasn't always under a self-imposed deadline, one that kept her on edge, kept her moving, kept her from wondering.

And now she was plunked right in the middle of the things she'd been avoiding.

There were questions that had been festering inside her for years. All the players were in place who could answer those questions if she could pry the answers out of them. She'd already learned some things. She could learn the rest if she really wanted to. All she had to do was go back to the Muses and demand the answers. Simple. "Who's for Fisherman's Den?"

They all walked down the sidewalk to the Den. Paolo and Chloe had paired off ahead of them and Ben and Issy walked comfortably beside each other.

"Just so you know. I always thought your cowlick was kind of cute," she said.

"I think you may have had enough alcohol for the night."

"I only had two glasses—oh, and one at the house."

"More than you're used to?"

"Yes. But I think I deserve it."

"Worth the hangover tomorrow?"

She nodded.

"You'll see your way through."

"With the hangover?"

"With the situation."

That was sobering. "I've only got another week. If I even want to go back to work."

"You wouldn't not go back to work because of what happened to Paolo?"

"I wouldn't go back because of my family. And that's a huge mess that I don't know how to fix."

He put his arm around her shoulders. "You'll figure it out. It might not be fun. And it may take more than a week. But you'll see your way through. And you have Chloe and me; we've got your back."

Ben nixed the Den and Issy knew it was because she was tired. She appreciated the gesture, but she didn't want the night to end.

They said good night to Chloe, and Ben drove them home.

It was nearly one when Issy and Paolo tiptoed into the old mansion. "Shh," Paolo said. They stopped in the kitchen, where he made Issy take two aspirin with a full glass of water. Then he poured out a teaspoon of olive oil. "A sure cure for hangovers from my granny," he claimed. Then they tiptoed upstairs and fell into their beds. Alone.

FAE SLIPPED OUT the doors of the conservatory and felt her way along the side of the house, until she was sure that Steph couldn't see her out of her bedroom window. She could feel someone watching her, but she'd waited for Steph to go upstairs, and made sure she didn't come out again. Even now she checked the darkened window.

She was feeling the anxiety in the house—the anticipation of time running out. She didn't like that feeling. She scanned the lawn, then made a run for the trees. She didn't turn on her flashlight. She was taking no chances tonight. The moon was waxing past the quarter and she was careful to avoid its light. In another week it would be full. There would be change.

She stepped on something sharp, a stick. Her feet found the path in the shadows, and she moved silently—or as silently as an old woman in the dark could manage—toward home.

When she could no longer see the mansion looming behind her, she turned on her flashlight, muted its light against her chest. Got her bearings and turned it off again. Darkness enclosed her and she hurried down the path to the light she knew would be waiting for her.

No looking back now. It had begun and the only way to go was forward. At least for one of them.

JILLIAN ADJUSTED HER light-blocking sleep mask. A week ago, if you'd told her she'd be lying in bed alone at the Muses, she would have laughed. But here she was with no prospects. The call to her agent had brought in zip. Only one query as to her availability. And that for a project she'd rather die than accept. There were no other prospects on the horizon. Her agent's advice was to get her butt back to L.A. and start making the rounds.

She'd happily do that. If she had a place to stay. If she could afford a place to stay or even a friend to stay with. If she had a working credit card. But she had . . . zip. Zip.

LEO PULLED THE combs from her hair and tossed them on the seat of the convertible. Her hair blew about her face like a whirlwind. She stretched out her arms; they'd just crossed into Connecticut and already she could smell the sea air.

"Oh Lord, I'm so glad we left early," she yelled over the noise of the engine. "Poor Andy, I feel sorry for him."

Wes looked over and smiled. Took her hand and pulled her closer. She put her head on his shoulder. Her hair whipped across their faces, and he laughed. "I can't see a thing."

She pulled her hair back and held it in one hand just so she wouldn't have to move away. They were going home.

Chapter 19

Issy, Paolo, Mandy, and Griff were sitting at the kitchen table when Chloe breezed in the next morning.

Issy lifted one eyebrow. Chloe looked . . . great.

Paolo nearly knocked over his chair getting up. This was not like her normally exotic, distant, passionate, funny . . . Actually it was just like him, only better.

"Croissants," Chloe said. "I didn't make them, but I did make lunch for you two day campers. Did you have breakfast?"

"Peanut butter toast," Griff said.

"Paolo made it," Mandy added. And smiled sweetly at him.

"Alas, it's the best I could do."

"Never mind," Chloe said. "Peanut butter is very healthy. Now chop, chop. I have to get to work. Ben said he'd try to get Al Dunn over to look at the elevator sometime this week."

"Great." Issy helped Mandy and Griff into their backpacks while Chloe and Paolo smiled at each other.

The children were out the door in a whirlwind. "Back around four," Chloe called as she followed them out.

"Whew," Issy said, sinking back in her chair.

Paolo was still looking out the door, smiling.

"Oh, brother."

He sat down. "I may be in trouble."

"Maybe. But don't mess with my sister from another mother."

"I never mess with women. I'm a better man than that. Plus I'm Italian."

"I thought Italian men were notorious."

"Not when they're the sons of my mother."

"Ah. You want more coffee?"

"Please."

While they were each studying their coffee, Stephanie came in.

"Feel like doing some cataloging with us this morning?" Issy asked her.

Steph reached into the cabinet and brought out a box of cereal. "Sure. I kind of made a spreadsheet that should make it easier to fit in Grammy's descriptions."

"Great." Issy pushed the milk carton toward her. "And this afternoon we'll go down to the beach and hang. Work and play. From now on, it's work then play."

Steph smiled. "What's up?"

"Well, I realized last night that you have the time you have and you'd better enjoy it."

Stephanie stopped pouring milk into her bowl and looked at Issy. "Don't worry, Aunt Issy. You and me. We won't let them take Grammy away and we won't let the Muses out of the family."

"We won't?"

Steph shook her head. "It's our family. And we're special."

"We are? We are," Issy said, remembering her talk with Steph about the book. Fae must have reinforced the idea.

"Where is Fae this morning? She's usually up."

"She's talking to Grammy. They said they'd be down in a few minutes and will help as soon as they've had breakfast."

"LET ME DO that," Fae said, and took the brush out of Leo's hand. She brushed the thinning white hair back from her face and put the brush on the dressing table. "We need to get a few things straight," she said, looking at her sister-in-law in the dressing-table mirror.

She twisted the tail of hair and pressed it against Leo's head. "You realize all hell is breaking loose around us, don't you?"

"Wes will fix it."

"From the grave?"

Leo's eyes filled with tears.

Fae let Leo's hair go and sat down beside her. "I'm sorry, dearest. So sorry."

She hugged Leo's thin shoulders and for a second she had the dreaded sensation that Leo was slowly disappearing before her eyes.

"We need you to be here, Leo. There's a young woman down there who needs a grandmother since her mother is lying in bed acting like a slug and hasn't said one kind thing to the girl since arriving. Not a touch or a hug. I could . . . well, it's not for me to do or not do."

Leo groped for her hand. Took it in hers.

"And three great-grandchildren who may be motherless. They need their Grammy. Issy will try, but there are some things only a grandmother can do and be. Can you do that?"

Leo shook her head.

"Don't you love them?"

"All of them with all my heart."

"But you love Wes more?"

Leo's mouth puckered and Fae hated herself for badgering her. Leo had been nothing but kind and understanding from the first day she'd walked into the Muses. She was good to everyone, but she loved her husband more than anything. And he left her without the tools to master the wayward Whitakers.

Now they were in a pickle. "Okay, this is what we're going to do. We're going to help Issy and Paolo catalog this artwork."

"Why are we doing that?"

"So we know what we have."

"We *know* what we have."

Fae took a cleansing breath. Time to make sure Leo really understood what was going on. "Wes left an estate to take care of the Muses. The house, the grounds, and you and me."

"He asked Dan to take care of it for him."

"Yes. And as it turns out, that was a big mistake."

"Just because Dan missed paying a few bills?"

"Not just a few bills. He's stolen it all. Every penny of the money Wes left. He's disappeared. I assume Vivienne went to look for him. I really hope she isn't party to it. She fired Mrs. Norcroft for stealing artwork, but it was her husband who was stealing it."

"That's why Issy's here. Trying to save our butts. And whatever she needs to do it, we have to help her. Agreed? Leo, do you agree?"

Her sister-in-law was staring into the mirror.

"Dammit, Leonore. Do you agree?"

Slowly Leo turned to her. Her eyes were dry; her face was

calm. "Agreed. I loved them all. I did. Max is dead. Jillian is a hard, empty woman. George an angry man. I don't know why he's so angry. Vivienne so unhappy. And dear Issy, should we send her back to New York? I loved them too much and I've failed them all."

"No, you haven't. You nurtured them to face life on their own. What their lives became was their choice. And you need to explain this to Issy. Tell her why you sent her away in the first place. I tried and she understands, but she needs to hear it from you. *And* why you didn't notify her of Wes's funeral."

"I wasn't thinking about her. I just assumed Vivienne would call her."

"Well, tell her. Somehow in her nutty Whitaker mind, she thinks you sent her away because you and Wes wanted to get back to your lives and each other, and that you didn't tell her about Wes's funeral because you wanted her to stay away."

"That's absurd. We loved her. Wes adored her."

"I know it's absurd. But she's a Whitaker. We are masters of absurd. It makes perfect sense."

Leo laughed quietly. "Bless her. She'll carry on for us. But what then?"

"Stephanie. She's a Whitaker through and through, if it doesn't get drummed out of her."

"So the Muses will continue?"

Would it? It didn't look likely. And if it didn't, what would be their family legacy? "I don't know, but we can't guilt Issy into staying or leaving. She has her own life. And she makes her own decisions. And you made that possible."

"And you and Wes. Is Paolo her young man?"

"Her friend and colleague."

"Oh, good, I like him but Ben . . . Ben would be perfect for her."

"Leo, it doesn't work that way and you and I are staying out of it."

"What? You think a couple of old broads don't remember about love."

Fae shrugged.

Leo laughed out loud. It was a welcome sound. One that Fae hadn't heard in too long. "Well, you certainly haven't forgotten. I saw you sneaking off last night."

"That was you? I knew someone was watching."

"Yes, right into the arms of your knight errant."

Fae smiled. "And why not? You don't lose your libido just because you turn seventy-five."

"I know, dear. And I understand."

They hugged briefly and Fae went back to pinning her hair. Would Leo understand when Fae told her she had to leave for good?

ISSY AND PAOLO set up the laptop in the library.

"We started in here the other day but didn't get very far. Leo had such great stories to tell about every piece. It was fascinating; it takes a really long time, but I don't want to lose that. We may have to break up the collection, but I hope not. Every object, every painting and drawing is part of the 'Life of Muses by the Sea.'"

She sighed. "But I just don't know how to keep it together."

"You could always apply for a grant."

"I know I could. But the competition is so stiff. And we would have to figure out a way to open the Muses to the public, which would cost a fortune we don't have. Millions probably.

At least have a curator who can loan out the work. But that sort of defeats the purpose of keeping it together."

"Well, let's start inventorying and find out what we have."

Issy pulled up the file that showed the room's layout. "We started on the wall. There are so many objects shoved onto every available surface, I don't know whether half of them are junk or fine art. Not my expertise.

"But I thought if Grammy—Leo—can give us an idea of what, when, where, and by whom, we could research it later. Now, a grant for that would be spectacular."

Paolo looked around. "You said Leo was telling stories about each piece. How did you record it?"

Issy stopped dead. "We didn't. It just happened organically. I asked what something was and then the stories started. Steph tried to write most of it down. I am such a fool, I should have been recording."

She looked around as if she'd find recording equipment among the artwork. Finally pulled out her cell. "Do you think we could get her to talk into the phone. I don't want her to be intimidated and clam up."

"Leo? She doesn't strike me as the type who would be intimidated by a little thing like a cell phone."

Paolo had guessed that one right, Issy thought, when Leo, Fae, and Steph came into the library and Paolo described what he wanted her to do.

The only thing Leo said was, "This little red circle?"

They spent the morning identifying objects, giving Leo ample rest time, during which Paolo fussed over her and talked art with her, and flirted with her, until her stories became inspired.

"Ah, that is a Vivian Maier photograph. Such an eye for

the stark side of Manhattan life. There were a whole group of them, the artists who 'depicted life.' They could have fun, though."

Issy hurried to give the photograph a number and position. Moved to the next item.

"That Murano glass vase was a gift from . . . Louis Pollock. He'd just finished making that movie . . . oh, you know the one, it was right before he was sent before that stupid man's Un-American Activities Committee. I was pregnant with Max."

"It was a miserable time. Everyone depressed and some of them sent off to jail. And I was so happy and in love. It didn't seem right.

"And poor Philip Loeb committing suicide. I don't want to remember that time."

Paolo sat by the side of the chair, unmoving. Steph had stopped typing and was listening, though Issy didn't know how she could know about the Red Scare. The only reason Issy did was because it was discussed in an art history course she once took at Columbia. She didn't remember any of her regular history courses covering it with more than a passing paragraph. But that was history for you. And that's why what they were doing today was important.

This was history, too.

"Well, don't remember it," Fae said. "Fortunately for us, they seemed to attack the theater and Hollywood people more than artists. Now, that tacky flamingo on the shell is a lamp; if you turn it over, there's a little tab to push. Remember that, Leo?"

"From Palm Beach; Wes and I went down to stay with the Kleinhoffs. We took the children. Wes bought this for them on the boardwalk one night. For a night-light. I don't know how it got down here in the library."

"You probably put it here to be with the photograph," Issy said. "Stephanie, come take a look at Grammy in a swimsuit."

Steph came over. She laughed. "The suit's a little weird, but you were hot, Grammy."

Leo's eyebrows dipped. Then her expression lightened. "Thank you, my dear, I think."

"I think it's time for a little break," Fae said. "Lemonade?"

Steph nodded. "It's getting hot already. I'll go help."

"Humidity," Fae explained. "We'll probably get a shower later."

"Not before I work on my thirty-minute tan, I hope," Paolo said.

"Bring back a dustcloth," Issy called after them. "I think we missed a few places the other day."

Paolo shut off the phone and began talking to Leo about life in New York and what he did at the museum. "Though I plan on staying for a while to help Issy, if that's all right with you?"

"Of course, dear boy, we're happy to have you."

"So many fascinating . . ."

Issy blocked them out and wandered about the room, picking up objects and putting them down again. Counting the paintings; there were over twenty and this was just one room. She would need weeks just to get through the first floor. And there were another two floors and an attic.

Fae and Steph came back with the lemonade and dustcloth. Issy went on to the next wall. Dead center, above a narrow table and in a place of honor, was a beach scape at night, painted from the knoll during a full moon. The pearlesence of the moonlight spilled across the waters, seeming to lift right out of the painting. *Moonlight on Painter's Cove*. It was the last canvas Adam Ellis ever painted.

Issy shuddered and decided to call it a day. No reason to bring up sad memories after such a productive morning.

Steph handed her a glass. "I love the way the moon looks, like it's lit up from the inside." She studied it a few seconds longer, her hands fisted on her hippie-clad hips, then continued on with her dusting. She stopped again, frowning at a photo on the table beneath the painting. "Aunt Issy, is this you and Mom when you were kids?"

Steph picked up a framed photograph from the table and laughed. "It is, and this must be Aunt Fae and—that's the E—" She broke off and looked at Fae.

The glass of lemonade slipped from Fae's hand and shattered on the floor. Fae stared at the framed photo in Steph's hand.

Issy looked closer, took the photograph, and said in a muted voice, "That's Adam Ellis, the man who painted *Moonlight on Painter's Cove*. He was a good friend of Fae's."

Issy returned the frame to the table, saying as she moved close to Steph, "He died in a car accident. It was quite awful."

"Oh."

"Not to worry. It was a long time ago. Take the cloth over to Paolo, please."

Steph ran over and handed it to Paolo, who moved everyone out of the way and sent Steph for a broom and dustpan.

"Stupid me," Fae said. "I wasn't paying attention."

Issy had never been told the whole story of Fae and Adam Ellis, but she was beginning to wonder how many other secrets lay waiting in the artwork.

"I think it's time for lunch," she said. "Shall we dine al fresco?"

ISSY, STEPH, AND Paolo changed into swimsuits while Leo and Fae filled an old wicker hamper with food, drinks, and a tablecloth. Paolo carried it down to the shore and settled Fae and Leo on the bench that Ben made.

"Absolutely magnificent," he said, taking a deep breath and scanning the coastline. He dropped the basket on the grass. "Last one in . . ." He ran down to the beach and into the water and let out a high-pitched squeal. "It's freezing."

"City boy," taunted Issy, running into the water and splashing him. Seeing Steph standing on the sand, arms crossed in front of her skimpy top, she and Paolo turned on her. Slowly they came out of the water.

"Oh no you don't," she said.

"Oh yes we do." Paolo and Issy each took an arm and dragged her into the water, where they all promptly fell down laughing and shrieking.

They swam out to where it was deeper, treaded water while they talked and laughed, and finally made their way back to shore for lunch and sunscreen.

Issy spread the tablecloth on the grass and began unloading the picnic basket. There was a feast of celery and carrot sticks, cheese and bread, apples and grapes, bottles of water, and big squares of a cake that Chloe must have brought that morning.

Paolo carried plates and drinks up to Leo and Fae. And Issy, for the first time ever, saw Paolo, to whom family was everything, in a family situation. Even though it wasn't his family, he treated them with such respect and kindness and care.

Actually he treated most people that way. Certainly Issy. And Chloe last night. It would be pretty cool if he and Chloe actually did hit it off. She was the epitome of how he described the wife of his dreams.

"And what, *bella,* are you grinning at?" He stretched out between Issy and Steph and reached for an apple.

"Nothing, just . . . happy." Weird. In the midst of total up-heaval, she was actually happy.

"That me makes me happy," Paolo said. "How about you, *bella* Stefania?"

"Me?" Steph squeaked. She shrugged. "I guess."

"What is it, *bella*?"

Steph looked up to where Leo and Fae sat near the two graves. "Tell me more about that painter. The one who painted the moon."

"Adam Ellis? He was very talented and really messed up. Drinking, drugs, a man of great passions but really on a down-ward spiral. I know he and Fae were good friends and she was trying to help him to stay sober."

"Were they, you know, like more than friends?"

"I'm not sure, maybe. He was married. They lived in Man-hattan, her family was super rich. I never met her, she never came up to the Muses.

"One night she called him and demanded he come home. He'd been drinking heavily as usual. Everyone tried to talk him out of driving home, but he was adamant.

"He drove his car through the guardrail and into the river. They found the car the next day downstream. The current had carried it almost to the sound and open water. Where it carried the body, no one ever knew."

"They never found the body?"

Issy shook her head. "No one talks about it." She couldn't stop herself from looking up the hill to Aunt Fae. "And look who's joining us," she said, shaking off the gloom.

Ben Collins was striding over the lawn toward them. Just

seeing him made Issy's day brighter. Made her glad to be home, even in crisis mode. You'd never find Ben driving his truck off the bridge in a drunken stupor.

Issy loved the people who came to the Muses, they were fascinating and challenging, but sometimes she just needed to escape to someplace comforting. In those times she went to Chloe's house, Chloe and her down-to-earth parents and her stinky, nerdy brother. Issy had forgotten how much they'd meant to her.

Ben stopped by Leo and Fae, and Issy called out, "There's lunch, come down."

He nodded, leaned over to talk to Leo and Fae, and came down to the beach.

Issy scooted over, the story of Adam Ellis lifting from her shoulders. "Have a seat."

"Ha," Ben said, sitting next to her and snagging a cluster of grapes. "I thought you were supposed to be working today."

"We did, and we will," Issy said. "We're on break. What about you?"

"I brought the plumber. I left him with a dripping faucet and Jillian on the phone making demands on her agent. Do you think he's safe?"

"From Jillian? Not likely. It's open season wherever she is. But she's really on the phone with her agent? Hey, whose phone is she using?"

"The house phone."

"Ugh. Using up Leo's long-distance minutes instead of her own."

"Probably. Have you talked to her at all?"

Issy shook her head.

"Only when she threw the dustcloth at her," Steph said.

"You've come to blows already?"

"No," Issy said. "Do we have to talk about this? I'll put a moratorium on phone calls when I go back. I shudder to think what she's rung up already. Why doesn't she call one of her friends to take her in?"

"You're going to have to talk to her, sooner or later. I mean really talk."

"No, I don't."

Ben rolled his eyes to the sky. Paolo and Issy burst out laughing.

"What?"

"You just did our Deirdre exasperation expression."

"What's that?"

"When she does something annoying or clueless, we look up to the third floor, where we're exhibiting the Cleveland Museum's copy of *The Thinker*. You know the one?"

"Yes, I know the one. Well, I'm glad to be part of the club." Ben stood up. "Try the cake, Chloe made it. Gotta run."

"You just got here."

"There's a storm forming that may make its way here. Need to secure my experiments, set up some backups. No time to loll with the idle artistic. I just came by to make sure the plumber got here today."

"A storm. Anything we should be concerned about?"

"Not yet. Gotta run." And he left.

"That was weird," Issy said.

"I think I make him uncomfortable," Paolo said.

"That's crazy. He was fine last night."

"Yes, but I think maybe today is different . . . different since last night perhaps."

"What happened last night?"

Paolo laughed. "Well, if you didn't see it, I certainly did."

"WHAT IS WRONG with Ben?" Leo said. "He barely got down there and now he's turning around and coming back."

"He's probably busy," Fae said. "There's a storm coming. I'm sure he has plenty to do to prepare for it."

"What kind of storm? One that you conjured?"

Fae snorted. "One that I heard about on the news, which you would have heard, too, if you hadn't been watching that SpongeBob character."

"Griff and Mandy love him. I confess I don't quite get what it's about."

Ben reached them, looking slightly perturbed. Fae wondered what was going on with him. She knew what she and Leo would like, but she also knew better than to get involved in other people's lives. There was always hell to pay.

"Ben, why didn't you stay and have some lunch?" Leo asked. "We made plenty."

"I'm kind of busy."

"So busy that you brought Scott Rostand over, when he had a perfectly good truck of his own?" Fae said.

"I don't know. Three's a crowd."

"There are already three," Fae pointed out. "You would make four."

Ben shrugged, scratched his head, leaving his cowlick sticking up. "What's between those two, anyway?"

"What two?" Leo asked innocently.

"Paolo and Issy. He paid attention to Chloe all night last night. But . . ." He frowned down at the group on the beach.

"You just want to make sure his intentions are honorable?" Fae asked, wrestling with a smile.

"I just want to know what his intentions are."

"He and Issy are colleagues. I don't know about him and Chloe. But I'd say he'd be a good catch."

Ben did a double take at Fae, and she nearly lost it. What happened to the days of free love and musical beds and fun? Though she supposed those were the days before sex killed you. A shame. It was painful to watch this generation barter for sex and love.

"Isn't that what you were asking?"

"Not exactly."

"Well, why don't you escort Leo and me back to the house and you can tell me exactly."

"Come, Leo. Ben will walk us home."

Chapter 20

F ae and Leo accompanied Ben back to the house. The others reluctantly packed up the lunch things and beach towels a few minutes later. No one was in a working mood. That tended to happen after you'd been out in the sun and sand and waves. But work needed to get done.

"Do you think my mother is ever coming back?" Steph asked as they trudged back to the house.

"I hope so," Issy said.

"Me, too, and now her voice mail is filled up."

Issy nodded. "I know; I've been calling her, too."

"Do you think she stole Grammy's money?"

Yes, she did. But how could she tell that to Stephanie? In just a few days the girl had gone from sullen to curious and helpful, even fanciful. Steph was special in that Whitaker way. And finding out that her parents were not only crooks but stole from their own family could ruin that for her.

Issy threw her arm around Steph's shoulders and gave her a quick squeeze, before letting go. "Whatever happens, we'll soldier on."

Paolo slowly turned his head to look at her. They both knew they wouldn't be able to soldier on without a major miracle.

Ben's truck was gone when they reached the house. They dumped the towels and shoes in the mud room and carried the hamper into the kitchen.

The plumber had left a note on the table that he had to get a part and would try to return tomorrow or the next day, which Issy filed under *this is going to take forever.*

While Paolo and Stephanie returned the uneaten food to the fridge, Issy went in search of Fae and Leo to see if they wanted tea or if they were interested in doing a little more inventory that afternoon.

She found Jillian instead, sitting at the escritoire in the parlor, with feet resting on a footstool that had been needle-pointed by Hazel Whitaker in 1843. The house phone rested between her shoulder and her ear as she reached for a glass of what looked like orange juice, but the vodka bottle sitting out on the butler's table suggested that happy hour had started at noon.

"Talk to you soonest. Good-bye. Oh, Oops. I'm glad you're here. I talked to George a while ago. He said to tell you he's dropping by tomorrow afternoon. Expect him at three."

Issy just stared at her mother. One didn't drop into Muses by the Sea from Hartford. Jillian must have put him up to it. How dare she butt into their business. And what did she think she could get out of it?

"Well, don't look at me; I didn't invite him."

"But you called him," Issy said, stepping into the room and immediately feeling at a disadvantage in her bikini. But she stood there, gritting her teeth, while Jillian gave her a quick once-over, before dismissing her. "Didn't you?"

"I just wanted to say hello."

"And how is Uncle George?"

"He seems fine. You can ask him tomorrow."

"Mother . . ."

Jillian gave her the eyebrow.

"Mother . . . Aren't you the least bit worried that your daughter Vivienne is missing?"

"Oh, she isn't missing. George's people traced her and Dan to Panama."

"Panama?" And why hadn't Uncle George bothered to communicate this to Issy? "Is she coming back?"

"I'm not sure they can."

Issy took her time to shower and change, trying to decide whether to warn Grammy and Fae that George would be coming to talk to them and that Vivienne had been found, or to wait until he confirmed what Jillian had said.

She was definitely telling Paolo and asking him to be there even though George would probably try to get rid of him for not being a member of the family. George could be a stickler like that. But Issy needed Paolo. She had a sneaking suspicion that Jillian and George were about to form a first and only partnership against the rest of the family.

And that's what it boiled down to. Issy was a part of the family and she had to make her stand where it counted.

She towel-dried her hair and went downstairs. It was time for a meeting of the minds—if they could just get rid of Jillian so they could talk freely.

Before she could gather the clan, Chloe arrived with Mandy and Griff. They dropped their backpacks and ran through the kitchen calling "Grammy, Grammy!"

Issy followed them in time to see them screech to a halt and domino off each other. She came up behind them and saw Jillian still sitting there, on the phone again, with an admonishing finger to her lips to be quiet.

Issy could feel them deflate. It broke her heart. Their mother had deserted them, and their grandmother was a cold fish.

She eased them back into the hallway. "Hey, guys, how was camp?"

"Good," Mandy said.

"Good," Griff echoed. "Where's Grammy?"

"I think she's still upstairs."

"Oh." Griff hung his head.

"Why don't we go up and see if she's awake?" said Issy. "But we have to be very quiet in case she's napping."

"Okay," breathed Mandy, and shushed Griff with a finger to her lips.

They tiptoed up the stairs and down the main hallway to Leo's room. The children crowded in front of Issy and she quietly knocked on the door. They opened it a crack and looked inside.

Leo was sitting on a chaise, a book turned over in her lap, her chin resting on her chest. But she opened her eyes and the two children took that as a cue to rush inside.

Issy came in, too. "Sorry, Grammy, they were so excited to see you."

"And I'm so excited to see them, too."

Griff crawled up on the chaise to sit beside her, and she patted his nose with one finger. "I heard you calling me, Max."

"Griff," Issy corrected her automatically.

"That's what I said. 'I heard Mandy and Griff calling me.'" Her eyes flicked to Issy's.

"Look what I made you," Griff said, and unwrapped a flat piece of dried plaster of paris. "It's my handprint. We can put it on the table and I can check every time I come visit to see if my hand is bigger."

"What an excellent idea," Leo said. "But this is such a big strong hand, does your hand really fit in there?"

"Uh-huh, watch." Griff stuck first one hand then the other until he got the right thumb in the thumbprint and fitted the rest of his hand to match.

"But look what I made, Grammy," Mandy said.

"My goodness, what is that?"

"I'm not finished with it yet. It's going to be a lanyard brace-let, you take these four plastic ties and you fold them over and you . . ."

Issy tiptoed out of the room.

STEPHANIE WANDERED DOWN the path through the woods. She shouldn't be here, but she wanted . . . She didn't know what she wanted. Aunt Fae had warned her about following the faeries but she didn't say not to follow the Elf King.

And Steph really needed to know.

She kicked at a stone that stuck up from the path. What was she doing here, thinking about Elf Kings and faeries? She didn't believe in that stuff. She believed in hanging out at the mall, not lurking in the woods hoping to catch a glimpse of things that probably didn't even exist. Her friends would think she'd totally whacked out if they could see her now. If she said to them the things she said to Aunt Fae and Issy.

But her friends wouldn't be allowed to associate with her because her parents were the worst kind of thieves, who stole from their own family and left their children behind when they fled—like one of those stupid television movies.

The woods suddenly got dark. A cloud passing over the sun; she knew that, and yet it was like her thoughts had brought on the cloud. And where was she? She didn't recognize this part of the woods. Had she veered off the path? No, it was there in front of her.

Still, her heart started pounding; this is what happened in time-travel books when the heroine is walking along and then suddenly she's not where she was. Steph quickly looked around. It still looked like Grammy's woods. But up ahead was something she'd never seen before. A cottage, a cabin, a Hobbit's hut.

She took a breath. Crept closer and nearly fell over with relief. It was one of the cottages Issy had told her about, where people used to store their supplies and meet for sex.

It didn't look very romantic. And it didn't look like anyone had been there for years. She tiptoed up to the door. Knocked quietly.

Stupid, no one is in there.

No one answered, so she tried the handle. It didn't open. Must be locked. She moved to the window, cupped her hands, and peered inside. Just a bunch of shadows. Pulled up the hem of her T-shirt and tried to wipe a clean spot on the pane. Looked again; a chair maybe, nothing much.

It would make a great hangout. Except she didn't have any friends here to hang out with. It could be her special place. She could write a novel or paint, except she'd never taken lessons. She could read her book. She was almost finished with it, but she could read it again, it was that interesting. Or maybe Aunt Fae had more books.

She moved away from the cottage. Issy had said there were several on the property. Maybe one of the others was in better shape. She'd ask Grammy if she could have it. Not have, but use it while she was here. She hoped that would be a long, long time. If she had to go to foster care, she would die.

Thinking that made her hiccup. If she didn't do something, the hiccups would turn into blubbering and she'd done enough of that the first week she and Mandy and Griff had come. No more blubbering. She needed a plan. But what about Mandy and Griff? Maybe if she promised to take care of them, Grammy would let them stay, too.

She started walking. Even if Grammy didn't want them, they could live in one of the little houses like Aunt Fae did. Steph would have to find some kind of job. An illegal one, since you had to be fourteen to work and had to get a special permit for it. She'd worry about that later.

First things first. Find a cottage big enough for the three of them.

She followed the path and found another nestled back in the trees. She couldn't see the first cottage anymore. Good. This one was more private. They could even hide here if they needed to. No one would find them.

She peered in the window. This time she could see a little more. A bunch of old paintings stacked against the wall. An old easel, a chair. Like on PBS where the archaeologists find a town under a volcano and everything looks like the people should still be there, only they've been dead for centuries. Steph shivered. She didn't like to think about things like that.

Kids who went to the mall and mooned over movie stars

were much better off. Her mind was always going places that ended up being scary. Like that thing Aunt Fae said about the galaxies. How could anything be that big? And how big was it? She moved away from the window. She wanted to go home.

But where was that? In the big brick house on the cul-de-sac where you couldn't even mess up your own room, like maybe some magazine would surprise them and want to take pictures. Was it Grammy's house, which was a neat freak's nightmare, but much more fun. And sometimes scarier.

Ugh. She just wanted things to be right, but she was afraid once they had started falling apart, they wouldn't stop.

Suddenly the woods weren't her friend anymore. Like they were angry at her. Wanted her out. It was just her imagination. She knew that, but still she turned around and walked—not ran, in case someone or thing was watching—but walked as fast as she could until she was back on the lawn at Grammy's. Then she sprinted across the grass and around the house to safety.

STEPHANIE BURST THROUGH the kitchen door.

Issy and Chloe both turned around.

"Whoa, I thought you were upstairs taking the longest shower in history. Where have you been?"

"Outside," Steph huffed. She went to the fridge. She came out with a bottle of water and guzzled half of it. "I was just exploring. I saw some of those cottages you were talking about."

"Cottages? Oh, the camps. I hope you didn't go inside. They're probably all rotten and unsafe."

"No, but they could be fixed up really nice, couldn't they?"

"I suppose. Why?"

"Do you think . . ." Her eyes flicked away.

"Think what?" Issy asked.

"That maybe I could have one—I mean just to hang out in?"

"Why? Isn't this house big enough? Plenty of quiet, private places."

"I know, I just think they're cool."

Issy sighed. "They are, and once they were really nice. I used to take my dolls out and play house in one of them. When they weren't being used."

"And we used to hang out there when we wanted to be private," Chloe added.

"Ah, the good old teenage years," Issy said on a laugh.

"Were they really good?"

Issy cocked her head. "Yeah. Filled with ups and downs and heartbreaks and ecstasy—the emotion not the drug. But yeah, they were good. And something you have to go through to get to the other side.

"Tell you what, one day this week we'll go take a look. Find one that's in decent shape."

"Thanks, that's great."

"In the meantime, are you up for some more cataloging this afternoon?"

"Sure. I'll go set up." Steph passed Paolo coming in.

Chloe lit up.

"If I were a painter . . ." he began.

"Fortunately, you aren't," Issy said. "Or Chloe and I would weigh two hundred pounds, have butts like a Rubens madonna, and would be surrounded by platters of homemade food we cooked while the bambinos were sleeping."

Paolo barked out a laugh. "Yes, you would. Lovable behinds with very low-cut peasant blouses and ample, very ample cleavage."

"Chauvinist," Chloe exclaimed, laughing.

"Classicist," Paolo countered. "My appreciation of the female form is tempered by a combination of my love of Baroque painting and my provincial upbringing. However, as it is, I'm an equal-opportunity admirer of women of all types."

"And on that note," Chloe said, "I'd best be going."

"Why?" Issy and Paolo said together.

"Why don't you stay for dinner?" Issy said. "You don't have to cook. There's plenty of food. I can cook, and you can visit."

"Thanks, but I have a few errands and Ben says he thinks you'd like to spend some time with your family."

"Ben likes making decisions, doesn't he?" Paolo said.

Chloe smiled. "Yes. But in his defense, he's used to working on his own and making all the calls. It's just a habit he's gotten into."

"No significant other?" Paolo asked.

Chloe blinked, frowned. "Not yet. He's had a couple that lasted for a while, but I think they got tired of specimens in the fridge. He sees women sometimes. He's not a total nerd. He just doesn't get very serious about any of them. He's a scientist. His work comes first."

"Always did," Issy said.

"Why do you want to know?" Chloe asked Paolo.

"Just curious. I know someone else whose work always comes first."

"And I know him right back," said Issy.

"Only out of necessity. Alas, *mio povero cuor.*"

"Don't listen to him. Women come into the museum just to look at him."

Paolo sighed. "But not to love."

Issy laughed. "I'll ask Leo if she minds us going out tonight again. That is, if you want to, Chloe."

"Of course. I'll call Ben. Tell him we're coming to his place to grill steaks. That way the guys can cook and we can have some girl time. I know it's selfish but I don't know when you'll be back."

Issy chewed on that while she went to look for Leo. Back? She'd forgotten for a minute that she would be leaving soon. When would she be back? If she didn't think of something quick, there might not be anyplace to come back to.

Issy passed Mandy and Griff running to the kitchen—after a snack, no doubt. Leo was in the library with Steph. They were sitting on the couch with a big photograph album opened between them.

They were bent over a page with a magnifying glass.

"Grammy, do you mind if Paolo and I go out for an early dinner with Chloe and maybe Ben?"

"Of course not, dear."

"Chloe and I can make a salad and put a casserole in the oven. Just check on it when the timer dings."

"You'll do no such thing. We can get our own dinner. Do it all the time. Now go on and have fun, but don't stay out late, because we have so many pieces to inventory tomorrow."

Issy smiled. Leo was actually enjoying the work—and the children. She looked more lively than she had since Issy's return. The kids and having something to do were good for her.

"What about you, Steph, want to come for dinner with us?"

"Thanks, but Aunt Fae and I are going to stream *Lord of the Rings*—if we can use your laptop."

"Sounds like a great idea."

Chapter 21

Chloe drove through the town and out Shore Road for several miles with Issy and Paulo following before she turned onto a smaller access road and finally into a short drive surrounded by scrub oak. She came to a stop in a wide parking area and Issy pulled in next to her.

"It looks rather like one of those houses where they greet you with a shotgun," Paolo said.

Issy nodded. The house appeared to have started life as a saltbox Cape Cod. Now it was a sprawling, ramshackle, wooden . . . Issy was at a loss for words. It was as if several architectural styles had been plunked down at random.

"It is rather interesting."

"An adventure at least," Paolo agreed, and got out of the car.

"I'm sure Ben would agree. He was always about adventure."

"The staid marine ecologist? I thought there was more to him than you mentioned."

Chloe led them around the house to a side door. "I know it doesn't look like much, but it's nice inside."

"And spotless, if you've been staying here," Issy added.

"I don't know about spotless, but it's clean. And not because of me. Ben is pretty meticulous at housekeeping, just like in his work. I have to say, he tends to leave the outside, outside."

They stepped into the house and Chloe turned on the lights. "I probably should have brought you in the front, but I'm so used to going through the mud room."

"This is the mud room?" Paolo said. "It's almost as big as my bedroom in Manhattan."

Chloe smiled, showing her dimples. "A lot of mud comes through this room."

Uh-oh, thought Issy, the dimples are serious.

The mud room also contained a large washer and dryer. There were two low shelves that held various types of boots in various states of dirty, a row of pegs for rain gear and waders on one wall and another on the opposite wall for nets, and various tools unfamiliar to Issy. A narrow door showed a bathroom complete with shower stall.

"Well planned," Issy said. "Strip out of stinky marsh clothes, put them right in the wash, and step into the shower. Come out clean and house-ready." And like any good exhibit, it told a lot about the owner.

The kitchen was small but functional with pine cabinets and newish but not upscale appliances. And not a granite countertop in sight.

Paolo put the wine Issy had snagged from the Muses cellar on the table.

Chloe dropped her bag on the counter and flicked a panel of light switches. "There's a cabinet with wineglasses and a corkscrew right outside that door."

Issy went through to a larger room, where a small dining table and low buffet sat at one end and a couch, easy chair, miscellaneous tables, and a large television were crammed into the rest of the space.

Very cozy, she thought. She found the corkscrew and the glasses and took them back to the kitchen.

Chloe was busy unwrapping packages of steaks. "Ben just called to say he was on his way."

"Where exactly does he work?" Issy asked.

"In the marshes? Actually I can show you." Chloe led them through another door into a room that explained the different architectural styles. It ran the length of the house and more, a simple rectangle with high ceilings. One side was all glass and the view took Issy's breath away. The house was on high ground with a cleared lawn that ran down to the water of the sound. On the right was a stand of trees. And to the left, scrub oak and a few houses not close enough to see their occupants. In the distance, marshes stretched to the horizon.

"Wow," Paolo said.

"Double wow," Issy agreed.

"Those are Ben's; not really, but I think of them as his. They're about fifteen minutes away, close enough to keep an eye on, but far enough not to smell them at low tide. The best of both worlds."

"Is this all his land?" Paolo asked.

"Not quite an acre. The property goes all the way down to the water. Though it's a triangular parcel, so there's really only about twenty feet of beachfront. It was a lucky buy; the owners had already started this room then couldn't pay their mortgage and bailed. Ben got it at auction. I confess I thought that was sort of bad karma—you know, taking someone else's house. But Ben said it gave them a new beginning without debt and gave him a house and debt. So they were even."

"Sounds like Ben," Issy said.

"It took forever to get him to put real furniture in here," Chloe said, indicating the couches and chairs and game tables and a heavy wooden dining table that was a work of art. "He spent his first two years here in an aluminum chaise longue."

"That also sounds like Ben."

When they returned to the kitchen, Ben's truck was sitting outside and the mud room shower was running. A few minutes later he came out, hair dripping, barefoot, and wrapped in a towel.

"Sorry. When I left this morning I didn't know I was having company and didn't bring any clothes downstairs. Back in a sec." He clasped the towel more tightly and hurried past them.

Issy got a glimpse of sinewy back muscles as he whipped past her.

Chloe smiled after him, then grinned at Issy. "It's just like Dad always said . . ."

"He'll fill out nicely when he gets older," they quoted together, in exaggerated, low voices.

Issy laughed. "And he has. What I could see. Not that I was looking."

Chloe gave her a know-it-all smile.

"Ben was always tall and skinny as a rail," Issy told Paolo. "Mrs. Collins was always trying to get him to eat more but their dad said . . . well, we just told you what he said. Shall I start on a salad or something?"

Ben came back a few minutes later, dressed and shod, and still looking pretty good.

"I suppose I have to grill the steaks," he said, looking at the platter Chloe held out to him.

"I'll come kibitz," Paolo said, and followed him outside.

Issy and Chloe set the table out in the room overlooking the sound and went back to the kitchen.

Chloe sank into a chair. "I feel like you and I haven't had a chance to talk since you've been home."

"I was just thinking that. I have to thank you again for dealing with Mandy and Griff for me."

"No problem, I just dump them off with Melanie Hathaway in the school office in the mornings. And take them home when she brings them back. How are things going at the house?"

"I don't know what I'm supposed to do," Issy said abruptly. "My vacation is flying by. And as much as I enjoy being here, and getting a chance to hear Grammy talk about the artwork in the house, time is running out. I'm no nearer to solving the problem of how to save the house from sale and Grammy and Aunt Fae from going to the old-folks home.

"And Jillian, who shows up like the uninvited guest, comes and goes at will, and doesn't lift a finger to help, but managed to expend enough energy to get in touch with Uncle George and he's coming tomorrow, probably with an ultimatum."

Issy pulled out a chair and sat down. "We are so screwed."

"You'll think of something."

"I've thought of a hundred things, but none of them are realistic."

"No sign of Vivienne?"

Issy shook her head. "Evidently George's people saw her with Dan in Panama. But I just can't believe it. Vivienne. Mrs. Ultimate Suburban Mom suddenly dumps her kids to live the high life in Panama? Panama? Why there?"

"No extradition probably."

"Of course. Which means she has no intention of coming

back. And what am I going to do with these kids? I can't really leave them with Leo even if she gets to keep the house.

"Fae's been staying there for the last few days, but I can tell it chafes her. She's used to being alone. I don't think she wants to give that up for great-nieces and -nephews or the old-folks home. I can't stay much longer, and I'm running out of savings."

The door opened and Ben and Paolo came back in with the steaks.

"Are you two still sitting here?"

"Just waiting for you." Chloe went to the oven, laying a hand briefly on Issy's shoulder as she passed by.

"What's that?" Paolo asked as Chloe carried a steaming casserole dish past him.

"Scalloped potatoes."

"Heaven." He took the dish from her. Issy followed with the salad.

They sat down and Paolo poured the wine. "Ben says he has a video camera we can borrow. I thought we could get some footage of Leo talking about the Muses if she doesn't mind."

"I think she'd love to do anything to help keep the Muses alive. That's a great idea." She turned to thank Ben only to catch him looking speculatively at Paolo.

Now, what was that about?

Dinner was delicious and Issy brushed aside her concerns to enjoy a couple of hours with friends. When Chloe and Paolo said they would do the dishes, the sun was setting and Issy and Ben were left alone.

"This is an incredible home," Issy said.

"A work in progress, not that I have much time to work on it."

"All those salt marshes calling."

Ben nodded. "I know everybody thought I was a total geek for being so fascinated with them, but they're vital to the survival of the shore habitat."

"I know. You taught me well."

"You actually were listening to me carry on all those years?"

"Yes. I know they protect shorelines from erosion, provide essential food, refuge, and breeding habitat for a whole bunch of marine species. And a habitat for birds and other animals. They reduce flooding and protect water quality and only stink at low tide—wait, wait, when they aren't aerated properly." She grinned. "And at low tide."

"Wow, you *were* listening."

"Of course; just because you were geeky didn't mean what you said wasn't interesting. Plus I grew up with paintings of shores and marshes. They don't call it the Coastal School of painting for nothing."

"Want to see something?"

"Maybe. Does it involve mosquitoes?"

"Maybe one or two."

"Nothing gross?"

"Nope."

"I guess," she said suspiciously, knowing the things that excited Ben were sometimes outright disgusting.

"Come on." He headed toward the far side of the glass room to a door that opened onto a wooden balcony where a set of steep, narrow stairs ran up the side of the house.

"They're safe," he said. "Just hold the rail."

He stood aside and let her precede him. She wasn't sure what she'd find, so at the top, she stopped and peered over the edge.

"It's a crow's nest," she said, and climbed through the opening to a circular deck perched at the apex of the roof.

And it was a spectacular view. To their right, the setting sun flared red, yellow, and orange, while the surrounding sky turned dark with streaks of mauve and gray.

"Wow," she said as she felt Ben come up beside her at the rail. "This is amazing."

"I can't take credit for it," he said. "But it was the thing that finally swayed me to buy a house this large."

"Not planning to inhabit it with more than yourself?"

"Not yet anyway."

The night grew darker except for a funnel of light that turned the marshes gold and the waterways that curled through them to deep ebony. Fireflies began to wink around the scrub oaks.

She sighed. "What a life."

"Cool, huh?" Ben draped his arm over her shoulders and a hundred scenes flashed through her mind. Ben and Chloe and her walking on the sand, walking into town, just stopping to look at the ocean, Ben in the middle, his long skinny arms slung carelessly over Issy and Chloe's smaller, shorter shoulders. Comrades. The Three Musketeers. Three nerdy kids.

It was a totally natural thing to do. It had made her feel at home that night at the hospital when he'd put his arm over her shoulder and pulled her along to the parking lot.

But somehow, in this private quiet aerie, alone and watching the sunset, it felt different. Comfortable. The same, yet different.

The sun slid below the horizon, leaving a nimbus of color, until it finally disappeared completely over the horizon. And they stood like captains on a ship among the stars.

"So how much longer are you going to be able to stay?" Ben asked.

The world came rushing back in. "I have a week left of vacation."

"And you think you can see things clear by then?"

"No." There; she'd said it out loud. "I've been here nearly a week and I'm no closer to figuring out what to do than when I arrived."

"Well, that's seven whole days more. Don't give up yet." He gave her a squeeze and dropped his arm.

She moved away. "I guess we'd better be getting back."

"How long is Paolo staying?"

"He hasn't said. But since he's at loose ends, I'm hoping he'll stay until I leave."

"He really quit because somebody said he was incompetent and only got the job because he was sleeping with you?"

"Yep. He may look totally metro but he's old-fashioned at heart. Honor, loyalty et cetera."

"Is he?"

"Old-fashioned?"

"Sleeping with you."

"No. That would be so unprofessional."

"Now that's he's no longer working for you? Not that it's any of my business."

"No, it isn't, but no I wouldn't and he wouldn't. We love, love, love each other to pieces, but not like that. We're friends. He wants to settle down to a comfortable home life. So do I, with someone steady, when the time is right."

"But not with him? I would think you guys would be dynamite together."

"We are. He's passionate and wild and it's wonderful working with him. He has an eye for art that is remarkable. And a special way with people. You should have heard him drawing Leo out this morning. That's why he wants the camera—to film her.

"Professionally we are an incredible team. Totally simpatico and hugely in demand for our inventive design. But personally? That special spark just isn't there. He wants someone to be comfortable with, a homebody. It's strange but he has a real domestic streak."

"And you?"

"Me? I don't know what I want. I'm counting on recognizing it when it hits me over the head."

"I guess it would be hard to give up your glamorous, exciting life in Manhattan to be a homebody."

"Glamorous? Long hours? Heavy lifting? Beautiful artwork. That's exciting enough for me. My mother had a glamorous life and look where it got her."

"For one thing, it got her back here. That's not such a bad place to be."

"No. And not for me, either. I like being home. It's going to be hard to go back, though I love my work, the artwork."

"You can't stay here and still design?"

"Not really, although for the last couple of days, I've had this wild idea. But no. I think the only thing to be done is to beg George to loan me the money to keep Grammy at the Muses. I'm not optimistic."

She turned away, the quietude disturbed by the reality of what awaited her tomorrow and the next day and the next.

They climbed back downstairs, but Ben stopped her before they went back inside.

"I thought if you do have some time before you leave, we might go to dinner or something, just the two of us."

She tried to see his expression in the dark. "Ben, are you asking me on a date?"

"Is that a dumb idea?"

"No. No, actually, it isn't a dumb idea at all."

IT WASN'T EASY prying Paolo away from his conversation with Chloe, which seemed to be about food, backpacking, and eighteenth-century painters. But finally he and Ben went out to Ben's workshop and came back several minutes later with a camera and tripod and several lenses.

"Boy toys," Chloe said, and gave Ben and Paolo a huge loving smile.

"Work toys," Ben countered. He carried them out to Issy's car and put them in back.

"I'll pick up the kids as usual," Chloe said.

They said their thank-yous and good-byes, and Ben gave Issy a look that at first she thought was meant to remind her of their date, but was actually about the weather.

"It's going to rain all tonight and maybe tomorrow. Probably starting in a few minutes. Drive carefully."

"Is this the beginning of that big storm you were telling us about?" asked Paolo.

"Associated weather is my guess," Ben said. "But I'm not a meteorologist."

"Should we be worried?" Issy asked.

"Hopefully it will veer out to sea long before it reaches us, but you should be prepared for some weather. After the weekend most likely."

"But you're preparing."

"I always prepare. I have delicate instruments that need protection. The first three storms of the season have missed us. No reason this one won't. Still, it's best to be ready. I have a bunch of stuff to do, but if you need help, call me."

It started to thunder as they drove through town, and by the time they pulled up to the door of the Muses, the rain was coming down in sheets.

"Do we sit it out or do we make a run for it?" Paolo asked.

"It could keep up for a while. I say we run."

They did and were soaked by the time they got to the kitchen.

"Ben definitely has the right idea about a shower by the back door," Paolo said.

They pushed off their shoes and left them to dry. It was later than Issy had realized. The rest of the house was already dark.

They climbed the stairs and said good night on the landing. Palo went off to his room and Issy to hers. Only one overhead light lit the hallway. All the rooms were dark except one at the far end. A thread of light shone from beneath the Impressionist Room door. Jillian's room. Issy didn't stop at her own room, but walked straight down the hall. They would have to talk sooner or later, and maybe this was as good a time as any.

As she thought it, the light went out. Issy crept back to her own room, thankful, relieved, and knowing that it couldn't be put off much longer.

FAE DUCKED HER head against the rain, only to have it roll down her neck. But she couldn't very well carry an umbrella while skulking around in the dark. It was ridiculous enough that she had to sneak out at night like some damn teenager. Something had to give, something was about to give. That business with the photograph this morning had almost undone her. There had to be some changes.

And she dreaded the only change that was possible. She couldn't leave. The life she knew and wanted would have to be jettisoned. She'd promised Wes.

She stopped under a tree. Thunder rumbled overhead. Lightning would soon follow. Why had she made that promise?

Because she'd never guessed at the ramifications.

She pressed against the bark of the trunk until her dress was soaked through and her tears were mingled with the rain.

Stupid old woman. You had some happiness. Let that be enough. Let it go, sever the past, your present, the future. Do it for Wes, for Leo . . . for Adam.

And the pain forced its way out and she wailed, slicing the sky with her acceptance. It had to be done, but not tonight, in the dark, in the rain. She turned and sloshed her way back to the house.

IN HER SLEEP, Steph dreamed the rumble of the gods at war, the wail of the banshee, the march, march, march of unseen soldiers, and she thought, It's starting, the end of the world as we know it, and she wanted her mother.

JILLIAN SAT BY her window in the dark. Rain slid down the panes, forming a curtain of indecision. Why had she come here? Had the thought of reaping money from the sale of the Muses really sent her scrambling back to the family bosom? She had a mother who was more icon than nurturer, two daughters she didn't even know, one a thief and missing, the other as skittish as a wild foal. Not that she'd ever seen a wild foal. Not that she'd really seen much of anything that was real.

Her life was a sound stage; the scenes changed but they were pretty much all the same, and in between, Saint-Tropez with

Henri, St. Moritz with Jonathon, Ipanema with Enrique. Even her last film, *The Sins of Eva Narone,* was the flip side of a film she'd done years before and whose name escaped her at the moment. She hadn't had a film in the last two years.

She touched her cheek and was glad it was dark. The skin was smooth; she paid plenty of attention and money to keep it that way. But there were wrinkles just waiting to show themselves. The toughness that came with age that all the derma peels on earth couldn't stop.

She wished she had a drink but she'd be damned if she'd get caught sneaking downstairs for a glass of courage. Her doctor had refused to renew her diazepam scrip. She sighed and sat in the dark, the rain came down, and Jillian York grew a little older.

Chapter 22

S teph and Fae were already in the kitchen when Issy came downstairs the next morning.

Issy stopped just inside the door and grinned. "You two look like a fragmented, dee-mented rainbow of love."

The two twirled around and struck a pose, which made Issy laugh out loud, something she hadn't expected to do today, not with what lay ahead.

Steph was wearing a T-shirt and a long gauze skirt that she'd turned into a pair of pants by pulling the back hem through her legs and rolling it into her front waistband. A string of brass bells rode low on her hips, and she jingled with every movement. Fae, for a change, wore a green-and-blue-flowered tunic over purple harem pants.

And with a stab of affection Issy realized she was attempting her not-batshit-crazy look since George was expected that afternoon.

Issy danced across the floor and hugged them both and they spun in the kitchen until the door opened and Griff and Mandy came in.

"What are you doing?" Mandy asked.

"Nothing, stupid," Steph said, and walked out of the room. Mood broken. Someday, hopefully, that would change.

"I want to dance, too," Mandy said.

"And so you will," said Fae. "In a few nights we're all going to dance on the beach."

"Why?" Griff asked.

"Because it will be a full moon and the Whitaker women— and one brave Whitaker male—always dance on the beach at the full moon."

"But I'm a Bannister," he said, his mouth puckering.

"That night, we'll all be Whitakers."

"What about me?" Paolo asked, coming into the room.

Fae shrugged. "Why not? It's the spirit that counts."

"If Mommy comes back, can she dance, too?" Griff asked.

Fae and Issy exchanged looks.

"Sure," Issy said. "Now, what do you two want for breakfast?"

As soon as Mandy and Griff had left for camp, Issy and Fae joined the others in the parlor. Paolo and Steph had set up the video equipment and both were in discussion with Leo, who had dressed in a light lavender suit that to Issy's semitrained eye appeared to be a Chanel.

"Doesn't she look fabulous?" Steph said.

"Beautiful," Issy agreed. And looked closer. "Are you wearing makeup, Grammy?"

Leo smiled. "Yes my dear. Fortunately, I didn't have to apply it myself. I had a wardrobe and makeup team."

Issy frowned and turned to Steph. "You and Paolo?"

Steph's gaze flicked to the archway. "Me and Paolo and, uh, Jillian."

On cue, Jillian swept into the room, slacks, silk shirt, hair back in a low ponytail. Her business costume?

Issy felt a sucker punch to the gut, straight back to the spine; she may have even taken a step backward. This was her project. Her idea. Her dream.

She did stagger back then. Her dream? What was she thinking? This wasn't a dream. This was an inventory, pure and simple. Except, one thing had grown out of another. Unfortunately, anything that might have been a dream had just turned into a nightmare.

Idiot. You just got too carried away. Possibly, but Issy had to stand her ground. To hell with the fact that she wanted to run to the nearest john and throw up.

She'd spent years trying to be something that was essentially Isabelle Whitaker, and not the leavings of someone better. Even though a newspaper clipping upstairs in a box reminded her that her birth was surrounded by salacious gossip and speculation rather than the joy of welcoming a new family member, a baby girl named Isabelle.

"Do you want to get started, dear?"

Issy heard Leo's question but she was having a hard time dragging her attention back to the room. It seemed to her no one moved. They were all staring at her.

Pull yourself together, Is. You've dealt with bigger divas than your mother, ones that were actually artists. And then she realized Jillian was gone.

"Sure, I was just thinking . . ." She turned to Steph and Paolo. "What do you think about having Leo sit in front of the fireplace?"

"Excellent," Paolo said, and offered his elbow to Leo.

They spent the morning, cataloging pieces and asking Leo questions. Sometimes the descriptions would ramble into memories associated with the artwork; sometimes they led to other anecdotes about the artist or the times. It was all fascinating.

At some point, Jillian reappeared with a makeup kit and sat at the side of the room. She stayed quietly in the background, running in to refresh Leo's makeup during their brief breaks. She didn't attempt to take over, but Issy was painfully aware of her constant presence.

"Leo's amazing," Paulo said after one hilarious story that had them covering their mouths to keep from laughing out loud during the taping. "You could make a whole PBS series with her."

"Hmm," Issy said, thinking, *Why not?*

With all of them working on the inventory, Issy's mind stayed off the fact that George was coming to "discuss" the situation with them. She was pretty sure he had no plans to discuss anything. He'd already decided what would be best. And she couldn't help but wonder if Jillian was a part of it.

Had the two Whitakers concocted a scheme to oust Leo and Fae from their homes? Was that why Jillian was suddenly staying so close? Spying on them? Looking for reasons that the house should be sold. Waiting for Leo to make some mistake as she drifted from past to present. So far she'd stayed focused, but she was getting tired, and when they stopped for lunch, Issy wondered if they should call it a day.

They didn't go down to the beach for a picnic but sat around the kitchen table. No one spoke much as they ate, but they reacted to every sound. On high alert. Looking, listening—as if they were waiting for a tumbrel.

Issy took her plate to the sink. "If we're all finished, I think we should get back to work. If you're up to it, Grammy."

"Of course, dear, I haven't had so much fun in I don't know when."

Issy smiled. She didn't doubt it. As Leo reminisced she came alive, her cheeks bloomed, she sat straighter, her voice sounded stronger. It was because her life had been exciting then; now it was lonely. She was enjoying the grandchildren, and Paolo, and especially reminiscing about the past.

It broke Issy's heart to think she would be turned out of her house. She didn't need that. Not yet. Assisted living could flock the wallpaper, and put in chandeliers and pretty couches, but it wouldn't be home, it wouldn't be filled with memories and artwork of the most creative minds of the era.

Would she sit at a communal table with the ladies and talk about how the Coastal School of landscape painting began and flourished at her home, Muses by the Sea. What kind of audience was that for a grande dame, hostess to the artistic and the infamous?

If Issy could just keep her here and bring a new audience to her . . . And there it was again. The perfect idea, a pipe dream that would cost a fortune she didn't have and would take too long to raise. She'd had an inkling of an idea before Paolo came with the plans for the Toulouse-Lautrec exhibit, which normally she would already be focused on. Instead those plans had just solidified the thought that the Muses could become a permanent collection of art, in situ, where it belonged. Not separated and sitting piecemeal in galleries and museums across the country, but as it lived. And now she couldn't get that idea out of her head.

Maybe she was the crazy Whitaker. Maybe Leo needed to be around other people, any kind of people, not sitting alone with the past.

But looking across the table at her grandmother, she knew it would make a difference. Leo's life, her reason for being, was back then, not making new friends because she had no choice.

After a quick cleanup, everyone went back to the parlor, where Jillian reapplied Leo's lipstick and gave her a few pointers on speaking to the camera. Then she placed Leo in a chair and started rearranging things around her.

"Wait," Issy said. "What are you doing?"

"Dressing the set. You don't want your grandmother to look like she's talking from a fishbowl, do you?"

"No, but you do realize this is for inventory purposes."

"Yes, I didn't move anything that you'd already counted. But really, Oops, even PBS has a set decorator."

"Some very good ones," Paolo said, then added, "do you think we should turn our inventory into an *Art in America* presentation?"

Jillian shrugged, thirties-movie style. "The idea has potential."

"As long as we don't have to pay for it," Issy said.

"Of course not, Oops. You need a producer—or two."

Issy fought not to roll her eyes.

"Do you know a producer who would be interested?" Leo asked.

Issy gave up the fight. Her eyes rolled upward.

"She might," Paolo whispered to Issy.

"In the biblical sense, maybe," she whispered back.

He grinned. "Whatever works."

It seemed like an inevitable losing battle and yet Issy wouldn't rush Leo through the smallest part of the inventory. Let her have her time with the artifacts of her life. They—and she—would be gone soon enough.

They'd filmed another hour when the room grew dark. Clouds scudded in to hang above the house, and Issy was hard put not to consider it an omen of the afternoon to come.

Paolo turned on a lamp, pulled the tripod over to take advantage of what light was left.

"You'll need more than a few little lamps," Jillian said. "There used to be some Fresnels in the closet somewhere. The painters used them in bad weather when they painted in the conservatory."

"That's right," Issy said, forgetting for the first time to bristle when talking to her mother.

"I think they got moved to the back storeroom," Fae said. "Come, Paolo, you can carry the light to the Whitaker cause," she intoned.

Paolo followed her but threw an amused "what have I gotten into?" grin toward Issy as he followed Fae out of the room. While they were gone, Jillian fussed over Leo and Issy, and Steph moved to one side and watched.

Fae and Paolo returned laden down with dusty spotlights, which they proceeded to set up on the floor and shelves.

"Mainly from low to high," Jillian ordered. "Makes everyone look taller." She seemed to catch herself. "If that's all right with you, Oops."

They stopped work at three. Issy wanted to have time to regroup before George arrived. She'd considered calling the first ever Whitaker family meeting to discuss a plan of attack, but decided against it. She couldn't keep Jillian out, and if Jillian knew their plans, she would have the upper hand.

Besides, Issy didn't have a plan. She opted for the wait-and-see approach.

They all heard it. The car turning onto the graveled drive. Everyone straightened.

"False alarm," said Fae, who had been watching from the window. "It's Chloe and the children."

There was a collective sigh.

Issy and Paolo went out to meet them.

They ran in as usual. "Is Grammy awake?" Mandy demanded.

"Yes, she's in the parlor. Why?"

"No reason." Mandy ran past her, followed closely by Griff.

"Wait," Chloe called after them.

"Relax. He hasn't come yet."

"Whew, I didn't know whether to bring them in or hold on to them. Not sure if I could even I'd wanted to. Field trip next week to Fun Town. Permission slips were sent home today."

"If there is a next week."

"Do you want me to try and take them back?"

"No, thanks. You go ahead. I'll call and let you know how it goes."

"Should I make myself scarce, too?" Paolo asked. "It's hard to remember I'm not one of the family."

"If you'd rather hang out with Chloe, sure, go ahead."

"*Cara*. Though I would love to run away with the lovely Chloe, I wouldn't desert you and Fae and Leo for anything. If you think I can help." He stopped. Listened. "Was that . . ."

Steph ran through the archway. "He's here. Aunt Fae said to hurry."

"I'll wait in the kitchen," Chloe said.

"I think I'll go with her," Paolo said. "Yell if you need reinforcements."

Issy pushed her hair back, tugged the hem of her T-shirt down, and went to answer the door.

George Whitaker was tall, like Wes, but more thickset, probably from years of sitting behind a desk. Issy hadn't seen him for almost a decade, but he hadn't changed much. The last time she'd seen him, he'd been carrying a briefcase. He was holding one now.

"Issy, how nice to see you." His voice was deep and full-bodied. No hugs, no perfunctory kisses, no pressed hands. "Shall we?" he said, and gestured ahead of him into the parlor.

The rest of the Whitakers were seated there, perfectly posed—even Mandy and Griff, who stood on either side of Leo's chair like figures in a family portrait. And Issy's first thought was of the Bennet women pretending to be busy at their embroidery when Mr. Bingley came to call.

Issy cleared her throat. "Steph, could you please take Mandy and Griff back to the kitchen for a snack?"

For a second she thought Steph would balk, but she stepped from behind the chair, took both younger children by the hand, and ferried them out the door.

George said a cursory hello to everyone as he moved several items aside to make room for his briefcase on the writing table and clicked it open.

"First things first," he said, taking out a sheaf of papers. He stopped to look at Jillian. "Can I assume that Leo has been apprised of the financial situation?"

Fae moved closer to her sister-in-law.

"I know that you say Dan has stolen the money that Wes entrusted to him." Leo lifted her chin.

Issy held her breath. Glanced at Fae. She should have told her grandmother to say nothing. What if she started talking nonsense? George would have additional proof that she belonged in assisted living. But she hadn't told her. She hadn't prepared any of them. She'd been too busy trying to get things inventoried, when she should have been planning a strategy to thwart George and Jillian.

George's mouth tightened. "I'm sorry, Mother. Father misplaced his trust in Dan Bannister. I warned him, but he wouldn't listen, and now we're all going to have to deal with the repercussions."

"Are you sure Dan took the money?"

"My forensic accountants have traced the money out of the country. And have traced Dan to Panama."

"And Vivienne?" Issy asked.

"There was a woman with him. I can only assume it was Vivienne."

Jillian, who had been standing, sank onto the arm of Leo's chair.

"We have to accept the fact that the money is gone for good. Even if we could freeze Dan's bank accounts, it doesn't mean that we would be able to recover the funds. I'm sure we'd all be glad to never see him again. Vivienne is another story. Jillian, if you want me to—"

"No."

"I don't think we want to pursue this in court," he continued.

"Why not?" blurted Issy. "He stole Grammy and Fae's money."

"Firstly, it costs too much. And secondly, think of the scandal."

"Really, Uncle George. You'd let your mother and your aunt live in poverty to prevent a scandal?"

"Well, if you don't care about the family's name, I do."

"We didn't do anything wrong."

"Oops, please, George is just trying to help."

Issy glared at her mother.

George cleared his throat. "Which leaves us with the problem of this house. Jillian and I have discussed this, and I'm sorry, Mother, but it will have to be sold. And since, unfortunately, Wes's will forbids the breaking up of the land in order to sell off any parcel by itself, the whole thing must go."

Leo's hand went to her chest. Jillian knelt beside her. "Mother, you can't keep this house up. It was impossible even with the money. Look at it; it's falling to pieces. You and Aunt Fae will be so much happier in a nice clean place where you can be taken care of. You can enjoy life instead of being strapped all the time."

"We do enjoy life," Fae said.

"Really, Fae, I think you should stay out of this."

"No, Mother," Issy said. "*You* stay out of it. You were never here. You don't get a say. If Leo doesn't want to sell, then we're not selling."

"How do you propose to keep it?" George asked.

"I don't know. I'm working on it."

"It's too late. Fortunately, I have someone interested in the property."

"Waiting in the wings with their millions?"

"Issy," Fae said on a breath, but it was too late for Issy to calm down.

"As a matter of fact. It's quite a nice offer."

"And how do you and Jillian plan on spending millions of dollars?" In her crazed state, Issy heard Leo gasp, Fae's bark of bitter laughter.

"It will be used to pay for Leo and Fae's keep."

"Our keep?" Fae exclaimed. "Leo and I are not barn animals."

"I didn't mean it like that, Fae. Truly, I only want to do what's best."

"Then leave us alone."

"I can't leave you alone. At best, you'll lose the house to back taxes. Better to cut your losses."

Leo pushed herself out of the chair and started toward the door. George went after her. "Mother, be reasonable."

She turned on him. "Max would never have sold the Muses."

"No, he just went blindly off to an unwinnable war and got killed for his effort."

"How dare you." And she slapped him hard across the face.

His hand came reflexively to his cheek. "I apologize, I had no right to say that. But that doesn't change any of the circumstances."

"Issy will figure it out."

"Issy has a job and a life in the city, don't you, Issy? How much longer can you stay here, a week? Ten days? Are your vacations even paid?"

"I—"

"They can't stay here alone."

"I'll stay with them."

"Issy, I admire your loyalty but—"

"I'll stay, too." Stephanie stepped through the doorway and came to stand by Leo.

"Who are you?"

"Stephanie Whitaker. I used to be a Bannister, but not anymore. And I'll stay here and take care of them."

"We will, too!" Griff and Mandy rushed in to join Stephanie and Leo.

Issy hoped Jillian was paying attention because as far as directing a scene, Frank Capra couldn't have done it better.

In spite of knowing it was a losing battle, she felt a fountain of pride and hope. She stepped next to the others. "And we Whitakers stick together."

"I'm a Whitaker, too," George said. "The children are not my problem. If you want to adopt them, be my guest. But they'll be better off going to the system."

"Nooooo," cried Mandy. "I don't want to be an orphan." She started to cry.

"I want my mommy," cried Griff.

Leo pulled them both close. Issy could feel Steph shaking beside her.

"That was gratuitously cruel, George."

"I'm sorry, Mother. I know you don't want to sell, I don't want you to, but the house is too expensive. I couldn't begin to keep it. And Wes has made it impossible for us to keep any of it.

"You can blame me if you must, but Wes, by trying to save it all, has lost it all. Trust me, you and Fae will both be happier once you have this behemoth off your backs.

"Issy. You can finish your inventory if you must and can do it in a week. But I'm having Sotheby's come in." He closed his briefcase. "Mother, Fae."

Fae didn't bother to acknowledge him.

He leaned over and kissed Leo's cheek. He could as well have been kissing wood.

He turned on his heel, and without looking back, left the room.

Jillian jumped off the arm of the chair she was sitting on. "George," she called, and ran after him.

The others stayed right where they were, but Stephanie started to cry.

Mandy and Griff clung to Leo, and Leo, swaying on her feet, held them tight.

Issy looked through the window where she could see George and Jillian standing at George's car. Talking intently. Probably over how fast they could divvy up the money. Issy knew she was being unfair; George might have Leo and Fae's best interests at heart. But the fact remained that the millions that Muses by the Sea would bring would go to their inheritance.

Jillian turned away and stalked toward the house, George jumped into the car and drove away.

Fae helped Leo to her chair and Mandy and Griff climbed up beside her.

"Perhaps Jillian and George are right," Leo said just as Jillian stepped back into the room. "I didn't understand. I was so in love with Wes. Our life together was so perfect, I didn't see how unhappy my children were."

"Mother." Jillian stepped toward her.

Leo stood, nearly dumping Mandy and Griff from their chair. "Excuse me, I need to talk to Wes." And she sedately left the room. They all rushed to the window and watched silently as she crossed the lawn to the knoll.

"Aunt Fae, do something," Steph begged.

"It's not up to me, child."

Steph turned on Jillian. "Why did you have to come? You've wrecked everything. You're not our grandmother, you're a traitor." She gulped back a sob. "And Aunt Issy isn't a mistake. She's the only one who cares. You're just like my mother and I hate you." She ran from the room. Mandy and Griff ran after her, leaving Issy, Fae, and Jillian alone in the parlor.

"Well," Jillian said. "Looks like it's a wrap. Who's up for a drink?"

Chapter 23

I'm sorry," Chloe said. "They heard George's threats and they just ran before I could stop them. It's amazing; kids just seem to have this sixth sense about stuff."

"They were pretty upset," Issy said. "Especially Steph."

"They all ran upstairs. Maybe you should go talk to them."

"And say what?"

Chloe shrugged. "Maybe just that you love them and everything will be all right."

Love them? Until a few days ago, Issy wouldn't have recognized them on the street. But Chloe was right. She did love them. But how on earth could she tell them that everything would be all right. Everything was going to hell. And there didn't seem to be one thing she could do to stop it.

But maybe the kids didn't need to know that yet. Maybe their mother would see the errors of her ways and return. Yeah. To jail; not to raise her children.

"All right. I guess I can do this. I love you. Everything is going to be fine."

Chloe nudged her toward the stairs. "I love you and everything . . ."

She found the three children in Steph's room, sitting on her bed, Steph in the middle with an arm around each of her siblings.

This was so unfair. Summer was a time for kids to have fun, not be deserted by their parents and left in fear of their future.

Mandy saw her and slid off the bed. "Please don't send us to be orphans, Aunt Issy. Please, please." She threw her arms around Issy's waist and clung there.

Issy caught Stephanie's eye and was hit with a staggering intensity of hope, defiance, embarrassment, and fear.

"You were fierce, girl."

"I'm not in trouble?"

What to say? They were all in trouble. "Nope. And thanks for sticking up for me."

"Well, it's true."

"Still nice to hear."

"So what are you going to do with us?"

"Uh, nothing for the moment. Wait for your mother to come back."

Steph flicked a look at Griff and Mandy. "I was thinking. We could live in one of those little cabins on the property. I'll get a job and take care of them. You wouldn't even know we were there."

"But I want to live here with Grammy."

"Shut up, Mandy. Do you want to go to foster care?"

Mandy shook her head violently. "No, no," she cried. "I'll live in a cabin. I won't be any trouble."

"I'll live in a cabin, Stephie," Griff said without taking his thumb out of his mouth.

"Nobody's going to have to live in a cabin," Issy said.

Griff's thumb came out of his mouth. "Are you going to take care of us, Auntie Issy?"

Issy looked at those three kids, the hopeful faces. She didn't think "everything will be fine" would work in this case. But what could she say?

Mandy looked up from where she was still clinging to her waist. "Are you, Aunt Issy?"

Issy's stomach turned over. "Of course I am."

Then all three were on their feet and hugging her and Issy wondered what she had just done. Actually she didn't wonder at all. She'd just sealed her fate—and theirs.

"HOW DID IT go?" Paolo asked as he handed her a glass of wine.

"We raided the cellar," Chloe said. "Hope that's okay."

"Of course."

"So how *did* it go?"

"I think I told them that they could live with me."

Paolo choked on his wine. "You mean like adopt them?"

"I guess. I mean, what else could I do?"

"Nothing," Paolo said. "It's what family does. But it's hard to imagine you with three ready-made children. What will you do when you're traveling? *Cara*, you do a lot of traveling."

"Hire a housekeeper?"

Paolo just looked at her. They both knew she couldn't afford a housekeeper on her salary. She could barely afford her one-bedroom unrenovated apartment.

"Or . . ." From the moment she'd walked into Muses by the Sea last Thursday, she'd had a feeling. A feeling that she was home, that she was where she belonged, and that there was a reason she was back. "I could try to save the Muses."

"How?" Chloe blurted.

"I don't know. Turn the rooms on the first floor into a gallery. Art as it looks in the home where it was created. I haven't really thought it out, because it seemed so farfetched. Not just hanging on a wall or numbered in a case, but in its historical context. With Leo giving the details. Not in person, it would be too tiring, but on video or a recorded audio tour."

"I doubt if the first few years would even pay your taxes," Paolo said.

"I know. I'd probably have to get a job."

"You could freelance," Paolo suggested. "Leo and Fae could watch the kids while you were gone. Dell won't like not having you around, though."

"Let's not tell Dell."

"No worries with that one."

Issy frowned. "He hasn't called you to apologize? That's so unlike Dell."

"Oh, he's called several times."

"Paolo! What did you say?"

"I didn't answer."

"Why not?" Chloe asked.

"I'm afraid he might make me an offer I can't refuse." He smiled at her and Issy felt a pang of affection and an echo of envy.

"Besides, how could I work for you if I go back?"

"If I had a dime you'd be the first person I'd hire, but I don't. You can't depend on me."

"Everyone depends on you, *cara*. You never let them down."

Issy sighed. "I might this time."

"You know, the sun porch would make a perfect little tearoom," Chloe said. "Come see the exhibit, stroll the grounds, have a light lunch. It's perfect."

Issy laughed.

"Or dinner," Paolo added. "I can see it. A string quartet playing. Twinkling white lights in the trees and the ocean views from every table."

"The sun porch doesn't look over the ocean," Issy reminded him.

"Not the sun porch. The conservatory. It would be magnificent."

"It would," Chloe said, her eyes growing bright. "And weddings. People would pay a fortune to get married here."

"And an artist retreat," said Issy, catching some of their enthusiasm. "Workshops and concerts and—it would take a fortune that we don't have and Leo would have to approve it. I can't imagine her okaying an idea that would have strangers tromping through the house. The amount of security needed would be staggering.

"Please don't even mention the idea to Leo. I don't want her any more upset than she is."

Paolo leaned back in his chair. "I don't know why everyone cossets Leo so much. When she's in the groove she's as with it and strong as anyone."

"I guess it's because my grandfather always took care of her—like she was a precious, fragile work of art. Everyone else just picked up the habit, I guess."

"And now she's used to it," Paolo said. "I get it. So who wants dinner?"

"You two go ahead. I think I'll stay with the kids tonight. A chance to bond."

"With Jillian, too?"

Issy made a sour face.

"You're going to have to talk to her, come to some kind of

peaceful coexistence or something. You can't just go about every day pretending she doesn't exist."

"I don't see why not."

Paolo shook his head and kissed her cheek. "I'll just get my wallet."

FOR THE NEXT two days Issy did manage to ignore her mother. They all still met in the mornings for filming. Jillian consulted with Leo over wardrobe and put herself in charge of makeup and stage setting. Issy longed to ask her why, but didn't. Maybe she was afraid of the answer.

They worked with a vengeance, turning on extra lights when the clouds rolled in, taking a break and going down to the beach when the sun came out again. Steph and Paolo worked furiously to upload the video to the computer.

Leo became more and more animated as she told the provenance of each piece of art. She retold the story she'd told Issy on her first day home from the hospital about Lois Long. Standing at the mantel and pointing gracefully to the dress as she laughed about the sight of Lois clad in her slip with her shoes in her hand as she ran to the car to take her back to Manhattan.

"A clergyman's daughter." She laughed delightedly. "Before my day, of course."

She flirted with the camera, glowed with happy memories, grew introspective at the tragedies that were bound to occur.

"He was such a young man. Heroin, they said. It was tragic. Such a talent and so senseless . . ." She trailed off, looked out the window to the sea.

As the hours passed it seemed to Issy that it was taking Leo longer and longer to come back from her memories. And she didn't think that was a good thing.

Maybe they were doing more harm than good by asking her to dwell on the history and past of the Muses.

They hadn't heard from George. Jillian swore she'd gone after him to persuade him to rethink his intention to sell the Muses. Issy had to admit that she'd been more helpful in the few days since his visit.

The weather continued to waffle between rain and sunshine. Whenever they weren't working and the sun came out, Leo went out to the bluff to sit with Wes and Max. It was almost as if she were saying good-bye. That she knew before any of them were willing to admit that she would be leaving the Muses. Then Issy and Paolo and Steph would throw themselves into work more than ever, as if determination alone could keep the Muses alive.

Until Saturday morning when Stephanie ran downstairs to report that Mandy and Griff weren't in their rooms. "I looked for them outside but they're gone. Where could they go?"

They divided up and searched the house. Issy took the west wing, thinking that curiosity might have led them to a part of the house that was no longer used. She looked in the first five bedrooms and was about to leave when she heard laughing and singing.

She stopped, listened again. Heard squeals of delight. She turned back and saw an open door at the end of the hallway. The entrance to one of the attics. How on earth had they found it? It hadn't even occurred to her to tell them what was off-limits. And the attic was bound to be dangerous.

Issy ran down the hall and climbed the stairs two at a time, then stopped at the open door. A light was on. An old steamer trunk was open and Griff and Mandy were galloping around a standing figure who, at first sight, Issy thought was Leo.

She was about to chastise her grandmother for climbing the steep stairs, when she realized that it was Jillian. She was wearing a ridiculously large-brimmed Ascot hat with a huge taffeta bow. A feather boa was wrapped around her neck and trailed nearly to the floor.

"Look, Aunt Issy," Mandy squealed. "Look what we found. A whole trunk of costumes. We're going to wear them to story hour. Grandma helped—"

She froze midsentence. The color drained from her face and her little body sagged. She exchanged a frantic look with Griff, then slowly turned her head to look up at Jillian.

Issy held her breath. So help her, she would scratch Jillian's eyes out if she snapped the kid's head off for having fun and forgetting.

"Well, we want to look our best for the parade to town, don't we?" Jillian said, surprising them all. Mandy and Griff slumped even more, this time in relief.

But Issy didn't relax. She knew from experience that Jillian knew how to wait until you were an unsuspecting prey. "Then you'd better hurry down and get some breakfast. Fae will be back from her cottage to pick us up in just a few minutes."

Mandy and Griff hurried to the stairs.

"Hold on to the banister," Issy called after them, keeping her eye on Jillian. "Do you need help putting the rest back?"

"Thank you, no. I can manage."

"Okay, then. I'd better go . . ." Issy couldn't think of anything else to say. So she followed the kids down the stairs.

When she entered the kitchen, Mandy, Griff, and Steph had their heads together.

"Did she really call Jillian Grandma?" Steph asked.

"She did." Issy could hardly contain her smile.

"Two thumbs up, sister mine," Steph said. "You sometimes amaze me."

"Is she mad?" Mandy asked.

Issy shook her head.

"I'm not in trouble?"

"No."

"Whew."

They just had time for cut-up apples and bran muffins before Fae came through the kitchen door. She was dressed even more flamboyantly than usual in a bright red ankle-length skirt. Her hair was tied back with a scarf filled with bronze- and silver-colored bangles.

Now Issy understood Steph's bright red harem pants and shiny silver tunic. She and Fae were color coordinated.

Just as Issy was about to go tell Leo they were leaving, she and Jillian appeared in the doorway, Jillian still in her wide-brimmed hat and Leo wearing yellow Chinese pajamas left from an earlier era. And right behind them, standing between the two ladies, was Paolo, wearing black shorts and tee with a white silk vest and bow tie. He cradled a top hat in the crook of his elbow.

Issy was feeling underdressed, when Paolo pulled his free hand from behind his back and produced a felt fedora, which he placed on her head.

Fae went to the door, turned around, and cast her gaze over her ragtag followers. "Never say the Whitakers went out with a whimper." She swallowed convulsively. "Onward and to the village."

They walked behind the red wagon, Paolo paying acute attention to Leo. But she seemed strong and they only slowed down once to parcel out the bubble mixture. Then they marched into town, bestowing smiles and bubbles on everyone they passed.

"Leo, good to see you out and about," called Howard Klein from the post office door.

"Brava," yelled someone else whom Issy didn't recognize but who Fae and Leo seemed to know quite well.

People applauded as they passed and Issy didn't know if it was for Fae, Leo, or Jillian York.

By the time they reached the square they had gathered quite a crowd. *Almost as if they knew they were watching a final performance.* Had they heard that the Muses was about to be sold, that the family would be turned out, and God only knew what would replace it. Condos and tennis clubs, restaurants that would send the Fisherman's Den and most of the other local establishments out of business.

For the first time in her life, Issy felt anger toward her grandfather, so consumed by his love for Leo and his desire to protect her that he hadn't taken care of the one thing that could destroy her.

Fae took longer than usual to find the spot for her drawing, but finally she pulled the wagon to the side, knelt on her gardening pad, and opened her chalk box.

"Today I'm going to tell you the story of Idril and Tuor."

Everyone looked blank, including Issy.

"Tolkien," Paolo said. "She never ceases to amaze." He moved closer.

"It's a story not often told. Tuor was born of man in the year 472 in the First Age of Middle-earth."

Murmurs from the crowd as they caught on.

"Born of man but left by his grieving mother with the elves before she died."

A swaddled baby appeared on the sidewalk, and with a few flourishes of color, the face of a grieving mother.

"He was raised by the elves of Sindarin and grew into a fine young man, fair of face and golden haired, tall and strong and valiant." One piece of chalk was dropped into the box, another taken out. A few deft strokes revealed a head and shoulders, a face and waving blond hair that reached to his shoulders. Fae threw the kneeling pad to the side and scooted back as she carried his torso and legs to the next concrete square. A tunic of white and blue, dark tights, and knee boots.

She spoke slowly and compellingly, mesmerizing her audience as her hand flew over the rough surface of the sidewalk.

"He was captured by the Easterlings, from whom he escaped after three years. He roamed the earth until the Lord of the Waters made himself manifest and gave him a cloak of shadow to hide him from his enemies."

And a warrior rose from deep blue waves. A wild beard rippled across the concrete and spilled into the grass.

"Together they went to the hidden kingdom of Gondolin, where Tuor fell in love with Idril, who returned his love."

She began drawing another figure, smaller and more delicate, who stood by Tuor's side.

"But it was not to be. She was already loved by another, an influential elf who turned others against Tuor. For she was elven and Tuor was man. She had eternal life, but he would age and die."

Under her fingers a woman appeared, also blond with hair wrapped around her head into a crown, her face turned toward Tuor's. Fae began to define the picture, finish off lines, fill in empty spaces.

No one left.

"When Gondolin was attacked and pillaged, Tuor and Idril fled with a small band of survivors."

Beneath their feet she drew red and orange flames shooting through the unfilled spaces.

"Tuor began to feel old and he built a ship to take him to the West."

Before their eyes and Fae's hand, Tuor's blond hair grew silver and longer, longer, until it reached his waist.

"And though Idril remained young, her hair grew silver, too. They left together for the west and it is said that Tuor alone of mortal men was granted immortal life to be with his lady love."

During her last words, the fire turned into a brilliant sunset beneath their feet. Fae scrambled on all fours to a square above the story picture, and almost magically, two small figures, hand in hand, turned their backs and walked into the future.

"And that is the story of Tuor and Idril."

At that moment Steph, who had been kneeling next to Fae, looked up, convulsed, and started to stand. Fae grabbed her by the arm and stopped her.

But their eyes met and held and Issy knew that some kind of communication passed between them, the eccentric great-aunt and the tween. Then they looked away.

It was a gesture so fast and so efficient Issy wasn't sure how to read it. Or if it meant anything at all.

She looked into the crowd, half expecting to see Vivienne hiding there, but there was no one but the spectators, who broke into applause that grew into an extended show of appreciation.

"Whoa," Paolo said. "Just whoa."

They looked to Leo, but she had tears in her eyes and they looked away. Jillian was gone.

FAE BEGAN PUTTING her chalk back in the tackle box. There were broken pieces and bits rubbed down to the nub scattered around her. She'd drawn with a vengeance today and she was tired. When she took her supplies back to the cottage, she would stay there for a while.

The story of Tuor and Idril was a story close to her heart, and if she had taken a little liberty with it, then so be it. Tuor and Idril deserved their life together. And Steph deserved a future filled with dreams and possibilities.

But dreams easily turned to nightmares and possibilities to disappointments. Fae and Leo had been clueless when Issy and Vivienne had come to them. Two middle-aged women, one who had given birth to three children but was sometimes hardly more than a child herself. And Fae, who had been too wrapped up in her own life and her own disappointments to be much of a guiding force.

But now she'd done her best for Steph. She'd sent her off with the others to get ice cream. It was hard to look into those blue Whitaker eyes and know that she might never see them again. It would all depend . . .

No. It had been decided. She pushed to her feet. Slower today even than last week. She returned the tackle box to the wagon and pulled it toward home. She stopped to look back briefly at her drawing, knowing that already it was beginning to fade, that it would grow dimmer with the first raindrop, and dimmer still with the next.

And with the storm it would disappear, and soon be forgotten altogether. And so, too, would she.

THEY WAITED FOR Fae outside the ice cream store. Another Saturday of dessert before lunch and Issy was considering declaring it a Whitaker tradition, except there might not be any more Whitaker traditions.

When Fae finally arrived, the cones were gone, and Jillian had joined them. Issy offered to get her ice cream, but Fae said she just wanted to go home, and kept walking. So home they went. Their little band of dressed-up ice-cream-stuffed Whitakers.

Fae led the way; Steph followed several feet behind her. No one attempted to catch up.

Today had been special. Fae was still in her own world and they knew not to bother her there.

The sun beat down and the day was humid and hot, and they were all hot and tired and a little depleted by the time they reached the gates of the Muses. Issy was considering declaring a holiday and spending the afternoon on the beach before her "date" with Ben, when she realized the others had stopped.

She peered past them to see two cars parked in front of the mansion. A black sedan and a squad car. A squad car?

Heart racing, Issy rushed past the others. She wanted to find out the news first in case it was bad. But before she could reach the vehicles, the sedan door opened. A man got out, walked over to the squad car, and opened the back door.

A woman got out. First one foot, then the other. Déjà vu, but Jillian was already there and these feet were wearing running shoes.

"Mommy!" Mandy and Griff cried, and ran to Vivienne's outstretched arms.

Chapter 24

W ell," said Jillian. "That's a relief."

Steph shook her head, once, twice, and kept shaking it, then she turned and ran toward the woods.

Issy started to run after her, but Detective Griggs was striding toward her. "She was picked up for breaking and entering. I heard it over the radio, recognized the address from my report. Did you know she was back?"

Issy shook her head. Stopped herself or she might be running into the woods after Steph. "This is the first we heard."

"But you didn't call me on Saturday like we agreed."

"My grandmother Leonore Whitaker—I don't believe you met her." Issy paused to bring Fae and Leo up to speed and introduce them to the detective. "Vivienne told her that she would be gone for a while and not to worry. Vivienne left a message on the answering machine to the same effect." She ended with a shrug. "You said breaking and entering?"

"Yes." Detective Griggs grimaced. "Into what she says she thought was her own home, but it turns out that Mr. Bannister had sold it without her knowledge."

"Can he do that?"

"I don't know the particulars of the case. One of the neighbors reported seeing someone breaking a window and climbing into the house."

"Is she under arrest?"

"The new owners were contacted and they won't pursue the case if she agrees to pay damages, which she did."

With what? Leo's estate money? And how can she even be back in the country without being arrested? *Because no one knows about the money.* Issy was so tempted to say take her back, because she didn't for a second believe that Vivienne had brought the stolen money with her.

"She won't have to post bail if someone here will promise she isn't a flight risk." Issy looked over to where Vivienne was fawning over her children. The caring, attentive mother, which conveniently prevented her from actually having to deal with the situation.

Jillian stepped forward and gave the detective a radiant smile. "She's my daughter, Detective. I can vouch for her."

Issy almost snorted out loud. Jillian was actually fessing up to the fact she was old enough to have daughter that age? And how the hell could she vouch for Vivienne when God only knew the last time she'd seen either of her daughters. At least as far as Issy knew; maybe Jillian and Vivienne had always kept in touch.

And in the midst of all their trouble, Issy choked on the humiliation of rejection and Vivienne's childhood taunts. *You're the reason Mommy dumped us here. You're ugly and stupid and nobody loves you. You're just a big oops.*

Issy fought the feelings down. She had a responsibility and the first duty of that responsibility was to find out about the money.

"Well, thank you, Detective Griggs. We're very appreciative."

Griggs nodded and walked back to his car. It galvanized the enchanted group into action. They rushed toward Vivienne, and they all walked toward the house together as the police cars drove away.

Griff and Mandy glommed on to Vivienne's side, each chattering over the other.

". . . and Ben took us to find the frog and Griff fell in."

"No, I didn't."

"And I tried to save him but he pulled me in and we both got wet and had to change our clothes."

"And we go swimming at the cove."

"Chloe picks us up every day to go to camp at her school."

"It's so much fun."

"Can we stay at Grammy's until camp is over?"

"Grammy doesn't mind, do you, Grammy?"

"I love having you," Leo said into the sliver of silence while Mandy and Griff took a breath.

"And we get to dress up."

"Guess what I am?" Mandy twirled around.

"Can we stay, please! Please?"

"Of course we can." Vivienne looked at Leo. She took after their mother, tall, lithesome, with auburn hair that she wore long until high school, when she styled it to every passing fad. Now she had one of those sleek suburban mom cuts. The kind of hair that swayed in the breeze but never seemed to get in their eyes when they were on the tennis courts.

Today the look turned Issy's stomach. And she wondered if Leo was seeing a younger Jillian. If she even knew who Vivienne was.

"Grammy, it's not my fault. He took all the money. I'm

sorry, so sorry." Vivienne fell on her knees at her grand-mother's feet. "He even sold our house. We have nowhere else to go."

"Guess I'm not the only actress in this family," Jillian said under her breath.

"You don't believe her?" Issy asked.

"Do you?"

"Of course you can stay," Leo said. "We'll make up the Harbor Room for you. How would that be?"

Vivienne sniffed, hiccuped, nodded.

Issy's fists tightened. Paolo, who had silently watched the show, moved a little closer, ran his thumb down her spine. *"Calma, sta' calma."*

She sucked in a breath, let it out slowly.

"You're welcome to stay as long as you like," Leo continued.

"Hooray," Griff shouted.

"Yay!" Mandy echoed.

"I need a bath," Vivienne announced, and started toward the archway, Mandy and Griff at her heels.

Issy started after her. If she thought she could just show up like nothing had happened, she was sorely wrong.

Jillian beat her to it. "And when you finish your bath we'll have happy hour. And you can tell us all about what you've been doing lately."

Issy doubted if anyone missed the subtext of her statement. If Jillian had ever had a *Mommie Dearest* moment, this was it.

Vivienne nodded reluctantly and let Leo help her up the stairs.

"Do you think Leo even knows who she is?" Jillian asked.

"I have no idea," Issy said, and left to search for Stephanie.

STEPHANIE RAN, SHE didn't know where, she didn't care. Her mother was back and she should be happy; she'd been so worried, but now . . . She didn't want to go back to her life in Guilford. She wouldn't go back.

She ran through the woods past the first little cottage. She didn't know where she was going, but she couldn't go back to the Muses now that she'd lost it in front of everybody. It was too embarrassing. She could only go to Fae's when Fae was with her. It was part of their bargain.

Her side started to hurt and there was snot running out of her nose. She wiped her arm across it but she didn't slow down. Once she tripped on a stone sticking out of the dirt. She barely felt it. She just wanted to be alone. Alone to turn back time. To make it so she would never have to leave the Muses or Grammy or Fae or Issy.

The pain jabbed in her side and she had to slow down or she was going to throw up. She saw the second cottage through the trees and ran toward it. Collapsed on the step, sucking in deep breaths of air.

She could live here. Even if Griff and Mandy wanted to go back home, she didn't. She froze. She heard something inside the cottage. Something being knocked over. A wild animal looking for food. A raccoon or something that might bite—or a psychopath.

She jumped up, and gripping her side, she started running again. Onward as if her feet knew the way. And they did. She burst onto the meadow just as the sun came out in a blinding light. The little blue flowers had just started blooming and she ran through them, mindless of the harm she was doing.

She collapsed on her knees just as a huge wail erupted from

her throat and she threw herself on the ground and cried until she was too exhausted to breathe. Then she just lay on the ground feeling nothing but that it was the end of her world.

She must have fallen asleep because the voice came to her through a haze.

"Why are you so sad, child?"

Stephanie knew that voice. It sounded like honey and coffee, and old and young. She'd never heard it but she knew it. She lifted her head but she already knew who would be there. He was standing over her, so tall, and strong, his feet planted, his arms crossed. The sun shone behind him, shadowing everything but his silhouette, but she knew him.

Steph sat up, started to rise, but he stopped her with a gesture.

"I want to stay here where I belong."

He chuckled. "In the meadow?"

She nodded. "With Grammy, Aunt Fae, and Issy. I'm like them, like you. This is where I . . . I feel like myself. Not in Guilford. None of that makes sense. This does. But my mother came back and she'll make us leave."

"Everyone has to leave eventually."

Steph sniffed. "You mean like die? You don't. Elves don't die."

"Hmm." His voice was deep but light, like lemon ice and chocolate cake. "In this world they do."

"But in the story—"

"Stephanie Whitaker, you are an important part of this story."

"I am?"

He nodded. "You are a special young woman and I know you are going to do something remarkable with your life."

"Can you make it so I can stay here?"

"No. I myself am moving on."

Steph's lip trembled. "Are you taking Aunt Fae with you?"

"I hope so."

"Then it's true."

"It's necessary."

"I understand. I guess. I'll miss her." Her mouth twisted. "I'll miss you, too." She thought he stepped toward her, but he stopped.

"Life is about change. Don't be afraid. Welcome it. And now, Stephanie Whitaker, I must leave you. Good-bye."

"Bye."

He stepped out of the light and Steph shut her eyes against the sudden glare. Even when she opened them again it took seconds for her to see more than the black dots left by the sun.

And when she could see again, she was in the meadow alone.

ISSY KEPT ON the lookout for Steph as she walked across the lawn to the woods. She was sure she must be watching from the trees. Maybe it was shock that had caused her to flee—that flight-or-fight-response thing—but wouldn't she want to be with her mother? Didn't she miss her like the two younger children did?

She took the path through the trees, thankful Steph was wearing red today. It would be easy to spot. She took her time, searching for any bit of color that might betray the girl's hiding place. It was an old woods, with some brush, but not so thick that it kept the light out.

She stayed on the path until she reached the fork that led to Fae's cottage. She wondered if Steph had been there before. If she knew the way. She took that path at a trot but stopped before she came to the clearing. Fae liked her privacy, and with

Fae back at the house, Issy didn't feel comfortable going any closer.

"Steph! Stephanie, are you there?"

Nothing. "It's all right, it's just me, you can come out." Issy waited, but Stephanie didn't appear.

She turned in a full circle, then retraced her steps until she got to the fork in the path; decided on the second fork and saw one of the old cabins off to the side. Steph had been talking about wanting to live in one of the cottages. Perhaps she already had a special place in one of them just as Issy had so many years before.

They'd all had names in those days. After the muses. She walked through the brush and climbed up to the tiny porch. Tried to make out the name above the door, but could only make out the faded color of the letters. She knew it spelled out Calliope, muse of epic poetry. It had once been Issy's kingdom of play. But it looked deserted now. She tried the door. It was locked. All of the cottages must be locked.

She peered in the window, saw only shadows, the window was stuck shut. She moved on.

"Steph! Where are you? Please come out. I just want to talk."

She walked away from the cabin, wondering how long Vivienne would be in the bath. Issy didn't want to miss one word of her story. And she had a few questions that she needed answered.

She tried the next two cabins; both were locked and looked as if they hadn't been disturbed in ages. Vines even grew over the porch floor of the one called Thalia. One day it might be completely covered in leaves.

She was getting deeper into the woods and farther from the

house and still no sign of Stephanie. There was one more cottage on this side of the main house. She'd check it out but then she'd have to go back. She doubted if Steph would have run this far.

This cottage was larger than most of the others, set back from the path, with room for chairs and a table and a narrow bed. It was a very popular place to meet.

She stopped just to look, then she walked up the narrow footpath to the porch. Up the steps, across the floor, and—the door was ajar.

"Stephanie?" Issy listened; hearing no reply, she tiptoed closer. "Steph?"

It was all well and good if Steph was really inside, but after having spent years in the big cities of the world, Issy didn't want to take any chance of stumbling over a squatter or worse.

She stepped up to the threshold, pushed the door open with her foot. No one came running out. She opened it wider. "Steph, are you in here?" She stepped inside.

Dust motes floated in the air, caught by the sunlight that radiated down from the skylight in the roof and created a nimbus of light around a wooden easel positioned dead center.

The smell of turpentine still hung in the air as if someone had finished a painting and gone home to dinner.

She peered into the corners. No Stephanie. But there were several easels, one holding a half-finished painting. Other canvases sat three or four deep around the perimeter of the room. The center spotlight made the corners murkier, but she could tell that some of the canvases had been painted and some were blank. And sitting on the single chair was a can of turpentine and a tackle box holding tubes of time-hardened paints. Left and for some reason forgotten.

She leaned down to look at a finished canvas. A painting of the sea and a secluded glade, the light playing impishly through the trees and spilling onto the beach. There was something familiar about it.

She picked it up and placed it on the easel, peered more closely. Stood back and looked again. Repositioned the easel under the skylight. One side of her brain was seeing one thing, the other denying what she saw. While her gut screamed. OMG.

There was no mistaking that play of light and dark, those brushstrokes. The subject matter.

She was looking at an Adam Ellis painting. She was sure of it. So this is where he had come to paint. There had been whispering about Fae and Adam for years before he died, and for years before that, if you could believe the things people said. He'd married young and stayed married until he drove his car off the bridge.

But maybe he came here to paint instead of to the conservatory and its diffused light, because it put him closer to Fae. Had they met here in secret? And more importantly. Were there more of these?

Because suddenly Issy could see a way out of their financial dilemma. If they could be authenticated as real Adam Ellis paintings, they would be worth a fortune. And since the Whitakers were in possession of them, wouldn't the paintings belong to them?

She picked up another painting, put it on the easel. Same brushstrokes, light and dark style, and there in the corner was Adam Ellis's signature.

Excitement thrummed through her and for a moment she forgot that Steph was out there alone, upset, maybe lost.

If the canvases really had been painted by Ellis . . . Heavens.

But if they were, why had they been left here all those years? It was bad enough that valuable artwork was left in the attic to disintegrate. But out here was little better than a shed.

How had they survived?

Her first thought was they hadn't. That they'd been stolen out of the house or attic and stored here by Vivienne and Dan. But there were a lot of paintings here. Many more than the Whitakers had ever owned.

There was another explanation for their presence. One she didn't want to contemplate. That someone else had painted them. That either Dan and Vivienne had hired someone to forge them so they could sell them as originals or that . . . Issy wouldn't believe the other possibility.

Fae could draw wonderfully but she only worked in chalk. *As far as you know, Issy. And why would Fae do such a thing? To keep closer to his memory?* It was possible. Leo sat out by the graves of her husband and her firstborn all the time. Maybe Fae felt closer to Adam painting in his style.

Surely she hadn't tried to sell any of them.

Issy needed to get a second opinion but she didn't dare. Knowledge of a cache of undiscovered Ellis paintings could create chaos in the art world. And if it turned out they weren't Ellises, it might implicate someone in her family as a forger. She couldn't even tell Paolo. She didn't want to get him in trouble by asking him to be an accomplice.

She'd just lock the door and take time to think. Do some research. Whether the paintings had been sitting there for the last ten years or whether they were newly painted by her aunt Fae, one more day wouldn't matter.

As earth-shattering as this discovery might be, she had more important things to worry about right now.

The mere thought that something could be more important than a find like this staggered her. The thought that a headstrong, "attitudinous" tween could be that thing finished her off.

Family. She was family.

Issy backed out the door, closed it, and realized she didn't have the key to lock it. But someone did. Someone must have been in the cabin recently or the door wouldn't have been left ajar. And they would be coming back. She wanted to wait to find out who it was. But did she really? She had to find Steph. That was what was important. She was out in the woods somewhere either too embarrassed and humiliated to return to the Muses or too lost to find her way home.

Issy could relate. She'd had some pretty tough years herself and she had to admit seeing her sister today had affected her pretty much the same way it had affected Steph. Run.

Then a worse thought struck her. What if Steph had discovered someone in the little cottage. The forger? Or a predator. Issy missed the step and fell to one knee. What if he had Steph?

Issy pushed to her feet and whipped around a full threesixty. No obvious signs of a struggle. *Sta' calma*. No one was here. Someone had been here. Probably just Aunt Fae, but maybe not. And she was wasting time.

"Steph!" she called. "Steph! Answer me!"

And there she was walking down the path that ran through the woods to the meadow and beyond.

Issy ran to meet her. "Are you okay?"

Steph barely looked at her, but Issy could see she'd been crying. No surprise there.

"I don't want to go back to Guilford."

"I know." And from the sounds of things, she wouldn't be.

"Mandy and Griff have pleaded to stay until the end of camp. That gives you some time."

"It doesn't matter."

Issy empathized. She'd felt the same way when she'd left for college, like Adam and Eve must have felt when they were kicked out of the Garden of Eden. The truck ride with Ben to the university, him carrying on about the future and adventure, and her only longing for the safety of the past and home.

He'd been right, of course. They all had. But it took years for her to realize it. And Steph was only twelve. Issy smiled thinking about that first morning at breakfast. Ben giving her grief about being a teenager and her confessing she was only twelve.

If Issy hadn't been worried about so many things, she would have known right then that she was committed to this family once and for all. They'd sent her to college, not just to get an education and not because they wanted to be alone together. But because they wanted her to return of her own free will, because she chose to be here above everywhere else.

She sensed there was another turning point coming up. She didn't know quite what it would be, but she knew who she wanted to share it with. The person who she now realized had always been there for her, who had helped her to see things clearly. Who'd always been a part of her life, even when she wasn't around. Fortunately, she was meeting him for dinner that night.

She and Steph began walking back toward the house; Issy slung an arm around the younger girl's shoulders. "Let me tell you a story about a girl."

Chapter 25

Steph balked at going inside the house.

"Trust me, I'm not relishing this any more than you are," Issy said, and steered them both up the front steps. But when they walked into the parlor, they only found Jillian and Paolo. Jillian held up her glass.

"A little early for happy hour, I realize, but really someone has to keep up appearances."

"Where's my—where's Vivienne?" Steph asked.

Jillian smiled slowly, accepting the hit. "In bed. Fae has gone off to her own cottage and said she won't be back until late. Leo is upstairs playing step-and-fetch-it for the prodigal grand-daughter. There wasn't a thing I could do, so I came down here. Paolo graciously offered to keep me company, though I'm told you're both going out tonight."

"There is still plenty of time to talk to Vivienne." Issy turned to go upstairs.

"There's plenty of time when you get back. I spiked her drink."

Issy spun around. "With what? How long is she going to be out?"

Jillian did the shrug she was known for. "Four to six hours, I imagine. I thought we might want to have a plan before we talk to her."

"Or time for George to get here?"

"Actually I didn't call him. And I thought we might want to question her once the kiddies are asleep."

"Oh," Issy said.

"I'm staying up," Steph said.

That shrug again. "Suit yourself. But it's not a good feeling to find out your mother isn't what you want her to be, is it, Oops?"

"You're awful," Steph said, and ran out of the room.

"Really, Jillian, was that necessary? The kid's had a hard enough day as it is. She doesn't need you rubbing her nose in it."

"Ah Oops, you have such a way with words. Paolo here has been telling me you've done quite well for yourself."

"Thanks for asking."

Jillian smiled. It actually looked genuine. "I'm a selfish person, Oops. You of all people should know that. Some people are just born that way. But . . ."

She got up and crossed to the drinks cabinet. "I think even I don't have the heart to separate Leo from Wes or Fae from whatever keeps her here."

"Leo keeps her here," Issy said. "She promised Wes before he died."

"Really? That is loyalty. Why didn't you come to the funeral? Even I left Henri—or was it Eduardo?— to make the trip."

"No one told me he was dead."

"Oh, that's right. It was during that big installation of yours in Paris. I think the consensus was they didn't want to bother you."

"Bother me? Did they actually think I would ever be too busy to come to my own grandfather's funeral? The only father figure I ever knew? Really?"

"I imagine they wanted to spare you from the catfight that ensued."

"What catfight?"

"The will," Jillian intoned, and shuddered dramatically. She took her newly poured drink back to the sofa. "It was like *It's a Wonderful Life* meets *Kill Bill*. Not pretty."

"Uncle George and Dan Bannister?"

"And poor John Renfroe trying to whereas and wherefore through the riot. Leo escaped to the freshly dug grave. Fae began to dance among the guests and George threatened to have them both committed just so Dan couldn't get his hands on the money. Looks like George was right."

"Maybe about Dan, but not about having them committed."

"No, they're perfectly happy in their bizarrely constructed existence. But even you have to admit they need to have—shall we say—help. Unfortunately, Dan Bannister put paid to that." Jillian took a sip of her drink. "And everything else."

"Maybe not," Issy said.

"Have a scheme in mind, Oops?"

"Perhaps. I'm going to take a shower and then Paolo and I are going out." No one needed to know they weren't going out together. "Be sure Vivienne is awake when we get back and don't ask her any questions until we do."

Paolo followed her out and caught up to her on the stairs. "Hell, the plot thickens. Do you want me to come back after dinner or make myself scarce?"

"I don't know. I mean . . ." She wanted so badly to tell him what she found—thought she found—but she couldn't take the chance. Not that she thought he couldn't be trusted, but there might be repercussions that could be the end of both their careers for sure. "Are you saying things are progressing rapidly with you and Chloe?"

"On the horizon, perhaps. But my first loyalty is to you." He grinned. "For now."

WHEN THEY MET downstairs at six, Issy had changed several times and had finally settled on her alternate gallery dress and strappy summer heels that she'd fortunately packed for the trip to D.C.

"*Mama mia,* as they say," Paolo said. "You look divine."

"Chloe said Ben was wearing a suit."

"Sounds serious."

"It's a little weird. He's Chloe's big brother."

"He's also a man, *cara.* Or haven't you noticed?"

"I've noticed. It's still a little weird. And I probably should stick around here in case Vivienne wakes up and tries to leave. I want to know what happened to Leo's money."

"I wouldn't worry. I'm pretty certain Jillian wants to know that as much as you do."

"That's why she's still here, isn't it? To get her share of whatever money there is."

Paolo opened the passenger door of the Alfa Romeo for her. "When she first arrived I had her pegged as a total mercenary, but I'm not sure. She seems to be going through a little softening. She actually helped Griff make a P, B, and J. It was a pathetic mess. I could have offered to help but it was vastly entertaining. So I just watched."

"Jillian and peanut butter? The mind boggles."

"Do you ever call her Mother?"

"Nope." They got into the car. "I'm a Whitaker, since I've never been sure whether I was born a York or something else. Speculation was rife. I consider Leo and Wes my parents and grandparents."

"I'm glad you appreciate them, but it's an awfully big chip to carry around especially wearing that dress."

She frowned at him. "I don't have a chip. Just telling it like it is." She'd been shocked, then angry at first, when she'd first discovered the tabloid article in a pile of old magazines.

"Uh-huh."

"Okay, maybe a little chip. But she did leave us."

"In good hands. Or at least in loving if not the most experienced hands."

"True."

They parked in front of Chloe's new house and met Ben crossing the street.

Chloe ran out to meet them. "Come in. It still smells a little like polyurethane but it's home sweet home." She hustled them inside.

One whiff of the new floors and Issy's mind flew to the cabin and the paintings. "It's charming," she said distractedly, then took in the living room, filled with chintz-covered furniture, comfortable and *Country Living* ready. "And it's so you. I love it."

"And you can give her the tour some other day," Ben said. "I have reservations."

Issy barely had time to say good-bye before Ben was leading her out again. Once they were back on the street, he stopped. "You look wonderful."

Amused, Issy said, "Thank you. You're cute, too. Are we in a hurry, really?"

Ben stretched his neck like maybe his tie was too tight. "I was trying to spare you the Cook's tour. It invariably leads to what's wrong with my house and my life."

"She loves you and your house," Issy said.

"She's driving me nuts."

"Is that why you asked me out? To appease Chloe?" Issy asked, surprised at her disappointment.

"No. No. It was after I asked you; she gets these notions."

"About marrying you off? I know. I've known you guys forever, remember? She's been trying to marry you off since you were sixteen. You don't know how many 'unsuitable' girls I saved you from when we were growing up."

"For which I'm forever in your debt." He opened the door to Chloe's car for her. "Thought you might prefer a real car tonight. Besides, the pickup hasn't been cleaned in a week or so. Been too busy preparing for the storm."

"Thanks for that bit of thoughtfulness. How is the storm progressing?"

"It hasn't made landfall yet. The models are disagreeing. It might just curve and peter out over water. Or it could keep traveling along the coast, gathering speed, and hit somewhere between New Jersey and Martha's Vineyard."

"I guess I'd better start making preparations," Issy said. As if she didn't have enough on her plate.

"I can come over and help with the heavy stuff, but you need to get the normal supplies ready, make sure you have plenty of batteries, water, the usual. Between the four of us, we should be able to get the plywood over the conservatory windows. How good is Paolo with a hammer?"

Issy shrugged. "We have installers to do those kind of things, but I imagine he's no schlepp."

"Which is women-splain for he's good at everything? So he and my sister—"

"Stop. You're just as bad as she is. Do you need help protecting the marshes?"

"I don't protect them, they do the protecting, their main enemy is man—people. I have to protect the equipment. My instruments make delicate measurements, and anything can upset them or break them. They're very temperamental."

"Little divas."

"Yes but nothing like the ones you face."

They both laughed and fell into an old familiarity, mixed with a new feeling of discovery. Issy felt her anxiety float away.

They drove to a nearby town, parked on a side street, and strolled down the crowded sidewalk toward the water.

"I didn't think you'd mind the crowds after being pretty much inside the Muses all week."

"It's a perfect choice. And after Manhattan this is just the right amount of crowd." As they walked down the brick path to the restaurant, Issy was acutely aware of Ben's hand resting on the small of her back. It was different from the casual arm slung over her shoulders of their childhood and teenage years; as comfortable, but with an added zing of something Issy wasn't ready to name.

La Moule was a small bistro-type restaurant at the end of a wide seawall.

It was crowded but muted, cozy with candlelit tables and a brick fireplace filled with antique oak kegs for the summer months. At the back was a large deck that overlooked an inlet and a wider view of the sea. In the west the sun was beginning its nose dive behind the coastline. The eastern sky was already midnight blue.

"I got a reservation for inside if that's okay."

She smiled up at him "Not in the mood for mosquitoes tonight?"

"I eat enough of my meals roughing it. This is sheer decadence on my part."

"Please tell me you don't still carry your lunch in with the first-aid supplies."

He laughed. "You remember that?"

"Not easy to forget. We were always afraid that you'd get involved with whatever it was you were doing and eat the gauze pads instead of your sandwich."

"Well, rest easy, the first-aid kit has been replaced by a sustainable, insulated state-of-the-art lunch bag."

They sipped wine and talked and ate and talked and the evening slipped into night.

"It's so weird being back," Issy told him over a shared piece of chocolate cake.

"Especially with your mother and Vivienne making guest appearances."

"It's crazy. When Jillian showed up the other day, I couldn't even look at her. I knew she was up to no good. And sure enough, she came because she needed money and probably saw Leo and Fae as easy pickings, especially with George as an ally. But there are moments when I forget to be angry.

"I mean I know she's totally useless, and I certainly have trouble accepting that she's my mother. But she did help with the filming, and she was in the attic with Mandy, and she made

Griff a peanut butter sandwich. She didn't lift a finger for the first few days, but there seems to be a bit of thawing. She can't be all bad, can she?"

"You mean, just sort of selfish and self-serving?"

"Then it wasn't me, Ben?"

Ben reached over and lifted her chin. "What are you talking about?"

"I grew up with Vivienne telling me I was the reason Jillian dumped us. That life was perfect before I came. That Jillian took one look at me and burst into tears."

"Oh, I remember Vivienne all right. Talk about divas. Chloe said she was mean to you, but you didn't believe her?"

"After a while, yeah, I did."

"I hope you don't still believe that."

"No, not rationally, but there's still this tiny little dark seed of doubt."

"Well, banish it. The problem is with Jillian not you. Believe that."

"I'm trying."

"And with that crybaby sister of yours. Chloe said she showed up today broke and in tears like always."

"Always?"

"Don't you remember? She always cried over everything. It was the Vivienne 'Don't Call Me Viv' show or nothing. Nobody liked her. I was only nice to her because Chloe said I had to be or she would be worse to you. My parents agreed."

"I had no idea."

He sat back. "Well, now you do, and let's not talk about your family anymore. What are your plans for the rest of the summer, or do you have any?"

"I told George that if he insisted Leo and Fae have someone to stay with them, I would." Her words fell into the space between them.

"Did you mean it?"

Issy shrugged. "I did at the time."

"But now?"

"I don't know. I love my job, but . . ."

"But what?"

Issy looked around the restaurant. It was a stupid thing to do. Spies weren't hanging on to her every word. Actually there was hardly anyone left still eating.

"There's something I need some advice about."

"From me?"

She nodded. "Maybe. But can we go someplace . . ."

Ben gestured to the waiter and paid the bill.

They walked along the water away from the crowds. Now that the time had come, Issy didn't know how to start. She stopped to look over the railing at the lights reflected in the dark water of the marina.

Ben leaned on his elbows, waiting.

"There's something I found." She told him about the paintings. The possible ramifications. "Selling them could save the Muses. But. What if they turn out to not be real?"

"You mean forgeries?"

"It's possible. It seems too good to be true, doesn't it? How could those paintings survive all these years untended in the salt air? They're not mildewed or anything."

"And if you could sell them, it would be enough to keep Leo and Fae at the Muses?"

She nodded, slowly and deliberately.

"And you would stay to set things up? Is that what you're thinking?"

"More than that. I'm thinking the Muses would make a great museum. Artwork in situ."

"Sounds like a huge project."

"It would be and maybe impossibly expensive."

"Is that something you would want to do?"

"I just don't know. Part of me wants to stay, but there's another part of me that loves the work I do for the Cluny."

"If you do stay, make sure it's for the right reasons and not because it's what you think you should do." He turned her to face him. "Wes and Leo didn't want you to be tied to the Muses. It drove all their children away and they didn't want it to drive you away, too."

"Oh, Ben, I don't know what to do."

"How about this?" He lifted her chin and kissed her.

FAE LOOKED INTO the darkened room one more time. This time Vivienne stirred in her sleep. If she kept this up much longer, Fae might be tempted to pour a bucket of ice water over her, but it would wreck the mattress.

Besides, Issy wasn't home yet. Good, maybe she'd stay out late. If Fae had her way, she wouldn't come in at all. But she knew Issy would be back. Somewhere in her unorthodox childhood she'd developed a keen sense of responsibility. Vivienne may have always acted like the responsible one, but her actions were merely knee-jerk reactions to a way of life she considered beneath her.

Vivienne couldn't wait to marry into the Bannister family. They were a staid, respectable old family. Much straighter than the Whitakers. But those were always the families who ended up with at least one doozy of a black sheep. Dan Bannister was theirs.

Well, Vivienne had made her bed, and Dan was evidently sleeping with someone else in it.

Issy, on the other hand, learned true responsibility, she would do what she thought needed to be done. Fae selfishly hoped she would stay, but not if Issy took over caring for her and Leo out of some mistaken sense of duty.

It was free will or nothing.

Please don't let it be nothing.

Fae glanced at Vivienne one more time. She would sleep a little longer. Fae needed to go home. Just for a while, she needed to go . . . home.

THE LAST THING Issy wanted to see at the moment was the gates to Muses by the Sea.

Ben had kissed her. More than once. And she was having unsettling feelings. He was Chloe's brother. He'd seen her in her Princess Leia underwear. She'd drunk his plankton experiment. She and Chloe had caught him making out with Jessica Redburn in the Collinses' basement. He'd gotten really mad and thrown a couch pillow at them. Jessica went home, embarrassed, and never went out with him again.

It hadn't saved him from girls. There were plenty waiting to take Jessica's place. Suddenly the nerdy boy-scientist who was their inseparable companion became Mr. Much in Demand. And then he was gone off to college, leaving an empty spot between his two companions.

And now? Now he was everything he was then, yet more.

Issy could feel it, relate to it, but she wasn't ready to act on it. Instead, she was going back to the Muses, feeling a little awkward and a lot aroused, and that made her feel more awkward. He'd been her friend since childhood. *He's Chloe's brother.*

And Issy didn't care. She let her hand drift over to his thigh. If this were Manhattan and Ben wasn't Chloe's brother, they might have ended up at his apartment. Though Issy could hardly remember those days, she'd been working nonstop lately.

Besides, she wasn't sure it was such a good idea to change the dynamics of their friendship. Issy, Ben, and Chloe. Except that Paolo and Chloe were definitely attracted to each other and might even now be settling in for a long night at Chloe's.

"Last chance for a night of reckless abandon," Ben said.

"As tempting as that is, and believe me it's tempting—though you have to promise to never tell Chloe—I have an interrogation to perform tonight."

"Really looking forward to letting her have it?"

"I was. But I'm feeling a little distracted at the moment."

"And I could shoot myself for reminding you." He kissed her hand and put it back in her lap. "And don't you tell Chloe, either. She'll just rub it in and say 'I told you so' in that annoying way she's always had."

He stopped at the front door. Got out of the car to open her door. "I see that Paolo isn't back yet."

"I told him he could have the night off."

"Lucky guy. You sure he's okay for Chloe? She's not a so-phisticated girl."

"He's lovely."

"And you're sure you two—"

"Me and Chloe?"

"You and Paolo."

"I love him dearly. But no, never have, aren't, and won't be."

He stopped her at the door, looked around, and pulled her close. This kiss took her breath away, and she was still dizzy when he reached around her to open the door. "Good night."

"Good night."

Issy went in and Ben went down the steps.

"That was lovely," Fae called. "Hold the door, Issy, I'm on my way."

Issy looked out the door. Fae was huffing her way across the drive. Ben had smacked his palm to his forehead. His cowlick was sticking up.

Chapter 26

"Well," Fae said when they were standing in the foyer. "I've waited years for that."

"For Ben to kiss me?"

"For anyone to kiss you beneath the porch light. It being Ben is just icing on the cake."

"Aunt Fae, I've been kissed before."

"I should hope so, but not under our porch light, not that I've seen."

Issy shook her head. She hadn't had a boyfriend until college. "Okay, now the porch light has been anointed, what does it mean?"

"Means you've come home."

Issy frowned. "Aunt Fae, it doesn't mean that I will stay."

"Oh, I know. It just means you can if you want to." She hurried on ahead, leaving Issy wondering what she was talking about.

Issy followed her into the parlor, where Vivienne was sitting in a wing chair with a light throw over her legs. She clasped a steaming mug in both hands. Leo sat in the other wing chair holding a nearly empty sherry glass and Jillian was on the couch with a tumbler filled with ice and gin.

Vivienne shrank back when she saw Issy.

"Hold that thought. I need to change. Don't start without me."

When Issy returned wearing yoga pants and a big tee, Fae had joined Jillian on the sofa and was drinking sherry with Leo.

Issy walked across the room and took a second to glare at Vivienne just for good measure. She took her laptop off the desk and pulled up a chair near the wingback where her sister sat.

"You don't mind if I take notes, do you?" Her tone let Vivienne know she didn't care if she cared or not. Vivienne hung her head and started whimpering.

Issy shifted in her chair. "Let's get this straight from the top. If anybody should be crying around here, it's Leo and Fae and your three children. So cut out the theatrics and tell us what you did with the money."

Vivienne reared out of the chair. "I don't have to—"

"Yes, you do," Jillian said. "Sit down."

Vivienne visibly deflated; she looked pitifully over to Leo, but Leo was looking past her and out the window so intently that Issy had to force herself not to look, too. Because she knew what—who—was out that window. On the knoll. She'd have to make sure Leo went upstairs to bed tonight and didn't go traipsing around the dunes at midnight.

"It wasn't my fault."

This was met by total silence.

"You don't understand."

"No, we don't, Vivienne," said Issy. "So explain to us why

you and your husband would steal millions from your own family, dump your children on two unsuspecting women, and then take off to Panama. Or why I got called away from work by your eight-year-old daughter, who begged me to come get her and her brother and sister, which I did only to find Grammy in the hospital and your three children in police custody."

"It's always about you," Vivienne spat.

"No, Vivienne," Leo said calmly. "It's always been about you. Now answer Issy's questions, please."

Vivienne's lip quivered. "You're ganging up on me."

"Oh, for Pete's sake." Jillian stood up and went to the drinks cabinet. Held up her glass, asking if anyone else needed a re-fill. No one did. She poured herself a large drink and sat back down. "Just answer Issy's questions."

"Why did you leave your children here?"

"I had to." Vivienne started to cry. Leo handed her a tissue from a box sitting next to her. She'd come prepared.

"I had to go after Dan. I accused Mrs. Norcroft of stealing and I fired her because I thought she was responsible for the missing items. But it was Dan.

"I didn't know he was stealing from the bank account. Oh God. He took all the money out of the bank and ran away. I went after him to try to get the money back."

Issy snorted. "Or help him spend it. Is that why you spent two weeks with him in Panama? Where were you going to jet-set to next?"

"Panama? I didn't go to Panama. I went to the family cabin up in the Adirondacks. I thought maybe Dan just needed to get away. Things hadn't been going too well between us. I thought he—but I was wrong. He hadn't been there. So I went back home. That's when I realized he'd cleaned out all the bank accounts and I saw red.

"I started calling his friends, everybody that he knew or might know where he was. One of them told me he'd just seen him in Miami. So I dropped off the kids and flew down. I couldn't take them with me. Grammy said it was okay, didn't you, Grammy?"

"Why didn't you answer your phone? We were all calling you and calling you. The children were frantic."

"I left a message that I loved them and I was coming back. And I *was* coming back. I was following Dan's trail and it took me some time to run him down in Miami, but by then he'd checked out of the hotel. I didn't want to give up without getting the money back, but I was out of cash, my phone was dead. I just couldn't come back and face everyone until I found the money."

"But you came back and broke into your house."

"I meant to slip in and out. Do some laundry and hit the trail again. But he'd sold the house. Can you believe it? He actually sold our house without consulting me. I couldn't figure out why I couldn't unlock the door. I tried and tried and finally I thought, Screw it. I threw a brick through the window and let myself in."

She took a sip of tea, probably cold by now. "I just went into my own house. I was just going to get some clothes and things I needed and take off again, only someone reported a burglary. And the police came. Thank God that Detective Griggs remembered you and got them to bring me here." She took a shuddering breath. "Oh God, what am I going to do?"

"Now, now." Leo leaned over to pat Vivienne's knee.

"Let Issy handle this, Mother," Jillian said, and Issy was so surprised to find her name on her mother's lips instead of her usual "Oops," she almost lost her train of thought.

"Are you telling us Dan took all the money and fled without your knowledge?"

"Yes. I didn't know what was happening at first, but when I did, I brought the kids here. I didn't want them to know what was going on. That their father was a—a—I can't even say it. I knew they would be taken care of here while I checked all the places where he might have gone."

"To Panama."

"Why do you keep saying Panama?"

"Because that's where he is. And you were seen with him."

From the corner of her eye, Issy saw Jillian grimace.

Vivienne shook her head. Then heat flared in her eyes. "That bastard! It wasn't me."

Oops, Issy thought, and almost laughed out loud.

"I can't believe he would do that to us."

Jillian leaned forward. "So you're telling us you don't have any of the money?"

"None. I don't even have our joint money. He took that, too. And before you ask, I didn't have a separate checking account. And now my credit cards are maxed out."

"What about the Bannisters?" Issy asked. If they didn't know where Dan was, maybe at least they would take Vivienne and the children in.

"They've already washed their hands of him—and me. Evidently there were gambling debts."

"And you were oblivious to all this?"

"Yes, why don't you believe me?"

"Because no intelligent, educated woman could possibly be that clueless about her finances."

"Well, I was. Maybe it was because instead of paying attention to myself, I was taking care of my children. Besides, Dan always took care of our finances. That's what husbands do."

"Lame, Vivienne, just lame."

"Girls, stop it," Leo said. "Wes hates—hated—when you argued. The money is gone and that is that. We'll just have to figure out a way to get some more."

Vivienne slumped back. "I didn't know. I was just trying to make it right."

Issy realized that she'd been holding on to a flicker of hope that Vivienne would return with the money. But that wasn't going to happen. Her sister had been betrayed just like the rest of them.

She thought about the paintings out in the cabin. She didn't dare mention them tonight. Jillian was just mercenary enough to find them and steal them. At this point she wouldn't even put it past Vivienne. Issy needed a lot more information about those paintings before she did anything with them, and even then she wasn't planning to share the information.

Vivienne blew her nose. "What do I tell the kids?"

"That you've decided to spend the summer with me," Leo said. "We'll have a lovely time."

So IT WAS true. Stephanie pulled herself up from where she crouched behind the archway and crept away. Her father was the worst kind of thief and her mother was clueless. He'd sold their house. They didn't even have any of their clothes or anything. They had nothing; they might as well have been swept away in the hurricane that was coming. They were such losers.

How could she possibly be important to any story with genes like that? She wiped her cheeks. They were wet, but today would be the last time she shed tears for what had happened. From now on she was her own person. No.matter how much it hurt.

She skulked along the walls to the back stairs, took them up to her room, and shut and locked the door. She meant to stay up until Aunt Issy came to bed, but it had been a long day and her feelings were all mixed up. And she had to cry just a little more before she never cried again.

"Does Grammy understand any of this?" Vivienne asked as she stood in the hallway with Issy and Jillian. It was the first time Issy had been close enough or cared enough to notice that there were dark circles under her eyes, and her face was puffy from crying and possibly sleeping tablets. Her perfect hair wasn't perfect, but near enough to prevent Issy from feeling completely sympathetic.

"I would say so," Jillian said.

"You think I've been very stupid."

"It seems to run in the family, except maybe Issy, and I have a feeling that she's about to do something rash."

"I'm standing right here, in case I really am invisible to the two of you."

Jillian raised both eyebrows.

Vivienne's mouth twisted. "I don't know why you have to be so bitchy."

"Bitchy?" Issy replied. "I passed bitchy a long time ago, somewhere between Manhattan and three frightened, deserted children. I'm fed up. I seem to be the only one in this house with a penny to my name and what I have is quickly being depleted by groceries and expensive liquor. Yes, Jillian, I did notice the empty box from the liquor store. So if you're both going to become a part of the household, I suggest that at least one of you come up with a scheme for earning some money."

"My dear Oops, one can't get anywhere earning money. You must attract it."

Issy just looked at her. "And how's that working for you . . . Mom? If you're both going to stay here, then make yourselves useful."

"Leo said I could stay. So to hell with you. It's not your house." Vivienne burst into new tears and stalked off down the hall.

"It won't be any of ours if somebody doesn't come up with a way to save it," Issy called after her. "Ugh. This would be a comedy if it weren't so gut wrenchingly pathetic."

"True," Jillian said. "I can't remember a more lachrymose scene. I feel absolutely waterlogged."

"Probably the gin and vermouth, Mother."

"Touché, darling, I think I'll just have another."

Issy sat in the dark of her room wishing she hadn't lost it in front of her mother and her sister, the two people she most wanted to appear cool before. She wished she'd just stayed away. She could be at Ben's house now, basking in the afterglow of what hopefully would be good sex.

Or maybe they'd still be talking, but about good stuff and not about how to stanch the hemorrhaging of the Whitakers. Maybe reminiscing. Even talking about recording saline levels would be better than this.

Actually just being with Ben would be good.

Which was a total nonpossibility, because either the family would miraculously save Muses by the Sea or they wouldn't, and Leo and Fae would go into assisted living, Jillian would go back to Hollywood or one of her men, Vivienne would get a job, and then Issy would go back to work at the museum.

Except she had a sneaking suspicion that Paolo wouldn't go back even if Issy got him reinstated. Loyalty only went so far when love was involved. And what was going on between him and Chloe was beginning to look like love.

It was pretty clear that he wasn't coming back tonight. So she sat in the dark. Worrying. She briefly considered asking Vivienne to stay in the house and be a companion to Leo, but she dismissed the idea summarily. She wouldn't trust her sister again.

And that still didn't solve the problem of the money. There were the paintings. If she could sell them and keep Leo and Fae at home, she could stay to oversee the opening of the Muses to the public, hire Paolo to run the museum. So much to do. Such a tangled mess to sort out. It could wait.

She decided to just linger on the memory of Ben's kiss and leave the rest until tomorrow.

IT WAS STILL early when Issy put on water for coffee the next morning. It was going to be another beautiful day. Hard to believe that a tropical storm was on its way and she vacillated between trying to rush through the filming of the parlor artwork or declaring a holiday and going down to the beach. It was the first time the whole family had been together in years.

She was watching the coffee drip when Jillian came in.

Issy's mouth fell open.

Jillian made a lifting motion with two fingers. "Not attractive, Oops."

Issy closed her mouth. "You'll have to forgive me, but the shock of seeing you up before midday was so overwhelming."

"Oh, I thought it was the outfit."

"That, too."

Jillian had tied what had to be an Hermès scarf around her hair à la *I Love Lucy* or perhaps she was going for Doris Day. She was wearing designer capris, with a button shirt that looked . . .

"Did you borrow that shirt from Grammy?"

"Thank goodness she still gardens. It was a necessity. I didn't have anything appropriate for a day of toiling." She twirled around then headed for the coffeepot. "Is that ready yet?"

The coffeepot beeped.

Jillian poured herself a cup. "Is there cream?"

Issy gave her a look and got down another cup from the cupboard. Jillian opened the fridge door and held up the milk carton. Issy shook her head.

They were both sitting at the table staring into their cups when Chloe and Paolo came in carrying pastry boxes and grocery bags.

Chloe blushed as she caught Issy's eye, but Paolo leaned over and kissed her cheek. Smiled charmingly at Jillian. "Is Leo ready for her close-up?"

"Fae is doing her hair," Jillian said. "But she's dressed and ready to dwell in the past."

"Excellent, I'll just set up the video equipment." He hurried out of the room.

Issy and Jillian turned on Chloe. She looked up and blushed pinker. "The two of you are wearing the exact same expression," she said. "And if you must know: totally wow."

"Get a cup down and tell us everything," Jillian said.

"Maybe not everything," Issy added. "I do have to work with the man."

Nonetheless, Fae and Leo found the three of them with their heads together a few minutes later.

"I can only guess what this is about," Fae said. "I'll just put the kettle on."

"Grammy, you look wonderful," Issy said, embarrassed to be caught in a tête-à-tête with her mother and best friend.

"Thank you, my dear."

"Where are Vivienne and the children?"

"Steph went in to help Paolo," Fae said.

"I told her to come have some breakfast as soon as she's done," Leo said, eyeing the pastry box.

Chloe jumped up. "I have fruit salad and pastries but I can make scrambled eggs."

"No, no, dear. You've done more than enough and we all have work to do."

"Where's Vivienne?" Issy asked.

"Still sleeping, poor thing. I'm afraid she's not feeling well. She's going to take it easy today."

Issy opened her mouth.

"We'll see about that." Jillian pushed her chair back. "Guilt is one thing . . . as I have cause to know," she added almost under her breath. "But avoidance—which I also know about—just makes it worse. Excuse me while I go have a little mother–daughter chat with my eldest."

She strode out of the room, the ends of her headdress flopping in the air.

The others stared after her, then stared at each other.

The kettle shrieked.

"Well," Leo said, "I never thought I'd live to see the day."

Chapter 27

After breakfast, they began what Issy hoped would be the last day of work in the parlor. They had cataloged at least a hundred paintings, sculptures, knickknacks, and miscellaneous objets d'art. Every time Issy was inclined to suggest an object didn't need to be kept, Leo came up with a story about it.

Around ten, Jillian made an appearance to say she and Vivienne and the two younger children would start cleaning the conservatory.

Issy thanked her and made a mental note to check in on them and make sure the two women weren't filching any of the more salable pieces.

Leo was in fine fettle, and several times during the morning, the taping erupted in laughter. But as the morning wore on, Issy became more distracted. Her vacation time would be up in four days; she needed to touch base with Dell. They hadn't discussed exactly when she was coming back, and Issy didn't see how she could get things settled and prevent the Muses and Leo and Fae's lives becoming further eroded by then.

And there were the paintings. They could solve all their problems, but even they couldn't solve them by Friday.

They were just wrapping up the inventory of the parlor when Chloe arrived, bearing food and a message from Ben. "He said that the tropical storm had been changed to a category-one hurricane. But it's still nothing to worry about. It looks like it's heading to North Carolina. And not to worry, because that'll knock the stuffing out of it. But he says we should start thinking about protecting windowed areas. He also said that if it's okay he'll bring food and we can barbecue tonight."

Chloe smiled at Leo. "I told him that was fine. Might as well eat it in case the electricity goes out. Is that okay with you?"

"It sounds wonderful."

Issy went back to the conservatory to see what, if any, progress the others had made. She found Jillian on a ladder dusting one of the many sconces that lit the walls. She was alone.

"What happened to your team?" Issy asked.

"Gone to read to the children. Honestly. You'd think these sconces hadn't been cleaned in a decade."

"Chances are they haven't been."

"You think George and I should have taken better care of Leo and Fae?"

"I think George should have. I know I should have."

"Ah, Isabelle, still so serious. I swear you were the most serious child I've ever met."

Issy flinched. "I'm surprised you remember."

"Of course I remember." She climbed down from the ladder and flopped back onto one of the rattan couches.

"Why the change of heart? Two days ago you couldn't wait to sell the Muses out from under Leo and put her in a nursing home."

"Two days ago I was still jet-lagged and had forgotten what a great place this was growing up."

"I thought you hated it here."

"Never. Growing up here was amazing. In those days Leo and Wes were the toast of the art world. One night the house would be filled with writers, the next weekend Andy Warhol would show up with his exotic and sexually migrating friends.

"George never really took to it, but Max and I . . ." She sighed. "Poor Max. He was a sensitive soul. He had the true artist's soul. Much more so than even Father. But he was patriotic and impressionable and he enlisted in that infamous war. A waste of great minds and spirits.

"But, Oops. We couldn't stay children forever. There was a world out there peopled with all the people we only glimpsed here. So I went to check it out."

"Fine, so why didn't you ever visit us?"

"I did, but if you're asking why I didn't visit you and Vivienne more often . . ." She shrugged. "I was busy, Hollywood is all-consuming. It's a mad wild, boom-or-bust business and you can't let your attention flag for a moment or you're forgotten." A cloud passed over her face and Issy didn't know if she had imagined it or if it was just the change of Jillian's mood.

"*We* didn't forget *you*."

"I know, darling. I did the best thing I could for you. Gave you the childhood I had with the best people I knew who could take care of you."

"Vivienne hated it here."

"Did she? Or did she just miss the bright lights and the attention she got from being a celeb's daughter? But she wouldn't have liked it. Eventually she would have ended up like a lot of these children do, fought over, dragged through the public eye, resentful. It's a horrible fate. You see it every day."

"Then why did you even have children?"

"Oh, it was the publicist's idea."

Issy reeled. "You mean you didn't even want Vivienne?"

"Oh, I wanted you both, once you were here."

"But not enough to keep us. Or at least keep Vivienne. Why didn't you take her with you?"

"And leave you alone?"

"I wasn't alone. She always said it was my fault you didn't keep her."

"Oh, that girl. The truth is, Oops, I just wasn't cut out for motherhood. I don't have the attention span. It was all worked out by the publicist, even the marriage. Trevor York and I would have a fairy-tale wedding. We were both philandering fools and having a great time, but Hollywood always needs change, so we got married. And actually he could be rather lovely when he wasn't screwing around. Of course so could I. That kept us on the front page of the tabloids for a while, but when the publicity started lagging, the publicist decided to put it out that we were planning to start a family. I got pregnant with Vivienne."

She frowned. "Hollywood loves babies. It eats them up and spits out the bones. And it didn't take me long to figure out that either I was going to have to leave Hollywood to raise my baby, get a real job like the rest of the weary world of women, or figure out how to protect her. She was already being fawned over and having her pretty little head turned. It was a nightmare.

"By then Trev and I couldn't stand each other; he moved out. I hired a housekeeper and threw myself into work. One night he came back to pick up some things he needed; one thing led to another and that led to you.

"But it couldn't last and we both moved on. It's Hollywood. We hardly saw each other after that. Never worked together again and some other 'packaged' couple took over the headlines."

"Then he really is my father?"

"Of course, why would you even ask?"

"There seems to have been some speculation."

"Who told you such a thing?"

"I have a newspaper article from the time." Issy spread out her fingers like a banner. 'Who is the real father of Jillian York's surprise baby?'"

"Ridiculous, they should never have let you see that. Of course you're his. You have the York eyes, everything else about you is pure Whitaker. Vivienne got the Whitaker eyes and the York everything else. Funny. I never thought about that before."

Jillian's cell rang. She fumbled in her pocket and snatched it out. "Saved by the—" She dropped her head dramatically. Turned the screen so Issy could see it, then swiped it open.

"Wait . . . George. How delightful."

Issy could barely hear his voice. Jillian touched speaker.

". . . Sotheby's to send someone up before . . . You do know there's a hurricane coming up the coast?"

"We're aware." Jillian rolled her eyes.

"Well, they can't come until afterward, the end of next week probably. Issy will be gone by then, and I expect you will be, too."

"Dear George, is that a question or a demand?"

Silence for a moment. "Just let Issy know that I'm making arrangements for the art appraisers. She can tell Leo and Fae. How's it going there?"

"Just fine, we're on our way to the beach."

"The beach? Good, good. Stay busy. Good. And make sure they move inland if the hurricane is expected to make landfall anywhere near there."

"I will, George. Thanks so much for calling."

If a viper could talk. Jillian's voice actually sent chills up Issy's arms and down her back.

Jillian hung up. "That ass expects us to do his dirty work for him? Really?"

"So what are you saying?"

"I have no idea. I just know I'm not telling those two old dears that they're going to be carted off to the check-in-but-don't-check-out old-folks home. I promised the Theater Fund ladies I would talk at the gala in September, so if my agent doesn't call, I'll be here until then. If you can stretch your vacation into a month or two, and if the hurricane doesn't carry us all off, maybe we can think of something by then."

"You're really going to help?"

"Be warned. I'm totally useless, but yes. I'll help."

Issy WAS IN the kitchen when Mandy burst in. "Mommy's crying again."

Issy had just gotten off the phone with Dell and she wasn't ready to deal with her depressed sister. Dell was fidgety. Worried that she wasn't coming back at all because of Paolo's quitting. Especially once she told him Paolo was at the Muses with her.

She assured him they had some great ideas for the Toulouse-

Lautrec exhibit and would start on the design in the next week or so.

She explained that things were more complicated than she'd realized, that the Muses' future was in jeopardy, and her grandmother and great-aunt had no one else to help them.

Dell was well aware of the Muses reputation as an artist's mecca and was sympathetic. Asked if he could help in any way; Issy was so tempted to say she had an idea but it might not be legal. She caught herself in time. She needed to act but she needed to be careful.

And she should be doing something more constructive about saving the house than taking inventory. But any grant money this year was tied up already and finding a wealthy patron would take time and would be in competition with her own museum, which would get her blackballed for sure.

She could at least get an appraisal on one of the paintings. Make sure that they were indeed Adam Ellis's work. She knew who to contact and how to order an appraisal by an anonymous owner. It happened all the time. Though not by her. Still, something held her back. And it was because of something more than the legal questions; she just wasn't sure what it was.

She needed to go back to the cabin and take a closer look. And then she needed to do something about ensuring that they would withstand the storm. Time was marching inexorably on. And her options were circling round in her head like a giant catherine wheel. And it kept stopping at the same place. *Ask Fae.*

And that was the last thing she wanted to do.

Mandy tugged on Issy's shirt. "Aunt Issy, Mommy's crying again and it made Griff start crying and they won't stop." She fisted both hands and stomped her foot. "Why is everything so messed up?"

Issy pulled Mandy's pigtail. "Sometimes things just get a little messed up. It will be all right."

"I want it to be all right now!"

"We all do. But we have to be patient."

"Ugh!" Mandy stomped out of the kitchen.

Issy didn't blame her. *Be patient?* Really, was that the best she could do? She didn't even want to be patient. How could she expect a ten-year-old—eight-year-old?—to be. She hurried out of the kitchen. Yelled up the stairs. "Mandy, how old are you?"

Mandy stopped and peered over the banister. "Eight and three quarters. Am I going to have my party here?"

"Sounds like an excellent idea." Eight and three quarters would put her birthday somewhere in October? "Would you like that?"

"How would my friends get here?"

"It's not so far from Guilford."

"Oh, okay. I want a bouncy castle and a pony." She skipped up the rest of the stairs.

"All righty, then," Issy said. *A bouncy castle and a pony. I'll just add it to the list.*

She wandered out into the hallway suddenly feeling at loose ends. Paolo and Chloe were coming out of the parlor. They stopped at Issy.

"I'm going to put potatoes in the oven."

"Need help?" Issy asked.

"No, you guys talk business for a while."

"Meaning stay out of my kitchen," Paolo said. "She's just perfect," he added as he watched Chloe walk away.

"I hope you're not taking advantage of her cooking skills to weasel your way into her affections."

"You know me better than that." He smiled so wonderfully that Issy knew she was right about them. It was love.

"You seem preoccupied this morning, *cara*. Anything wrong? It's not about me and Ben's beautiful sister."

"Of course not. I think the two of you are lovely together."

"Then what is it?"

"I don't know. I had to ask Dell for more time off; my mother is either playing a new part as scullery maid or she's not who I thought she was; my sister is upstairs crying about poor her. And the thing that bothers me most is I kind of feel sorry for her."

"So ignore them."

"They're my family."

"That's what I usually say."

"I guess you're finally getting to me."

"Well, let me say this. You can love them, or hate them even, but you can't get rid of them. And you can't fix them. Families are not beautiful, or curated like a good exhibit."

"It would be better if they were, then I could just fix everything and be done with it."

"Oh, *cara*, you're the best designer I know. But people aren't like art; you can think you fixed them a hundred times but they never stay fixed. Let them be your family and love them warts and all. It's their job to live their lives. Yours to live yours."

"For a young guy you sometimes sound really wise."

"Pffft. I'm Italian. I was raised by a bunch of know-it-all, in-your-face, wise men and women who came from wise men and women. It's kind of a family trait. I'm stuck with it."

He went off to help Chloe, even if she didn't need his help, and Issy walked outside. It had been sunny and cloudy in alternating parts all day, brightening the parlor, then casting it in shadow. At first Paolo had tried to compensate for the changes, then decided it would just add more ambience to the interview.

Somewhere along the line, they had all forgotten the original point of the videoing. They were still cataloging, but the experience had taken on a life of its own. Listening to Leo talk about the artists who had shared not only the rooms but their talents, dreams, and stories while at the Muses was fascinating. Something worth keeping no matter what happened.

Finding herself alone, Issy walked to the cove, stopped at the bench, and looked out to sea. It was warm and humid but there was a definite heaviness in the air that said a storm was on its way.

They probably should have spent the day at the beach. It might be the last day they had for a while, especially if the storm continued to progress along the coast.

And suddenly she had a wild desire to swim in the cove where Wesley Whitaker and Leonore Eberhart fell in love and began it all. And where Isabelle Whitaker York might be the one who lost it.

She ran down to the beach and along the sand to where the waves had dug out a cup shape of rock. And there she pulled off her sandals and clothes and threw them onto a bush. Then she waded in until the water was thigh-high, dove in, and swam until she had to come up for breath.

There was no Wes waiting for her, so she turned over on her back and basked in the reappearing sun.

It had been a long time since Issy had swum naked in the

sound. Been a long time since she'd swum anywhere. Not even a hotel pool. She didn't remember swimming naked since leaving the Muses for college. She made a dolphin roll, something she had perfected in a younger life, then breaststroked her way toward open water.

She wouldn't go far; the water was surprisingly deep in the middle of the cove, currents carving away at the rocky coastline for eons on one side while leaving a sandy beach on the other. The best of both worlds.

Leave it to Mother Nature to get it right. And if Issy had her way, she'd continue to do so. The Whitakers had never tried to encroach on their natural surroundings. There was once talk of building an auditorium for dance, music, and theater performances, but the idea had been nixed. This was a painter's paradise, secluded and serene.

And that's the way it would stay. She would call her contact tomorrow and arrange for him to authenticate one of the paintings and make an appraisal for an anonymous owner. If it was a forgery, she'd say the owner had found it in his attic.

That should cover all her bases. She wouldn't have to show it to Paolo; that way she'd keep him out of any possible scandal. And she certainly wouldn't tell Leo or Fae. Fae was still scarred from her relationship with Adam Ellis and his untimely death. And she didn't trust Jillian enough to make her privy to the secret.

She was in this alone. And it was about time she did something about it. She pushed her feet down in the water until she was treading water.

And saw Ben's head appear over the crest of the knoll and was surprised by the thrill that shot through her. When he was in full view, she waved. "Come on it. The water's great."

He didn't answer. He seemed to be staring at the opposite side of the cove.

Issy twisted around just in time to see a figure slip into the woods next to the meadow. Not Fae or Steph; this was a man. He was tall and dressed in white or ecru.

She held her hand up to shield her eyes but he was gone. Like a wisp of smoke.

"Did you see who it was?" she called to Ben.

"No, but I think you should get out now. I'll take a look in the woods later."

"Probably just a hiker, they sometimes wander onto the property. Wes never minded."

"Still, would you get out?"

Issy had already been making her way back to shore. And was in a dilemma. Having Ben join her in the cove was one thing that she could readily imagine turning into more. But Ben standing on the land watching her unceremoniously climb out of the water, butt naked, and hobble across the stony outcropping to the bushes would be more like *Flamingo on Velvet* than Pelagio's *Venus Rising from the Sea.*

"Would you turn your back?"

He grinned. Shook his head.

"Then you come in."

"No can do. I left Paolo manning the grill so you better hurry."

"You'll pay for this."

"Looking forward to it."

He crossed his arms. She walked out of the water with head held high, and teeth clenched so as not to show the pain her feet were feeling as she crossed the pebbles to her clothes.

Ben didn't say anything when she reached him where he

waited on the knoll. But he had a big grin on his face, and several times as they walked to the house, she heard him snorting back a laugh.

By the time they reached the house, she was laughing, too. He threw his arm across her shoulders and pulled her close. Friends. More than friends. Almost lovers.

THEY MET CHLOE and Steph coming out the kitchen door; both were carrying huge bowls of food. Chloe looked from one to the other. "I won't ask what has you two in the giggles."

"Wise girl," Ben said. "Chloe, have you seen any strangers around here lately?"

"No. Why?"

"I saw somebody across the cove."

Stephanie bobbled the salad bowl.

Ben snatched it from her. "Easy there. It was just somebody hiking through the woods. Still, it would be a good idea if you kids didn't go wandering out there alone. That goes for you big kids, too."

Ben narrowed his eyes at Steph. "Have you seen anyone out there?"

"Nooo." She pulled the bowl away from him and continued on her way.

"That was odd," Ben said.

"She's a teenager . . . almost," Issy said.

"That must explain it."

They ate in the pavilion out on the east lawn, which someone had thought to have screened in since Issy had moved away. As soon as they were done, Ben excused himself to go check his instruments now that the barometric pressure was doing whatever it was doing.

Chloe began to gather up food and dirty plates. "I'd better get this mess cleaned up and go, too. I have to work in the morning."

"You go ahead," Issy told her. "You cooked, we'll clean. And take Paolo with you. He's a dream in the gallery, a nightmare in the kitchen." It wasn't true, Paolo was a good cook, too, but she wanted him to have fun and a reason to stay near the Muses.

As soon as they were gone, Vivienne declared that the children needed baths.

She'd tried to coerce Steph into coming, too, but Steph refused, and after a couple of threats and glaring looks, during which Steph held her ground, Vivienne took the other two into the house.

"Afraid she'll have to do the dishes," Fae said under her breath.

"At least she's beginning to show some interest in her children's welfare," Issy said just as quietly.

"Good for you, Stephanie," Jillian said at full volume. "Your mother is a mess and a bully. I can only say she learned it from the best."

This won a fleeting smile from Steph.

"It's how some people act when they feel guilt, anger, remorse, and the need to blame anyone but themselves. I should know." Jillian leaned over and patted Steph's knee. "It will pass and she'll be your mother again."

"I'll just keep the sage handy until then," Fae said, and patted her pocket.

It was true, Issy admitted. Vivienne cast bad energy wherever she went. Everyone had tried acting like everything was fine, but they each had sighed with relief when she left the pavilion.

The sun set; the fireflies came out while they sat finishing the last of the wine.

"Lord," said Jillian. "Do you realize that there are four generations of Whitaker women sitting around this table?"

"Wow," Steph said.

Issy echoed her wow. She hadn't expected to see this anytime—ever.

"And the moon is full." Fae stood. "Jillian, go get your daughter and her children. The rest of you stay here. I'll be right back."

Chapter 28

Jillian cast a curious look around at the others, then followed Fae into the house.

"What's happening?" Steph asked, curious and a little apprehensive. "What about the full moon?"

"More sage burning," Issy speculated. "Grammy?"

Leo smiled, a mixture of mystery, memory, and regret. "Oh, Issy, don't you remember?"

Issy shook her head. But she did.

Jillian returned accompanied by Mandy and Griff, wearing clean pajamas and sneakers. "Vivienne doesn't feel up to it. I told her to come later if she changes her mind."

"What is it?" Mandy asked. "Are we having a sleep-out?"

"No," Leo said.

"Are we having ice cream?" Griff asked.

"Something even better."

"What, Grammy? What?"

"Wait and see." She stood and went to meet Fae, who was carrying a heavy tapestry bag.

"We're going to town?"

"No. But I have these." Fae brought out sparklers that must have been left over from a Fourth of July years before.

She lit them. They sputtered then caught and she handed them around.

"What are we doing?"

"We're going to the cove for the Last Great Whitaker Full Moon Family Dance and we're doing it in style."

Fae led the way as always when there was an adventure to be had. The others followed, Jillian supporting Leo by the elbow. It was a side of her mother Issy had never seen and it spoke volumes about the woman she was and not the woman Issy thought her to be. Mandy and Griff went next, though they wanted to run ahead. Until Fae told them if they broke ranks they'd be sent home and miss the fun. Issy and Steph walked together, not touching but close, the last two generations of a great family whose patronage had helped some of the best of American painters.

It might all be gone soon. This might really be their last Full Moon Dance, a tradition at least a hundred years old whose origins might be in folklore but probably more likely in a gin or vodka bottle. But like Fae said, they would go out in style.

Leo slowed as they passed the bench and the two graves she visited every day. Slowed even more as they helped her down the incline to the sandy beach, where they all shed their shoes and Fae pulled a boom box out of her bag.

Fae turned on the music, took Leo by the hand, while the others stood by. Issy sensed she was watching something she was not likely to see again and she wanted to etch every detail in her mind and heart. Jillian took Leo's other hand. And Issy stepped forward to take Jillian's. Stephanie, who had to be an old soul, had taken both her siblings' hands and was holding them back until Issy and Fae reached for them and they all three ran to join the circle.

The music was an eclectic mix of classical, reggae, folk, and popular tunes from the sixties, all collected by Fae over the years. It always started with something tame, with them holding hands in a circle. And the circle started to move and they danced and danced, and laughed and split apart and came together again. They went wild with dancing and laughing until Issy suddenly felt someone watching them and turned around.

Vivienne stood at the edge of the trees and in a moment of sisterly affection Issy ran to her and pulled her to the beach, where Mandy and Griff immediately took her hands and turned her in a circle.

And all the Whitakers danced while the moon rose and the night grew dark. And hope burst into little starlets in the sky.

The clouds rolled in and, with the clouds, reality. It beckoned to them as they packed up and walked up the beach to the lawn, wrapped around them as they crossed the lawn to the house. And just as they reached the door, the clouds passed over the moon and the first drop of rain fell.

"It's starting," Fae said.

"Did we make it rain, Mommy?"

"No, Griffin. We were just dancing."

Issy sighed. For an hour Vivienne had actually seemed to shed her bitterness, but now it was back, Issy could hear it in her voice. The resigned, defeated, and perhaps just a little rueful woman who was her sister.

There was nothing Issy could do about her. She could try to save the house and the paintings. She should have gone back to secure them today instead of going to the beach. It was too late now. She knew the woods but didn't relish being there alone in the dark and rain. She would go first thing tomorrow.

But in the morning she had no time to get away. Ominous black clouds crowded the sky and the waves cut across each other and turned the water gray. The beginning of the wave surge.

As long as it didn't strengthen beyond a category-one or -two hurricane, they should be safe from flooding. But she wondered about Ben.

Chloe called to say camp was being canceled until after the storm.

"Ben's moved some things to my place."

"He was ordered to evacuate?"

"No, he's just being a big brother. I told him I'd be fine, and that I was coming to weather the storm with you."

"And Paolo, don't forget him."

"I didn't. But Ben said if you guys are staying he'll come over later and help Paolo with the shutters and heavier stuff."

Issy smiled. "Uh-huh. We'd love to have you, both of you. The more the merrier. And I'm sure Paolo would be glad of the company."

They canceled the rest of the inventory to prepare for the storm. Fae brought out the emergency radio and put in new batteries. She kept Mandy and Griff busy collecting blankets and carrying them to the central stair hall, where they would sleep as a last resort if the storm became stronger.

"We should go inland," Vivienne said, clinging to her children.

"Nonsense," Leo said. "We've weathered two hundred years

of storms and this isn't even one of the big ones. Mandy, come help Grammy decide which snacks we want to have. I think I saw some marshmallows. We can make s'mores."

Mandy abandoned ship and went with Leo. Griff released his hold on Vivienne's pant leg and followed them.

"No need to frighten the children," Fae said.

Issy knew she meant it sympathetically, but of course Vivienne bristled. "You would be worried, too, if you'd ever had children."

Issy wanted to smack her.

Fae just smiled and wandered off into another room.

Issy sent Steph to fill the bathtub in Mrs. Norcroft's bathroom.

"Why? How long are we going to being stuck inside?"

"Hopefully not more than a day, maybe two, but the power may go off, and the town water supply might shut down. We want to be able to flush, right?"

Steph made a face. "I'm on it."

Paolo spent the morning bringing wood into the mud room. The last two loads he carried straight into the library, where they always sat out the storm. The library had a fireplace, north-facing windows for the most part, and direct access to the central hall, which had no windows at all.

"This should do it," he said, passing them with his armload of wood. "It looks like night out there."

Issy moved her computer and the specs for the Toulouse-Lautrec exhibit. From nowhere—though probably her subconscious—the room was suddenly peopled with mannequins in period dress, standing and sitting among the artwork. Not the nineteenth-century denizens of Montmartre and Pigalle of Lautrec, but their American counterparts, who peopled the history of the Muses. It would make a good opening event if the Muses ever became a museum. They could use real actors in costumes for the opening, maybe even as docents.

"Stop it." She found a safe place for her laptop, plugged it in, and pulled up a weather link. Watched the hurricane moving up the Jersey coast. It was moving east. Was there a chance it would miss them?

"Steph, are you back?"

Steph stuck her head in the library.

"Go turn on the television and see what the weathermen are saying."

EACH TIME FAE was near a window—and she made sure she was near one often—she'd look out on the knoll and then to her cottage. She just wanted to go home. Be in her cottage. Resume her life. But she couldn't leave Issy with this brood. And she couldn't leave Leo.

Already twice this morning she had tried to get out to be with Wes. Fae had stopped her both times. But Leo was stubborn and she wanted to see Wes before the storm hit.

Leo lived between two worlds but she wasn't stupid and she hadn't lost her marbles, at least not when she was "here" with the rest of them. But Fae knew how much the past was calling her, how loud Wes's voice could be even from the grave. A gothic thought maybe, but true.

Didn't she hear it every day?

Soon, soon she would have to make a choice. Maybe as soon as the end of the storm. And she was so afraid that she knew what it would be. She tried not to be bitter; after all, it was her choice. And she'd made it long ago.

She started when she saw the figure running across the

lawn. She was wearing an old rain slicker, the hood pulled low, and carrying a roll of painter's plastic and a big flashlight.

Not Leo, but Issy.

So Issy knew. Fae had suspected it for the last few days. There was no use going after her. She watched as Issy took the path through the woods, watched until the rain became too intense to see more than the moving shadows of the trees. A chance for the Muses to survive.

And Fae's heart began to break.

SHE SHOULDN'T HAVE let this go so long, Issy thought as she fought the slicing sheets of rain. She should have done something about preserving the paintings the day she found them. But she'd had so much else to deal with.

It was a relief just to get into the woods. The ground was slick, but she hurried down the path, anxious to complete this chore and return to the house before someone saw her and she had to make up some reason for being outside.

The rain seemed to be letting up, but that might be an illusion because of the trees. She could see the cabin up ahead. Dark, forlorn in the darkened light. She hurried onto the porch, and pulled out the key ring that held the keys to all the cabins. She'd shut the door the day she'd found the paintings. She assumed that it would still be locked.

It was, and it took several awkward tries of inserting the keys in the lock while holding a heavy flashlight before she found the one that worked.

She left them in the door and stepped inside. Shone the flashlight around the floor. The canvases were still there, where she'd left them. She propped the plastic roll against the wall, aimed the flashlight toward the first stack of paintings, and reached into her mackintosh pocket for tape and an X-Acto knife. She meant to put them on the easel to keep them from getting lost in the dark, but when she reached for the ledge she found there was a canvas already on it.

Strange, the central easel had been empty. Her stomach clenched as she realized someone must have been here since her discovery of the paintings. She snatched the flashlight off the floor and shone it on the canvas. It wasn't finished, but it had been painted in a hurry, as if the painter didn't want to forget the scene. The cove, the night sky, the full moon. And the eight figures dancing in the moonlight.

For an eternity, Issy just stood there, looking at it as disappointment clogged her throat. The paintings wouldn't save Fae and Leo from the old-folks home. They wouldn't save Muses by the Sea. But they might send Fae to jail.

She wanted to throw that last painting across the tiny room. But what good would that do? They had been her last hope. Even if she applied for every grant and loan for the following year, Leo and Fae would be long gone by then. Sotheby's would have come in and taken what they thought valuable enough to auction. The local dealers would be given the next shot, then the Vets, and whatever was left they would pay to have carted away.

"Nooooo!" She snatched up the flashlight. Let the storm have the damn things, but she wouldn't let anybody get the Muses. Somehow there had to be a way.

She locked the cabin. She'd have to confront Fae. Make sure she hadn't sold any of the paintings. They'd fooled Issy. She wasn't a trained authenticator but in her line of work you learned to spot obvious forgeries, and these were good. They just weren't real . . . Like so many other things about the Muses and the people who lived there.

She took the path back to the house more slowly. Her sense of urgency washed away in the downpour. She'd have to tell Fae that she'd seen the paintings, make sure she hadn't tried to sell them. Or maybe she already had as a last-ditch effort to save the house. Maybe that's why she seemed so complacent.

And if one of those fakes was on the market now or even waiting to be sold . . . It would cause an uproar in the art-world rumor mill and a scandal for her family when the truth came out. But Issy hadn't heard a thing, and if even a whiff of a rumor was out there, she would have heard about it. They were still safe for now.

Ben's truck was parked outside the kitchen when Issy got back. Her heart lifted a little bit, but she really didn't want to see anyone. With any luck he and Paolo would be putting up the shutters and everyone else would be having tea somewhere other than the kitchen.

She threw her raincoat on a peg in the mud room, pushed off the galoshes that were kept by the door, and slid into her espadrilles.

And ran smack into Chloe, who was putting on the kettle.

Leo was sitting at the table, cutting pieces of what looked like zucchini bread. "Where have you been?"

"I just remembered that Steph had been exploring those little cottages in the woods, the other day. I just wanted to make sure she closed the windows." *Sorry, Steph.*

"And had she?" Chloe asked.

"What? Oh yes. False alarm."

"Sit down; I'm making tea. The others are already having theirs in the parlor, but I put on a second kettle for Ben and

Paolo, who are bound to be soaked when they get in. And I've hardly gotten to talk to you all week."

"Hey, not my fault that someone here has moved in on my favorite design assistant."

"Or that someone else has moved in on your brother," Leo said. "Fae caught them kissing on the front porch."

"She didn't." Chloe was smiling, but she turned serious. "Are you and he . . . like an item?"

"Chloe," Issy warned, cutting her eyes toward Leo.

Leo threw back her head and cackled. "You think you invented sex? Ah, the things we did. The goings-on at this house." She shivered. "They were wonderful. And Wes was wonderful." She pulled herself back. "So? Are you?"

"Am I what?" asked Issy, blushing.

"An item."

"Depends on what you mean by an item. We had a good time at dinner."

"And he kissed you," said Chloe.

"Well, I did kiss him back . . . for the record."

"Oh, good." Chloe got down the second teapot from the cabinet, poured in loose tea and hot water.

"But don't get ahead of yourself," Issy warned. She pointed a finger at Leo. "And don't you, either."

"You two would be perfect for each other," Chloe said, ignoring her.

"You always say that about anybody."

"No, I don't. There have been several women I warned him about."

Issy laughed. There was a hurricane on the doorstep, the family was broke, the Whitaker legacy was crashing down around their ears, Issy wasn't even sure she'd have a job waiting when she finally got back to Manhattan, and here they were, talking about men. "Do you know you're the best friend and best grandma anybody could have?"

"No, really. I mean it," Chloe countered. "About Ben."

"He's my best friend's brother."

"Which is why it's so perfect. You know all the good parts and the weird parts about him, too."

Issy smiled. "I guess I do."

The mud room door crashed open and Ben and Paolo pushed inside. "It's torrential out there," Paolo said, jumping up and down to shed the excess rain water from the mack he'd borrowed.

Ben was dressed in professional waterproof pants and coat, bright yellow. "He's not kidding," he said, deadpan.

"Well, come in. I just made tea."

"Tea?" Ben crossed to the fridge. Pulled out two beers. Held them up for Paolo to see.

"Definitely. And maybe a couple of sandwiches."

"Just bring that cold roast out of the fridge," Leo told him. "Paolo, you know where the bread is."

They had an impromptu picnic at the kitchen table, just the five of them. With the steam fogging up the windows and the wind howling just outside the door, Issy forgot about the conversation she would have to have with Fae soon. Forgot about most of her troubles as they laughed and reminisced and Paolo entertained them with some of his and Issy's more ridiculous museum-opening moments.

Chloe and Issy switched to beer. Leo had a glass of Chardonnay from a bottle Chloe found in the fridge. Ben moved his chair closer to Issy and gave her a kiss on the cheek. And for a few minutes they forgot about the world.

FAE LISTENED TO the latest weather report and turned off the television. She made a final round of the windows in that part of the house and returned to the parlor, stopping to close the double pocket doors behind her.

"You'll all be glad to know that the storm has been downgraded to a tropical storm and it has veered east without making landfall."

"Does that mean we can go to camp tomorrow?" Mandy asked.

"Probably not tomorrow, we're still in for some rain and flooding. We'll be housebound for a day or two but we have plenty of food and games and Chloe and Ben are staying to keep you occupied."

"Well, that's a relief," Jillian said. "Come have tea. Chloe made us a pot not long ago. I think it's still warm. Where's Leo?"

"I thought she was here," Fae said, looking around.

"She was here a minute ago," Vivienne said. "Kids, where's Grammy? Steph, do you know where Grammy is?"

Steph shook her head, and went back to the book she was reading.

Fae hurried to the window.

"Can you see her?" Jillian asked, joining her at the window. "You don't think she went outside?"

"I don't see her."

"Vivienne, take Mandy and Griff and go look upstairs. Steph, go—"

Steph shook her head.

"Stephanie," Jillian repeated. "This is serious. We need to find her."

"She told me not to say anything."

"Oh my God, she's gone to Wes. We've got to do something."

Steph looked up from her book. "Chill, Jillian. She's in the kitchen with Chloe. She told me not to tell because she needed a break from us."

Chapter 29

The rain kept up a steady assault all afternoon. Since the hurricane had been downgraded to a tropical storm, Leo went upstairs for a nap and Ben and Chloe decided to go home.

"Take Paolo with you," Issy said.

"No," Paolo said. "You may need me for the heavy lifting."

"Thanks, but I think any heavy lifting can wait until the rains pass. We'll be fine. The Muses is like a fortress. Go off and enjoy the storm with Chloe."

Ben lingered after the two had left. "I can stay, if you need me."

"Thanks, and you're always welcome, but I know you're anxious to check on your instruments."

"It's just I'm at the culmination of two months of observations and data collection."

"Go, but be careful. And call me to let me know you're okay."

Ben looked surprised, then he grinned, and kissed her.

Fae came in while Issy was sitting at the table, wishing she hadn't been so quick to send Ben on his way.

"What is wrong with those children?"

"Which children?"

"Mandy and Griff. They're sniping and whining and picking at each other. I've never seen them like this. It must be the barometric pressure."

"More likely boredom," Issy said. "I think dinner in front of the television is in order."

"If the electricity doesn't go out. It usually does. Comes from all the new housing construction and a very old grid."

Issy was always surprised that Fae could go from burning sage to oust evil spirits to discussing barometric pressure and old electrical grids in a heartbeat. The pathways of her mind were always fascinating.

"Well, if it does go out, my laptop is charged, though I imagine Wi-Fi will be out, too."

"Mandy and Mini Me are hungry," Steph said, coming into the kitchen. "They're driving us all crazy."

"What happened to those kids?" Fae asked. "Do they always whine and fight like that at home?"

"Yes."

"And are you always so morose?" Issy poked Steph in the ribs to lighten the question.

"Me? I'm not morose."

"Have you even spoken to your mother yet?"

Steph shrugged. "Why should I? She stole Grammy's money and she's being a bitch to everyone else. I wish she'd go back to stay with Dad instead of making everybody miserable here."

"Oh, dear," Fae mumbled to herself.

"Well, it's true." Steph's lip trembled. In a second she would be running off somewhere to be alone, hopefully indoors.

Issy wanted to tell her it didn't do any good. But Steph was already heading for the door to the hall. She ran right into her mother, holding a stack of plates. Steph backed up reflexively. And bumped into Fae.

"What's the matter?"

"Nothing," Steph mumbled.

Vivienne put the plates on the table. "What is wrong with you? You've been acting worse than normal since I've been back."

Steph hung her head and eased closer to Fae.

"Vivienne, cut her some slack, why don't you?" Issy said. Wrong thing to do. Vivienne turned on her.

"What do you know about raising children?"

"Well, I'd think those who have been through the trauma of being left by their mother without explanation—you should be able to relate to that one—find themselves in police custody, and have to call an aunt they hardly know to help them deserve a little slack."

"Like we got?"

"We landed in a cushy life with people who loved us. And took care of us."

"And knew nothing about what we really needed."

"It's what I needed."

"Well, goody for you. Look at her."

Issy couldn't tell if she was pointing to Steph or Fae because they were standing so close together and were dressed almost identically today in their favorite patchwork overalls and tie-dyed T-shirts. Issy had gotten so used to seeing Steph copying Fae and Leo's dress code that she'd almost stopped noticing.

"She's turned from a typical teenager to a flower child in a few short weeks. And the trash she's reading. Oh yes, I saw it in your room."

"I'd hardly call a Victorian classic trash," Fae said calmly. But Issy could see her fingering the sage stick in her overalls pocket.

"I just hope you haven't done irreparable harm. George is right, you should be locked up."

"Wait a minute," Issy said. "George never said that. He suggested assisted living because he thought it would be easier for both Fae and Leo and because there isn't enough money to even pay the taxes on the Muses. And who can we thank for that? Oh. You."

Fae eased away from Steph and came to Issy. "It's all right, you don't have to stick up for me. Vivienne's allowed her opinion."

"My opinion? Everybody thinks you're crazy, no matter what they say to your face."

Stephanie lunged before Issy or Fae had an inkling of what she was doing. The force of the impact made Vivienne stagger backward.

"You're horrible. You don't care about anybody but yourself. I hate you!" Steph slammed out of the room.

Fae moved toward the door, but Vivienne stood in front of it. "Don't you dare go after her. Haven't you done enough harm already?" She turned and stalked out of the room.

Fae sagged and Issy just managed to pull out a chair from the table before she crumpled into it and covered her face with both hands.

LEO STOOD LOOKING out the window and closed her ears and her mind to the noise. The television, the arguments, even the rain hurt her head. She touched the windowpane as if she could touch Wes through the glass, but it was slick with a river of rain.

How she needed him, when the family was falling apart. To lie quiet in his arms as the rain beat against the house, safe within his love, within his world.

We loved storms, didn't we? Making love beneath the thunder and lightning, Wes slick and sweating and powerful, crescendoing with the storm, not stopping with the calm. *We were immortal, god and goddess of all that was beautiful, passionate, iconic.* The bedcovers falling to the floor, Wes and Fae falling with them and laughing. *We laughed so hard and wrapped ourselves together in the quilt like a cocoon and waddled to the window to watch clouds roll in and the rain pound down and we couldn't stop from tumbling to the floor and taking each other once again. Your hands are everywhere and mine—*

"I've had it with you. You'll go upstairs and change into something normal."

Leo's palm slid from the window. Wes was gone.

"I DIDN'T MEAN to cause that," Fae said.

"You didn't," Issy assured her. "Vivienne is angry at everyone but herself. She's like that donkey in *Winnie-the-Pooh*."

"Eeyore."

"Yes." Issy smiled at her. "I hope you didn't take all that stuff she said seriously."

"About me being crazy and needing to be locked up? Dear Issy, it's been said for my whole life. I never tried to change because I just didn't understand how to do it. Nor did I want to. I don't see anything wrong with me."

"And I don't, either." Issy leaned over and kissed her cheek. "Now I'm going to fix a tray for those little hellions that should keep them buzzing for hours and send their mother into a fit of apoplexy. Do we have any Cheez Doodles?"

Mandy and Griff ate in front of the television. With their mouths stuffed and the sound blaring, Issy couldn't tell if they were fighting or not.

Everyone who hadn't eaten managed on their own and by the time it grew dark they were all back in the parlor attempting to appear like a family while the storm raged around them. Leo look rested but preoccupied. Fae had brought out a bag that held yarn and a crochet hook, which she used with fierce concentration. It was surprising. Issy had no idea she'd taken up crocheting.

Jillian stood by the window looking out at the rain while nursing her gin and tonic. Steph had yet to make an appearance. Issy caught herself reaching for her laptop—very rude. Eyed the tube of Toulouse-Lautrec specs. No place to spread them out. For a moment she even considered checking out whatever was blaring from the television.

She did none of them. Just sat there.

Stephanie finally came downstairs, still dressed in her Fae clothes, which Issy had to admit she was glad to see. Time for that kid to start making a break from all that bad energy.

Issy smiled at her thought. She was beginning to sound a little like Aunt Fae herself.

Stephanie crossed the room without acknowledging anyone and blatantly ignoring her mother, sat in the chair she'd been using for her reading, and picked up a book.

Issy stole a glance at Vivienne, who had been looking at the same page of an old issue of *Town and Country* for the last twenty minutes.

"It seems like the rain is lessening," Leo said.

The lights went out.

Screams of "Mommy!" pierced the darkness. "Mommy!"

Someone lit a lantern, handed it to Vivienne, who held it awkwardly in front of her as she went to collect her children.

The rest of them sat in darkness. No outside lights, no lights from afar, no stars or moon, just dark.

"This is nice," Fae said as the room slowly began to take on shapes of dark and darker.

"I was watching that," Griff complained as his mother carted him on her hip into the parlor. Mandy trailed alongside, clutching at Vivienne's belt.

"But I was watching it," whined Griff.

"The electricity is out. There is no television or lights." Vivienne's voice was soothing, but it had no effect on Griff. She placed the lantern on the coffee table and slid Griff down to the floor. "Can someone get some more light?"

"But I want to see it," and he started to cry.

"Play a game," Jillian said, and blew out the match that she had just used to light the storm lantern on the reading table beside her.

Issy was so astonished that she stared at her.

"It won't work without television," Mandy said. "And he never lets me play anyway."

"Don't you know any regular games?"

"Like what?"

"I don't know."

"Leave Jillian alone," Vivienne said. "She doesn't know any children's games."

Jillian raised an eyebrow. Issy couldn't really see it in the lantern light but she felt it.

There was a brief standoff between mother and daughter,

then Jillian said, "Of course I know a game. I used to play with you and Issy."

"Really, Jillian? I don't seem to remember any games. I just remember being here with a famous mother somewhere else."

"Do you really know a game, Gran—Jillian?" Mandy slid off the couch and came over to Jillian's chair.

"I want to play." Griff followed Mandy.

Jillian sighed. "I do. I hope I don't screw this up," she added to no one in particular. "Okay, hold out your hands."

They held out their hands.

"Just one. The left one."

Mandy held out her left hand. Griff watched then held out his left hand.

"Okay. Now look at your palm. No, like this." She turned Griff's palm to face him. "Now you—here, come around like this." She pulled them both around to stand on either side of her chair.

She held up her own hand, fingers splayed. Everyone looked on to see Jillian York play a child's game.

"Okay, take your other hand and count your fingers."

"What? That's not a game." Mandy put down her hand.

"Sure it is. It's called the Oops game."

Issy started. Steph closed her book and sat up.

"Griff and I will demonstrate. Point to each finger and follow me." She pointed to her pinkie. "Griffin." Next finger. "Griffin." Next. "Griffin, Griffin—" Then a slide down the slope between index finger and thumb. "Oops Griffin." Back the way she'd come. "Oops Griffin, Griffin, Griffin, Griffin."

"Now you try."

Griffin bit his lip; it was slow but he got it done, and had barely finished his last "Griffin" when Mandy interrupted. "I can do it faster. Watch."

"Mandy, Mandy, Mandy, Mandy, Oops Mandy, Oops Mandy, Mandy, Mandy, Mandy."

"Very good." Jillian stifled a yawn.

"Let's do Mommy," Griff said. "Mommy, Mommy . . ."

"Let's do Aunt Issy, 'cause her name is Oops and it will be Oops, Oops, Oops, Oops, Oops, Oops . . ." Mandy and Griff dissolved into giggles.

"I've created a couple of monsters. I'd forgotten this part. The giggles."

Issy gripped the arms of the chair she was sitting in. Steph jumped up. "That's not nice."

Jillian frowned. "It's just a game."

"Aunt Issy wasn't a mistake. She's the best aunt anybody could have."

"Of course she is. What is all this mistake business? You said that before."

Steph looked to Issy, clearly torn. Issy couldn't help her; she was paralyzed with humiliation—again.

"Issy said you called her Oops because she was a mistake."

"Ridiculous. I never said such a thing. This was Issy's favorite game and she giggled more than those two put together. She loved it so much she called herself Oops Issy and it caught on. Issy's wrong if she thought that."

But Issy noticed she didn't look her way.

"Mom said it, too."

"No, I didn't."

"Uh-huh," Mandy said. "You said it was Aunt Issy's fault that Jillian gave you away."

"I didn't give them away. What utter nonsense."

"I'm sure you misunderstood," Leo said.

"Nuh-huh," Griff said. "She says you did give her away because Aunty Issy was a mistake."

Jillian turned to the others. "Is that what you all think?"

"Well, it's true," Vivienne blurted out. "Everything was fine until she came."

Issy just sat there as snippets of memory crowded before her mind and passed on like an old-fashioned newsreel, the good-byes, the newspaper headlines, the taunts by Vivienne and then her schoolmates, egged on by her sister. The recent talk about saving them from Hollywood. The game. Oops Issy. It sounded so familiar and then she saw it. She was wearing a pink dress with lots of ruffles, sitting on Jillian's lap, laughing, and holding out her chubby fingers, and saying, "More, Mommy."

"Is that why you left us with two old ladies we barely knew? You drove away without a backward look. I was happy with you in Hollywood. People were nice there, we did fun things. It was awful here. I wasn't like the other girls anymore. Their mothers picked them up in nice cars and wore tennis outfits and took them to the mall.

"I just had an old witch in a broken-down station wagon smeared with paint and making a spectacle of herself while all the kids laughed at me.

"I just wanted to be a normal kid, go to the mall, sit down with a family and not a bunch of crazy artists arguing about things I didn't understand and who didn't care about children or know how to talk to them."

"Maybe I should take her back to Hollywood with me," Jillian told Issy under her breath. "She certainly has the flare for drama."

"We had no idea," Leo said, rising from her chair, but collapsing back on the seat. "I'm so sorry, dear. You're right. We had no idea how to raise children."

"Bullshit," Stephanie said. "You and Aunt Fae are great with children. We've had a great time here, haven't we?" She looked wildly at Mandy and Griff, daring them not to agree. She didn't have to.

"We love you, Grammy," Mandy said, and ran to hug her. "You, too, Aunt Fae."

But Fae was looking out the window.

No doubt longing for her cottage.

And Issy saw red. "Yeah, they were so bad at raising children that you dumped your own children on them and it's twenty-something years later. But did they turn you away? No, they took them in and it nearly killed Leo."

"No, no, Issy. It was a silly accident, my fault for not paying attention." Leo's hand went to her chest and Issy gaped in horror that she'd just given her grandmother a heart attack. But Leo just shook her head. "Mine."

"No, Grammy," Issy said. "It's Vivienne's. Isn't it, Viv? You robbed her of millions of dollars, destroying the family legacy. So you have your revenge on us all."

"I didn't. Why won't you believe me? I didn't know what Dan was doing. He stole from me, too. He took everything. I have nothing left."

"The hell you don't. You have a family that accepts you even after all this."

"That's not what I meant."

"Then what do you mean? You willingly jettisoned your children, but according to you, that's what this family does."

"I didn't. I was always going to come back for them. Not like . . . like . . . our mother."

"Stop it. Stop it, both of you." Jillian rose to theatrical heights before their eyes. "I know you blame me for everything that went wrong in your lives. Though until Dan's sleight of hand I would say that neither of you had anything to complain about. But before you fling around any more accusations, let's start back at the beginning and get it right. I'll tell you exactly what happened. Hollywood is a hard enough place on adults who have their wits about them. But it eats children alive. I saw it and knew I had made a big mistake. Not having you but having you and thinking I could also have Hollywood.

"I was gone for weeks, sometimes months, at a time and left you with nannies and nurses. Do you remember those times?

"Probably not, but I did. I remember the screams and the tears, and the flailing each time I left, the pitiful little voices begging me to come home until I couldn't stand it. And I knew one day I would leave town and the drugs and money and all those devouring things would move in to take my place, and I knew I had to choose.

"Well, I chose. I chose Hollywood. And your father for my sins. You wanted to know all this. Well, here it is all laid out with a bow.

"I didn't get motherhood. It was a publicity stunt arranged by someone else. But I got acting. So I brought you to the most wonderful place on earth with the most loving interesting people I knew; crazy, wild, nonconformists but with true hearts, something else you rarely find in L.A. Something I may have lost most of along the way.

"Vivienne, I'm sorry you think you had a rotten life. And I'm sorry if you, Issy, think you were a mistake. But trust me, your life was a lot better here than it would have been with me."

She walked slowly over to where Leo sat and knelt down. "I'm sorry, Mother, to have caused you so much anguish. I was selfish. I still am. I meant to tell you before, but this seems as good a time as any. My agent called yesterday. She has a part for me and I'm afraid I have to leave as soon as the storm lets up.

"I'm sorry if I set this all off. Greed and desperation brought me here." She stopped, smiled. "We've welcomed a lot of desperate people at the Muses, haven't we?" She glanced around the darkened room. "But once I got here, I realized I was home.

"Issy, do what you have to do to keep the Muses in the family. I'll see what I can do to get George off your backs while you figure it out." She stood and walked from the room, managing to hit all the hot spots of lantern light, Issy noticed—but didn't realize—until many minutes later.

Vivienne was crying, balled up on the sofa like a little girl. Leo struggled out of her chair and went to sit beside her.

"Now, now," she said, and to Issy's amazement, Vivienne melted into her shoulder while Leo rocked her and stroked her hair. Issy motioned to the children and led them into the central hall, snatching up a lantern as she walked past.

"Whoa," Steph said.

"Is our mommy crazy?" Mandy asked with real fear flickering in her eyes.

"No, hon. Just a little upset. Let's get out the ice cream and eat it all before it melts."

FAE BENT HER head and pushed her shoulders into the storm. The wind had died down; the storm was passing off the coast. She couldn't wait any longer. All her life, happiness had been just beyond her reach, a tantalizing gift not given, but nothing could be changed. She'd been a fool to think it could be.

UPSTAIRS IN HER bedroom, Jillian hauled out her designer suitcase and packed in the light of one candle. Her agent *had* called. With a character part, the aging neighbor of one of the bright young stars of the day. It was a good part as character parts went. She'd said she'd think about it. She'd meant to call her agent tomorrow and say no. But she'd just called her back and accepted.

IN HER BEDROOM down the hall, Leonore floated in the cool blue water of the cove. She couldn't see him, but she knew Wes was on the other side, waiting for her.

Chapter 30

L eonore stood at the crest of the knoll as the sun rose above the horizon. She wasn't alone, she was never alone out here.

Another storm, not so bad, this one. Not like some we made it through. There doesn't seem to be much damage, not to the house. Oh, but to the Whitakers, my dear. They are so unhappy. Well, Vivienne is unhappy. I suppose you know that you were wrong to place your trust in Dan.

Ah, we were wrong about so many things. But how can you always choose wisely when you're having so much fun and when you love and are loved so deeply. Is it wrong to love that much?

I know it must be wrong for you to be there and I, here.

Can you see little Issy? She's finally come back and is trying desperately to save the Muses. I should tell her to go, not let herself be encumbered by the past, but we did that once and she almost didn't come back at all.

Remember the first time we met? Of course you do. The day was so warm, the sun beating down on the rock and the water so cool and inviting. I didn't know you were there, not consciously, though I must have felt you waiting in the wood.

I stood with the rough granite heating my feet. Dropped my shift; it had little owls on the fabric.

Then I stretched my arms to the sky, lifted my whole being, and dove. Were you watching me then? Worried that I stayed under so long? I was always a good swimmer. I swam the width of the cove before coming up for air. And there you were. Socks and Birkenstocks. I fell in love before my eyes even traveled to the rest of you.

Was it like that for you, too? Of course it was. Though I miss hearing you say it. And I know you're waiting for me. And when I get there, you'll be there with your hands outstretched to take mine. And lift me to you, safe and untroubled again.

Just reach out my hands . . . like this . . .

ISSY BRACED HER arms on the kitchen counter and watched the coffee drip into the glass carafe, thankful that the electricity had come back on during the night. She hadn't slept well; too much stuff was going on in her brain, worrying about her family members who after her confrontation with Vivienne had scattered in the dark to their own rooms.

So much for a cozy familial camp-out in the parlor. It had ended in disaster. Issy wouldn't be surprised if Leo kicked them all out when she woke up this morning. It was pretty clear that her grandmother was tired of them all.

Part of that was Issy's fault. She'd inadvertently brought down Jillian and George's wrath on her grandmother and Fae's heads. Vivienne was out of her control, but she could have tried to be more sympathetic. And what? Let their feelings fester another ten years, another twenty, until they were both left virtual orphans? Their children without relatives. Maybe this was for the best, just get it over with.

At least she had finally come home to the Muses, met her nieces and nephew. Maybe even bonded a little with Steph. Gotten to know Jillian just a bit, and stupidly, ridiculously, learned the most important thing of all—that she'd gotten her name Oops from a game and not because she was a mistake.

She almost laughed out loud. How could a grown woman live under such misapprehensions? In the early-morning light, it didn't seem possible. Or why it could have mattered so much.

Someone came in, interrupting her thoughts.

"Steph. What are you doing up this early?"

Stephanie padded into the room. She was wearing jeans and one of Fae's old tie-dyed T-shirts and Issy wondered if this was the beginning of the reconciliation with her mother. Because reconcile they must, somehow.

She came to stand beside Issy, not looking at her but staring at the slow-dripping coffee. The kid didn't even drink coffee.

"You want breakfast?"

Steph shook her head.

"Anybody else up?"

Steph shrugged.

"Well, I expect Fae will be up in a bit."

"No."

Issy turned to look at her.

"She went home last night. I mean to her cottage."

"Are you sure? During the storm?"

Steph nodded. "I told her it was dangerous and she said she couldn't wait any longer. To at least give her that."

Issy frowned. "At least give her that? Do you know what she meant?"

Steph shrugged, but her mouth twisted and she turned

away. Her back lifted in a deep breath. "I made her take my cell in case we needed her, or . . . vice versa."

Issy checked her own phone in case she'd somehow missed a call. Nothing. "She must be okay."

"I think it stinks."

"What?"

"Nothing."

Jillian came through the doorway.

"Wonders never cease," Issy said.

"Excuse me, miss, but I'm often on set by this hour and that's after two hours in hair and makeup, so don't give me a hard time. But I'd kill for a cup of coffee."

Steph got down another mug. "Here, Jillian."

"Thank you, dear." She sighed. "And you may call me Grandmother if you like."

Issy and Steph stared at her.

"Alas. I wasn't ready to confess last night, but the part I'm called for is a supporting role. A character part of a retired CEO and neighbor to the star. Damn her. No, really, I'll be nice. I have to accept that my ingenue days are over."

"Well, Mother . . ." Issy tried the word on for size. "You *are* over sixty."

Jillian shuddered dramatically. "Gracefully," she intoned as she walked over to the fridge for the milk. "Gracefully, will I go into that dark night of maturity."

"I doubt it," Steph whispered to Issy.

Jillian turned and laughed. "You, my dear, are a Whitaker through and through." She pulled out a chair and sat down. "I thought I'd find Leo here."

"She must still be asleep. I think these last weeks have tired her out."

"No. I checked her room and the bathroom. Oh Lord, you don't think—" Jillian was already hurrying into the hallway. It only took a second for Issy and Steph to follow, but when they reached the parlor, Jillian had already pulled back the drapes and was peering out the windows.

"Why are these panes so dirty? It's impossible to see."

Or maybe it was her eyesight. Issy squeezed in next to her. She knew right where to look. There was someone sitting on the bench on the knoll. "There she is."

"Where? Let me see. What's she doing?"

Steph nudged in between them.

"She's stretching out her arms," Jillian said. "Is she falling?"

"No," Steph said. "No. It's like in the story she told us of how she and Wes met. She dove into the water and he was waiting to take her hands on the other side."

"The other side? No!" Jillian pushed Issy and Steph out of the way and ran for the front door. They all crowded onto the porch. A branch had fallen across the steps and they had to slow down to navigate across it. By the time they reached the lawn, they saw Fae coming out of the woods.

"It's Leo," Jillian screamed. "We've got to stop her."

Fae didn't even ask where to look, but started running toward the knoll.

They met Leo as she was coming back across the lawn.

"Oh, Grammy, are you okay?" Issy asked.

"Of course I'm okay."

"It looked like you were about to—to fall," Jillian said, trying to sound concerned, not frightened.

"They thought . . ." Fae huffed. "They thought . . ." She held up one finger, then braced her hands on her knees and heaved a few deep breaths.

"I needed to talk to Wes. I miss him dreadfully, but I told him he'd have to wait. That the family needed me. He'll be there when I'm ready. He would never let me down."

"Oh, Grammy, we do need you." Steph threw her arms around Leo.

"Thank you, Stephanie. It's always good to be needed. Now, we have lots to do. But first on the agenda is for you all to go back to the house and put the coffee on, then we'll all sit down to a nice breakfast.

"We have to agree about how to help Vivienne back on her feet. And how to help Steph reconcile with her mother. I'll try to make it up to all of you, but first I must speak with Fae. So go back to the house now."

Issy wasn't sure she wanted to leave them outside, but when Steph started back toward the house, she did, too. Jillian was the last to give in, but finally she followed the other two.

FAE WALKED WITH Leo back to the bench.

"They were afraid you were going to jump, you know."

"Ridiculous."

"They thought you were going to rejoin Wes in heavenly bliss."

"Heavenly? Wes? I doubt if that's where we'll be, but who knows."

"Were you?"

"Going to jump from the knoll? I'd end up facedown on the beach with a mouth full of sand. I won't go yet. During the storm, I felt so alone. But I couldn't, not with the family and the future of the Muses at stake. Though sometimes it is tempting."

"What if there is no heaven or hell, what if it just ends?"

"This coming from you?"

"Will you be disappointed?"

"Frankly, heaven or hell? Wherever I'm going, Wes will be there to take my hands. Of that I'm certain. And for you, my dear, it's time."

Fae shook her head.

"It was a promise kept too long. I have my whole family back and I've depended on you for too, too long."

"Are you sure?"

"Yes. You are the dearest friend and sister anyone could have. I'll miss you, dearest, but either here or there . . ."

The two shed a few tears, hugged, and sat there while the sun took its place in the sky.

Leo pulled away. "And now I think you need to talk to Stephanie."

"I can't tell her."

"She's a Whitaker; you won't have to."

Issy sat at the kitchen table watching Vivienne, Mandy, and Griff cutting fruit for breakfast.

She vacillated between apologizing for the argument the night before and pretending like it didn't happen. She decided on the latter.

Evidently, so had Vivienne. "Chloe called and said they had electricity and no damage. And she and Paolo were on their way to help with cleanup."

"Great," Issy said. "I'll get some eggs and bacon started. I'm famished."

Paolo and Chloe showed up a few minutes later. "Ben's in the salt marshes all day today. He lost some experiments. But he knew he would. Still, it's a lot of work and he said not to clean up anything until tomorrow and he'll come help."

Issy stifled the bit of disappointment she felt knowing she wouldn't see him today. But there was plenty of work to be done and plenty of relationships to readjust.

They'd have a busy day.

After lunch, Fae announced that she would be returning to her cottage. Her bags and case were packed and she asked Steph to help her get them home.

Jillian had called a car to pick her up at three. She had an evening flight to L.A. Issy had to pay for it with her credit card, and give Jillian money for tipping and a cup of coffee at the airport.

"Allison will send a car for me at LAX. She's my agent, but we've been together so long that we've become friends. I'll stay with her until I get settled. Hate to leave you with the mess, but duty and a paycheck call."

At three o'clock, they all said good-bye and Issy and Vivienne walked their mother out to the limo.

The driver placed the luggage in the trunk and opened the door for Jillian to get in.

She looked from one daughter to the other. "I made some mistakes. I'm sure I'll make more. But better to have tried and all that. It's time to let go of it, blame me if you must, but stop blaming each other."

Vivienne sniffed. "Will you be okay?"

Jillian trilled a laugh. She was already in actress mode. "Of course I will. It may be a character part, but I'm not the first actress who has had to segue during her career. And hell, if it's good enough for Meryl Streep, it's good enough for me."

She kissed them both on the cheek, then got in the limo, first one foot and then the other, which lingered in the opening, showing off her four-inch heels and several inches of well-toned leg.

"I may no longer be an ingenue, but I've still got the ankles to drum up some serious money for the Muses Museum.

"You'll be hearing from me. And I guess I'll have to come back in September. I did promise the ladies of the Theater Fund I would be their hostess for the gala. Maybe you can offer the Muses as venue for their patron party. I'm sure we could pick off some of their heavy hitters while we're at it.

"Ciao, darlings. Be good."

The driver shut the door and jumped into the front. Soon the limo was out of the gates and gone.

Issy and Vivienne turned and walked back to the house, but Vivienne stopped Issy before they went inside.

"I really didn't know about Dan."

"Okay."

"I know I have't been very nice, but I was so miserable. I would never hurt this family."

Issy gave her the Jillian York lifted eyebrow.

"I was just too self-involved to realize what I was doing."

"Is that your excuse?"

"No, it's me saying I'm sorry. I went after what I thought was the perfect life. And it turned out to be anything but. Now I'm homeless, with two children who'd rather stay with their great-grandmother than me, and one daughter who despises me."

"She doesn't despise you."

"Do you think she'll ever come around?"

Issy looked out at the empty drive, where once again a limo had just taken their own mother away. "We did. Give her time."

THEY ALL SPENT the rest of the day setting the house to rights. Paolo insisted they wait until Ben and he came over the next morning before they attempted to clean up the outside property. The storm had done minimal damage around the house at least. A few downed branches were large enough to require a skill saw, but most were smaller pieces that could be carried or dragged to the curb outside the gate.

But no one really felt like working. It had been a trying couple of weeks and now a strange lassitude settled over them. They needed time to assimilate. Time to decide what path to take. Mandy and Griff were back to their boisterous selves after learning that camp would be held the next morning.

With Jillian gone and Fae back at her own cottage, the house seemed a little larger—maybe even a little empty. Twice Steph forgot to ignore her mother, but Issy wasn't sure if it was because things were thawing between them or if it was because Steph was definitely preoccupied.

And Issy wondered if something had happened between Fae and her on their walk back to the cottage. Had she insisted that Steph reconcile with her mother? Is that why the girl was making such halfhearted efforts?

Or was there more trouble brewing?

Not something Issy wanted to contemplate tonight, so she took her laptop back to the music room. Rolled out the Toulouse-Lautrec specs and started making notes. She was down to her last paycheck. It was time to get back to Manhattan or figure out a way to afford to stay.

Chapter 31

The whole household was up the next morning, dressed in work clothes and with a new resigned, if not enthusiastic, energy.

Chloe dropped by to take Mandy and Griff to camp. Ben and Paolo arrived with truck and saws a few minutes later.

Issy went out to meet them, mainly because she wanted to see Ben. He took her right into his arms like they knew they were meant to be there. She hadn't thought that far ahead. And she was pretty sure he hadn't, not with him worrying over his salt-marsh measurements.

"What are you laughing about?"

"I'm not. How are the marshes?"

"*Mezza, mezza.* Once again they saved the lowlands from some major flooding." He sighed, totally over-the-top. "But they just don't get no respect."

"Well, they do around here." She kissed him, just to remember how it felt. It felt right. "Okay, boss men, where do you want to start?"

For a couple of hours the sound of skill saws reverberated in the air. Limbs and bags of twigs and garbage were hauled out to the street. Midmorning they took a coffee break, and before they could start up again, Fae arrived.

"I need to borrow Issy for a minute," she said, and motioned her outside.

"Can I help?" Ben asked.

"No, just Issy. I'll send her back soon."

"What is it, Aunt Fae?" Issy asked as soon as they were in the yard.

"Just come with me. I have something to show you." She struck off toward the path that led through the woods.

They didn't talk until they took the fork toward Fae's cottage. Issy slowed down to glance at the cabin where she'd found the paintings.

"They're not there," Fae said, and kept walking. She didn't stop until they came to the edge of the woods and the beginning of the meadow. "I had no idea Vivienne resented me so much."

"Don't pay any attention to her. She resented everyone."

"But everyone didn't show up in public with her. And I was just trying to be a good aunt and maybe mother substitute, but I only embarrassed her. I didn't understand. I kept trying to do more and more and she wanted me to just go away. Please tell her I'm sorry."

"You have nothing to be sorry for, but if you want to talk to her, you should, not me."

"I won't be here."

Issy began to be afraid. "What are you going to do? Please, Aunt Fae, if anything happened to you, Grammy, me, all of us—"

"Oh, my dear. I have no intention of throwing myself off the bluff. Life is a precious thing. But I won't check myself into an old-folks home, either. Old folks should be free, should be allowed to soak up the last of their days like there was no tomorrow, because one day, there will be no tomorrow."

That brought a smile to Issy's mouth at the same time tears flooded her eyes. She didn't want that day to come for Fae or Leo or any of them. Unless she went, too. What would she do without this family?

"What are you going to do?"

"I'm going away."

"No, we'll see this through. I have a plan. If you can just be patient."

"I've been patient long enough."

"I don't understand, what do you mean? Where are you going?"

Fae didn't answer but motioned her forward. They walked past the meadow to the point of rock where the little yellow cottage had withstood one more storm.

There was a van parked in the rutted footpath that led to the road.

"Whose van is that?"

"A friend's."

"I don't understand. If you're in any kind of trouble, we'll see it through."

Fae shook her head and went across the porch to the door. Opened it and motioned Issy inside.

It had been years since Issy had been in this cottage. Still, it looked different. Then she realized that the bookshelf and all the books were gone. Moved to a back room? Or moved to the van? All the things that belonged to her great-aunt . . . the photos, the found marine objects, the books, cushions, pottery . . . all gone.

"Are you really leaving? But what about Leo?"

"We've talked. It's all good."

"But why? How? Where are you going? Is your friend who owns the van going, too? This doesn't make sense."

A chair scraped across the floor in the next room. Footsteps and a tall lithe man wearing all white with silver hair flowing almost to his waist ducked his head and stepped into the room.

Steph's Elf King.

Not a king—elfin or otherwise—but a painter. A painter who had been dead for almost a decade. Aunt Fae hadn't been forging his paintings. Adam Ellis had been painting them. Issy sank onto the couch.

"You're alive?" Adam Ellis was definitely alive and well and living in Aunt Fae's cottage. "But how? What are you doing here?"

He chuckled, a low rumbling melodic sound she remembered from childhood. "We're eloping."

Issy just stared while her brain tried to engage. "Like . . . *eloping* eloping?"

Adam smiled over at Fae and the love in his eyes hurt Issy's heart. "But—"

"We've had a . . . what shall we call it, Fae? An understanding, for decades."

Issy tried to remember them as younger, but to her, Fae had always been an ageless fairy child. And Adam, she remembered him. He often came to visit, sometimes staying in the main house, sometimes sleeping out in one of the cottages where he painted.

"How many decades?" She slapped her hand over her mouth. "Sorry, not my business. It's just such a shock."

"Three . . . four . . . more." His eyes twinkled and Issy saw a glimmer of the young man, playing at pirates on the back lawn, sipping kirs, and reading the latest *New Yorker* reviews. Often happy, but also sometimes deeply troubled. That's what Leo had called it when once he'd taken a carving knife and slashed his newly painted canvas to shreds right in the middle of dinner. Issy had read later about his drug and alcohol problems. One of those people who couldn't take the attention or the pressure. "Even before I blindly married Harriet Payne. I was such a fool."

"And you've been here ever since the accident?"

"I finally made my way back here."

"And lived here ever since?"

"Yes."

"And no one ever recognized you?"

He shook his head. "How many people would recognize any painter on the street? We're not movie stars. And after a while I was so changed, no one even looked twice. Even you."

"Me?"

"I passed you on the street in town. And stood right across from you when Fae was doing her last drawing."

"Tuor and Idril. But if no one recognizes you, you both could stay here."

"No," Fae said. "Once the new paintings are 'discovered,' speculation will be rife. We can't take the chance."

"I can't go back, Issy. I couldn't handle the pressure, the temptations. It should have killed me, it almost did. And that saved me. In that split second when you know you're going to die and it's too late to do anything about it, I saw myself and I was glad to go. And I went straight through the guardrail and into the river.

"Imagine my surprise when I woke up miles downstream and not dead yet."

"And so you decided to stay dead?"

"Not at all. I was dead. And I was glad."

"But what about your family?"

"Hardly had any. My wife and her family had given up on me as soon as they realized they couldn't profit by my success. But they certainly profited from my death. They made a fortune on my paintings. I'm sure they're quite happy."

"Doesn't anyone have a normal family?"

Adam and Fae both looked shocked.

"Why on earth would you want a normal family?" asked Fae. "Besides, there's no such thing. That was Vivienne's mistake; behind those tennis outfits and trips to the mall are just people with all their warts, their fears, their disappointments, their anger."

Adam and Fae moved a little closer together.

"Our lives aren't perfect, maybe they're worse, but that's art for you. Heaven or hell and hardly ever anything in between. Fortunately, Fae has generously offered to give up her home, her way of life, to go with me."

"Where?"

"Somewhere."

"Somewhere? That's a song not a place."

Fae reached out and took Issy's hands. "I'm sorry, Issy. We're just going to go until we find the right place. I know you think I'm deserting the family. I promised Wes I would always take care of Leo, but Leo doesn't need me anymore. Actually she never did. She's always had Wes, even in death. Now it's my time. Please let me go and do it without the guilt. My time." She rolled the two words on her tongue like a fine wine.

Her time. She deserved it.

"I've left you the paintings," Adam said. "All but one and I'm taking that with us."

"The Full Moon Dance," Issy said.

"Yes. The rest are finished, they're all signed. Sell the older ones first, say you found them in the attic. They should bring enough to do necessary renovations and get the museum up and running."

"But what about you? How will you manage?"

"We knew this day would come, we've made provisions. The paintings are yours but we've moved them to a secure climate-controlled storage unit." He reached in the pocket of his pants and handed her a locker key on a braided loop of leather.

"If you're leaving because the paintings will lead to your discovery, keep them, we'll find a different way."

He and Fae smiled at each other.

"She said you would have this reaction. We're ready to go . . ." He glanced down at Fae. "More than ready.

"And in view of her astute knowledge of her family—of you, to be exact—I took the liberty of sending the oldest painting to a friend of mine to put up for auction. He knows my story, he won't give me away. He thinks it will fetch at least seven hundred K after his fees. You should be receiving a check within a few weeks.

"I just ask that you leave the newer ones hidden as long as you can. Someone is bound to figure out that some of them were painted after I was dead. And after they go through the series of tests to prove them forgeries, they'll realize Adam Ellis the painter lives on.

"So it's a good thing that I finished them and fled before you ever came back or you might have found me out." He smiled, as if he had no cares in the world, and maybe he'd just jettisoned his final earthly burden.

He reached in his shirt pocket and pulled out an envelope. "Put this in your safety deposit box. If it ever comes to it, this states that I gave the Whitakers these paintings in thanks for their unwavering support."

Issy took the envelope and Adam wrapped his long arms around both Fae and her in an embrace Issy knew was good-bye. And she held them both as another piece of her life's tapestry was ripped from her. But this sacrifice she was willing to make, not for the money the paintings would bring, she had no intention of selling any more than necessary. The Muses would have an entire room dedicated to Adam Ellis, who inspired an entire Coastal School generation and who loved her aunt.

Issy left after that, carrying a rattan case meant for Stephanie. Fae didn't walk her back, and when Issy asked her what she was supposed to tell Stephanie, Fae said, "Nothing, You and Stephanie really are special. She'll understand."

Issy was teary-eyed as she made her way along the path, the meadow grasses, and the cornflowers, a hazy mist of blue and green.

She thought about never seeing her aunt again. Or Adam now that she'd been introduced to him again. But she understood, and hopefully Steph would, too.

When she came out of the woods onto the lawn, she saw Steph standing on the knoll looking across the cove. She already knew. Either Fae had prepared her or she had been expecting just this outcome.

Issy came to stand beside her. They didn't speak, just looked across the blue, blue water to Fae's faerie cottage. The bright yellow paint already looked as if it were beginning to fade, the cottage wavering in the sunlight, wavering and bleeding into the air like one of Fae's chalk paintings on the village sidewalks. Soon there would be nothing left but memories.

Would it be enough? Would they someday be reunited? Could you be arrested for impersonating yourself?

And what about Steph? Fae had taken on a sullen, jaded almost-teenager and helped her to blossom. And now, in great Whitaker fashion, she was leaving her, and Issy's heart ached for the child who was about to learn she'd been deserted, not just left behind while her mother looked for stolen money, not left by a mother who had no time or interest in raising two young daughters. But deserted forever maybe, by someone she trusted and someone she loved. And suddenly all the old hurt and sadness and yes, anger, bubbled up inside Issy, not for herself but for her niece.

As they watched, two people came out the front door of the cottage, hesitated on the porch, and Issy thought maybe they were saying good-bye. Then they walked around the house and a minute later the van drove away and out of sight.

Issy cleared her throat and hoped words would come. "You know what's happening?"

"She's going away with her Elf King."

"Do you know who the Elf King is?"

"I think so. He painted that painting in the library. He was in the photograph."

"Yes."

"Aunt Issy, we must never mention this."

"Why do you say that?"

"Because she needs to be free. They both need to be free."

"Did Aunt Fae tell you that?"

"She didn't have to. I just knew."

Issy handed her the little flat box. "She left you this."

Steph took the box and hugged it to her chest, not surprised or curious. "I'll miss her."

"I will, too. What do you think we should tell the others?"

"The truth, Aunt Issy. She went away with the Elf King."

"They'll all think we're crazy, except maybe Grammy."

"Of course they will. We're Whitakers."

ISSY DIDN'T STOP when they returned to the house but went straight to the music room and closed the pocket doors. She knew no one would disturb her and she wanted to work and think and make some decisions.

When she came out two hours later she found everyone but Mandy, Griff and Steph seated around the kitchen table. The table was covered in food, wine and beer bottles, and notebooks.

"For a house that has fifteen bedrooms, a conservatory, two parlors, and all sorts of miscellaneous rooms, we sure do sit around the kitchen a lot."

"Come in," Chloe said. "We gave up waiting for you, but there's plenty left."

But Issy just stood in the doorway and looked them over. Her best friend from school, who had stepped up to help without even needing to be asked. Ben, who had always been more than a big brother and was now what Issy was beginning to think could be an indispensable part of her life. Paolo, one of a kind, the best assistant a designer could hope to have, a good designer in his own right, and a good friend. Grammy, who deserved to be happy in her own home for as long as she wanted, and Vivienne. They were sisters, for better or worse . . . could they ever be friends? Maybe, maybe not. But they were both part of the family and Issy was determined to start over again.

Chloe poured out a glass of wine. Ben moved his chair over and dragged an extra chair to the empty place beside him. Issy sat down and took the wine.

"We've been talking while you were gone," Paolo said. "I at least have come to a decision and I think I should tell you before we go any further. I've decided to stay here, see how Chloe and I get on. I'm perfectly willing to watch out for the Muses and Leo, if we can figure out a way to keep them here."

"No more museum work?" Issy asked, trying to hide her smile. She'd seen this coming since day one and she was so happy for them.

"If I can get some pickup work, unless of course you can come up with a way to make the Muses open to the public, I'll be the first one to turn in my résumé."

"Well, if you're sure . . ."

He looked at Chloe and that answered Issy's questions. "In that case, I think I've found a way to keep it going for a while longer. Maybe even implement some of the plans we've been throwing around."

"How?"

"An anonymous donor," Issy said.

"Is that what you were doing all afternoon in the music room?" Chloe asked.

"Partially."

Issy raised her voice. "And yes, Steph, that means we're going to open a museum."

The door to the housekeeper's quarters opened a few inches and Steph stuck her head out. "That's great. Can I come in?"

Vivienne started to say something, but Issy beat her to it. "Come in, Steph, you're part of this family."

"What about your job at the Cluny?" Paolo asked.

"That's the other part of what I was doing this afternoon. I talked to Dell. Told him our plan. After the initial dead silence, and then after he stopped yelling, he decided it might be a good idea. It would be a satellite of the Cluny, Whitaker owned and operated under the Muses complete control. A sister museum, if you will. Under one condition." She looked at Paolo.

"What condition?"

"That you would agree to curate the Muses collection, Paolo, in order to give me the freedom to freelance for the Cluny as well as administer the museum here. If that's okay with you, Grammy."

"I think it sounds like an excellent idea, but we won't have to leave, will we?"

"Absolutely not," Issy said.

"Oh, good, and, Ben, perhaps you could drop by every now and then."

"An honor and a pleasure," Ben said. "But, Issy, will you be living here or in Manhattan?"

"I've thought a lot about it and now I've stopped thinking. I'm staying here to run the Muses by the Sea Museum of American Art. But I'll still work for the Cluny on special projects.

"Which means, Paolo, that we'll sometimes be doing double duty."

"Nothing we haven't done before, *cara*. The best of all possible worlds."

"In that case," Chloe said, "and if it's okay with you, Leo, I was thinking the little sun porch would make an excellent tearoom for visitors, close to the kitchen, cozy but lots of light. It will be perfect."

"What happened to culinary school?" asked Issy, only half teasingly. Everything was suddenly moving way too fast.

"This sounds a lot more exciting."

"Yes," Paolo agreed. "And the conservatory for weddings and debutante balls. I can see it now."

Everyone laughed, except Ben, who leaned over and said, "Can we talk for a minute?"

"Sure."

"Outside?"

Issy stood up. "Excuse us for a minute."

They walked away from the house, out toward the sea, then he stopped her. "Are you sure you're doing this for the right reasons? Do you know how hard it will be to make any money from the few visitors you'll get?"

"I won't be counting on just admission income, but grants and that other resource I told you about."

"So they're legitimate?"

She nodded.

"Wow. And they really will bankroll the whole museum and house and everything? But is it what you want for yourself, not because you think you should do it but because this is what's best for you?"

She frowned at him. "What are you getting at?"

"I'd be glad if you stayed. Really glad. But not if you're going to regret your decision when it's too late to go back. I want you to stay for the right reasons."

"Let me see, now. What would those be? My family, the art, the history, and . . . Wait. I'm sure there was something else . . . Oh yes, Chloe and the beach and—"

"Okay, cut it out. I get the point. So do you think there might be room in your entourage for a levelheaded, sometimes marshy-smelling marine ecologist?"

"Actually, I just might have an opening. Let me check the job description. Hmm. Must have cowlick."

"That works for me." He took her shoulders and kissed her.

"And that works for me," Issy said when they finally pulled away.

"Good. Let's go back in before they—or we—get completely carried away."

He slung his arm over her shoulders, a gesture of a hundred memories, a gesture of home and security and the next adventure.

Sometime later

NEW ADAM ELLIS BRINGS 1 MILLION AT AUCTION

A recently discovered oil on canvas by Adam Ellis, one of the most noted of the late-twentieth-century Coastal-style painters, was auctioned off by Sotheby's for one million US dollars.

The painting, titled *The Muses at Sunset*, portrays the shoreline at Muses by the Sea, the neo-Gothic mansion of the Whitaker family, fondly called the Muses and a place popular with many of the painters and other artists of the day.

Found in the attic of an anonymous owner, it was appraised at $700,000. But the mystery and tragic death surrounding the troubled genius and rumors that possibly there are more of his paintings as yet undiscovered led to a bidding frenzy.

Mr. Ellis drove his car off the bridge into the Connecticut River on August 5, 2007. His body was never recovered, which police chief Roland North said was a common outcome of drowning victims at that location due to the strong currents and proximity to the open sea.

JILLIAN YORK, A bottle of water in one hand, her cell in the other, checked her makeup in her dressing trailer mirror. "Yes, Harry, just make it out to Muses by the Sea Museum of American Art. We'll put your name on a plaque. Divine. Gotta run, I'm wanted on set. We'll do lunch soon. Ciao."

STEPH RAN THROUGH the door of their new apartment in Painter's Cove and followed the smell of fresh-baked cookies to the kitchen. "Mom, I'm home. I told Chloe I would come out and help her and Paolo set up the sun porch for the historical society dinner tonight. I'll take my bike."

Vivienne placed a hot cookie sheet on the stove and turned to hug her daughter. "Fine. You can take this tin of cookies to Chloe."

Steph took the tin, snagged two cooling cookies for herself. "I'll be home in time for homework. See ya."

"I'M NOT SURE I'm cut out for this," Issy said as she tried to follow in Ben's footsteps through the sucking mud.

"Sure you are. Even the palest museum curator needs to get out in the fresh air every now and then. Here, hold this." He

shoved a metal rod and an instrument box at her, and while she
had both hands full, he pulled her close.

"Dr. Collins!" she said, laughing.

"The plankton won't mind." And he kissed her.

    To: George Whitaker
    From: Felix Pretto
    Re: The matter in question

    George:

    As you requested, the local bank here in Panama has
    frozen the particular funds under discussion. The subject
    is en route to Grand Cayman, where additional funds
    are still available. He will be taken into custody on ar-
    rival and the Cayman authorities will await your decision
    about prosecution. Your contact there is . . .

LEO LIFTED HER face to the setting sun. "You wouldn't believe
it, Wes. We have so many people coming through the museum,
I must lead five or six tours a day. It's so invigorating. It's almost
like the parties we used to have."

FAE STOOD ON the porch of their new cottage. The ocean
stretched as far as they could see. She leaned into Adam.
"Happy?"

"Very. You?"

"Oh yes." They were standing at the end of the world and
the beginning of a new life.

Acknowledgments

As always thanks to my agent, Kevan Lyon, and my editor, Tessa Woodward, as well as Nicole Fischer, Elle Keck, and my always supportive William Morrow team.

To my Beach Book Buddies, who are always ready to jump in to help navigate the growing pains of a story as it develops from idea to novel.

People always ask where writers get their ideas. Sometimes we have specific incidents in our lives, sometimes it begins with a vague feeling that takes shape as we work. For *The Beach at Painter's Cove* it was a photo I saw on Facebook posted by a friend from my Manhattan days. That life came flooding back and there it was, the beginning of my story about the Whitaker family and their love of art. To those friends from a former life, my deepest thanks and appreciation.

Book Club Questions

1. When Issy answers the phone call from her niece, she drops everything to drive to Connecticut even though she's pretty much estranged from her family. Yet when she arrives, she takes charge even while juggling her professional and family life. Why do you think she feels compelled to do that? Is it from love or from duty? Why is she ambivalent about her place in the family?

2. A statement in the book says that generations of Whitakers had nurtured artists but drained the life out of each other. Do you think that was true at least with the last four generations that are portrayed in the novel? And how did it happen? Do you think that it's a problem that any philanthropic family encounters, caring more for the greater good than for each other?

3. In Chapter 12 Fae says Leo and Wes's love consumed them and singed those around them. What did she mean? How was the family, especially their children, affected? Was

their love a good thing or a bad thing or is love something you can judge? Is it possible to love too much?

4. Leo and Wes's children—Max, George, and Jillian—all grew up at the Muses, and all chose very different paths in life. How were their feelings for each other, their parents, and their life choices shaped by living at the Muses surrounded by artists, nature, and the family history?

5. Jillian left Issy and Vivienne to be raised by their grandparents. How much of her decision was selfish and how much a genuine concern for their well-being away from the snares of Hollywood? Do you think she could have been happy and a good mother if she'd given up her career? Do you think her feelings about family changed during the story or was it the others' perceptions of her that changed?

6. Fae has been living a secret life for years. Do you think she and Adam did the right thing to live as they did? Do you think they will find continued happiness? If you had a chance to live a totally different life, do you think you would take it?

7. Vivienne's bitterness at being left at the Muses as a child colored her whole life, overflowing into resentment of her sister and aunt. How did those feelings affect her as well as the rest of the members of her family? Can the feelings of one person change the dynamics of a whole family? Will she be able to overcome those feelings?

8. Fae and Steph have a special relationship. Why do you think Fae took her under her wing? Did you have someone like this in your own childhood? How important is this kind of relationship?

9. Issy and Ben have been friends since childhood, but now their interests and lifestyles are different. Do you think they can have a future together not just as friends, but as a family? Why?

10. Did you have a favorite scene in the book? Who was the most interesting character? Is there someone you really connected to? Loved? Couldn't stand? Someone you were inclined to make excuses for?

11. Do the Whitakers remind you of your own family even though they might be very different in some ways? Are they people you would like to know or who you would try to avoid?

About the Author

New York Times bestselling author Shelley Noble is a former professional dancer and choreographer. She most recently worked on the films *Mona Lisa Smile* and *The Game Plan*. She is a member of Sisters in Crime, Mystery Writers of America, and Romance Writers of America.

BOOKS BY SHELLEY NOBLE

THE BEACH AT PAINTER'S COVE
A Novel

FOREVER BEACH
A Novel

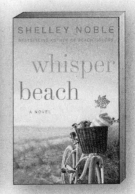

WHISPER BEACH
A Novel

BREAKWATER BAY
A Novel

STARGAZEY POINT
A Novel

BEACH COLORS
A Novel

ALSO AVAILABLE • E-NOVELLAS BY SHELLEY NOBLE
Stargazey Nights
Holidays at Crescent Cove
Newport Dreams: A Breakwater Bay Novella
A Newport Christmas Wedding

Available in Paperback and E-Book Wherever Books Are Sold